When the War Ends

Jenny Prater

Choosing a dedication for this book was hard and sort of painful. I've been working on it for fifteen years, and during that time, I've planned a lot of dedications, all of them to people I no longer have relationships with.

So. This one's for the people I know I'll never lose. For my family. All of you. Love you lots.

The princess stepped into the hallway. Glanced to the right. Glanced to the left. Reached back to grab the hand of her young soldier, and pulled him, giggling, down the hall. She opened a closet door, and tugged him in before slamming it shut.

"Eloise," he whispered in the dark. "We shouldn't—we shouldn't—"

She kissed him.

"Eloise," he said again a moment later, in that reverent but anxious voice she loved so much. "Eloise."

Chapter 1

She was a fool. She was a fool, and soon she would be dead.

She should never have left the palace grounds at all. Certainly not without telling anyone, riding an elderly mare meant for the training of frightened children. She had her sword; she always did. But her training had been for recreation, not necessity, and she had never trained on horseback.

She was a fool, and she would die, and it would be because she had let Joel get to her, again, as she always did, even a decade later.

There would be a little time, before she died. She would be recognized before they could kill her, today. But they would kill her eventually. There would be no ransom; the royal coffers were empty. She had a little time left. It would not be a pleasant time.

There were four men, all on horseback. Their clothing was an odd mix of styles—one man wore a worn wool jacket with the kind of clasps they used in Olion, with the wide legged linen trousers favored in Ibanar, and the style of boot that was fashionable in Aliria a few years ago, which certainly shouldn't be worn with wide legged trousers. Another wore the special mountain-climbing boots usually seen only in northern Olion, near the mountain range, and a shirt cut in the Ibanari fashion. A decade ago, the mishmash would have indicated a traveller, or someone from a border town. Now, it was more likely to mean a deserter or a bandit, wearing whatever he could steal, often off the corpses of men he killed.

She drew her sword, but was still trying to decide whether to dismount and put herself below her enemies, or do her best with Tulip's head in the way, when a man yanked her out of the saddle and threw her to the ground.

She tossed her sword aside to avoid landing on the blade. Tulip reared, and nearly stepped on her coming back down. She landed on her left side, and felt her ankle twist beneath her.

She couldn't defend herself against so many, and couldn't hope to run with horses in the mix, even if she hadn't twisted her ankle. She forced herself to her feet and collected her sword, despite the futility. Her reputation was bad enough already; she wouldn't add cowardice to the list.

The man who'd thrown her from her horse dismounted himself. She took a moment to study him, aware that the other men were catching Tulip. (It wouldn't be difficult. She was the elderly pet of a princess, not a warhorse.)

He wore a mask which obscured the upper half of his face, except for slits cut out for his eyes. He was tall, with the dark skin and, when he spoke, the achingly familiar accent that labelled him Ibanari. There was something familiar in the shape of his forehead, his chin, which she attributed to his ethnicity as well. (She'd not known many Ibanari men. The one she'd known best, she tried not to think of.) His nose had been broken in the past, and there was a long scar on his right cheek, starting behind the covered part of his face. Dark, glossy curls escaped from the bottom of his mask.

"Princess," he said.

Eloise didn't bother denying it. She had her father's nose, which had also been her grandfather's nose and her uncles', and the same golden-blonde ringlets as all three of her sisters and several cousins. She might get away with claiming to be a duchess, but no one with a passing knowledge of the royal family would believe she wasn't part of it.

"Eloise, isn't it?"

That did surprise her, a bit. While the women of her family shared a few distinctive features identifying them as royalty, it was not often a stranger could tell immediately which of them was which. It meant that this was deliberate, that they had come looking for her. It meant that they had expected her to be here, which was impressive as she had not, this morning, expected to be here herself.

Of course, she was the princess with the reputation; if any of them would be foolish enough to leave the grounds alone during a war, it would be her.

She wasn't foolish. Usually. But she was perpetually restless, and edging toward desperate as the rumors flew.

It didn't matter if she was foolish or not. There was no one but these four men to defend herself to. These men who would kill her and, if she was lucky, not do anything worse, first.

She didn't deny her identity. She didn't confirm it, either. It was largely irrelevant. Any princess—any duchess, too—would be worth a fair ransom, theoretically. But it mattered little how much she may be worth, when her family could never afford to pay it.

They stood there, staring at each other, Eloise's sword useless in her hand, until the other three men returned, leading Tulip. Eloise tightened her grip on the sword, pointlessly, as they surrounded her.

"You won't hurt my horse?" she asked.

"We won't," the masked man assured her. "We'll need her yet."

She was skittish, still; the masked man took her bridle from the others, stroking her nose to sooth her. Tulip was, unfortunately, easily soothed. A horse more wary of strangers would have been more useful, in this situation.

(Any horse but Tulip would have been more useful, as dearly as Eloise loved her.)

"I'll take that sword now," he said. "Do I need to tie your hands as well?"

"No," she said. "I know my limits—I won't outrun your horse." Especially not with a twisted ankle.

"Your sword," he said again, and she held it out to him, hilt first. She couldn't afford to antagonize him. Not now. Not yet. They were in the woods, miles from the city and the palace both.

He took the sword easily, and held it out toward another man, who took it gingerly.

"Now what?" she asked.

"One of my men will take the ransom demand to the palace."

"And how much is it?"

He named the price. Eloise wished uselessly for her sword. Her father couldn't have paid that a year ago. He couldn't have paid that two years ago. Now, this deep into the war, the only jewels left were too precious, too symbolic of their kingdom, to be sold, and the taxes had been raised as high as they could be, with the people at their breaking point.

Even the jewels left—if they sold the sunset diamonds (if anyone would buy them), if they melted down a crown or two—

Her father would do that, for her. But they were at war with the only countries nearby, and with growing risk of a civil war as well—who would buy their heirlooms? Who would want to help them? The time it would take to find someone, for the exchanges to be made—

She could not count on a ransom. Certainly not at that price.

If he had noticed her distress, he didn't show it.

"We'll be travelling a way. I assume this girl can be compelled to follow the others? Compliant enough, isn't she?"

"She'll follow your horses. And she can't outrun them."

This man would kill her, in time. She shouldn't be grateful that she could keep her utterly useless horse.

"At least you're dressed sensibly," he said. "That will make things easier."

She had worn breeches for this outing, not out of any need to disguise herself, but because they were more comfortable for riding. Her clothing was undyed linen and brown wool, because their kingdom was out of money, and the nicer clothing—the bright colors, the embroidery, the silks and velvets—couldn't be risked on something like an outing in the woods, had to be saved for special occasions.

"I dressed this morning with kidnapping in mind," she said lightly, and he smiled, brief and tight.

"I'll need your seal ring," he said, holding out a hand expectantly.

"Whatever for?"

"Proof we have you. We'll stamp the seal on the ransom note."

One man left, with the ransom note and the ring. Another had retreated some distance into the woods, and seemed to be consulting a map.

Eloise glanced at the other man still here—a boy, really. He couldn't be yet twenty. Too young, she thought, to be a dangerous criminal.

Of course, Joel had been far younger.

She had to stop thinking of him. Thinking of him had already gotten her kidnapped—she'd never have gone out like this if his name hadn't followed her in whispers for days now.

Ten years, and he was still causing trouble.

She spotted a downed tree and went to sit on it—she didn't like to appear weak, but her ankle was paining her. The masked man's eyes followed her closely, but he didn't otherwise react.

He was very calm, very confident. Likely he had plenty of experience with this sort of thing.

The younger man was fidgety, eyes darting wildly. He held her sword awkwardly. If she were ever left alone with him, she might have a chance of escaping.

She may get such a chance. They were travelling some distance. That was good. The longer it took them to reach their destination, the more chance she would have of getting away.

Although the next step, after her escape, would prove difficult. Could she make her way back home alone? What if they left the country? What if civil war did break out? She could easily exchange one captor for another.

She would worry about that when the time came. She couldn't escape now—there was no sense in getting ahead of herself.

"He'll catch up with us when we make camp for the night," the leader said. It took her a moment to realize he was referring to the man with the ransom note. "It's many hours yet to our meeting place."

He urged Eloise back onto her horse, and she complied, not wanting to be lifted and slung about if she didn't.

Tulip was attached by a long rope to one of the other horses, and made no fuss about it. She was a very compliant horse, which was, along with her age, why she remained in the royal stables that had been mostly cleared now, the other horses out on the battlefield. Eloise stroked her neck, and turned her injured ankle carefully, painfully, trying to decide whether it was broken or only sprained.

It was a long ride, hard on an elderly horse who'd already done more galloping that day than she ought to have. Eloise had planned to spoil her thoroughly at the end of their ride.

The little clearing where they stopped was, to Eloise's eye, indistinguishable from a dozen other clearings they'd passed. They had never left the woods; there had been no villages, no other people, no particularly notable landmarks. She had been watching carefully for all of these things, for any chance of escape.

This clearing must be special, though, for they all dismounted and made themselves comfortable. There was a fallen log, and a space that had clearly been used in the past for a fire. The men began unloading the horses, then drove a stake into the ground and tied them to it. Tulip followed the others, and Eloise remained on her back.

"Coming down, Princess?" the masked man asked.

She knew she would have to, eventually. But she was not confident she could stand on the ankle, and didn't want to collapse or cry out in front of them.

The youngest man stepped forward. He was tall and gangly, with a curly head of light brown hair and a friendly face.

"I can help you dismount," he offered, and she accepted.

Fire raced up her leg as soon as she put weight on the ankle. She clung, embarrassingly, to the boy for a moment, until the first shock of the pain passed, and she could stumble a few feet to sit on the fallen log.

The boy hovered for a moment, until the leader called, "Chris! Did you pack this bag?"

"I did."

"Then come unpack it; it's a disaster. I need the maps."

It was not yet terribly late in the day. The men went about their business, or two of them at a time did, while the third watched her. She didn't move. Now would be a foolish moment for an escape attempt, in a terrain they clearly knew well, when she could scarcely walk.

The sun had just set when the fourth man rejoined them. He and the leader went deeper into the woods, out of her hearing, with the boy—Chris—trailing behind. He had started a fire not long ago.

(The smoke would draw no attention, or no attention that was helpful to her. The countryside was rife with refugees and deserters.)

The last man remained, still watching her.

She studied him carefully. He was darker than the leader, with dark, short cropped hair. Older than the other two men, at least—she could not guess at the masked man's age. He might be Ibanari as well, but she thought it more likely he was from across the sea. It would be easier to tell when he had spoken more; Ibanari accents and across-the-sea accents were quite different.

"We'd best check that ankle," he said, after a few minutes of uncomfortable silence. She couldn't quite place the accent. Not quite like the leader's, but not like her brother-in-law's, either.

"It's fine."

"It should have been checked hours ago."

"It's fine," she repeated.

"It's not fine, and hiding it away because you don't want me to touch you won't make it better."

"Forgive me for not wanting medical care from my kidnapper."

"I'm half a doctor, if it helps."

"It does not," Eloise said, unsure what half a doctor even meant.

"Princess. We've a long way to go yet, and you needn't spend the whole journey in pain. We don't want you to—in fact we won't let you. If I tell them you wouldn't let me look, they'll make you, and that will be unpleasant for both of us."

"You're saying your leader will hold me down while you rip off my boot and stocking? To spare me pain?" She didn't mind the pain. It was certainly preferable to letting any of them touch her, but the combination of pain and touching was—

The man nodded. "He hates doing this kind of thing. Not that it'll stop him from slitting your throat if you get annoying, but he'll feel bad about it later. And he'll keep you in good health while you're in his care. Kidnapping's a tricky business, you know. People tend to get attached, if the ransom takes too long."

Eloise didn't dignify this with a response. She had no intention of becoming attached to any of them.

"I have bandages, and an ointment that will ease the pain. I'll touch nothing above the ankle."

Clearly there was no way out of this. She began undoing the laces on her boot. Slowly, she eased it off, hissing as she did so. He was right—it should have been wrapped hours ago. At least the boot was tightly fitted. She rolled down her stocking next, bunching it all below her heel so at least she wasn't completely barefoot. The ankle was swollen and discolored.

The man approached slowly, and knelt on the ground in front of her. He took the ankle gently in his hands, and twisted it in various ways that did not feel gentle at all. Eloise breathed carefully through her mouth, resisting the urge to make any sound, to express any pain.

At last, he let her go, but he was back a moment later with the bandages and ointment.

"Well, it's not broken, thank the gods. We'll keep you off it as much as possible—if all goes to plan we should be on the horses for some time."

"If all goes to plan, shouldn't I be safely home, and you safely paid, before much time passes at all?"

He shrugged. "We ride for our destination. Our men in the capital wait for the ransom. If they send word it's received, we bring you back. Until then we keep going. It's not safe to stay put, here. Your father's men will be looking for us, likely your fiancé's men as well. And the battles are constantly moving, the borders always changing. You stay put too long, you're liable to find yourself on the frontlines."

They were still so close to the palace—just one day out by horse. Could the war really be so close?

He finished applying the ointment, and began wrapping her ankle.

"Half a doctor?" she asked, to fill the silence, and distract herself from the pain.

"I was halfway through my training when I had to flee the noose."

"What charges?"

"Murder," he said, very casually, as he tied off the bandage.

Eloise pulled herself hastily away.

"Pull your stocking back up, and see if you can get the boot back on over that."

She could, though it required loosening the laces significantly.

"Good. We'll check it again tomorrow." He glanced back into the forest, where the others had disappeared to. "They should be back by now. Can I trust you not to run blindly into a dark forest if I turn my back on you to dig through our food pack?"

She nodded. He found what he was looking for, and began to cook. The uncomfortable silence returned. At last, she decided she would rather make polite conversation with a murderer than just sit there.

"Are you Ibanari? Or from the continent?"

"Both," he said. "I crossed the sea from Geth as a child, but it was Ibanar I fled."

"And how did you decide to become a murderer?"

"He murdered my sister first—it seemed only fair."

"Oh."

He pulled the food off the fire, and turned away from her to call, "Chris! Fuller! Come get your dinner, or I'll give your shares to the princess."

All three men emerged from the woods shortly after; presumably it was the masked one he hadn't named. The four of them chatted quietly as they ate, and Eloise ate as well, watching in silence.

If the battle lines were really so close, escape would be even more difficult than she'd anticipated. And the man had mentioned her fiancé—she'd not even thought of Jeremy all day. She would be the second girl to die after accepting his hand.

He would come looking for her, of course. And it would end badly for these men if he found her. She knew he had a temper, though she'd never seen it herself.

Perhaps her best chance was to delay things as much as possible, to give the inevitable search parties more time to find her before they travelled too far afield.

Her father could not pay a ransom, but he could send an army after her. A small one—most soldiers were off in battle somewhere. But her captors were four, and it wouldn't take much of an army to defeat them.

She could try, perhaps, to release their horses or destroy their supplies while they slept.

It was a foolish idea, she realized, not long after, when three of them laid on the ground around the fire to sleep, and the fourth sat up to watch her. Of course they would not leave their prize unattended. She moved from her log to the ground, careful of her ankle, and tried to sleep as well. It had been a long day, and the next—likely the next several—would be no better.

Chapter 2

Eloise did not sleep. Surrounded by strange men—all kidnappers, and one a confessed murderer—she was too anxious, and the ground was uncomfortable, besides.

The only night she'd ever spent on the ground had been with Joel and her brother Ben, in the forest just outside the palace grounds, under a poorly-constructed tent. No one but the three of them had ever known about it. She still wasn't quite sure how Ben had come to be there—maybe he'd invited himself, as a sort of chaperone. Far too many of her outings with Joel had been unofficially chaperoned by her brother, something she'd come to be grateful for in hindsight.

If she had been anyone but who she was, she would have been— one did not just kiss a man to whom one was not married, especially in public. One certainly didn't spend a night with a man to whom one was not married, or take him into one's private chambers.

It was her title that had saved her from utter ruin. She had been so incredibly lucky, and had taken it all for granted. It wasn't just that she hadn't cared; it was that she had absolutely delighted in trailing scandal wherever she went.

She had been a stupid little girl, and she would spend the rest of her life paying for it.

That night in the forest had been horribly uncomfortable. Joel had slept soundly, but she and Ben had sat awake for most of it. Clearly her indecent notions wouldn't have come to fruition even without Ben's presence; the forest floor was not conducive to romance.

She did not sleep. She watched the sun rise, red gold snaking up through the bruised blue sky. The leader was on guard by then; the watch had shifted several times.

There was a quick breakfast. The man from Geth—Alem, she'd heard Chris call him—let her apply her own ointment to the ankle, and then rewrapped it. They were up on their horses and off again a few minutes later.

Last night's anxiety was wearing away, no match for the exhaustion of the day, and Eloise found herself dozing on Tulip's back. She lost most of the morning to a half-asleep state, interrupted by brief bursts of panicked wakefulness.

At midday she was woken by a tentative hand on her shoulder; she jerked back, nearly losing her seat, and Chris leaned away, looking apologetic.

"Lunchtime, Your—um, Highness? It's just dried meat; we haven't time to stop."

She took the meat, and tried to take stock of her surroundings, but it was only trees, and more trees, and the four men who were her unwanted companions.

"Thank you, Chris," she said, and stuffed half the meat in her pocket—thank all the gods for a pocket, today—when he turned around. It wasn't likely she would escape, but if she did, some small supplies stashed away would be helpful.

Not as helpful as her sword, but that was in the leader's possession now, and unlikely to be easily reacquired.

~

The second night, like the first, was spent in the forest. It was a large forest, spanning hundreds of miles all told, with sections belonging, at least theoretically, to Olion and Ibanar both, as well as her own kingdom. Of course, it was hard to enforce boundaries in the middle of an empty wood. Since she had no idea in which direction they were moving, she had no way to guess how long they would be in the woods, or what country they would be in when they left it.

If she had been more alert throughout the day she might have been able to pick out their direction by the position of the sun; now, the sky was dark. Likely they had been moving in the same direction all day, but she wasn't certain. She could ask, but she didn't know whether she could trust the answer. She would take note of the sun's position tomorrow, and hope that they had been moving steadily in the same direction right along. She hadn't noticed any circling or doubling back, at least.

But then, she wouldn't have.

She should have been awake and watchful, earlier today. It was only her most recent mistake.

She had been so stupid. So stupid.

For a third of Eloise's life, her kingdom had been consumed by war. And no one would ever forget that it was all her fault. She'd gotten used to that, mostly. But these last two weeks—it had been years since Joel was last so much in the court's mind.

She didn't know where the rumors had started. She didn't know who in the palace had first suggested that Eloise might betray them, again, for a man she'd loved as a foolish child, and hadn't seen in nearly a decade. Her father had given strict instructions to cease the gossip, and if the originator could be tracked, he would have seen them punished. But rumors were impossible to trace or control.

She had just needed to be alone for a bit. Truly alone, away from not only the gossip and suspicious glances, the hastily cut off whispers, but from her family's pity, her lady's maids' sympathy, her fiancé's endless patience and understanding.

And now that solitude would, if she was lucky, cost her only her life. If she was unlucky, if these men were being paid by an enemy, or chose to offer her to one when no ransom arrived, it could cost her kingdom the war.

She had been so stupid.

~

They built another fire, the second night, Chris and the other man—Fuller?—tending to the cooking while Alem checked her ankle, and the leader disappeared into the woods. He was joined shortly by Fuller, and she could make out their voices—hushed, but frustrated— though no particular words.

They were frustrated. There was tension between her kidnappers. Perhaps that would help her.

She woke in the morning to find the leader much too near her, already awake.

This was why she hadn't slept the night before.

He hadn't touched her. He likely wouldn't, until he knew the ransom wasn't coming.

Eloise swallowed her fear, and attempted a smile.

"I've met Chris and Alem, and Fuller I've been introduced to by your shouting. But what shall I call you?"

"Nothing."

"Surely I must call you something? How else shall I shout at you when I'm angry?" She paused. "Or beg you for mercy, if you prefer?"

"Call him the Bandit King," Chris suggested. The others, she noted belatedly, were just waking, and gathering around them.

The leader laughed—a brief, quickly stifled sound. "Don't, please."

"I shall, if you give me no better option."

He didn't answer right away, turning to fiddle with the remains of last night's fire. Finally, when Eloise had given up on a response, he said, "You might call me Senam."

The name seemed to fit oddly in his mouth, and fit oddly, too, with what she could see of his face. He did not look like a Senam. Or perhaps it was only that he did not look as if he felt like a Senam. Either way, it was clearly a false name, provided as an alternative to Your Bandit Majesty.

It was, however, still a king's name, a name from an old Ibanari story, one of many that Joel had used to tell her. King Senam and the mermaid. A name from stories, a name that had likely been given to no real person in a hundred years or more.

She waited until they were on horses to resume the conversation. "Why be so protective of your own identity, when your men share theirs freely?"

"I happen to be significantly more wanted than anyone else here," he said.

"Oh? And what are you wanted for?"

He pointed at Chris, Fuller, and Alem in turn, then at himself. "Petty theft, repeatedly. Poor romantic choices. Murder. Light treason."

She raised her eyebrows. "Light? Is that as opposed to heavy treason, or dark treason?"

"Have you met the king of Ibanar?"

"Not personally."

"I have, unfortunately. He didn't like me much. They say he's grown temperamental in his old age—I never knew him younger to compare."

Realizing that she would get no interesting story from him, Eloise changed the subject. "Poor romantic choices?"

The leader opened his mouth to answer.

"No," Fuller said. "Absolutely not. I'm not doing story time with the hostage."

He sped up, riding a little ahead of them. When he was a sufficient distance away, Chris leaned close to whisper, "She was married. To a duke."

"Which duke?" she asked Fuller when he slowed down again. She'd had to memorize all of the names of all of the dukes on the island, for diplomatic reasons, before they were at war. It would be someone in Olion, she assumed. He was obviously not Ibanari, and she would obviously have already heard his story, if it had happened in Aliria.

He scowled. "I lost everything I had, narrowly escaped a beheading, and was forced to fall in with criminals just to survive. None of that is for your entertainment. Chris, why don't you tell your own damn stories?"

"Sorry," he said.

"You don't have to make friends just because she's a princess. A few days, maybe a few weeks, and she'll be out of our lives for good."

He rode ahead again. Alem and Senam didn't comment, Chris appeared ashamed of himself, and Eloise gave up, for the time, on conversation.

That mask worried her. What did she care about the face of an Ibanari traitor? A man wore a mask because he feared being recognized. If not by Eloise, then by someone she might describe him to, once safely home again.

And a recognizable captor meant a politically motivated kidnapping. Which made little difference to Eloise, kidnapped either way, but could matter a great deal to her father.

It would explain why they were moving south, as she'd worked out this morning, instead of staying near the palace, waiting for the ransom to be paid.

They would be pretending to be more interested in money than politics to lessen her panic, make her easier to manage.

Who was he behind the mask?

He could be one of any number of Ibanari noblemen or high-ranking military officials. Or, if he was telling the truth about his treason charge, he could be the king of Ibanar's cousin, exiled on pain of death over a decade ago. He could be working now for Olion, or even the Alirian rebels that may or may not be slowly organizing.

It didn't matter who he was. Not if she would never go home to identify him.

But any information she could learn, any scrap of an advantage she could snatch, would increase her chances of escape and survival.

If he was the king's cousin, they likely wouldn't be heading south, toward the kingdom he'd been exiled from.

Unless Eloise was a peace offering for the king, and the mask was to get him far enough into Ibanar to present her.

She had been told they were travelling far. She had time to figure it out, if she couldn't escape first.

~

They moved steadily southeast for the next three days. Eloise was unsure how many miles per day they travelled, and equally unsure of the exact national borders in an unoccupied forest during wartime. She suspected they remained in a nebulous area somewhere between Aliria and Ibanar.

If she was going to escape, it needed to be soon. Before the nearest villages were definitively Ibanar.

She had been docile and quiet, all her attention on watching and listening, waiting for any slip-up. Hints at the leader's identity, opportunities for escape.

So far there was nothing. And her time was running out.

She got her chance that night. It rained, for the first time since she was taken, a dreadful downpour.

Fuller and Alem put up a tarp. It wouldn't keep them dry, but it might keep them drier. One tarp, and not overly large. Which meant

Eloise would have to sleep pressed close to the men, unless she wished to be directly in the path of the rain.

Chris was the weak link. She'd known that from the beginning. He was also her favorite. Young, kind, respectful. Not safe, but safer than the other, older men. It was a surprise to no one when she positioned herself toward the end of the tarp's reach, with Chris between herself and the others.

He'd have the third watch tonight. They rotated. Three watches each night, and the fourth man allowed a full night of sleep.

None of them would have a restful night, with the rain pounding above them, and the ground below them slowly soaking. But Chris would have the worst time of them all. Throughout the first two watches, Eloise feigned an extremely restless sleep, jostling him awake again and again.

And just after the watch changed, she received a miracle.

The rain stopped.

In the sudden quiet, it took poor, exhausted Chris even less time than she'd expected to dose off on his watch.

Her plan had been to take Tulip and go. Now, she had another advantage to press.

When she was sure all four men were asleep, she untied all of the horses, shooing the outlaws' three away, toward the west. They wouldn't have left the comfort of the tarp, if it had still been raining. It would have made catching her much easier, having horses still.

She took her sword back from where the leader had left it, then took most of the food and water, as well, and a knife she thought belonged to Fuller. She swung onto Tulip's back, and pointed her east.

It was the longest of long shots. She had no idea where the nearest village was, or even where the forest broke. She had no idea how long it would take for Chris to wake, or how far the horses might roam in that time.

If she was very lucky, she would be found by one of the search parties doubtless scouring the forest for her, or she would find a town occupied by Alirian citizens, and not ones currently furious with their ruler. If she got far enough, she might find an Alirian army post.

She was unlikely to be lucky. She would probably be retrieved within a few days by men more familiar with the terrain than she was, or by other men, more dangerous than these.

It was possible she was making a terrible mistake.

It was the only chance she had, and she would be a fool not to take it.

Even if the kidnappers recaptured her, she would have delayed them a while, and that would increase the chances of a search party finding her.

~

She rode through the night and all the next day, stopping only at streams for Tulip to drink, never even dismounting. She knew she was being hard on an old, tired horse. She couldn't afford to do anything else.

It took them less than a full day to catch her.

The sun was setting, and she was thinking about finding a place to camp, about giving Tulip as much of a rest as she could, when she saw him. Senam, alone, on his brilliant black horse. They moved quietly—he was almost on top of her before she'd seen him.

His sword was drawn.

She remembered how Chris had held her sword, like a snake that might bite him. His leader held a sword like a man who knew how to use it. He held his sword like a man who intended to use it, and Eloise realized, looking at him then, that she had never before seen him angry.

Her training never included fighting on horseback. Her training was never finished at all.

She looked at his face, what she could see of it below the mask. She looked at his grip on the sword. She wondered if he would kill her.

He smiled, and somehow it only made him look more vicious.

"Eloise," he said, "you're marvelous."

In the few seconds she took to process this unexpected statement—compliment and insult both, for he should never have used her given name—he snatched Tulip's bridle with his free hand. His other hand, his sword arm, dropped slightly, his attention on the horse.

They were too close together. She hardly had room to draw her sword. Instead she slapped him, hard.

He reeled back, pulling Tulip with him, putting Eloise dangerously off balance.

She righted herself and reached for her sword. But it was in the saddle scabbard, on the same side of Tulip as her enemy.

He cut the sword from the saddle before she could draw it. Tulip reared, and made a sound like a scream—he must have cut her, too. Eloise closed her eyes and clung to Tulip's neck until she was certain she wouldn't be thrown off.

By the time the horse was calm, it was all over. There was no more chance of escape. Senam had her well in hand, disarmed, her horse injured and the bridle in his grasp. His men were doubtless close behind.

At least, she told herself, looking up at him, he didn't seem so angry anymore. At least he would not kill her now.

For a long moment, he stared at her, and she stared back, unwilling to be the first to break the gaze.

"You're too smart to make a proper escape attempt," he said, at last. "You're hoping to delay us long enough to be rescued. It won't work, princess. Would you like to know why it won't work?"

"Oh, do tell me, please."

"If we are caught, we are all dead. There will be no bargaining, no alternative options. If we are not killed on the scene, we'll be taken back and hung. If we are caught, I will have nothing left to lose. And my last act will be to kill you, as well. I rather think I'd slit your throat, though of course I may need to improvise."

Eloise didn't answer.

"Perhaps one of your soldiers could shoot me before I could kill you—they carry crossbows, don't they? But I shall be riding right alongside you, from now on. It won't be much of a reach for me to drive your own sword through your stomach before they can react. Do you understand, Princess?"

"I understand."

"Remember they'll kill Chris and Alem and Fuller as well. I know you're fond of Chris, at least."

She didn't want that.

She shouldn't care. They were criminals. Kidnappers. Outlaws.

She did care. Her father had been right to de-prioritize her training, to ban her from the battlefield. She didn't want to see men dead.

"Dismount," he said. "Collect your sword and give it to me. Then get back on and I'll take you to the meeting place. We'll see about treating that gash on your horse when we find the others."

With little other option, Eloise did as she was told.

~

She was beautiful when she was angry.

Well, she was always beautiful. But she had so often since they caught her been so stiff and quiet she seemed scarcely to be real; enraged, she was bright and vivid and alive.

Chapter 3

"You found me more quickly than I expected," she said, as they made their way back to the camp.

"Our horses didn't go far. And they went west. I thought you would go east—put as much distance between yourself and our horses as possible. Although I sent the others searching in different directions, in case I was wrong."

Eloise didn't answer. It didn't occur to her, until they had been riding several minutes, to worry about Chris. If a guard at the palace had let a prisoner escape, he would be punished. And surely her father was more civilized than outlaws—who knew what form punishment might take, here?

He looked unharmed, when they joined the others, gathered around a small fire.

"You found her," Fuller said. He didn't sound pleased.

"Any injuries?" Alem asked.

"The horse. I cut it disarming her."

Eloise slipped down from Tulip's back, and went to sit by the fire, while the leader unloaded the food she'd stolen, and Alem checked the cut.

"I'm sorry," she said to Chris. She wasn't sorry for trying to escape, for taking advantage of the only weak spot she could find. But she was sorry it might have hurt the person here she liked best.

He shrugged. She turned her attention to the fire, staring into the embers as she tried to think what to do next.

She couldn't escape. She didn't want to die. No other option had presented itself, yet.

~

The princess had vanished, and all anyone knew was that she had saddled her own horse, and left the stable under her own power.

Search parties had found nothing. Spies had no information. Soldiers had been called from battlefields that could not spare them to hunt for her. Messages had been sent to her siblings at the frontlines, and those who could were coming home to help.

It had been a week. If she had been taken—and she must have been taken—there should have been a note by now, or a body.

People in corridors whispered that she must have gone to join her lover. Jeremy, the baron who was her betrothed, ignored them.

That Eloise would have gone to Joel, after everything, was absurd. That she would have left for some other reason was possible, if unlikely. That she would have done so without telling Jeremy was unfathomable.

She knew that she could trust him to keep her secrets. And she knew how it had been for him, last time he'd lost someone he cared for, coming home to find her whole village burned down and still smoking, without a single survivor.

She would not have left him without word.

He had slept four hours since the last search party checked in. It was enough. He had to keep looking.

~

There had been tension among her kidnappers since her escape attempt. It was not, she thought, related to her escape; none of it seemed related to her, or to Chris, who had let her escape. Whatever was happening, it was between Alem, Fuller, and the leader—particularly Fuller and the leader. There were pointed looks, angry whispers she couldn't hear.

There must have been some fight, in those few short hours she was gone. It seemed she should be able to use it to her advantage, but she had not yet worked out how.

Now, Fuller's horse was limping, badly. They'd paused to investigate, Fuller holding the horse carefully in place while Alem checked the hoof, grumbling about how he wasn't a horse doctor.

Eloise watched them work. The leader watched Eloise.

"Chris," he said abruptly, "take the princess on a walk. Don't go far."

Chris wandered into the woods; Eloise followed reluctantly.

"They'll only yell at each other a bit," he told her. "Long journeys put people in bad moods."

He didn't seem upset with her. They had not interacted much, these last few days, the leader keeping his promise to stick right beside her, and the other men riding before or behind.

"What are they fighting about?" Eloise asked.

"What to do with you," Chris said, and she was surprised that it seemed an honest answer.

"I thought they meant to ransom me," she said, struggling to keep her tone light. What might they want to do instead?

"Fuller thinks you more trouble than you're worth. I think Alem agrees."

What did you do to a prisoner not worth the trouble?

Did you release her? Or did you kill her?

They were outlaws. The latter was undoubtedly more likely.

~

"You're making a mistake," Fuller said.

The leader shrugged. "I'm making half a dozen, at least."

"You could still fix this."

"I am fixing it. Everything will be fine."

"You are not," Alem said. "Every day your window narrows. You must make a choice, and soon."

~

Eloise had not been out in the forest with Chris for long when Senam joined them, scowling, breaking more twigs with his passage than was his usual habit.

"Go help them with that damned horse," he told Chris. "I'll watch the princess."

In a moment they were alone. If what Chris had told her was true, her life was in this man's hands, more truly than it had already been, these last several days. Chris did not have the authority to save her. She could not afford to further antagonize the leader, if he was now keeping her alive against the wishes of half his band.

They didn't speak. Eloise wandered aimlessly between the trees, and the leader followed closely.

Then she heard voices. Not the other men. New voices, coming from ahead, not behind.

Voices that could belong to her rescuers, if only she could reach them.

Eloise wasn't much of a fighter, especially without a weapon. She could have taken Chris, maybe. If she caught him by surprise, and didn't make the mistake of trying not to hurt him. Joel had taught her a few dirty moves, before—

Chris was gone. She had no chance of taking this man.

Perhaps she could outrun him. But if she couldn't—

Perhaps if she just shouted—

Before she could make a choice, he wrapped one arm around her, pinning her arms, and clamped his other hand over her mouth. He dragged her behind the cover of the nearest tree. Her caution overwhelmed by the indignity, she attempted to kick him, and to shout past his palm.

"Shut up, you little fool," he hissed. "They're Ibanari."

The voices came close enough as he spoke for her to recognize the accent, and realize that he was right. She stilled in his arms; he didn't loosen his grip.

It felt like a very long time before they were out of hearing distance—walking, thank the gods, in a direction that would not lead them directly to the other men and horses.

Senam released her slowly, cautiously.

"So are you," she said.

"What?"

"You're Ibanari, too."

"Well, so are a lot of perfectly decent people. I'm not one of the king's own soldiers. What were you going to say to them? 'Help me, help me, I'm the favorite daughter of your greatest enemy, and I'm lost alone in the woods'? 'Please take me home'? I just saved your worthless life."

She wouldn't have said anything, once she realized who they were. She wasn't an idiot.

"Worthless? I'm a hostage. Dead I would be worthless. You just saved your payday."

"I'm sorry, did you want to die today?"

She shook her head. "Where are you taking me?"

"Not to Ibanar."

"We're moving south," she countered. There were three countries on their island, all in a neat little row. They had started their journey in the middle, in Aliria. The only thing south was Ibanar.

He stared at her, thoughtful, for a long moment. "There's an island in the Sea of Tears. Our best access point is down south. Was down south. If there are Ibanari soldiers this far north, we'll never make it. We have to reassess. I can't be caught by Ibanar. You can't be caught by Ibanar. Alem—we have to move."

His face went pale as he spoke, and he turned to run back to where they left the others, seeming to forget about her. Eloise followed. She had no desire to fall into the hands of Ibanar, either.

"Is the horse all right?" he asked when they got back.

"I've removed—"

"Good. Load up. We have to move. North. Now."

"Ibanari soldiers," Eloise said, as she helped load saddle bags onto Fuller's horse.

She was actively helping her kidnappers. She shouldn't be—

She was doing the only sensible thing, no matter how foolish it felt. These kidnappers had not yet harmed her. She didn't know what others might do.

They rode through the night, due north, not pausing until the sun had crested the horizon, a dull orange piercing through the trees.

"We're far enough, for now," the leader said. "The horses need rest. I'll take first watch."

~

Eloise was the last one to wake. Fuller had a large piece of parchment that appeared to be a map, and was studying it carefully, Senam leaning over his shoulder. Alem was eating. Chris was digging through one of their packs.

"Princess is awake," Alem said as she sat up.

Senam sighed, leaning away from Fuller. "Chris, get her some jerky."

Eloise ate quietly. Chris and Alem sat near her. Fuller made marks on the map with charcoal, and the leader paced.

"Now what?" Alem asked, when several minutes had passed.

Senam turned to Fuller. "What are our options?"

"There aren't many. Not with the princess. The whole coast will be crawling with soldiers. Battlefields shifting every day. We could sneak through, pass for refugees if not soldiers. But a word from the princess, and we're all dead."

"The mountain port. Surely that's secure?"

"It'll add weeks to our journey."

"I know."

"We'll have to leave the horses," Chris said.

"I know."

"Half the pirates hate you, and there's no telling who'll be there," Alem said.

"I know, damn it. We have to get home, don't we? Does anyone else have a better idea?"

"Find the Alirian soldiers," Eloise offered. "Let me go to them, and I swear I won't send them after you."

Senam stiffened. The other men exchanged glances. Alem opened his mouth, then closed it.

"Chris," Senam snapped. "Watch her."

The other three men vanished, deeper into the woods. Eloise stayed with Chris.

"He won't agree," Chris warned her. "The others will try to convince him, but he'll never agree. He has too much riding on this."

~

"I can't," the leader said, when they were safely out of the princess' hearing range.

"This is more than we signed on for," Fuller said.

"I know."

"It gets more dangerous every day."

"I know. I just—you know how much this matters."

"We could still go back to the original plan," Alem suggested.

He frowned. "Give me a few days to think. We'll keep moving north, meanwhile."

~

Chris was right. When the men returned, there was no more talk of releasing Eloise. They packed up their horses and continued north. It was three cold days before they dared to light a fire again.

~

They used to play at being bandits in the woods, as children. Eloise, and her brother Ben, and their cousins. Their older siblings didn't care for such games, and the younger were too young, then, to be included.

Cousins came and went. Mostly it had been Ben and Eloise. And for a little while, Ben, Eloise, and Joel—they had been too old, by then, for sneaking into the forest to play pretend, but they had done it anyway.

Travelling with real bandits in the woods lacked much of the charm and romance they had once imagined.

She would likely never see Ben again. Not Ben, or Jeremy, or her parents. Not her cousins, or her siblings, or her little niece and nephew.

Her best hope of escape now—her only hope of escape—was the map Fuller carried.

He had marked the location of the soldiers they'd seen. If Eloise could get a look at that map, she could use his fresh markings as a starting point. They had been moving due north; if she could estimate how many miles per day they travelled, she could find the nearest village on the map.

If she could look at the map. Which, thus far, she couldn't. Fuller kept it on his person at all times. When he brought it out to consult, Eloise was shooed away.

The leader was always right beside her, as they rode through the days. At night, Chris was now always vigilant, as were the others. Whatever they had fought over, the tension had dissipated.

She had no opportunities to escape, no advantages to press.

Her father could not pay the ransom. She would die with these men.

Days passed; she lost count. It hardly mattered. There was nothing she could do but wait for an increasingly unlikely rescue.

Fuller and Alem had seemed agreeable, when she suggested that they set her free. So perhaps Chris had not meant that they would see her dead, perhaps any lack of cooperation would not be an immediate death sentence.

But there were enemy soldiers in the forest. She had seen them.

It was better to stay here. These men might only hurt her. If she fell into the hands of Ibanar or Olion, they would certainly use her to hurt all of Aliria.

Eloise remembered being sixteen, her mother telling her, "Don't let them see you're hurt. Don't let them see you're ashamed. You'll want to scream, and cry, and rage. Do it in your own rooms, and dismiss the maids first. You can't undo what's been done. But you can control how you're seen, moving forward. And they should never see you weak."

She remembered. Don't let them see you weak. Don't let them see you afraid.

She forced herself to be cheerful, friendly, talkative. This was easiest with Chris and Alem, who were willing to engage in small talk and casual joking. Fuller kept any direct interaction with her to a minimum. Their leader would speak with her more easily than Fuller, but more often he would just stare, expression inscrutable behind his mask.

She decided she would make him like her. He would be more difficult than Chris and Alem, certainly, but not nearly so impossible a prospect as Fuller.

He was the most important.

Chris and Alem were reasonably fond of her. But Chris was young, inexperienced, not yet a hardened outlaw, but largely enthusiastic in his apprenticeship. Alem was the oldest, she thought, and the only one Eloise was certain had killed a man. But he followed the masked man's lead. She thought either of them would be reluctant to do her harm. But ultimately they would do as they were told.

Winning the leader's favor would be a difficult task. Largely, she thought, because he had a special knack for upsetting her. But not as difficult as it would have been, at the beginning. Senam was different, after the foiled escape attempt. He had, it seemed, used all his capacity for cruelty and rage in that one incident. Now he was quiet, and seemed often lost in thought. She caught him staring at her often, expression unreadable with the mask around his eyes. It was not the kind of stare that made her skin crawl, though. It felt like being stared at by—by someone who liked her. It felt...fond, perhaps. Which perhaps she should have disliked—what right did he have to look fondly at her, a woman he had kidnapped?

But his eyes didn't make her skin crawl. That was something.

"Senam," she said, and had to repeat it twice before gaining his attention. It was definitely a false name. And he was not accustomed to using one.

"Do you think it will rain?" she asked him.

"Will you try to escape again, if it does?"

She didn't answer him.

"Do please consider it; I could use the excitement of chasing you down. Kidnapping's grown boring, lately."

"I'm so sorry you don't find the utter destruction of my life entertaining," she said, and then turned her attention quickly to Alem, knowing that, for her, sarcasm was one short step away from shouting.

"Ignore him," Alem said. "The rest of us crave no extra excitement."

She let a few days pass, entertaining Chris with stories of her cousins, before attempting another conversation with the leader. She should have known better. Having failed at the weather, she was not sure, in hindsight, why she had aimed next for politics.

"You were exiled from Ibanar," she said. His identity remained a mystery, but she was at least now confident that he was neither working for Ibanar nor seeking to regain their favor.

"I was."

"Surely, then, you would not see them win the war?"

"I would rather they did not," he agreed.

"My kidnapping will cause chaos in Aliria. It may allow Ibanar to gain the upper hand."

"Perhaps I'm rooting for Olion."

"You are not," Fuller called from up ahead. ("Fuller hates Olion," Chris had told her, two days ago. She still suspected it was where he had been outlawed, though she'd learned no further information.)

The leader shrugged. "Perhaps I don't care who wins, so long as I get paid."

"People are dying every day in this war."

"In all three countries," he said. "And your father's killed far more of them than I have."

"My father didn't start this."

He had been relaxed, calm. Suddenly he was rigid—with anger, she thought, though his half face could be hard to read. "No. That was you. Wasn't it?"

Her own anger rose just as quickly. "It wasn't."

"Then who was it, princess?"

"You know. Everyone knows."

"I know," he said. "But who let him in?"

Eloise dug her heels into Tulip's sides, sending her forward until she was at the front of their band, beside Fuller, who, predictably, ignored her.

She had been fifteen years old.

She had been in love.

She had been a fool.

And had it not cost her enough? She had plenty of this, in whispers through the palace. She shouldn't have to take it from outlaws, too.

She had been a child. There had been dozens of adults about, better equipped than her to see a traitor for what he was. Why should the responsibility fall all to her, who had loved him?

~

He had led his band for two hard years, his position increasingly tenuous. He had been a part of the band for three years before that. This was his first kidnapping.

It was a desperate move. With the entire island consumed with war, there was little money left to steal, and soldiers, better trained than most of the band, were everywhere they turned. His men were losing faith in him, and deposed leaders died. He'd taken his most trusted friends and left, promising to return with a fortune. And if he didn't deliver, the others would track him down and kill him.

He hated every moment of it. He hated the feeling of her eyes on him, hated the sound of her crying on the rare nights when she let her guard down. He hated the secret he carried, which he knew would break her. He hated how angry she made him, when he was trying to be kind, trying to make this as easy on her as he could.

When he killed people, they were dead. When he stole from them, he took their gold and left, and never had to see them again. He'd never had to carry a victim with him for days on end—the memories of them, the feeling of blood on his hands, yes—but never the victim herself, a constant, inescapable reminder of just how low he could stoop.

The plan had seemed so simple, when he whispered it to his friends that night. Two ways it could go, and either would be a triumph. But he hadn't had to look at her, then. It had all gotten so complicated.

Chapter 4

She tried again, as the forest thinned. "What was your life like, before you were an outlaw?"

"Hard," he said, after a long pause. "My family was impoverished, and I picked pockets for supplemental income. My father abandoned our family when I was very young, and my mother was sickly. I worked when I could find jobs, but I could often get more money picking one pocket—if it was the right pocket—than working from sunup to sundown."

"And how did a pickpocket come to the king's attention, to be charged with treason?"

"I had travelled north, near the start of the war, to seek better opportunities. There were none to be found, so I came home. At that time, it was Ibanar's habit to question all those crossing the border about any enemy movements they'd seen. As I had passed a posting of the Alirian army, I was brought directly to the king to make my report. He was dissatisfied with the level of detail I provided. I foolishly talked back. It was discovered that a courtier—his cousin, it turned out—was missing a ring. The ring was found in my pocket; I'd taken it mostly by habit. I failed to show the appropriate level of remorse. I do think treason was rather an exaggeration, but that was the charge the king chose. He quite dislikes me."

"It does seem an overreaction," Eloise agreed.

35

"It was shortly after his wife had died. I'm sure it was—I shouldn't have shown so little respect for my sovereign lord, I suppose, but I never—I'm afraid I don't much care about respecting my betters. But I wouldn't have been so difficult, if I had known he was in mourning. As I said, I'd come down from Aliria; the news had not yet travelled north."

Weather, no. Politics, no. Questions about his personal life, yes. Odd; she'd certainly have expected the weather to be the safest of those topics. Perhaps it was only that he had been in a bad mood that day, and Eloise—understandably, she thought, given the circumstances— lived constantly on the edge of a bad mood, and was pushed easily over it.

Indeed, their next conversation about the weather was without incident.

"Ugh, fog," she said, as she woke up to find it thick all around her.

"Ugh," Senam agreed. "You'd think, looking up at them, that walking through clouds would be a pleasant experience."

"It makes one so…damp, stuck outside when it's this bad."

"At least we're not on a battlefield—imagine being unable to see your enemies clearly, or even your comrades."

"Stop whining," Fuller said, "and get packed up. We need to keep moving."

Senam smiled at her, small and sincere and unexpected, and she felt pleasantly flushed as she had not in years.

It was ridiculous. He had kidnapped her. He had threatened her.

He had never actually harmed her, and he was fond of her horse. He was quite handsome, from what she could see.

Well. She could find him handsome; that was harmless enough. Just so long as she didn't do or say anything about it. She was an engaged woman, and he was a bandit, a kidnapper, and a liar.

~

It was easier, with the leader, after that. He was annoying, at times, but at times he was pleasant, and she found that as long as neither of them lost their tempers—which, granted, they were both prone to doing—they got along well enough. When she was not in a mood to make nice, she settled instead for snide, sniping comments which he returned in kind. It was oddly enjoyable; few enough people would argue with her, these days, or show anything resembling disrespect. (At least to her face. The whispers were another matter. She'd have rather they said it to her directly.) They avoided talk of politics and war, and if he did not share Chris and Alem's fondness for her, she thought he at least did not hate her.

She did not attempt escape again, though she hadn't given up on catching a glimpse of the map. They did not come into true conflict until they reached the edge of the forest, which was the foot of the mountains.

She had never seen the mountains in person, only in paintings and drawing and jagged lines on maps.

Legend said they were the petrified corpses of dead gods. They were the mountains of Olion, and it was an Olin legend.

Olion told stories of gods and devils, of creation and destruction. They told them in rhymes, simple poems that children memorized at bedtime, details and complexities added as the children grew. A grown man or woman in Olion could recite the longest, most complicated epics from memory.

Ibanar's stories were histories, for a given value of history; whether they were strictly true was debatable. They said the third king was anointed by the gods with a crown of fire. They said the pirate queen of the second age had united seventy unique ships into a loose kingdom by killing the last of the sea serpents. They were mostly ballads.

Eloise's kingdom had few stories of their own. They retold the myths and legends they'd learned from the empire they had started from, stories based on a land they'd never seen. It was…lonely, sometimes, Eloise thought.

It was almost exciting, the thought of going up through the mountains, of stepping into one of the stolen stories of her childhood.

And then Senam said, "We'll need to leave the horses, here. Fuller, find a town where we can sell them?"

"Sell them?" Eloise echoed.

"They'll never make it through the mountains. The terrain is all wrong. Besides, they're too expensive to transport by ship, and there's nowhere to keep them, on the island. Our detour gave you a little extra time with your Tulip, at least."

Eloise patted Tulip's sleek neck. She hadn't thought—she had forgotten they'd have to leave the horses. Tulip had been her friend since she was a child. Tulip was the only horse she'd ridden in years, since everything more impressive was redirected to the battlefields.

"You'll sell them," she said.

"Yes."

"And who do you suppose will buy them?"

"Men who need horses, I imagine," he said, turning away from her to join Fuller at the map.

Eloise went to look over his shoulder; he turned and took a step to block her view.

"Princess," he said.

She gave up on the map, for the moment. They were certainly in Olion by now; any escape attempt was doomed. Besides, she had more pressing concerns.

"I'm quite fond of my horse."

"I'm rather fond of mine," he said. "Stole him from an Alirian general—that was a fun day."

"Is there no way we could—"

"Look at your horse, Princess. Now look at mine. Which do you think might have a peaceful future pulling carts, and which do you think will be sold back to the army, to die in pain on a battlefield? I would much rather keep them. But they'll break legs in this terrain, and die painful. Better to leave them here, where they'll at least have a chance."

Eloise nodded, slowly. She didn't like it. It was some comfort that he didn't, either.

"When?"

"In the morning. Say your goodbyes, and I'll ask Chris to look for someone kind, all right?"

"Someone—someone with children. She loves children."

"I'll tell Chris," he promised.

In the morning, Chris and Fuller took the five horses into town. Eloise sat with Alem and the leader in the foothills, waiting.

She had learned to ride on Tulip, as had Ben, and their little sisters, and at least six cousins. She had taught Joel to ride on Tulip. She had taken Tulip when she went riding with Jeremy—it was socially acceptable time alone together, time they needed to make their plans, and she refused to cause a second scandal with her second courtship.

If they had sold the horses a week ago, or two, someone might have recognized Tulip, and at least have started in the right direction to find her. Someone might have recognized Tulip and taken her home, even if they couldn't find Eloise.

She was truly alone, now.

They returned in a few short hours, with a fresh supply of food, and the men spent some time rearranging all their supplies so that they could carry everything themselves. Eloise's sword remained at Senam's waist, and he handed over his own to Fuller, who seemed not quite sure what to do with it, two swords on one belt being impractical.

Eloise's offer to carry it herself was, of course, not accepted. At least they made her carry little else, only the bedroll she'd been sleeping on, and some of the food.

With the supplies all rearranged, they stepped into the mountains. They would be safe here, at least, from soldiers and armies, though not other dangers; reaching any politically or economically significant part of Olion through the mountains was far more trouble than it was worth.

She missed Tulip. She missed her home, her life, her family. She put them out of her head, and tried instead to recall the names of all the gods who made up the mountains.

~

"You left a man in town to collect my ransom," Eloise remembered, suddenly, when they had been two days in the lower hills that started the mountain range. She should have thought of it days ago.

"I did," the leader said.

"We've changed courses. How will he find you to organize my return?"

It didn't matter that there would be no return—they should be prepared to keep their word, collect their ransom, and send her home.

"It only means that you are guaranteed a few extra weeks in our company. He was always to meet us at the base; with this detour, he may beat us there. But we will still meet up, and you'll still be sent home."

"This seems a very inefficient kidnapping."

"It is a kidnapping that has thus far caused you no worse harm than a twisted ankle; you might consider expressing gratitude, instead of criticism."

"Gratitude."

"Your father is known to love you; he would accept you back in any condition. But we have kept your condition good. We have fed you the same food we eat. We have touched you in no indecent way, and have allowed you privacy for your needs, even after your escape attempt. We have laid hands on you only to prevent escape. We have not sold you over to your enemies, who would gladly pay dearly for an Alirian princess, though it would doubtless have been much easier than collecting a ransom from your father."

"All cares you needn't have taken, if you had only refrained from kidnapping me in the first place."

"We could make this trip far less pleasant for you than it has been thus far."

She knew this was true. But Senam poked at her temper in a particular way that made common sense take flight.

"I doubt anything could be less pleasant than waking every morning to the sight of your face. I am blessed, I suppose, to be subjected to only half of it."

He made a frustrated sound. "Princess," he said. "Eloise."

"Don't call me that."

He reached up and pulled off his mask. She stared for a long moment at his revealed face. The scar, uncovered, ran up along the side of his face, past the eyebrow; she thought the original injury must have come very close to blinding him.

He must be very near in age to her—older than Chris, certainly, but much younger than Alem, and likely younger than Fuller as well. How, she wondered, did a man come to lead a group of hardened criminals older and more experienced than him?

He was quite handsome, and somehow familiar.

She realized suddenly that he had been staring just as intently at her.

"Why the sudden loss of interest in identity protection?" she asked.

He stared at her for a moment longer before answering. "I think, when you go home, I am not the man you will be interested in tracking down and having killed."

"And why is that?"

"The man who arranged this, who told us how to draw you out, where to find you when we had? His name was Joel."

It hurt like a knife to the stomach.

It shouldn't have. She knew what he was; she'd known for years. She already knew he had the power to hurt her still; it was rumors of his return that had drawn her out of the palace. Rumors he'd started, she realized now, with this goal in mind.

"And what does he get in exchange?" she asked. "I assume the joy of hurting me wasn't quite enough incentive."

"A quarter of the ransom."

"That's quite the sum, for insider information that anyone with half a brain could guess at."

"The whole plan was his idea, and every step along the way. Without him, there would be no ransom."

There still won't be a ransom, Eloise thought, and didn't say. When they knew she was worthless they would kill her. Or, worse, sent her to Ibanar or Olion.

Her father couldn't pay money he didn't have. She didn't know if he would surrender to his enemies to save her. She didn't want to find out.

"So you're just a lackey? What happened to the Bandit King?"

"Anyone can have ideas, Princess. His happened to be quite good. But he never could have carried them out."

"I see. Only the best of bandits can carry out a kidnapping."

"Do you ever wonder about your lover? Would you like to hear how he lives, now?"

"No," she said, and though the question itself had been cruel, he did not wound her further by forcing an answer.

"A word, please, sir," Fuller said. "Senam." His voice was like ice, and it was the first time any of the men had addressed him by the false name he used.

The leader glanced between Fuller and Alem, then back at Eloise. He sighed. "Chris—"

"Watch the princess?" he guessed.

"Yes."

The other three men walked away. They couldn't get out of sight, with the cover of the forest gone, but they went far enough away that she couldn't make out their words. She watched their body language instead.

They seemed angry with the leader. She couldn't see why—it was only his own face he'd revealed. The scar was impressive, and could likely be used to identify him. But why should it matter so much to the others?

"I didn't recognize him," she said to Chris. "Ought I to have?"

"It's not the mask they're fighting about. Well, not only the mask. We weren't to tell you about Joel."

There was something about the way he said the name—"Do you know him?"

"We've met."

"When you planned my kidnapping?"

Chris nodded. Eloise turned away. She couldn't cope with any of them. Not now.

It wasn't fair. It wasn't fair. She had been a child, and he had been a mistake, and she had spent a third of her life trying to come back from where he left her. She would always be the wild, reckless, foolish princess. It didn't matter that, had she not been kidnapped, she would have been sorting out the final details of her wedding to a perfectly respectable baron, didn't matter that she had followed every stupid rule, official and unspoken, since she was sixteen. It didn't matter that she had successfully petitioned the court to raise the taxes by ten percent instead of fifteen when the war costs rose, and made up a good amount of the difference by selling off most of her jewels, and convincing her sisters and cousins to do the same. She was infamous in three kingdoms for a childhood romance gone sour, and even here, miles from the court, she couldn't escape his ghost.

He had coordinated her kidnapping. Senam shared his chin, his skin tone, his accent. She heard him in songs Alem sang by the fire at night, saw him in Chris' clumsy movements, a young man still adjusting to his own height. She would never be free of Joel.

She thought of him, as he had been when they were children, of his warm dark skin and faintly accented voice, of his quick nimble fingers and coltish clumsiness and anxious, adoring eyes. She thought of the soft breathy laughs she used to startle out of him, and imagined that laughter turned on her, imagined him laughing that little laugh as he plotted her kidnapping—the rumors that would upset her, the door she would choose to slip through and the horse she would take with her and the way she'd never learned to fight on horseback, because she'd learned from him, and he'd only ever been trained as a foot soldier.

She'd told herself and anyone who asked for years that she had hated him, and meant it at least half the time. But this—but this—

She hadn't hated him like this, yesterday.

~

"That was a stupid thing to do," Alem said.

The leader didn't answer.

"That wasn't the plan," Fuller snapped. "That was never the plan."

"I was sick of lying to her."

"So you gave her another half-truth. Blaming it all on—how are you going to work your way out of this mess?"

"I don't know," he admitted. "I just—it wasn't fair, what we were doing to her."

"I told you that at the start," Alem said. "But we've come too far now to offer her anything better."

"I don't know what to do."

"Of course you don't," Fuller said. "You just destroyed three backup plans."

"I'll figure it out. Just—let's just keep moving toward the base, all right?"

"Fine," Alem said.

"You're just damn lucky she reacted the way she did," Fuller said, and they both walked away from him.

The leader allowed himself a moment to regain his composure before rejoining the others. The men, angry, avoided his eyes. The princess was quiet, pale and pensive. She kept her eyes on her feet as they resumed their journey, all of her attention apparently going toward planning each step.

He'd hurt her. Badly.

Better she learned it now than later.

It was true, though, that with her aware of Joel's involvement, none of their existing plans were feasible.

He didn't want to see her hurt. She'd been angry with him, plenty, and he didn't mind that. But the look on her face now felt wrong in the same way as hearing her cry in the night. This was bad enough—he could not bear how much it would have hurt her, learning the truth later, learning the truth too late.

He would make a new plan. He just needed the time and space to think, away from her. He needed to be home.

~

The night was warm, and they did not light the fire. Eloise fell asleep on a bed of heather. She dreamt of Joel's hand in her hair, his voice murmuring, "Don't cry, Ellie. It'll all come right in the end."

When she woke, dried tears stained her cheeks, and she cursed Joel for everything he could still do to her. She had not dreamt of him in over two years. She caught herself thinking fondly for a moment, remembering the rare "Ellie," a name he'd used only at the best of times.

She saw Senam in the corner of her eye and was startled, badly, for a moment, with Joel so on her mind. They had the same skin tone, and similar jaws and chins. Of course, they were otherwise quite different. Senam was several inches taller, and the way he spoke, the way he carried himself—

He was handsome. She'd known that before, but revealing the rest of his face was an improvement.

It wasn't his fault Joel had proven his continued awfulness. Telling her had been a kindness, even if he'd done it in anger.

It was a relief when he sauntered up, tossing her a bit of stale bread before he opened his mouth to drive her mad.

"Rough night?" he asked, not completely without sympathy.

"I could do with a proper bed, sometimes."

"Ship'll have mattresses. Hard ones, full of bugs no doubt, but mattresses."

Eloise smiled. "I look forward to it. Surely the bugs are better company than you."

He smiled back, his uncovered face young and appealing. "I expect you're right. Good morning, Princess."

He walked away, leaving her to the task of shoving Joel from her mind.

She was glad he had told her. He had done it to hurt her, but it was better to know. All her anger at him from yesterday was gone, pushed aside as everything always was by Joel. He didn't seem angry anymore, either.

She wished she didn't like him so much. All of them. When she'd planned not to get attached, she'd expected them to be crueler. Only Senam was ever cruel, but only in word, not deed, and it was—she enjoyed their fighting. It went too far sometimes, but the sniping and argument was a welcome distraction.

Chapter 5

She liked the mountains. It was a relief, after so many days on horseback, to be walking. It was good to be out from under the trees, to see the sun and stars and sky again.

Fuller and Alem had been tense since the leader removed his mask. Chris was excessively chatty to counteract this, and Senam himself seemed largely as usual, occasionally bad tempered, but generally not unpleasant.

No one seemed particularly concerned that she would run, now. They had become much less vigilant. Unfortunately, this was because any escape attempt now would be futile.

They were thoroughly, indisputably in enemy territory. They were also in a territory known to be occupied exclusively by brigands and deserters. Without a horse, she couldn't go far, and with so few trees, she couldn't hide if she did leave. There were large rocks and such to hide behind, but spread loosely across the landscape, easily found and searched.

They kept watches, still, but Eloise thought this was more for fear that someone else would come, than that she would go. Whoever was on watch always had a weapon within easy reach, something they hadn't bothered with in the forest. A sword, for Senam and Fuller. Alem had Eloise's sword, now, but he and Chris had each a wicked club, as well.

47

Legends of brigands in the mountains had, however, apparently been greatly exaggerated. There was not another person to be seen.

"Careful of your ankle," Alem said, as she picked her way through the rocky terrain. It was the first time he'd spoken directly to her since the men had argued.

"It's healed."

"And let's keep it that way, shall we?"

"Yes, let's," the leader said, and offered his arm to lead her over a difficult bit. She accepted. Fuller and Alem exchanged looks, and neither spoke.

~

"Your men are angry with you," the princess observed.

"Looking for weaknesses to exploit?"

"Just making conversation."

"Alem hated the idea of a kidnapping from the start. Fuller is friends with Joel. Chris hates when we fight, and he's fond of you, besides."

"Were you—why did you tell me? About Joel?"

"I think—I think that your lives will intersect again. And when they do, you deserve to know what kind of man he is."

"And what kind of man is he?"

"A coward and a fool."

"That's hardly a surprise."

"No. But he's also a skilled actor."

They had gone off course. They had abandoned the plan. Joel would not stage a rescue, would not win back her favor, would not weasel his way back into the Alirian court on her arm. And her kidnappers would not be paid.

And if the kidnappers were not paid, the men he'd left at the base would revolt. He had to find a fortune, if he wanted to keep himself and his friends alive. He could not just run; if he collected any more people to hide from, he would scarcely be able to turn without being found.

A fortune would not come from Aliria. Ibanar or Olion might pay him, but that would doom the princess.

Returning to base would at least make him appear he knew what he was doing; it would be better than waiting for the others to track him down. He would make a plan from there.

"Why did Joel have me kidnapped?" the princess asked.

He shrugged, waiting to answer until he was sure his tension would not come out in his voice. "Because he's scum, I suppose."

She asked no further questions on the topic.

~

There were mountains across the sea that reached heights beyond climbing, mountains whose tops disappeared into the sky on even the clearest of days, mountains so magnificent they were said to house the gods, and climbing them was forbidden, for they were sacred.

Eloise's brother-in-law had told her, once, that the mountains of Olion would be mere hills by his homeland's standards, and not particularly impressive ones, at that.

But Eloise had never left the island, and likely never would. They were the highest heights she'd ever seen, and to her they were magnificent, miraculous.

"Fuller," Senam said one day, "you've been all through the mountains. Tell the princess where we are."

"The high point ahead, just to our right, is the head of the god Hyg. We're walking now on his body, entwined with the goddess Breya's. Some say they died in battle, others that they died embracing. There's a valley we'll cross soon, the space between their heads. Hyg's head deteriorated in an avalanche, so the valley's full of large rocks, but still passable. The lumpy crest we've just come over is their clasped hands. The next mountain, after the valley, is their son Gir—we'll be crossing at the legs. To the left is his cousin Onin."

"How many gods are there, in the range?" Eloise asked.

"Some say a dozen. Some say over twenty. I counted eighteen, including the ones that fell into the sea. But erosion makes them hard to distinguish."

"Fuller's a cartographer," Senam told her. "He participated in the first official mapping of the mountains in over two hundred years."

"They're lovely," Eloise said. "It must have been a great deal of work."

Fuller smiled—a rare sight. "It was. But worth it. From the cartography standpoint it's all settled, but priests are still arguing about it, or were, last I could get word. We brought three of them along, and they all signed off on the work, but of course you can never get all the priests to agree on anything, and the ones who didn't see it for themselves just won't accept the data; half of them are convinced we made up extra mountains that aren't really here, and the other half think we must have missed several."

It was the most animated, and the most willing to engage with her, Fuller had been. He must have cared a great deal about his work, before he was outlawed.

"Was it a very large party?" she asked.

"Five mapmakers, three priests, and a troop of soldiers, to handle the criminals who roam the mountains."

"Were there criminals? I thought it odd we haven't seen any, given the stories."

"There's no need to hide in the mountains anymore," Senam explained. "The whole island is coming apart, and men have better things to do than keep constant watch for outlaws wandering."

"There were, then," Fuller said.

"When will we get to Sigga?" Chris asked. "We are crossing Sigga, aren't we?"

"We are," Fuller said, and the conversation moved to stories of the gods. Chris, Eloise had already learned, was Alirian. Sigga was the most well-known of the dead gods of Olion, and likely the only one a young Alirian thief was familiar with.

She slipped on a crack in the rocks, then, distracted. Senam caught her, and it felt nothing at all like when Alem had caught her a few days earlier. They stared at each other for a long moment, her foot still half in the crack, his hands both on her waist, hers both on his arm, until someone cleared his throat. Eloise tightened her grip on his arm—just to better get leverage to free her foot, no other reason—and as soon as she was clear he released her, and stepped quickly back.

"Thank you," she said.

~

The nights were cool and moonless, the days hot and bright, the clouds that darkened the night sky promising rain that never came.

Often, thinking of friends she would never see again, Eloise could not sleep, and woke to see the outline of the leader, staring into the darkness. Often, she would go to sit beside him. They did not speak. He seemed to take on a disproportionate amount of watches—she seldom woke to find one of the others on guard, and when she did she did not go to them.

Their days were long, and her legs ached from far more walking than she had ever done, but though her body tired, her mind did not, and she was often too restless to sleep.

"The base you're taking me to," she said, one morning as they walked side by side. "Are there—are there more of you there?"

"Bandits and brigands?"

"Yes."

"There are. A few dozen at a time, usually."

"And they all answer to you?"

"In theory, at least. Outlaws, shockingly, tend not to excel at following rules."

"How did you come to lead a band of outlaws?"

"I killed a man," he said. "Several, actually."

"Oh."

They walked in silence for several minutes, Eloise half listening to Chris and Alem's conversation ahead. Fuller was somewhere behind them, likely taking note of any little changes to the landscape of the mountains, as had become his habit in recent days. Either Chris or Eloise would ask, each time they reached a new crest, whose body they walked on, and he seemed glad to tell them, though he otherwise acknowledged Eloise seldom, and she thought he still did not like her.

Friends with Joel. That would, she supposed, explain it.

She studied the leader, his profile sharp against the rising sun. She decided to take a risk.

"Senam?"

"Yes?"

"If—if no ransom was paid, what would happen to me?"

He stared at her for what felt like a very long time. "I would get you home. I don't—my men wouldn't like it. Not these men, but the rest of them, waiting at our base. It would be—difficult. But I promise you,

Princess Eloise, no matter what happens, I will personally see you to safety."

She nodded. Their silence resumed, less fraught, and a quiet hope rose within her.

~

Fuller caught him, fallen several feet behind the others. The princess, ahead, was engaged in animated conversation with Chris, and would not hear them.

"I am beginning to suspect your new plan is to keep her," Fuller said.

"I wouldn't—not unless she—"

"Unless she wanted to?"

He didn't answer.

Fuller sighed. "What happened to the last queen of the sea, when she gave her heart to a deckhand?"

"She died, and her kingdom fell."

"Your princess has already fallen for an unsuitable man once, and paid dearly for it. Do you think she'll make the same mistake twice?"

No. He did not think she would.

Chapter 6

The baron dismissed his men, and went to find the prince. They were not friends; in fact, they were practically strangers. But they were bound by their affection for the missing princess.

"Any word?" the baron asked.

The prince shook his head. He did not bother asking how the just-finished search had gone; if they had found something, Jeremy would not be asking him for news.

"It's been weeks," the prince said, "and not so much as a ransom note or a subtle threat from the enemy."

"I'm sorry, Ben."

"I'll have to go back to the front soon. They could hardly spare me in the first place, and reports say Olion is advancing."

"I'll keep looking. I won't give up on her."

"I know," Ben said.

Jeremy had lost one fiancée already; he could not bear to lose another. His love for Eloise was unromantic, but no less sincere for that, and her absence had torn open old wounds, as well as creating new ones. He had so few people to love; he did not think he could survive losing another one.

Chapter 7

There was hope. She may yet survive this; she did not think Senam a liar.

Well, she did. She thought he had lied every time he had threatened to harm her. She did not think he would lie about keeping her safe. She thought she would survive, if he had any say in the matter. There was hope, and she allowed herself peace. She allowed herself to enjoy the beauty of the mountains, the freedom of being so far from home. She made conversation with the men not in an attempt to draw close to them and save her life, but because they were interesting to talk to.

"Have you seen the great hills of Geth?" she asked Alem.

"If I did I don't remember it; we came to Ibanar when I was quite young."

"My sister's husband grew up in one of the lesser palaces, nestled between Jun and Mirac."

"I didn't know the newest prince was from Geth."

"He's not the newest prince anymore. Not for a while. He and my sister have twins. A boy and a girl, four years old."

~

"Have you done much other travelling, for your maps?" she asked Fuller.

"I would have gone across the sea for a project, but I was charged before we set sail."

He did not say anything else on the matter, and Eloise left him to try talking with Chris, instead. Chris had few interesting stories to tell—he had been a petty thief in the capital of Aliria until two years ago, when his crimes had piled to such a height that he was to be pressed into the army. He had been given leave to say goodbye to his family, and had run instead, then had met Senam and joined his band a few weeks later. But he was more pleasant to talk to than Fuller.

~

"How did you get your scar?" she asked Senam, when she woke to find him stoking the fire, and the others still asleep.

"It was a fight. A foolish fight over foolish things." He poked at the fire, eyes fixed on the coals. She did not think he would say more. But he did.

"I loved a girl, and I wasn't fit to clean her boots. We all knew it, and we all knew it couldn't last. But she loved me too, once. We were separated, and I told some men I met how I felt—they thought I was lying, they thought I wanted something from her, and I took offense. They took offense at my taking offense, and they attacked. I fought back, and got the better end of things, overall. But I never saw the girl again."

"I'm sorry."

He looked up at her, briefly. "Not the exciting outlaw story you were expecting, I'm afraid. It can't be all theft and fun and murder, you know. We all had lives before we were the dirt beneath your feet."

"You're—you're not—"

"Oh, I was always dirt. But she made things grow in me. And then I was a fool, and I lost her."

"I'm sorry," Eloise said again.

"Don't be. It was years ago now. Come on, let's see about breakfast."

~

Once the leader asked, in the dead of night, breaking their unspoken law against speaking before the sun had risen, "Do you miss them?"

"Who?"

"Your family."

"It hardly matters."

"It does," he insisted, his voice gentle and familiar in the dark. "Tell me about them."

"Everyone knows everything about my family," she answered, almost bitter.

"Humor me. You know I'm not Alirian."

She took a few minutes to answer. "I have three brothers, two older, one my twin. And three sisters, one older, two younger. My older sister is the only one of us married. My mother and father are beginning to worry, I think, that none of the boys are married yet. Especially Theo, since he's the heir. But he says he'll bother about that when the war is over and we all have some space to breathe.

He doesn't care much about marrying for love—who can afford to in this world?—but he doesn't want it to be something purely political, in the midst of war. He wants the space to choose a girl he can be comfortable with, at least."

"And what about you, Princess? Would you marry for love?"

"No. I've tried that way already. I'll take comfort, too."

"Our Lord Jeremy is comfortable, then," he said, something in his tone she couldn't identify.

"Yes, Jeremy is comfortable."

"Tell me about your twin."

"He's been in the war, on and off, these past few years. I haven't seen him much. I haven't seen anyone much. But we were always close, when we were children."

"He was involved in some of your scandals, wasn't he?"

"Several. He never meant to be. I dragged him into the most outrageous things when we were young, him and Joel. My boys." She caught herself smiling, as she thought of it, and she stopped for a moment to collect herself. "But that's all done with. He's away at war. Maybe not now—I imagine most of them will come home to search for me. Waste of good soldiers. They'll never find anything."

"I'm sorry," he said, and he sounded like he meant it.

"No, you're not. No one expects you to be—this is what you do, isn't it?"

"You'll be back with them soon."

"Perhaps."

~

She had long since lost track of the days, but it occurred to her, as the sun rose golden over Hedi's braid, and she thought of their conversation the previous night, that she must certainly have missed her wedding day.

Hedi's braid was the customary hairstyle for an Olin bride, a tradition Eloise had planned to adopt in honor of Jeremy's dead Olin mother, despite their war. The mountain did not much resemble the drawings she'd been shown when making this plan; likely Fuller would blame it on erosion.

Jeremy must be going mad with worry.

They were not done yet with their outgoing journey; they would have to make the same way home again, as well. She would likely have missed her younger sister's wedding, too, by then. Though not as galling as missing her own, this would be more a cause for sadness. She had looked forward to supporting Annabelle and celebrating with her.

Both marriages were for safety, not love. A princess already married was a princess who could not be forced to wed an enemy to solidify an alliance, if they lost the war. But Annabelle was young and romantic still, engrossed in wedding plans, eager for the next stage in her life.

Eloise had not thought much about her own upcoming wedding, beyond the decision for her hairstyle. And little would change, for her, with the marriage. They would be able to enter each other's chambers without scandal, and not much else. Annabelle would move to her new husband's estate, but Jeremy's manor had been burned down in the war, and he had lived in the palace since, for nearly two years now. They had not the time or resources or workers to rebuild; they could not begin until the war was over, and then it may be years before they could move in.

Anger rose, sudden and unexpected. These men were pleasant enough, to her, and she had been promised a safe return. But what they had done to her family was unbearably cruel. They may well have given her up for dead by now, as weeks passed and search parties found nothing, as no sales or loans or taxes could produce the funds for her ransom.

So many people, so frightened for her, while she gallivanted about the island, having the time of her life.

Her anger at the bandits passed, replaced by anger with herself. How could she have such fun, while they would worry so?

But then, had she not worked endlessly for a decade to be exactly what they wanted? Would she not continue to do so, for the rest of her life? Could she not have this one adventure, enjoy this strange, rare time in her life?

Conflicted, she withdrew from the others, and a few days passed quietly.

"All right, princess?" Senam asked, and she nodded. "We'll be at the coast, soon."

"Good."

"Are you—are you sure you're all right?"

"Fine."

He left her to speak quietly with Fuller, and she hung back, trailing behind the others. She was excited, despite herself, to reach the coast.

Within another day the air had changed, growing faintly salty. In three more, they passed between the mountains Wen and Yunak, and could see the rocky shoreline. There was not much of a dock, but multiple ships were anchored in the shallows, and she could see at least two more, tiny in the distance.

"Wait here," Senam said. "Princess, Alem, Chris. Fuller, come with me."

They waited at a collection of large rocks a few miles from the shore, Chris and Alem talking about—about ships, she thought. It wasn't a conversation she could follow. She looked out at the shore, wondering which of the dead gods had fallen into the seas, and whether Fuller would point them out to her.

A few hours passed. The three of them had unpacked and eaten their lunch before Fuller and Senam returned. Senam dropped to the ground and dug more food out of the pack, handing some up to Fuller, who remained standing.

"The captain is Ibanari," Senam said. "That's good."

"Why?" Eloise asked.

"Foreigners can get odd, about women on ships." Foreigners had, when Eloise was very young, meant off-islanders. These days it was hard to say whether one meant only off-islanders, or also the residents of whichever two countries on the island the speaker was not a citizen of.

"You never know, with pirates," he continued. "What you're going to get. What they'll decide to be difficult about. But an Ibanari captain will have grown up on stories about the pirate queens of old. He won't hold with keeping anyone off the water for silly superstitions."

"When do we leave?"

"In the morning. We'll stay here until then—we've picked a good ship, with a good crew, but there are many men about today that I do not trust. It's safer you stay far from them."

It was the most relaxing day Eloise had experienced in weeks, long hours where she was not required to walk or ride, and Fuller was talked into reciting a poem on the death of the mountain gods, while the rest of them lounged about and listened.

The night was cool and pleasant. She fell asleep to the sound of Fuller and Alem exchanging myths, and woke to the sound of Chris attempting to explain the Alirian spiral of the gods. It was not a good explanation, but Eloise was not in the mood to correct him.

"Ready to go, Princess?" Senam asked her. The sun had barely peeked over the horizon; they would have to leave now to reach the ship when the tides were right for departure.

She took his offered hand, and he pulled her to her feet. They gathered their supplies and began their walk to the shore.

There were last minute arrangements to be made, friendly-sounding shouting to be done between Senam and the ship's captain, and Eloise stood atop a large rock to take in the view, while she waited to be let aboard the ship. Alem waited just below her rock, standing guard, she assumed, against the untrustworthy men Senam had mentioned.

The shore was beautiful, if very rocky. The ship they were to take had anchored well away from the shore, where it could rest without being impaled. They would have to wade out to it. Eloise didn't mind; she was thoroughly filthy, and would enjoy bathing up to the knees, at least. Perhaps she could duck fully under the water, and rinse away the worst of the grime.

They were in the Sea of Tears, which filled the curve of their roughly crescent-shaped island—it was a large basin filled with the tears of the sky, who wept when his children, the gods who became mountains, were killed. The windy season was supposed to be the anniversary, when the waters became rough with the force of the sky's renewed sorrow.

Fortunately, they were far off from the windy season. Eloise looked out at the horizon, but there was nothing to see but water. The continent to the east, the other handle of the basin in Ibanar, and the island Senam claimed they sailed for were all still invisible in the distance.

"Ready to go, Princess?" Senam asked, for the second time that day, and she turned on her rock to find he had taken Alem's place watching her.

She took his hand to hop off of the rock, and followed him for a while into the water, until it reached her knees, and she broke away to slip beneath the surface, and run fingers through her filthy, tangled hair.

"The tides," he reminded her.

"Yes, yes, I'm coming." She swam to the ship, though it was shallow enough she could easily have walked. She wanted the cool water running over all of her, not just her legs.

There was a rope ladder to get from the sea to the deck, and she climbed ahead of Senam, joining the men as they wrung out their clothing and checked their packs for damage. Eloise herself had carried nothing, and had stuffed her shoes and stockings into one of the bags before stepping into the water.

"Come below deck," Chris said. "They hate having people underfoot when they're getting started, usually. I'll show you where we'll sleep, and you can come out and see the deck once we've gotten going."

~

Eloise's seafaring experience, thus far, had been limited to rafts and rowboats in the lakes and ponds that dotted central Aliria, and once a barge, on the river Trell. She had welcomed visitors and seen them off at their main port on the western border, but had never herself set sail from there. She had never been far enough out on the open water that the shores grew hazy in the distance. She had never been caught up in winds and waves and tides. She had never been seasick.

She was, it turned out, very prone to seasickness.

As staying below deck made her feel trapped and anxious, Eloise made a habit of sitting at the edge of the deck, so that she could lean over and be sick into the water, rather than making a mess for the sailors to clean.

She liked to look out at the sea, watching the movement of the waves, the passage of the sun. It had been a long time since she had been near the water much.

When she was fifteen, she and Ben had snuck off in a rowboat to show Joel the small lake at the edge of the palace grounds. Joel's seafaring experience had been limited to falling into a fountain in the royal gardens, and Eloise had delighted, as she always did, in showing him something new.

Joel's own home had been landlocked, but he was Ibanari, descended from the pirate kings and queens of legend. He had told Ben and Eloise, as they rowed, the stories his mother had told him, of sea monsters and battles, ancient warriors and explorers.

He had told them of the last queen of the sea, a story Eloise had loved until the end, which she hated, and she had played at shoving him overboard. He had panicked, for he didn't know how to swim. It had never before occurred to Eloise that there were people who couldn't swim.

(Often, in the coming years, she would wish that she had truly pushed him in.)

They'd spent most of their summer in the water, Ben teaching Joel to swim, while Eloise gathered around her what little dignity she had, at fifteen, and watched them from the shore, or occasionally the shallows. Mixed swimming was indecent, past certain ages and family relationships, and while Eloise had not particularly cared, then, if either Joel or her brother saw her with fabric clinging, wet, to her body, one could never be sure of privacy at the edge of the lake, during their unauthorized swimming lessons, and she didn't want anyone else who might pass to see her in such a state.

When Joel could swim safely in the depths of the lake, where no one on the shore could see what they were doing, they'd taken the rowboat out again. Eloise had joined the boys in the water, playing with Joel at being King Senam and his mermaid, or the lady Eisha and the dolphin who'd guided her home. Ben had laughed and made faces at their antics, and Eloise—Eloise—

She wished she could stop thinking of him.

He had haunted her since first the leader had said his name.

Jeremy had taken her on a lakeside picnic, once, last year. Conscious always of eyes on her, Eloise had not dared even to kick off her slippers and dip her toes in the water.

The reason she could never stop thinking of Joel, she supposed, was that all the most interesting things she'd done involved him.

She had been wild, then. And she had been happy. In the aftermath—all nine years of it—she'd tried always to be on her best behavior.

This was an incredible adventure. And Senam had promised she'd end it safely, and she believed him. If only she had not her family to worry about, this would be the most fun she'd had in years. Perhaps when she was home again, she could think of this, of him, instead of Joel.

Senam. She thought of the false name, of the story.

> 'In the days when Senam ruled the sea
> On the night of a red tinged sky
> The mermaid stepped aboard his ship
> Her fin split to form a standing disguise
> He knew not from whence she'd come or why.'

It was a ballad, though the original tune had been lost to time, and she'd heard it set to three different melodies. She'd known it by heart, once, but the details had been faded by time. The broad strokes of the story, she remembered still. How the mermaid had fallen for King Senam, but could not bear to live aboard his ship:

> 'For though I love you, dear and true,
> Your home I cannot abide.'

How eventually she had revealed her true nature, and taken him to her home beneath the sea, and there they had stayed, together, while Senam's brother took charge of his kingdom.

Her brother Julian had told her, when she relayed the story to him, that probably the real Senam, if there was a real Senam, threw himself overboard, and they made up the story to soothe whatever frightened children might have witnessed it.

Her brother Julian had never been much fun, and she hadn't appreciated his interpretation. Of course, she hadn't appreciated anything Julian said and did, in those days. He was—sensibly, it turned out—disapproving of her relationship with Joel, and she'd had little patience for anything he'd said to her.

Senam joined her, as she was thinking these thoughts—the Senam who was the leader of a band of outlaws, not the Senam of myths and mermaids.

"Is it getting any better?" he asked her.

"I've not been sick since you came by last," she offered, not entirely certain if that was an improvement or not. It had been an exceedingly unpleasant day.

He sat beside her, arm on the railing, feet dangling over open water, and handed her a jug. "Here, drink this. Should help."

Eloise took the jug, studying it carefully.

"Oh, don't look at it like that. You think I'm going to poison you this late in the game?"

"What is it?"

"I've no idea. One of the sailors said it would help with seasickness."

She took a cautious sip. It was disgusting—usually, in her experience, a good sign, when it came to medication. "How much do I need to drink?"

He shrugged. "Sailor didn't say."

She took another sip, and set it carefully aside. "Will we be many days at sea?"

"Not many. They've never been to the island, so I couldn't get an exact arrival date. But Fuller showed them a map, and we should have no trouble getting there."

"I didn't know there was an island in the Sea of Tears."

"Not many people do. Odd, really—it's very significant, historically. But then it's quite small, with no natural resources, in a strategically useless location."

"Historically significant?" Eloise asked.

"Now it's just a neutral, forgotten island where outcasts—most of us nasty—wind up. But a few hundred years ago it was a military base for your kingdom, and a generation or two before that it was the birthplace of Ibanar."

"Ibanar was born in the sea," she said. Everyone knew that.

Ibanar was debatably the youngest of the three countries on their large island. Olion and Ibanar had both started out as disjointed collections of people under assorted chieftains, frequently coming together and breaking apart, but Ibanar's collections of people had all been always on the water. Eloise's kingdom was the remains of an abandoned expansion attempt by an empire that had, at the time, been one of the greatest world powers. It had since faded into near obscurity, and the outposts it had left behind had coalesced, becoming a country in their own right, while Olion had solidified into one people, and eventually Ibanar had come up from the sea, settling in the south.

"Ibanar was born in the sea," he agreed. "While Olion roamed the lands, and your emperor ruled you still, Ibanar roamed the sea. Their young queen wasn't as restless as her ancestors, perhaps—she chose this island to settle on. Your emperor found that a threat, killed her, and burned all the docked ships. The remaining sailors scattered, but most moved north, toward Olion, since you still held the southern half of the island then. The queen's younger brother led a rebellion, eventually, and he did his best to drive the empire off the island—he didn't succeed, but he did drive them north, and the southern half became Ibanar. This island, though, was the first land that was ever called Ibanar. No one remembers, of course."

"And why do you remember? How did you come to be here?" She knew of the last queen of the sea, Ishan, who had died, and been betrayed, but had never heard of her landing, first.

"I inherited the island with my position—outlaws have settled here for generations. The history, I learned when I was living in the south, before the war got so bad. There are stories down there you'll not hear anywhere else in the world. No one in Ibanar will come here now—

think it's cursed. And it's too far south to be of interest to Olion, or to you, without the influence of the empire; it was a good place, strategically, for them." He smiled at her—not his usual smile, but something softer and almost sad. "She reminds me of you a bit. That last queen. First and last, on land and on sea."

"How?"

"She had a young lover, far beneath her station. A boy in the crew of her ship. He betrayed her to the empire. Told them about the island, led them right to it."

Joel again, always inescapable. She knew this story, or most of it—not about the island. She knew this story. She hated this story. "And what happened to him?" she asked. For the deckhand's story ended, usually, with the death of the queen.

"No one seems to know. Some say he died, some say he sailed across the sea, and some say he married the daughter of one of the emperor's governors here."

"I hope he died."

"Well, I'm sure he has by now." He stood. "If you'll excuse me—I have work to do."

~

She sat often at the edge of the deck, and Senam often sat with her. The others she saw seldom, saving when the four of them slept each night in one small room. They were occupied, she supposed, with their own business, now that they had a little freedom to do more than walk, and walk, and walk all day. The sailors mostly ignored her, which suited her well enough. If she had questions about seafaring, she addressed them to Senam, and he could usually answer them.

Seasickness persisted, but it was not so severe as it had been the first day or two, and she was enjoying the adventure enough that it bothered her little.

"How many days will we be at sea?" she asked him again, on the third day.

"No more than a week now. Perhaps five days. The seasickness is better?"

"It is better. Is it nice, your island? Will I like it?"

"Perhaps."

"Will we be there long?"

"It depends. We'll stay there until we get word of the ransom going through, and have to return you home."

"And if—if it doesn't go through?"

"Then we sneak off the island in the dead of night, and I still return you home."

She nodded. "I don't—I don't—"

"Don't worry, Princess." He smiled at her, and changed the subject abruptly. "Have you ever been in the Sea of Tears before?"

She shook her head. "The western coast is closer to the palace; it's the only harbor I've been to."

"They say it's the saltiest water in the world—all those tears the sky wept, I suppose. Does Aliria have any stories of the basin? Or is everything civilized too far west? I know it's mostly forest on your eastern border."

"We've nothing special. We've no local stories, really. Nothing but more recent histories. All of our early stuff comes from the empire. Does Ibanar have stories of the basin, too? I thought it was only Olion."

"All of Ibanar's stories are stories of the basin. When we were seafarers, we spent most of our time in the basin. We had to go farther afield sometimes, of course. But this was the base of everything, even before we tried to settle the island. Senam and his mermaid were here; the center of the mermaid kingdom is right below us, or near enough. Of course, no one's seen a mermaid in two hundred years, except Dubar the fool, eighty five years ago, and when he caught it and brought it home—"

"It was a dolphin, wasn't it? Or a seal?"

He shrugged. "Certainly not a mermaid, at least. The body is in a temple in Ibanar. I've never seen it. They say the skeleton is like a dolphin's, but the drawings from before the flesh deteriorated showed it larger, shaped differently."

"Do you think the mermaids are still below us?" Eloise asked him. "Do you think they ever were?"

"Perhaps. I suppose none of us are worthy of their attention anymore—we cannot all of us be Senam."

"No, we cannot. I think—I think that when you take me home, you should tell me your real name. Before you leave again."

"You don't believe my name is Senam?"

"Did you expect me too?"

"No," he admitted. "We'll see. When the time comes."

"Have you more stories of mermaids? There are only a few we know, in Aliria, and most of those I learned from Ibanari visitors."

"I know a few. Maybe some you haven't heard. Do you know the princess Irena?"

"I don't."

"Then let me tell you. She was the youngest daughter of the king of the sea, in a time before counting, when the mountains had not yet fallen into the sea."

~

He found her watching the sun set, and sat down beside her. And for a moment she thought—

She could kiss him. There was no one about to see the indecency. It would be only the once, and Jeremy wouldn't mind, not until after the wedding; it wasn't a love match. She could kiss him, and she was fairly certain he would kiss her back.

She leaned forward. The ship jostled as it hit a wave, and instead of kissing him, she clung to his arm for balance. Somehow, by the time she'd swallowed down the resulting nausea, Senam had rearranged them so that his arms were around her, her cheek against his shoulder. It felt, somehow, even more intimate than a kiss. Not just romance and scandal but a sense of comfort. It was too much, and she forced herself to pull away. Neither of them spoke.

Senam left her, after a few minutes, to watch the setting sun alone. Their destination was visible in the distance; they would certainly reach it soon, and she had missed her chance. She would not kiss Senam in front of an entire island full of outlaws, and so she would not, it seemed, kiss Senam at all.

~

Eloise stood at the stern, watching the sun rise, and the small shape growing on the horizon. Senam came up behind her; she recognized his step, and did not bother turning to face him.

"Princess," he said softly.

"Yes."

"We'll reach the island tomorrow. I—I promised I would see you safely home. And I meant it. Wait on me. Don't try to escape. My control of my men is not what I would wish it."

"All right," she agreed easily—she trusted him.

~

As soon as they drew close enough to the island to see the undersized, overrun dock, the attitude of the leader changed dramatically. They had been standing at the rail in companionable silence, and suddenly he was stiffer, standing straighter, with a new distance between them. The silence was no longer companionable.

"Are you—"

"Don't speak. We're nearly there."

He went to talk to Chris and Fuller and the sailors, and he gathered their equipment, and did not address her again until the ship was docked.

"Get out."

She made the jump unassisted, since no assistance was offered, unsteady still on her sea legs. It was Fuller that caught her when she stumbled, while the leader watched impassively. When the ship was unloaded and departing he spoke again, and his voice was cold and unfamiliar.

"This is a very small island, Princess, and it's all mine. The boats you see here are the only way off. And I'm sure you're intelligent enough to realize that none of them can be manned by a single person. Or even by two. Now, you'll be under constant supervision, but I can only spare so much attention for you, and I'm quite sure you're capable of slipping your guard. Be sensible and don't. You couldn't get far—you couldn't get off the island—and when we found you I would have to be angry. Understand?"

"I understand."

She did. She understood that he was a bandit king and a kidnapper first, and her friend—if he was her friend at all—a distant second. How foolish, to grow fond of a man when she was his prisoner. She did not think her taste in men could be worse if she tried.

There was always Jeremy. But she would never see him again.

~

It was a small island, apparently occupied only by criminals. And only male criminals—she had not yet seen another woman.

She was brought to the ruins of a castle. It stood well enough, in many spots, that the men were able to live in it. She walked past several of them, saw the small personal spaces they had carved out, for there was little privacy in ruins. The dungeon area, being lower down, was still mostly intact, and there was a cell for her.

The ceiling was low and rounded, and it felt more like a cave than a room—this, for some reason, was comforting. Many other cells were occupied, though their door hung open, and she thought men must have chosen them as the most comfortable areas in the ruin to sleep.

Her door, barred with rusted iron, was kept closed, and a man stood guard. He did not speak to her; he hardly looked at her. She tried to ignore him, and paced the limited space available, not noticing the small, high window until she did.

There was a large, roundish stone on the ground, which she found she could roll with some difficulty to sit more directly below the window. The guard did not react to her efforts, presumably because he knew the window was too small for any escape.

She stood on the stone to look out. There was nothing of note to see, only rocks and sparse trees, and many large men milling about. She could see the dock from here; there were a few small rowboats pulled up onto the shore, and the ship she'd arrived on had already vanished into the distance. She was trapped. She was alone.

Chapter 8

"The men are growing restless. You're running out of time."

"I know."

"Have you thought of a new plan?"

"No."

"You know what you must do, then."

"I know. Just—just give me a few more days. Please."

~

The leader did not come back. Days passed, alone in her dark little hole. Food was brought with the changing of the guard. The guards were never men she knew, never Chris or Fuller or Alem, and there was never news—she didn't expect a ransom or even a rescue, but lived half in dread, half in longing, for the announcement that the bandits had given up on ransom, and had a new plan for her.

Sound travelled well in the ruins, and outlaws were a noisy bunch, though they never seemed to speak of anything important. She occupied herself mostly with listening, trying to pick out the familiar voices of the men she'd travelled with. Occasionally she was successful.

She shouldn't have trusted Senam.

Chapter 9

Eloise was a fool. She had thought nothing could be more humiliating than her kidnapping, utterly her own fault, except that it was also Joel's.

She was a fool. She should have known. She should have known.

Hardly a day had gone by, all these years, without a thought of him, despite her best efforts.

And yet she hadn't known. Somehow, she hadn't known.

It was the familiar voice of Chris, echoing through the caverns, that told her.

She hadn't seen him—hadn't seen any of them—since the day they arrived at the island. And the guard had grown lax, since she was so well behaved. Still, it was three days after learning the truth before she managed to escape. There was no real lock on the door; there was only the iron bar and the guard.

The guard had taken to sleeping, instead of watching her, at night. It mattered little. She had been told there was no way off the island, and as far as she could tell it was true. Leaving her cage and her guard behind would only put her in the path of many other outlaws, and she was not entirely sure whether the guard was to contain her, or to protect her from other men.

It was a risk she would take. After all, she was not seeking to truly escape, only to speak to one man.

Her guard slept. She waited until it was nearly morning, until she could see the first rays of sunlight when she looked out her little window. The iron bar was not so heavy. It was ancient and discolored, and when she lifted it she could feel rust crumbling onto her hands.

She lowered the bar carefully to the ground, and pulled the door open slowly, wishing she could remember, from that first day, if it creaked.

It did not creak.

Most of the outlaws slept late. She slipped carefully down the winding halls, hoping desperately that none would wake.

None woke.

She did not go in the direction she had come, the day they arrived. She went instead across the other side of the building, where the ruins were far more ruined.

It took longer to find her way outside again than she had expected, and the sun was high, and painfully bright after days of darkness. They would be looking for her by now—they had probably been looking for her for several minutes. So she chose a nice, visible place to await developments. He would come out for her himself. He had to. She only had to wait.

She was sitting on a rock on the beach, in a little patch of sunlight, when he strode out. He stopped between her and the sun, arms crossed.

"I told you to wait for me," he said.

She studied him carefully. She could see it, now that she was looking for it. She should have seen it before.

"You've told me a lot of things. Haven't you, Joel?"

His face went white in a gratifying way. "Eloise," he said, and he sounded so young.

"You must have known I'd find out eventually."

She stood, not wanting him above her, and watched him collect himself, drawing confidence around him like a cloak, that brief glimpse of a boy she'd known hidden again behind the bandit king.

"Eventually, yes. Frankly, I expected it much sooner. I'd rather given up, by now, on you ever working it out."

"What the hell is wrong with you?"

He grinned. "Come on, don't say you didn't want to see me again."

She slapped him. If he'd ever grinned at her like that she'd have known. Nine years. Closer to ten now. But she should have known, she still should have known.

He reeled back. "All right, I deserved that one. But El. Really." It was a different smile that he smiled this time, and one she didn't like. He reached out to touch her shoulder, and she flinched.

"Don't touch me. Do not touch me, or I swear I'll—"

"You'll what? Glare at me? Yell some more? You're powerless here, Eloise. You are my prisoner, on my island, surrounded by my men. Your sword is in my scabbard. The only reason you have legs to stand on is that I have been kind enough not to have them chopped off at the knee. Now sit down."

She sat. "This was all done with years ago. What game are you playing?"

"What makes you think I have a game?"

"Oh, please."

"How did you find out?" he asked.

"Chris. He called your name. You answered. I recognized your voice." She'd recognized Senam's voice, and realized it was also Joel's voice, deeper than it had been, distorted by an accent he'd never let her fully hear, but still his voice, his voice that she should never have forgotten. "Of course it was you. As soon as the idea occurred to me— well, obviously it was you. I'd have seen it right away if it hadn't been so completely absurd. That even you would do something so abysmally stupid. It's astounding."

"Well. It worked, didn't it?"

"I found out."

"And how does that change anything? Oh, it was fun enough, watching you not knowing. But your knowing isn't going to magically set you free."

"Nothing is going to set me free. You idiot. Our treasury is empty. Completely. If they raised the taxes again they might be able to pull together half the ransom. Maybe. But we're already on the verge of rebellion. Taxation is not a viable option. You will get no money for me. I will live and die with you." She laughed, suddenly, hysterically. "Oh, gods. I'll live and die with you. Just like we always planned when we were children. Don't expect to have the same kind of fun you could have had then."

"As if you had any ability to control the fun I have with you. Powerless, remember? You always did want to be the one in control. But you can't expect the old rules to apply here, El." He took her arm and yanked her to her feet. "Come on, then. Back to the cage. I'll come and visit you soon."

"Please don't."

"Of course I will. You know, I've missed you terribly."

He left her, and she sat in her little corner of the cave, under the suddenly watchful eye of her guard, trying to plan an escape that could not be planned. There was no way off of this gods-forsaken island. Not alone. Three people, he'd said, when he was someone else, when he had not been Joel and when she had almost cared for him. Three people. She was only one, and there was no one here to turn to. They were all his.

And he would—she had loved him.

Dying, she could manage. But to be hurt at his hands, and after all this, after it was finally all over—it was too much.

She was—Joel was—Joel was—

She hated Joel. She had loved him, once, for a brief and beautiful time. She'd had near a decade since for her hate to fester.

She had liked Senam. She had known he told her lies, known he could hurt her, badly, if he wished. But she had trusted him.

~

The first thing he remembered, after, was a boy staring down at him. He didn't know how long it had been—hours? Months? There had been the trial, and then there had been Eloise, and then they had taken him away. He didn't speak to the boy, but let him take his hand and pull him upright, then into the village. They had been in a forest. It had been a forest, hadn't it, where they dropped him off? He thought those trees had been a different color. Silver—no, that had been Eloise. Silver and gold. That had been a very long time ago. Time didn't make sense now.

They didn't know who he was. He didn't tell them. He learned, when he bothered to care about things again, that he was in Olion, and that they wouldn't have cared, anyway.

They did know that he had been tortured—not too long then, since he'd left. Not if they could still see it on him.

They told him he was fine, and he tried to count the scars they couldn't see.

They told him they were at war. Several of them went to fight, and invited him: "It would take your mind off things. You could get revenge."

He'd never told them he needed revenge. He'd never told them where he was from—what kingdom he'd need revenge on. Obviously he wasn't from Olion, but he looked far more Ibanari than Alirian.

Maybe they had known who he was. He'd never bothered with a name, false or true. He'd never bothered with anything. He didn't go to war. A month later he left.

At first he thought he would kill Eloise. That would be good. Scars didn't heal—that was the point of scars. But maybe he could tattoo his own pattern on top of them.

He had decided against it, in the end. It wasn't good enough. It wasn't right.

~

Eloise woke to a hand over her mouth and Joel's voice in her ear. "No one who could hear your screams would care. So keep quiet, and things don't have to get ugly." He removed his hand.

"What do you want?"

"I want you to come with me. Very quietly. And stop looking at me like that—I'm not going to hurt you."

"You can't even see me."

"I know your looks, El. I can feel them. Now come on. I've still got your sword, and half a dozen small knives, but I really suggest you don't try to take them from me. Nothing is going to happen here that you wouldn't want."

"You think you know what I want?"

"I know I do. And I'm not going to touch you. Now shut up and follow me, or I'll knock you out and carry you."

They crept through the caves and across the beach. It was a dark night, cloudy and moonless. Joel stopped in front of a rowboat, sitting lower in the water than the others. She saw the outline of a hand move, and squinted. There were three men in the boat.

"Get in."

"What are we doing?"

"Escaping."

"Really."

"I promised I would see you home, Eloise. I will see you home. I'm sorry about this morning. But they were all watching, and I didn't get to be leader of a band of outlaws by getting on my knees and begging for forgiveness from my captives. You can't believe I would ever really—" He broke off abruptly. "Just get in the boat and be quiet. I'll explain when we've gone a way."

She climbed in, trying without much success to put space between Joel and herself. She stared out at the landscape, though there was really nothing but darkness, and waited.

Finally Joel said, "Eloise." She looked up. "I'm offering you a deal. I'll get you home, unharmed, and I'll tell you everything I know about the conspiracy—everything I didn't tell all those years ago—in exchange for full pardons, for me and for everyone on this boat."

It was the best offer she was likely to get. "Deal. Shall we kiss on it?"

He laughed. "Let's not." He took a ring from his pocket; she reached out, and he dropped it in her outstretched hand. Her seal ring. She hadn't seen it since he'd taken it the first day of her kidnapping. "Sign of good faith," he said. "Get some sleep, Princess. I'll wake you when we reach shore."

"It took us days to get here. You can't possibly make it back in a rowboat."

"It took us days because we came through the mountains. Our little island is at the bottom of the sea, not far from the Ibanari shore. We're going to where we meant to come from, last time."

"We couldn't get to it, last time. Can we get away, once we land?"

"The landing point is clear—we can see it by telescope. I don't know about the surrounding terrain, but it's a safer chance than staying here." He stood carefully, and the boat rocked. "Move, Chris. I want to row."

Eloise woke at midmorning, and saw that the other two men in the boat were Fuller and Alem, who she hadn't seen since the first night.

The whole band, back together. Alem waved when he saw she was awake.

"So. Here we are where we started. What happens now?"

Joel answered, "There's another hour or two of rowing. Some of us worked all night, while you slept."

"I've more than earned my sleep. The things you've put me through, Joel."

"When we get to shore. We'll work from there."

~

Her determination to ignore the lot of them lasted not even until midday, when the shore came into sight.

"Will anyone follow us?"

"I drilled holes in most of the other rowboats," Fuller said. "Not all of them—they would die, with no way off the island. But I think they will be too busy worrying about the boats, or fighting amongst themselves, to come after us immediately."

"And what would happen, if they did?"

"They would kill the four of us," Joel said. "They might kill you, too, or they might sell you to the highest bidder. Depends on who they choose to replace me."

"Not exactly a beloved leader, are you?"

"Do you think your civil war has started yet?" he asked in response, and she renewed her attempts to ignore him.

She had been thinking furiously since the moment Chris called his name, and trying desperately not to since the moment he woke her. She had succeeded, for a while. Now all the thoughts were back.

She was a fool. Exactly the idiot everyone thought her to be.

How could she have failed to recognize him?

She hadn't wanted to recognize him. She'd been infatuated with Senam—infatuated for the first time since Joel, which made a horrible kind of sense in hindsight—and she'd spent a decade alternating between trying to despise Joel and trying to forget him. She had been having an adventure, an exciting journey and a harmless rush of pleasant but ultimately meaningless feelings. She had intended to enjoy herself until her real life resumed, and recognizing Joel would most certainly have ruined everything.

She'd known he looked familiar, and she'd talked herself out of it. She hadn't wanted to recognize him. She was so sick of being haunted by that particular memory. Joel had been a childhood mistake. A rather spectacular mistake, with far-reaching consequences, but she'd only been fifteen when it started.

It was a mistake she had no intention of repeating.

She remembered the dream she'd had—not a dream, of course. His hand, his voice. Not a dream.

Damn him.

Senam—Joel—his voice now—his voice was Ibanari, accent clear and proud. He'd had just the faintest trace of it when they were young, though looking back she thought it had been too carefully absent, his tone too closely matched to hers.

In the dream that was not a dream, the accent had been gone completely. He'd overcompensated, almost developing the lilt of Olion. She should have noticed. She would not have dreamt of him speaking in an accent she had never heard him use.

Every word she'd heard from his mouth had been a lie, and he had forgotten how he used to pretend.

She hadn't even noticed.

She was such a fool. And this whole stupid mess was entirely his fault, and she was entirely dependent on him to get her out of it.

Chris finished his turn at rowing, and tried to talk to her. She didn't want to talk. She liked him—had liked him. She had thought he was a sweet boy, essentially harmless.

He had participated in kidnapping her, he had known all along who his leader was to her, he had not seen her once during her captivity on the island, and he was apparently among the only few of his men Joel actually trusted.

If Joel could trust him, she could not.

She'd been such a fool.

~

They docked, unloaded, and let the little boat drift back into the sea.

"We need the lay of the land," Joel said. "Alem, Fuller, see what you can find out; we'll wait in the grove."

Alem and Fuller left. Joel and Chris made their way to a little grouping of trees not far from the shore, with an ease that suggested they had both been here before. The beach was deserted, the docking area just a brief stretch of shore not obstructed by rocks.

Eloise followed them. She considered, briefly, the possibility of breaking away, of finally escaping. Joel was down half a band, there were no horses in play, and her ankle had long since healed. But where would she go? Joel was awful, but Ibanar was likely worse. She would never find her way home alone, and any goodwill the average citizen may have would evaporate if she was recognized as an enemy princess.

She would stay, for now. She would trust Joel, for now. With her return home, if nothing else.

The three of them sat silently on the mossy ground for a few minutes before Chris stood. "I'll just—um. Find something useful to do."

"Did you tell me anything true?" Eloise asked when he was gone.

"How I got the scar. That was true."

"Nothing else?"

"Everything else. Everything but my name. And the threats."

"Yes. Your name."

"Senam was your favorite story. You might have recognized it—recognized me—instead of complaining about my deceit."

"I knew the name was false—I'm not a fool. I didn't think you would—"

"Have I changed so much?"

She studied his face. The broken nose, the scar. She thought of the calm confidence he had carried, until she learned the truth, though it had vanished, now. She thought of his hands, which had killed several men to earn leadership of a band of outlaws.

"Yes," she said. "You have."

"Maybe so. I didn't mean to."

"I don't suppose anyone does." That was untrue; Eloise herself had put a great deal of effort into changing, into becoming the sort of princess who would not fling herself foolishly at a budding traitor.

"Why did you choose Senam?" she asked.

"Why do you think?"

"I don't know."

"Perhaps it was a clue," he said. "Or perhaps it's only that it was my favorite story, too—'And the mermaid kissed his bonny face, and laughed at his dismay. She drew him gentle beneath the sea, where her world unfolded from the waves, all bright as—'"

Why Senam? She thought of how she used to catch him staring—the fondness of it. The fondness that had emerged when she'd done the sort of stupid, reckless thing so characteristic of the version of herself he'd have remembered.

Why Senam?

....because he still loved her, or wanted her at least.

No. No. She could not deal with this. Not here. Not now. She cut him off abruptly. "Is that what you thought would happen to us? Having failed spectacularly to integrate yourself into my world, you would merely drag me down to yours? Or am I the mermaid in this arrangement, bringing you back to my jeweled home? Senam and the mermaid never betrayed each other, Joel."

"So you see the betrayal was mutual, at least."

"I never betrayed you."

She didn't realize she had shouted it until Chris reappeared. "There might—I'm sorry, I'm trying not to eavesdrop. But there might be soldiers nearby."

Her face burned. She hadn't known he had stayed near enough to hear their conversation. He slipped away again, and a few minutes passed in painful silence.

"The day of my trial, Eloise."

"You want to talk about that now?" she hissed. "Really?"

"You said you never loved me. You said it was a game. You told me to go to hell."

"And you just couldn't listen, could you? Couldn't even get out of the country like they told you to."

"You know that's not the part I was talking about."

"Fine. I lied. I loved you. Is that what you need to hear? Is that what it will take to make this conversation end?"

"Is it true?"

"Yes. I loved you. A very long time ago. Let's move on."

"Come on, El. What's the rush?"

"It's been months. They'll think I'm dead by now. Mother and Father and Jeremy and the rest."

"Jeremy. Do you love him?"

"That doesn't concern you."

He grinned. "You haven't even kissed him, have you?"

"We are fond of each other. We will be comfortable. He makes me feel safe."

"You didn't feel safe with me?"

"Well, now I don't. Jeremy is trustworthy. He's loyal. We do love each other, and we know where we stand, and what we have will be real."

"You think what we had wasn't? I loved you, Eloise."

"You betrayed me. You used me."

"I loved you. Nothing else matters."

"Really? Because, see, we're at war now, and I think a lot of things matter. If this is how you show affection—"

"I was framed."

"Really?" she asked. She felt suddenly frozen. She felt—she felt—

"Yes. No. Did the possibility never occur to you? You said you loved me."

"Were you framed or not, Joel?"

"It's complicated."

"Tell me the truth."

All three of his men returned before he could answer.

"We need to get moving," Fuller said. "Have your lover's spat later."

"We're not—"

"Later," Joel said, standing and offering her a hand. She ignored it, standing alone and following the men out of the grove.

"How's our route?" Joel asked as they walked.

"Battles have moved farther inland, allegedly. We haven't seen any soldiers, but that doesn't mean there aren't any. Nearest village is jumpy but not dangerous. They say the next village north was razed as the soldiers moved; they saw the smoke, and took in some survivors. We bought some supplies—overpaid, but they need the money more that we do. We'll need to walk a few days through the hill country to reach the woods. It'll leave us exposed, but there's no other safe route."

They walked for many long hours, all five of them silent, the tension between Joel and Eloise so strong it might as well have been a sixth member of the party. They walked mostly near the shore, moving very slowly inland, following some invisible trail set by Fuller. She ached to ask Joel what he had meant, what could possibly be complicated—either he had been framed, or he hadn't been. But it wasn't a conversation she wanted to have in front of the other men.

It wasn't a conversation she wanted to have at all. She wanted nothing in the world so much as she wanted to never again spare a single thought for Joel. But the question would haunt her until it was answered.

She did not speak, and she did not look at the men, and they passed the village, and the remains of the next.

Night fell, and food was distributed quietly, and a watch was set. Eloise was given a place in the watch, and given her own sword back, as well. They lit no fire, as they could afford to draw no attention.

She slept, and woke for her watch, and slept again. In the day they continued their journey, in the same uncomfortable silence.

Joel and Fuller discussed their route, consulting Fuller's precious map again. Joel and Alem discussed something—she knew not what, only that they were all speaking in only whispers. Chris tried to whisper to Eloise, perhaps feeling left out, or perhaps worrying that she did, but she was a mess of dread and fear and rage, her anxiety over the razed villages consumed by further, unwanted thoughts of Joel, and was not a good conversationalist.

At last Joel, having made his rounds with the men, fell back a little to talk to her, his voice still cautiously low, but not quite a whisper— perhaps they had reached a slightly safer leg of the journey.

"You didn't recognize me," he said. "I knew you wouldn't, with the mask. I thought you would, without it."

"Why hide? If you wanted to hurt me, all you had to do was be honest."

"I had a plan. It was a foolish plan, and when I abandoned it I gave up the mask. You didn't know me, so I didn't tell you."

"You've changed so much. You were a child, the last time we met."

"So were you, and I didn't have any trouble recognizing you."

She ignored this. "And what was your plan?"

"It doesn't matter anymore."

"Perhaps it matters to me."

"Perhaps I don't care much what matters to you. You, who claimed to love me, and yet couldn't remember my face."

"I have expended a great deal of effort on forgetting you, and have not succeeded as well as I would have liked."

"You should have known me."

"You have no right to tell me what I should or should not have done."

"I have—"

"Joel," Alem snapped, and Joel closed his mouth, turned around, and walked away. Eloise stared after him, puzzled both by Alem's tone and Joel's response.

"We've no idea how far we may be from any enemies," Alem explained quietly. "We can't afford a loud argument, and Joel knows it. You'd best learn it too."

Eloise resisted the childish urge to point out that Joel had started it, and their quiet trek resumed. They still followed the shoreline, though they were no longer close enough to smell the salt, or hear the beating of the waves.

As the waves of the sea disappeared behind them, the waves of the ground began, rolling hills growing slowly larger as they continued north.

~

"I would have expected more people," Eloise said quietly to Chris, as they walked for the third day through the hill country of Ibanar.

"They used to live mostly in tents and caravans here—the weather's so nice. So when the war came to the hills they picked up their houses and left. At least, that's what Joel says, and Alem agrees." He shrugged. "Joel's from much farther west than this, and Alem from much farther south. But they know more about Ibanar than I do, at least."

"I don't want to talk about Joel."

"He's un-kidnapping you."

It wasn't enough. It would never be enough. Every time she saw him she was filled with so much anger. And with so much hurt, which was absurd. He ought to have lost the power to hurt her long ago.

Was it Joel, she wondered, in one quiet moment, who still hurt her? Or was it Senam?

She had long since learned what Joel was. But Senam—she had trusted him. She had liked him. It was a whole new betrayal. It felt like being betrayed by an entirely different person. Joel was a traitor. But Senam had been a friend, if an unconventional one. And then he had turned into Joel.

They had, over the last few days, come to the silent but mutual decision to ignore each other. Joel would speak quietly with the men, and Eloise with Chris and Alem, though she still had not built a relationship with Fuller. She trusted him, at least, to navigate them safely back to Aliria.

Another day passed, and another. They timed their stops for the night in the valleys of the steadily growing hills, where they were less likely to be spotted. Fuller consulted his map. Alem measured out their food supply carefully. The shoreline fell out of sight, and the ground grew rockier.

"Let me," Joel said, taking her elbow to help her over a particularly difficult outcropping of sharp stones.

His hand on her arm, careful, respectful, felt just like Jeremy's. She shook him off as soon as she could do so safely.

"Don't touch me. Don't ever touch me."

He didn't argue, which was somehow even more upsetting. He walked silently ahead to join Fuller, and Eloise fell into step beside Alem.

"You needn't be so hard on him," he said. "He's escorting you home at great personal risk—none of us can return to the band, now."

"Such sacrifice would not have been necessary if you simply hadn't kidnapped me in the first place."

Alem shrugged, and they fell back into silence. It occurred to Eloise that she should be just as angry with the others as she was with Joel— had they not also kidnapped her? Had they not also concealed Joel's identity? But it wasn't the same. The others could not produce in her that same mess of hurt and anger. The others were not Joel. The others had never pretended to love her, when she was a foolish child.

Chapter 10

The illness had swept through Joel's village when he was ten—an earlier strain of the same sickness that would devastate Olion a decade later, both brought over from Kire on the continent.

It had killed his father, and left his mother permanently weakened. Without his father's income, they had relied primarily on the money his uncle sent, but his uncle cared only for Joel, and sent only enough to support him. His mother had done what work she was strong enough for, which was not much, and that slowly. His sister had been too young to work. Joel had worked what small jobs he could, and had made up the difference with petty theft.

They had survived like this for a few hard years, until Joel's uncle had summoned him to the palace. He would train to be a soldier, and the crown would support him, freeing up his uncle's finances for less embarrassing expenses than a bastard child. Joel had agreed to go only for the wages, which he could send home to his mother and sister. He had thought he would stay there until he was big and strong enough to work a proper job, with decent pay, then go back home to find one. Once he was an adult, or nearly, his uncle would feel no further obligation, and would allow Joel to vanish from his life without a fight.

Instead he had been exiled, and he could never go home, though home was—barely—in Ibanar. They'd left him in Olion, after all, and the only way back to Ibanar was through Aliria. His uncle was doubtlessly delighted to be able to write him off, to have a legitimate reason to despise him. He would expect Joel to go home, and would have men watching for him, to drag him back to the capital and hang him, thus finally erasing the evidence of his infidelity.

He could never safely stay at home again. But he'd used the chaos of war to eventually pass back through to Ibanar. He had managed one brief meeting with his mother and sister before moving further south, where he had gotten into the fight that gave him his first kill.

Somehow he'd been recognized near the capital, moving back north, and he'd been captured and taken to meet the king, who'd demanded any useful information on the Alirians. Joel hadn't had any useful information—he'd only been a minor princess' pet soldier—and had found himself exiled from Ibanar as well. They'd dumped him back in Aliria, despite knowing he wasn't allowed to be there either.

It hadn't mattered, as it turned out. By then the war had gotten bad enough that he felt safe to move as he pleased through all three countries—there were more important things to watch for, like deserters and enemy armies, than one exile just passing through. He'd been up near the Olin border again when he fell in with the band of outlaws he would someday lead.

He hadn't enjoyed it. He'd never enjoyed it, though he felt as if he ought to. Killing people had been awful. Leading other killers of people, who did so with less remorse, had been more awful. But the higher up one was in the band, the safer one was from other outlaws. And he had liked being safe.

When he was frightened, and needed to put on a show, which was nearly always, he had tried to act like Eloise. It had been difficult, as the thought of her hurt the way the torture had hurt, in the dungeons beneath her palace, in the weeks following his arrest. But painful or not, her breezy confidence, her utter lack of concern for what anyone else thought, her complete comfort in who she was and the respect she commanded, had been a mask he could wear, when he felt his real face had been ripped off, leaving him skeletal and exposed.

He had never stopped loving her. And it had never stopped hurting him.

They had a conversation to finish. He waited a day, after helping her over the rocks, hoping in vain that her temper would cool. And then he instructed his men to walk ahead a bit, to give the illusion of privacy he knew she would want.

"You asked if I was framed," he said.

She glanced over at him, barely; she didn't make eye contact, and didn't slow. "And you didn't answer. Do please explain how complicated a framing could possibly be."

"I was in the conspiracy. If you could call it one. Half the young people in the palace were, it wasn't anything—anything real. It was a space to vent about how difficult it was to be—to be that close to royalty, and that far. It was a game. Just this stupid game we were playing, a group of the new recruits. I was a child when I joined, El, and it was never supposed to mean anything, I swear. I was—I never did anything. I loved you. The group was real, more real than I thought, a space for adults to gain our trust and use us to destabilize things if we ever became important. I became important. I failed to destabilize anything on my own. So they planted the evidence—I'm sure it was real documents from the real conspiracy that I was technically involved in, but I'd never seen it before my court date."

"So you're not the bad guy here."

"I'm not the bad guy here." It was true. He knew it was true. But he didn't think it would be true enough for her.

"Then who kidnapped me, Joel? Justify that."

"I can't."

She walked ahead.

~

That night he took first watch, and watched the moonlight on her curls, and marveled that she trusted him enough to fall asleep.

He should find her a hairbrush. There were Chris' clothes in one of the packs—they would fit her. She wouldn't trust him enough to bathe, probably. Her own fault, then, that she would have to stay filthy. Still, he felt guilty. He always felt guilty.

She turned, eyes open, and smiled at him, and he nearly smiled back before realizing she was still half asleep. It was a few minutes before she sat up and came to sit by him.

"This is going to work, isn't it?" she asked, and she sounded like a girl he'd fallen in love with, and not a woman who hated him.

"Of course."

"I hate you," she said.

"Of course."

"But I can't sleep."

"You can't trust me."

"Something like that."

She was sitting beside him, though, on the log, and staring at something he couldn't see, far away on the horizon, and maybe he couldn't trust her, either, but they were close now in a way he thought they could never be in daylight.

~

He remembered his first view of the palace, a filthy exhausted child who'd spent weeks walking, and often in the wrong direction, from his village at the border. His uncle had wanted him at the capital, but not enough to arrange any transportation, or send him the money to arrange it himself.

Not, admittedly, that he would have used any transportation money sent for its intended purpose. With Joel gone, his uncle would no longer send money to his mother and sister. He did not know what pay soldiers in training received, or how often, and was nervous to leave them with only what his mother could scrounge up, until the necessary arrangements were made.

He had never seen a palace before. He had never left his city. He had seen the mayor's estate, and the temples, and the barracks at the edge of town. On his long walk he'd seen more temples and manor houses, but nothing like this.

How strange, he thought, that a king should have a home as large as a village, when the gods had homes scarcely larger than a common man's.

There was a wall, made of large, smooth, white stones that glowed where the sun hit them. Inside the wall was a gate, which was open, and large enough, he thought, for a dragon to pass through without ducking. Not that he had ever seen a dragon. But he imagined them to be very large.

He spent several long minutes outside the gate, working up the courage to step through. This was a gate for kings and gods and dragons, and he was only a boy, a barefoot pickpocket with torn trousers and a father who despised him.

But that father—his uncle—was waiting for him inside the gate, and Joel was nearly certain that he was late, for he had spent some time wandering in the wrong direction, and had lost track of the days.

No lightning struck him when he walked through the gate. No soldiers chased him back out again. So he continued on.

From outside the wall, he had seen only the highest parts of the palace, mostly towers that reached the very heavens. From inside, it was even more impressive. The palace was made of the same white stones as the wall, and there were a dozen towers—a dozen, he remembered vaguely, was a sacred number to the Alirians. He knew little of Alirian religion, but his village was very near the border, and sometimes he heard small details.

Between each tower was a long stretch of stone wall, dotted with windows that he would later learn were paned, every single one of them, with glass. But he would not set foot in the palace until Eloise. His place was past the palace, past the gardens, in a wooden building where the least important of the future soldiers were kept.

He did not see his uncle the day he arrived. He wandered the long, paved road between the gate and the palace for a long time before he dared to approach a man who looked as if he might know what was going on. That man had consulted another, who had consulted another, until eventually they found one who knew that the general's nephew, when he arrived, was to be escorted to his dorm in the barracks, where the general would call on him at his convenience.

It was nearly two weeks before calling on him was convenient for the general. In that time he built fragile friendships with his dorm mates and fellow soldiers, who were shocked and horrified that he knew so little of the kingdom he had come to serve.

"It's bad enough," one had said, "that you look Ibanari. I suppose you can't help how you look. But you've got to at least act Alirian, or you'll never survive basic training."

"We'll work on your education," another said. "You work on your accent."

From his fellow trainees, he had learned that he served not only a king and queen, but three princes and four princesses.

He had been just barely fourteen, and just barely adjusted to living in palace barracks a hundred leagues away from anyone he loved, on the day he first saw Eloise. They had been wandering through the courtyard, in their limited free time, Joel and three or four other young soldiers, when someone had noticed her behind them, following them, all pink and gold and satin. He had been the one to whisper, "Who is she?"

They hadn't known. Someone important. Someone that had no business hovering behind them, in the soldiers' courtyard. A duchess or a princess or a lady. And she didn't go away. And finally, when it was time for them to split up and go about their work, she had continued to follow him. Him. And then she had approached him, so close he could hear the fabric rustling as her skirt moved.

"I'm Eloise."

He had bowed, or attempted to—he'd never bowed before. The others had helped him memorize the names of the royal family in their first week—Theodore, Julian, Erika, Benjamin, Eloise, Annabelle, Maria.

"This is the part where you tell me your name," she'd said.

"Right." He'd never spoken to a princess before. "Joel."

She'd smiled like he was the sun after a month of darkness. "You have a lovely voice, Joel," she'd said, and he'd felt himself reddening, aware as he'd never been before of his Ibanari accent.

"I'd like you to teach me to use a sword," she'd said next.

"I don't really know how to." He'd felt he ought to use some form of address, here, but couldn't remember if she was a highness or a majesty.

"You're carrying a sword; surely you must know how to use it."

Joel had glanced down at his sword, which was wooden, tucked carelessly under his arm. So far he knew to hold the handle, and aim the pointy end at his enemy. "I'm—I'm only just learning. Your. Um. Princess."

"Then your masters shall teach you, and you shall teach me. It will be like learning together."

"There are people much more qualified to teach you than I am," he'd said, and it was more words than he'd wanted to say, for the longer he spoke, the more pronounced his accent became.

"But I want you to do it. Please, Joel?"

Please, Joel. Those two words, over the next year, would get him into more messes than he had ever imagined possible.

"You'll have to change clothes."

She'd stared down at her pink satin dress, then smiled up at him again. "Of course. I'll be back. Wait for me?"

"I have—there are things I'm supposed to be—"

"Oh, just tell them I wanted you for something. Father won't mind."

"It's not your Father that I—"

"Well, he'll tell everyone else not to mind, too. It'll be fine."

She'd dashed away, and he'd remembered, when she was halfway across the courtyard, and called out, "Tie up your hair, too."

One more time she'd turned and smiled, and then he had waited there, stubborn and determined, and half convinced it was all a lie, for nearly an hour before she returned in men's clothing a few sizes too big.

"My brother's," she'd explained. "Ben. You should meet him."

"The prince?"

"Well, I'm the princess. You've met me. And we are going to be very good friends."

"We are?"

"Yes. So naturally you'll have to meet my entire family."

"Oh." He just wanted to train and stay out of everyone's way. "Wonderful."

"Yes, isn't it?" She'd smiled again, oblivious, and he'd decided that maybe it was.

Chapter 11

Days passed. They skirted around the few small villages they encountered. The occupied ones. They walked directly through two that had been abandoned and destroyed—likely, Eloise realized, not in that order. She wondered if it had been her army, or some other, that had passed through here, that had left the scorch marks climbing up the stone walls of the temple, that had torn the doors and windows off a row of small houses, that had dumped refuse into the spring that watered the village.

War was an ugly thing. She'd been told so, often enough, these last several years. She had never seen much firsthand.

There had been days—early days, mostly—when she had longed to join her siblings and her cousins on the battlefield. Those had been the days when war had been a new adventure, before Ben had come home on his first leave, and told her the sound a sword made, driven through a man's gut, before her brother-in-law's eyes grew haunted, before her cousin Sylvia described the warmth and the wet of an enemy's blood, trailing down her hands and pooling, sticky, inside of her elbows.

Eloise was glad not to be at war. But most of her family was, still. She missed them, though she did not wish to join them.

She wondered how many harmless fishing villages her brothers and sister might have destroyed, for whatever reasons, in war, one destroyed things like harmless fishing villages. She wondered if any of them had been here, if it had been Erika that desecrated the temple, or

Theo that drove little children out of their homes, ripping the door from its hinges and throwing the furniture out into the street.

"We're on the same side, now," Joel said as they walked. "We might try getting along."

"You betrayed Aliria. You betrayed me."

"I was fourteen years old."

This was so unexpected, so patently untrue, that she stopped walking abruptly, and Chris ran into her.

"Sorry," he said.

Eloise waved him away. "You were sixteen."

Joel stared at her, apparently as baffled as she was. "All right, I was fifteen by the arrest, but all of the—the trouble happened, really, when I was still fourteen."

"I celebrated your sixteenth birthday with you, Joel."

"I—oh."

"Oh?" she repeated.

"I lied. I…had forgotten that lie."

"I see. It must be difficult to keep track of so many."

"The age to join the army is sixteen. They let me in a year early, because of my uncle."

"Yes. I know that."

"He lied to them about my age. I joined two years early. I had just turned fourteen when I came to the palace."

She stared at him. "I feel sick."

"Right. Not only did I conspire against your father, but I lied about my age. The boy you loved was a full twenty two months younger than you. How heinous. Did I mention I'm a bastard?"

"Joel—" she started.

He laughed. "This is the day for confessions, it seems. My uncle is my father. When your high position in the military is partially due to your marriage to the king's beloved cousin, you can hardly have a mistress and a half-Ibanari bastard back home. He convinced his brother to marry the girl before the baby was born."

And now she could hardly be angry at him. "Did you know? Before the—"

"I've known all my life."

"You never told me."

"And when, exactly, should I have mentioned it, Eloise? Where in the course of our relationship would that information have fit? After you made me teach you to kill people? Not that you would ever need to know, but it would be fun to learn. Maybe we could have talked about my parentage before you dragged me into that first court dinner full of royalty, in a uniform I'd been wearing three days, so you could look like a rebel. Or when you pulled me into your bedchamber to help you change clothes? How about after Julian got me for that, and before I had to explain to my uncle why I had missed an entire day of training when I had to chase you into the city?"

"Maybe you could have mentioned it at the same time you mentioned the conspiracy against my father?"

He didn't answer her. She watched him walk away, and waited a moment before catching up.

"Was it really so bad?" she asked. "I thought you loved me."

"So did I. It seems we were mistaken."

Eloise did not try to catch up when he walked away again. They did not speak for two days.

"At least they're quiet," Alem said, as the second day stretched on.

"Perhaps you could continue not speaking to each other?" Fuller suggested. "At least until we reach the forest."

He was speaking to Joel, but Eloise was near enough to hear them easily.

"How far is it?" she asked.

"To the forest? Three days, if we're lucky. Maybe five. We'll have to restock our supplies before we reach it, which means going off track to the nearest large town. The bigger it is, the less we'll stand out. There's no proper big cities, out here, but Kahir will do well enough."

Eloise remembered Kahir. She'd attended a festival there, when she was young, and Aliria and Ibanar were not yet enemies. "I didn't think the forest was between Kahir and the capital."

"It's not, really. It's a bit of a detour, but it's safer in the woods."

She nodded. This was, she thought, the longest conversation she'd yet had with Fuller that wasn't about mountain gods.

"Fuller," Joel said before she could ask another question. "Come help me with something."

~

As the third day of silence between Joel and Eloise progressed, she decided that, whatever Fuller and Alem might like, she could not actually avoid talking to him for the entire journey. There were conversations to have, arrangements to make, before she could fairly ask that her father pardon him.

She finished a conversation with Chris, and jogged to the front of their little group, where Joel was leading the way.

"Why do you even want a pardon?" she asked. "You're the bandit king. You're giving that up to do what, go back to being a foot soldier in my father's army? In war time?"

"No, I won't go back to being a soldier. I never wanted that in the first place. But with a royal pardon, I could safely, legitimately get the training for any job that appealed to me. I hate being a bandit, Eloise. Being the leader of a whole band of them—I'm responsible by proxy for every crime every one of them commits. You've known me since we were children—do you really think I'd enjoy that? I hate hurting people. I hate taking from them. I hate killing them, even the ones I hate. But I do it anyway, because I would hate dying more, and I haven't had any other choices, here."

"What will you do, then?"

"I don't know," he said, and lengthened his stride to put distance between them.

~

He had killed his first man when he was seventeen, desperate and terrified and in self-defense. It had happened so quickly, and he had run, and run, and had never let himself think of it again.

He had killed his second man at nineteen, in a fight he hadn't wanted and hadn't known how to get out of. For a long time afterward he had stared down at the blood seeping into his shirt, and when he looked up the man's friends were all around him, and he was dead anyway, and could have spared himself the fight. But they had been impressed, not angry, and so he had gotten his first glimpse into the mind of an outlaw, hardly remembering that he was one, and when they had invited him to join their band he had accepted, because what else was there to do?

Within three years he had earned the right, dragged through chaos and blood and fire, to lead them. He had no desire to continue such a life. It was a life for children and men who couldn't help it, and only the children found it exciting.

All he had ever wanted was to keep his mother and sister housed and clothed and fed. He had never truly considered the specifics, beyond a vague idea, at fifteen, that he would marry Eloise, and do whatever it was that prince consorts did; the details of that particular career had always been unclear to him.

Well into adulthood, he still had no particular ambitions, just the confidence that being officially an honest man would open new opportunities. He would figure it out. He always did. Perhaps he could work in construction—surely, demand would be high, as the war came to an end and rebuilding began.

Eloise had been willing to speak to him. He should not have pushed her away again, even if exactly what she chose to say had made him feel, achingly, like a stranger to her. He slowed his steps until they were side by side again.

"We should talk about the conspiracy," he said, reluctantly. Better to have it all out now. Make sure he'd thoroughly finished destroying their relationship before trying in earnest to rebuild it.

"I suppose so," she agreed, her voice unreadable in a way it had never been, when they were young.

"I never gave out any information I gained from being with you. Nothing, at least, that couldn't have come just as easily from one of the others. Nothing personal. And nothing I would ever have thought could be used against you. Things like the size and layouts of rooms. Complaints about the endless wealth you hardly noticed, not—not— just complaining. Because they were my friends. And I was a child, overwhelmed by opulence while my family starved."

"You expect me to believe that your only role in a vast conspiracy against my family was to, what, describe my bedchamber? Whine about my jewelry?"

He shook his head. "They recruited me before I became close to you. They liked to gather frustrated, overworked young people who came into close contact with politically important figures. They gave us a space to vent, and they listened to us. We were just talking, not—not giving up state secrets. But we did give them up. Affairs. Conflicts in relationships. Army maneuvers. Secret passages that could be used for spying. We were complaining about people who treated us poorly, or making fun of them to relieve tension. We were talking about the insane construction of insane rooms that we were made to clean. Well, not me, personally. On the cleaning. And I never mentioned that hidden room you showed me; I didn't want anyone to find us there.

"But they tapped me because of my uncle, I think. Anyone could see we didn't get on, and that was a weak spot they should have been able to use. I suppose they were hoping he'd mention military plans in front of me, or fights with his wife. Maybe they suspected I was his bastard, and hoped I'd talk about that. But we never interacted if we could help it, so I was useless to them. Until I met you."

"And what information might you have accidently let slip that was later used against us?"

"Nothing, Eloise. Nothing. I was useless to them, and they worried I would tell you or Ben about them—which I wouldn't, because I didn't understand until I was arrested that there was anything real to tell. They needed to get rid of me, before I became more trouble than I was worth."

Eloise stared at him for a long moment, and it felt, though Chris was scarcely a yard away, as if they were the only two people in all the world.

"I remember how I loved you," she said. "I wish—I wish—"

"You might trust me."

"I did," she said, and the moment broke. "Twice. And see where it's gotten me?"

~

"Give her some space," Alem advised.

Joel frowned. "I gave her nearly a decade of space, with no notable improvement."

"All right, less space than that, this time. But you know why she's upset. Don't push her into more fights."

"I don't mean to. It seems the only way we know how to interact, anymore."

"Don't pretend you haven't provoked her, a few times," Fuller said, inserting himself, uninvited, into their conversation.

Joel's frown deepened. "She just gets so quiet, sometimes. She never used to be quiet."

"Perhaps it's a sign she's matured," Alem suggested. "Perhaps you should do the same."

"I'm going to go talk to Chris. Chris will be nice to me."

"Chris is currently telling the princess all about your first trip to Kahir together," Alem said.

"Ugh. Do you think they'll remember me?"

"Does it matter?" Fuller asked. "They were some of the rare people who actually liked you."

"I hate you," Joel said.

"I know. Here, give me your pack. I'm hungry."

~

They approached Kahir in the midmorning. It would be, Eloise realized, her first time among people who weren't criminals in months.

"There should be a stream about a half mile east," Fuller said. "We'll all bathe, and change, and by the time we reach the city we should be dry."

It occurred to Eloise that she had not bathed properly since her kidnapping, and had not even rinsed herself since they boarded the ship, up in the mountains. She'd not changed clothes once, either, in all that time.

Did she trust these men enough to undress in their presence?

She wouldn't have cared, ten years ago. If Joel had never seen her unclothed, it was in spite of, not due to, her best efforts.

Now, the thought of Joel seeing her naked made her skin feel more itchy and awful than the weeks of dirt that covered it.

The men waded into the stream, removing items of clothing and tossing them to shore as they did. Eloise waited, grateful that there was nothing really to see, from the shoreline, with all four of them up at least to their waists in water.

She should not, she supposed, be seeing their bare chests and backs, either. She turned away as this thought came to her, but not before she saw a new mess of scars on Joel's back.

When they were children, playing in the lake—not on the shoreline nearer the palace, but the other side, once they'd rowed over—Joel and Ben had discarded their shirts, while Eloise had hiked her skirts up to her knees, and abandoned her stockings by the shore, and they had enjoyed the warm sun and the cool water, and spared not a thought for modesty.

Joel's back and chest, then, she remembered, had been smooth and lovely, untouched by any of—

What had happened to him? How many things had happened to him? How many times, when she was seventeen and hurt and angry, wishing him dead, had her wishes nearly come true?

"Coming out," Alem called, and she continued facing carefully away, listening to the rustling and idle conversation as they dressed themselves in fresh clothes.

"All right," Joel said, coming to stand behind her, close enough that his wet hair dripped down onto her shoulder. "Your turn."

"What happened to your back?" she asked, without turning to face him.

"I was whipped. And stabbed. On two separate occasions, of course. But they both left scars."

"Who stabbed you?"

"A pirate."

"And who whipped you?"

"Someone in your father's prison."

"Oh."

"Yes. Come on, get up. Bath time."

She turned, slowly, to face him.

"We've got clothes of Chris' that should fit you. No one will look, because Alem and Chris, at least, are gentlemen, and will see to it that we behave."

"You wouldn't, without their interference?"

"I'll behave. But you trust them more than you trust me. Don't you?"

She stood and walked toward the stream without answering. The water was cool and clear, and she ducked under to wet her hair, carefully not turning around to see whether Joel had kept his promise. She knew how her temper ran away from her, and she knew that if she turned to find one of the men looking, she would storm out of the stream to have at him, thus worsening the issue of her sullied modesty. She could trust them. With this, she could trust them.

She scrubbed at herself with the bar of cheap lye soap Alem had provided, and ran fingers through her hopelessly tangled hair, and seriously considered hacking it all off with her sword, when she got out of the water. She looked out toward the west, where the forest was finally visible. It was—

"Joel?" she called.

"Yes?"

"Come look at this."

"Eloise—"

"Oh, don't be a baby. I'm up past my shoulders in the water. Just turn around and look toward the west, would you?"

"That's—"

"It looks like fog. But it's too late in the day for—"

"It's smoke," Fuller said. "Damn it."

Eloise turned to face the men, body still carefully submerged. "How did you not see the smoke, when you were all out here bathing not a quarter of an hour ago?"

"That would be because Chris and Joel were—"

"Oh, shut up, Fuller. El, get clean quick. We need to get to Kahir."

~

The clothes taken from Chris fit surprisingly well, and Eloise enjoyed the feeling of clean fabric on her skin as she struggled to keep up with the men, who were in a great hurry ever since she'd spotted the smoke.

Joel slowed enough, at least, to prepare her for their arrival.

"Kahir is an Ibanari city, but it's not far from the border, and they've long been used to seeing people of all kinds passing through. That hasn't changed much, since the war. But in Ibanar we—"

"You're not even Ibanari," Eloise interrupted him. It had been bothering her since she learned who he was. True, she had often thought of him as Ibanari—he nearly was, and it had made the betrayal sting less, somehow, reminding herself he wasn't properly Alirian. But he'd never described himself as Ibanari, before.

"I didn't want to be Ibanari, when I was a fourteen year old in the Alirian court. But I was. My mother was. My city was. But my father wasn't, so it was easier to just—to say I wasn't, either. It wasn't so hard, because we were on the outskirts. Like this, really. A border town. I'm surprised Kahir is still doing so well. Border towns are not a safe place to be, in times of war."

"Like Jeremy's first fiancée."

"Who?"

"The girl Jeremy was to marry, before she was killed. Her village was too near the Olin border, and we attacked it by mistake. Jeremy's men attacked it by mistake." Poor Jeremy. As if he didn't have enough sorrow in his life, without her being kidnapped. "I doubt he'll ever recover, but at least our histories mean no one expects us to fall in love."

"Would that be so bad?"

She hadn't really meant to say that out loud. "Yes. It would. We've had enough of drama, both of us. Romance has come and gone. We'll take comfort and companionship now, gladly."

"And what an exciting ending for the princess they wrote bar songs about."

She flushed. The drinking song was as enduring in the people's memory as Joel was, and equally embarrassing in an entirely different way. "I've grown up, Joel. People are known to do that, on occasion, though you seem to be headed in the opposite direction."

"We become who we must to survive, El."

"And outlaws must become children. I see."

He shook his head. "Do you really not love him?"

"I don't need to love him. I've had enough of that."

It had been rather difficult to arrange a marriage. She'd earned a reputation in her wild youth, which she'd never been able to shake, and it was widely assumed that she was not a virgin.

(An incorrect assumption, though not, admittedly, for lack of trying on her part. Joel hadn't wanted to.)

(Which, in hindsight, was likely because he'd been only fourteen. This new knowledge still made her feel vaguely ill if she lingered on it for too long. The difference between fourteen and sixteen seemed monumental. She wasn't sure why—the space between fifteen and sixteen had never bothered her.)

(Perhaps it was only because she herself was no longer sixteen. She'd felt like an adult at the time, but knew she had not been.)

(Perhaps it was less the actual two year difference, and more the difference between her current understanding of fourteen, and how very mature she remembered feeling when she was sixteen.)

(Really, she thought, it wasn't about their romantic relationship at all. It was about all of the other things. She had allowed herself to think of her relationship with Joel as the foolish mistake of a child. She hadn't allowed herself to think of how Joel himself was also a child—how he was, in fact, more of a child that she was. Fourteen was so young. Fifteen was so young. How much of that betrayal could he possibly have been responsible for? Had he any real understanding of the severity of the situation? How had they come so close to hanging a child? How had they tortured him? How had they banished a child with no resources, no support system, nowhere else to go?)

She pushed these thoughts away. The situation had been mishandled. But that had been years ago. The Joel standing before her today was an adult, fully understanding and fully responsible for his own actions. This Joel was a thief and a killer, and she wouldn't let herself be distracted from that by the past.

The marriage had been difficult to arrange. She had not, for many years, been particularly motivated. She was far enough from the crown that there was no real need to produce heirs. She had experienced quite enough romance for a lifetime. Her father had not pushed her to wed. But as the war dragged on—

Unwed relatives of the deposed king were a valuable resource for conquerors. It was better to be married quickly while the war still waged, than to wait until it had been lost and find herself tied to some Olin or Ibanari noble, possibly one who'd killed other members of her family.

Jeremy had been a great blessing. They would never be in love, which was more a relief than anything else. He was in mourning, he would remain forever in mourning, and he had proposed to her as a kindness. They were friends, and they would be happy together.

They would.

"Jeremy isn't your concern. Didn't you have things to tell me about Kahir?"

He nodded. "Don't speak if you can help it—you sound too polished. Looking as rough as you do, we're hoping anyone noticing a royal resemblance will dismiss it as coincidence. A strong Alirian accent and excellent diction won't help with that. I don't—maybe you should wait for us outside the city. We don't all of us need to go in. Chris could—"

"I am coming into Kahir. I'll try not to be too obviously a princess, but I'm not going to sit and wait for you. We're a team now. I'm not your prisoner, and you don't get to hide me."

"All right. Into Kahir. Thank the gods your hair is an absolute mess. No one has ringlets like the royal family's ringlets."

~

In Kahir, they purchased supplies and spoke with locals and the few other travellers they encountered, and Eloise watched and listened, as much as she could.

They all, on the island, shared one language, but when men with strong Ibanari accents got to talking quickly, it might as well have been Geth. She supposed she would have the same problem in Olion. Mostly Joel talked, while Fuller listened and made notes on his map, and Chris and Alem ran about purchasing food and whatever else they needed. Eloise did not pay them much attention, more interested in trying to decipher Joel's rapid speech and Fuller's increasingly dire expressions.

"We'll stay at an inn tonight," Joel said when all their work was done. "It's been a long time since we've had much comfort, and it will be a while still before we have more. We can make a new plan, and no one searching for us would think us foolish enough to rent a room."

"A new plan?" Eloise asked.

Joel nodded slowly. "They've burned large swathes of the forest, these last few weeks. Everything is too exposed, and there may still be fires going. We can't pass through, at least not as we had planned."

"Who burned it?"

"I don't know."

"There are trees in this forest older than Aliria. Older than Ibanar. This forest has fed and housed a hundred generations."

"I know, Eloise. I can't change it. And we're still in public, where your accent can still be heard. We'll figure something out at the inn."

"I stole someone's cap," Chris offered. "Here, put it on, Princess. We can pretend you're a boy, and no one will ask why we're trying to get a room for four men and a woman."

Joel shook his head. "She'll never pass. We'll get two rooms—one for the princess and one of us—we'll pretend we're married. We could hardly fit five in one room, anyway, and we'll not likely have a use for our money again until we reach our destination. Might as well spend it where we can. Who'll you have for your husband, El? He'll sneak into the other room to sleep, if you like."

"You," she said, and almost regretted it. But she—she still trusted him the most. Perhaps she shouldn't. But she did.

They purchased one night at the inn. They ate tasteless stew for dinner, and retreated to their two rooms. Eloise sat on the edge of the bed—the first time she'd been on a bed, on any sort of padded furniture, in weeks, and found her body lying on it before her brain had agreed to the idea.

"How's the bed?" Joel asked, and she remembered herself, and sat back up as quickly as she could.

"It'll do. Had we better join the others? For planning?"

"We'll wait until the rest of the inn is asleep. We don't need the other guests overhearing us. Rest, for now."

She collapsed back onto the bed, and a few minutes passed in silence.

"Well, you might as well lie down with me. I trust you'll behave yourself—if you don't I'll scream the house down."

Joel lowered himself slowly onto the bed. She turned to meet his eyes, briefly, then looked away again. Neither of them spoke. Several minutes passed.

"When did you stop loving me, Eloise?" he asked. It didn't feel like an accusation, just a question, and she considered it seriously, and didn't lose her temper.

"I don't know. I suppose I just—grew out of it. I was hurt. And then I was angry. And then it all just seemed very far away." She looked over at him; he was staring at the far wall. "When did you stop loving me?"

"I'm not entirely sure that I ever did."

It took a moment to understand what he was saying—the closest thing to a declaration of love she could expect from a man who wore scars on Joel's face and blood on his hands. "We can't go back, Joel."

"Why not?" He turned, finally, to look at her, and meeting his eyes was almost painful, in a way she couldn't quite understand.

"Why not? Aside from the kidnapping and conspiring, you mean?"

"Yes. Aside from all that. If I could make all of that go away. Then why not?"

"We—we've grown up, Joel. We were children. And I would like to believe that we could have been happy together, but as it is we've grown in different directions, and even if the person I am now could fall in love with the person you are now, I think that I would always be afraid that—that it was only dust and shadows. I would not want to marry a stranger because I was in love with the memory of a boy who no longer existed."

"I'm still me, El."

"No. You're really not. And I'm not me anymore, either, and we hardly know each other. Don't—please don't do this to me, Joel. I just want to get home and end this war."

"All right. I'm sorry. Forget it."

He stood and walked across the room. She heard his footsteps pause at what must have been the door, and she tried not to care. He had always been the rational one. She did not have time for a lovesick outlaw clinging to the past. They had work to do.

Although as far as her love life went, there had been less romantic moments than "I'm not entirely sure I ever did." Her engagement, for example.

She had been on a bench in the hallway, and Jeremy, coming out of an audience with the king, had taken a seat beside her. "Your father wants you married. So that when—if—if we lose the war…"

"Is this you proposing?"

"I suppose it is."

"All right." Jeremy was a friend, and a good one. Eloise was the closest unmarried woman to the throne, and she would not risk being married to an enemy.

It would be peaceful. Jeremy would not love again, and Eloise had no desire to be loved like that. Not anymore. He was a far better match than she had any right to hope for. It would be good.

"I'm going to find the others," Joel said, now, and Eloise started to sit up. "No, stay. We won't make any plans yet—I'll come get you, for that part."

~

They had been on the field when he was arrested, training. She had just knocked him to the ground, twice, and hadn't understood what was happening. He had understood, and had not had the heart to explain it, except for the lie that everything would be fine. It was a lie she had repeated back to him confidently, reassuringly, unable to comprehend treason in him.

When next he had seen her, two months later, she had not been Eloise. She had walked slowly into the courtroom, the last in a long train of women, wearing grey silk, her hair bundled up, somber and almost severe.

There was blood on his face, on his clothes, in his hair. He thought his arm was broken. He had known, or had tried to convince himself he knew, that she would have lost her faith in him, that she would hate him. He had told himself not to expect that smile, that flourish of gold and pink and rustling skirts as she dropped into his lap, as she liked to do in a roomful of witnesses. But he had not prepared himself to be looked at like a stranger, and he had certainly not prepared himself to look back in the same way, all the things between them so distant he could half believe they had been a dream.

It would be quite a dream, for a traitor in a torture chamber to convince himself a princess loved him.

Had he been a traitor? The room was too bright, with sunlight streaming in past Eloise, and he could not think, now, exactly what he was.

There had been no hesitation over his guilt. Of course. It was the punishment that left something to chance. The king voted banishment. Everyone in the room had the right to vote—he had never thought, when Eloise told him, that he would ever need this particular bit of trivia about court politics—but most would follow the king's lead.

Eloise was last. It didn't matter what she said. Enough people had spoken already, and his fate was decided. But still, it mattered. It mattered so much.

"Hang him."

She had stood and begun to walk away, and it had been then that Joel had discovered, by trying to fight them off, that no guards were actually holding him. He had run forward to catch her arm, and she had stopped and turned to face him.

"El, please."

She shook off his hand and asked, her voice like ice, and wholly unfamiliar, "Please what?"

He hadn't known what to say, hadn't known what to beg for in the face of this stranger. "Two months ago you loved me."

She had laughed. Laughed. "Loved you? You? It was a game. We had a good time, Joel. But that's all we had. You can't have thought it mattered?"

"Eloise. I love you. No games."

"Go to hell."

He hadn't noticed much after she left. The verdict was set, anyway. There had been more talking, questions he hadn't answered. The king looked disappointed—well, Joel had given him plenty to be disappointed in. They'd taken him somewhere, somewhere far away, and then he had been alone, and nothing else had mattered.

~

"I thought you'd be enjoying your time alone with the princess," Alem said when Joel let himself quietly into their room.

"Another fight?" Fuller asked.

"No. No, it wasn't a fight."

"Joel, did you—"

"I didn't tell her anything I shouldn't have. Well—well, maybe I did. But not—I'm not that stupid. I just told her—I told her—" He stopped, and sunk slowly onto the edge of the bed.

"What did you tell her?" Chris asked.

"He told her that he loved her," Alem said.

Fuller shook his head. "It was too soon, Joel."

"I know."

"All right. Rest a little—you've hardly stopped moving since we took her. We'll handle it. Just give it an hour or two."

~

It had been Eloise that had initiated their first kiss. Of course. It had been Eloise that had initiated everything. Except for his downfall. They had been in a crowded hall, surrounded by noble people still annoyed at his presence, but beginning to be accustomed to him. She had taken his hand and pulled him along, and he had followed blindly, not realizing, until years later, that she was deliberately leading him to the place where the most people possible could see them.

She had stopped abruptly in the crowd, and turned to face him, and he had been puzzled, and then she had leaned forward, standing on her toes, and kissed him.

"Ellie," he had murmured, red faced, and the whole room had gone quiet enough to hear him. The queen had cleared her throat and suggested that they all go in for dinner, and Eloise had taken his hand again.

Prince Theodore, as he walked past them, had bent to whisper something in her ear, and she had shrieked, "Theo!" and turned nearly as red as Joel had.

He had been, on that occasion, too embarrassed to think about what else he might have felt. He had decided later that he quite liked kissing. But he liked doing it when they were alone. Eloise seemed to like it best when they had a sizable audience, all of whom would be shocked and horrified.

It hadn't—he knew it hadn't always been about making a spectacle of herself. He knew that she had loved him in the quiet times, in the private times, too.

But she had always loved him loudest in a disapproving crowd.

He must have fallen asleep; the next thing he knew was Chris shaking him awake.

"We need a plan," Alem said.

"I promised Eloise I'd fetch her for the planning."

"Well, fetch her then."

He shook his head. "Chris, you go get her."

When they were all assembled, Fuller brought out his precious, much-marked map, and began running through the many problems they didn't want to face. The active battle sites. The spots where armies had gathered for rest and planning. The burnt—and possibly still burning—forest. The very real possibility that the other outlaws from their band were tracking them down, planning to kill the men and recapture the princess, likely to sell her to an enemy nation.

"That's a lot of problems," Joel said, studying the newest marks on the map. "Do we have any solutions?"

"We can't go through the forest. The deeper in the forest we are, the safer we are, normally. But now—"

"Yes, we're all aware the forest is on fire. I asked for solutions."

"Well, if you would shut up and listen for a minute—we still need to stick as close to the edges of the forest as we can. We'll move north, clinging to the edge of the wood. We don't know which army burned the forest, but if it was Ibanar or Aliria—and it was probably one of them—they may have alerted their citizens beforehand, to get out of range of the fire. Which means we may be encountering a string of abandoned but only partially burned down villages, near the outskirts, where we can hide and restock. Along the western edge of the forest, once we're in Alirian territory, we'll hit the line of temples that runs straight from the southernmost territory the empire ever claimed to the northernmost—one temple every twelve miles. Temples promise sanctuary from war, and few soldiers will disregard the threats of immolation, on that front, even deserters, which means a safe place we can stop and hide every night until we reach the capital."

"All right," Joel said. "How quickly can we make it?"

"More quickly than we would have travelling through the forest. But it'll mean taking proper roads, which means a higher chance of encountering threats."

"It's fine. We'll make it. We can all of us wield a weapon well enough—don't look at me like that, Chris, just because you're useless with a sword. You're decent with a club, and if we're attacked, your job will be to get the princess to safety while the rest of us fight."

"I don't recall agreeing to getting myself killed so your pet princess could escape," Fuller said.

"And I don't recall agreeing to run and hide while everyone else fights," Eloise added.

"Fine, we'll all die together. Go back to your room, El—we'll fetch you in the morning."

~

She woke to a soft knock on her door, and was surprised, for a moment, to find the bed containing only herself. She had forgotten that Joel hadn't come back to the room with her.

He loved her still. She had known he did, or thought he did, but having it out loud, hanging in the air between them—

It wasn't good. It was best she pushed him away, now—she had been too friendly, these last few days, had made him believe that maybe there was a chance she would—he was best pushed away now, before they reached the palace. She could not continue being friendly.

She didn't engage with the others as they ate breakfast at the long wooden table in the main room of the inn, and followed behind them as Fuller led them on the new route he'd planned, occasionally glancing down at his map to be sure they were moving in the right direction.

She had her sword strapped to her back, now, in a leather harness Alem had purchased the day before, instead of tucked into the top of a pack. They knew not who they might encounter, and weapons were best kept near at hand.

Eloise closed her right hand into a fist, running her thumb along the seal ring she wore. As they moved from Ibanar into Aliria, this would be her true weapon—she had only to show it to any soldiers they encountered before the bloodshed could start. It wouldn't work, of course, for any bandits or deserters they met, but she would not have her friends attacking or being attacked by her own army.

Were they her friends, she wondered.

Fuller wasn't. Chris, perhaps. Alem. Joel—Joel could not be her friend. Senam had been.

Senam had never existed.

Joel could not be her friend.

Ignoring him, while the most comfortable option, was not enough. She needed to put any delusions of pleasant feelings between them to rest, swiftly and firmly.

She lengthened her stride to catch him, at the front of the group, hanging over Fuller's shoulder to study the map. After a few minutes Fuller shook him off, and he slowed just enough to put him at a pace with Eloise.

"About yesterday afternoon," she said.

"We needn't speak any more of it. You needn't think of it, or worry—"

"You betrayed me, Joel. You hurt me in a way that I can never forget, can never forgive."

He stopped walking, for a moment, and she continued. He caught up with her shortly, and when he did he was near vibrating with some strong emotion she no longer knew him well enough to identify.

"All right, you want to talk about how we hurt and betrayed each other? You want to talk about that? Fine; let's talk about how you abandoned me. Let's talk about how you left me to rot in prison for two months without a single word, then tried to get me executed when I finally got out. Let's talk about how you just believed it all—never mind that it was true—you said that you loved me, and you couldn't even trust me enough to believe I was innocent."

"It wasn't like that, Joel." Always, she was surprised by the creative new ways he could find to hurt her. She had not thought of those two months—had not let herself think of those two months—in years. He might as well have ripped the fresh scab off a still-healing wound.

"Fine. What was it like?"

"I was trying to prove you innocent. I didn't want you to go to court until I was sure you'd get the right verdict. So I delayed the trial, and spent two months combing through the evidence, looking for the proof. But there was nothing there, Joel. Nothing. You were guilty."

"Yes. Yes, I suppose I was."

"You could've told us. You could've told us what happened."

"When? Two months in prison, El, and no one let me talk then. Even if I had any brain left by the end, you saw how the trial went. Did they even ask me if I had anything to say? I can't remember."

"They must have. Didn't they?" She shrugged, trying for indifference, and if his face was any indication, succeeding. They must have. They must have. How could she admit to the man who had once been a boy she loved that she had no idea, that she had not noticed whether he was ever given a chance to defend himself? She had spent the trial trying not to look at him, trying to convince herself the wounds she'd seen were deserved, reminding herself again and again how she hated him. It was easy enough to vote for his execution, when she knew he had more than enough votes already for banishment, no matter what she said. She could never have cast that vote if her vote had mattered at all; she had never been quite that successful in hating him.

He didn't answer, and they walked in silence until their arms brushed each other. None of the other men spoke, or even looked at them—she was sure this illusion of privacy was more for his sake than hers. As long as they did not raise their voices, they would be allowed to continue this awful, awful conversation.

"Joel?" she asked, very quietly, as their arms touched.

"Yes?"

"How many people have you killed?"

"Twenty-two."

He kept his eyes on the ground. She took one careful step away; he looked up, as she did, and she felt guilty, though she had the right to stand wherever she pleased.

"I've never been on the frontlines. I'm sure your siblings have killed more. I'm sure I'd have killed more, by now, if I had never been exiled."

"If you'd never been exiled, we'd never have had a war."

"If you've listened to a single word I've said since we landed in Ibanar, you know that's not true. I'm not taking responsibility for a whole war's worth of death. What evidence did they even have, Eloise? What were the incriminating documents? What did they say I did? No one bothered telling me the details of the charges."

"They said you were sharing state secrets."

"If you were keeping the kind of state secrets that can start a war, I think that's on you."

He walked away from her, rejoining Fuller, and she hung back until she was in step with Alem, unsure whether or not she'd succeeded in pushing him away, or why the thought she might have made her stomach feel so tangled and heavy.

~

It was another day before she approached him again, this time to share the evidence he'd asked about. He should have been glad—he'd always wanted to know—but he didn't want to be near her at all, then. Everything about her overwhelmed him, still.

"There were dozens of documents—letters and order forms and all sorts of things—buying weapons, bribing foreign government officials, things like that—all signed by my father or brothers, and all finished with my seal."

Each member of the royal family had their own seal, but they were similar enough that an outsider wouldn't recognize the difference, that Eloise's could easily pass as her father's in the Olin and Ibanari courts. She'd given it to him, saying she hardly ever had to manage official documents anyway. Saying it was a promise.

"Your seal," he repeated. "Do you know what I did with that seal, when I got back to the barracks that day?"

"What?"

"I begged some parchment and a pot of wax from a bookkeeper, and I made seals until the wax ran out. Because it was fun." Fun on its own, and he'd been so giddy and excited knowing what it meant that she'd given it to him—playing with it had seemed the best use of his energy. "And then I put it under my pillow when it was time for training, every day for weeks, because I didn't want it to distract me or get in the way."

Eloise frowned. "You wore it when you trained with me."

"Yes, well, you weren't in the habit of yelling at me every time I made a mistake, were you? I was much less concerned with distraction, then. The point is, it would have been incredibly easy for someone to borrow it. Everyone knew you'd given it to me. Anyone could have noticed I didn't wear it during training."

"I suppose I should never have given it to you."

It hurt for a moment, even though he knew it was ridiculous, knew she wasn't even talking about the sentiment behind it, but the more practical aspects. And she was right. "So. I allegedly forged your father's signature, too. And, what, Theodore's and Julian's?"

"That was the idea. It wasn't exactly a stretch—you could do mine and Ben's."

They'd had dozens and dozens of thank you letters to write, after their birthday. He'd helped. With the letters and the signatures and the seals, which he'd carried out with a great deal of enthusiasm—that was before Eloise had given him hers.

Honestly, he probably could have forged the king and the other princes' signatures. He'd always been good at things like that. Anything with his fingers, really. He could have. But he hadn't.

"It sounds like I sent a lot of mail to a lot of people I've never heard of. I was quite the mastermind in my youth, wasn't I?"

"Well, obviously it wasn't all you. But since you wouldn't give us any other names..."

"Give who the other names, Eloise? I didn't know that any of this was happening. And the only person who ever questioned me was probably the leader of the whole damn conspiracy."

He walked ahead again.

~

The air was smoky and strange; the fires were gone, but they'd made their mark, lingering not just in the burnt trees and stones and occasionally houses, but in the very sky.

The sky had wept, she thought, when the mountains died. She wondered if he wept for the trees. She wondered if the smoke made the sky god cough, and what it might feel like to stand on the ground while the sky above you had a coughing fit. She wondered if any of the temples had burned—they had not yet reached the start of the holy line—and if the gods would take their revenge on the army who burned them, or whether they had returned to the continent, and cared not for what monuments their worshippers had left behind.

The forest was as essential a part of their island as the dead mountain gods, as the Sea of Tears, and it was the only magnificent, essential piece of the island that had been hers, that she had known for herself, and not just through stories. She thought of the trees she'd climbed, and the bushes she'd picked berries from, and she wondered if all of them were gone. She wondered if her brothers, her sister, had been in the army that set it to flame.

It was still intact; she could see trees still standing in the distance, though everything within a few miles, at least, was black and crumbling.

Fuller wanted to walk closer to the edge, where the forest was still more or less a forest, but Alem was worried about the smoke in the air, worried that something not too far away might still be aflame, or that the burnt air might make them ill.

They picked their way carefully over the blackened ground, and none of them spoke. It was a hallowed, haunted path they walked. The mountain gods were all long dead, but the trees were freshly killed, and their ashes clung to Eloise's skin, her hair.

They had been killing each other for years. Now they killed their home. Soon there would be nothing left. Soon they would kill themselves.

They encountered no one. Whoever had once lived here had fled or died. The armies need not come back through here—they would know that no one could have survived, and they would not expect travellers to cross this burning wasteland.

As the days passed, and they walked on, covering their mouths and noses with spare clothing so they would breathe in less smoke, her sorrow turned to rage. They would reach the first of the temples today, if it still stood; it was likely it did not.

With no other target available, she turned her fury on Joel; after all, she had still to push him adequately away.

"Don't," he said, as soon as she was walking alongside him.

"Don't what?"

"You're going to shout at me, because you're angry at the world, and I'm convenient. You're upset that I love you, which is hilarious, because it's not as if I had any choice in the first place."

"What are you talking about?"

"Does anyone say no to a princess? When we were children, you decided that you loved me, and you would have me, whatever I thought of it. Now we're grown, and I'm not even allowed to love you, but then—but then—"

"Whatever you thought of it? Did you not love me?" Always, always, he found new ways to hurt her.

"I did love you. I just don't think it would have made any difference, if I didn't."

"How can you say that? How can you think I would ever—ever have—what, forced you to be with me?"

"Eloise, you wouldn't have noticed if I didn't love you back. I wasn't even a person to you, at first. I was just a chance to make a spectacle of yourself. The fact that we actually liked each other was secondary."

"That's not true."

"You wandered through the barracks in your pink satin until you spotted the boy who looked most out of place—well, most out of place after you. You dragged me to court functions and even private family dinners. You made a point of draping yourself all over me whenever we were in public, and never spared a thought for the fact that I couldn't say no to a princess."

"You proposed to me."

"Because I did love you—I did. And because I wanted to be married as quickly as possible, in case your father got sick of your antics and had me executed for defiling you."

"You never defiled me."

"You did every damn thing you could to convince the entire kingdom otherwise."

"I never—"

"Shut up, both of you," Fuller said. "We're in unfamiliar territory, and I'm not dying for your lovers' quarrel. Look—the temple is still standing. You can just see it ahead."

They walked in an oppressive silence as the temple grew steadily larger in their vision. It was the first Alirian temple, coming from the south, dedicated to the first god, and it was made of grey stone. The more elegant temples were in the city; out here, they were built to last. Even, it seemed, through forest fires.

The sun was low in the sky, and the air, still smokey, was cooling, by the time they could see that though the building still stood, the door, which must have been wooden, was gone.

"We'll sleep here tonight," Joel said.

"Will you?"

The voice echoed from within the temple, and for a moment Eloise thought the goddess was at home, for surely no priestess was foolish enough or brave enough to stay.

But no, it was a god in this temple, not a goddess.

A woman stepped out from the shadowed doorway. The right side of her face, extending down her neck until her skin disappeared beneath her clothing, was covered in bubbly white scarring, likely from a burn. Her hair, pulled back in a long, tight braid, was the shade of white blonde Eloise usually associated with small children. The left side of her face was lovely and young.

She carried a quarterstaff with the confidence of one who knew how to use it, and she scowled at them.

"Get your own damn temple."

Chapter 12

Sylvia watched from the window as the travellers approached. Four men, one woman, though she didn't realize until they were quite near. She wore men's clothes, as did anyone sensible, out here.

They were armed. Swords, staffs. Anyone sensible was. But they looked comfortable with their weapons, looked as if they knew how to use them. Men who were confident with their weapons were, in Sylvia's experience, not to be trusted.

She sent the others to the back rooms of the temple, the space where once oracles had hidden, waiting for divine messages. She warned the women to hush the children, and positioned herself just under the window, where she could best hear when the travellers came close enough for their voices to carry.

They intended to sleep in the temple. Her temple.

Well, many people did. But not without her permission. She grabbed the best of the quarterstaffs they'd assembled, and stepped out to face the intruders.

"Get your own damn temple," she advised them, and watched as the men with staffs tightened their grips, and the men with the swords reached to unsheathe them.

"Oh, stop it," the one woman among them said. She took one cautious step forward, her own sword remaining strapped to her back. "They won't actually attack you, though they'll defend themselves if you attack. Everyone is stressed; that's all. We didn't know the temple was occupied, and we don't mean to intrude. We'll go on to the next one." She glanced briefly back at the men, who'd moved silently to fan out around her. "That's only, what, twelve miles? And the sun's not yet set. We can do it."

"That temple will also be occupied," Sylvia told her. "All temples will be occupied, or near enough. You didn't know?"

"Who would occupy them?" the woman asked.

"People like you. People running or hiding from something—you are running and hiding. No one passes this way who isn't, unless they're in an army. The priests have abandoned this temple, but the gods have not. Or at least, no one is sure enough they have to risk attacking it. No soldier sets foot past these walls. Past any temple walls."

She considered the travellers. Their clothes were not too worn, not too dirty. But they had the weary, resigned look of those who had travelled too far and seen too much. (Not likely as far as she would otherwise have guessed, though, if the woman thought they could easily travel another twelve miles tonight.) They did not seem dangerous—not dangerous to her, at least. The woman was noble. Sylvia could see it in how she held herself, how she spoke, even if she didn't recognize her profile from coins. It didn't matter; she wasn't the first noblewoman Sylvia had seen living like a refugee. But she was going to get herself killed. The whole lot of them were, if someone didn't take them in hand.

The others wouldn't like it, but Sylvia knew her wishes would be respected.

"You'll want to stay, at least for the next few days. There's an army coming east. You can continue on your way once they're past. Most of the abandoned temples are full of refugees; most of them will let you stay with them a day or two. Some will be frightened of armed men, and turn you away. If you force the issue, word will spread, and all the refugees, runaways, and rebels across the island will be against you."

"We understand," said one of the men, the dark, young one. It was the first time any of the men had spoken since she'd come out of the temple. "Thank you."

She nodded. "Leave your weapons inside the door. There are only women and children here tonight; they shan't hurt you, and you needn't frighten them."

"I am Sylvia," the woman said, as she led them into the abandoned temple.

"El—Elisabeth," Eloise answered, "and this is Senam." She gestured to each of the men in turn. "Alem. Fuller. Chris."

Sylvia nodded, leaning her quarterstaff against the wall where several others, of varying quality, already sat, and gestured for them to do the same. Joel and Eloise exchanged silent glances as they set aside their swords. She had taken charge of the situation the moment the woman had appeared; in their old lives, it had been natural for her to take charge of every situation, but here, now, he was used to leading.

She did not think he minded. He didn't seem upset. He likely knew as well as she did that a woman alone in a war zone would be better talked down by another woman, with empty hands, than by a man who had already automatically drawn his sword.

"Did you really just name yourself after my sister?" he whispered.

"I'm sorry; I forgot. It was the first el name I could think of."

Sylvia gave them a tour, ending with the oracles' chambers, where the other inhabitants of the temple had collected—half a dozen women, and about the same number of children, all of them too thin, in ragged clothing and with large, frightened eyes.

"They'll only be here until the army passes," Sylvia assured them. "And they're all unarmed. And none of the men will dare cross the boundary."

She meant the raised stone border that separated the oracles' chambers from the rest of the temple—it was said that for a man to cross was instant death, for only the god himself could join his most beloved servants in this, his most sacred space.

Eloise was fairly certain some of the scattered children were boys; she was unsure if this meant that the legends were untrue, or if it meant that the god had made an exception considering the dire circumstances. Regardless, the women seemed only slightly comforted by the barrier.

"You'll sleep in the courtyard behind the temple," Sylvia decided. "It's walled in, and still part of the sacred grounds. But I won't have you any nearer the women than that. Elisabeth, you may choose to sleep with your friends or with the women."

Eloise chose to stay with Joel and the other men, and they were sent out into the courtyard. Sylvia settled herself in the doorway, where Eloise suspected she would remain all night, protecting her women from the unknown men.

She wondered why Sylvia had invited them to stay at all. It was an unexpected kindness, especially considering she had begun their introduction by swearing and demanding they leave.

More concerning than Sylvia's behavior, though, was the information that she had shared. If most of the temples on the islands held groups of refugees like this one—

The island was littered with temples.

Olion had a near infinite pantheon, comprised of gods dead, alive, and not yet born. Hundreds, perhaps thousands of temples had been built all across the island, dating back to the times before Alirians or the Ibanari had set foot on its shores.

Ibanar was born from the seas, and most of their gods were of the seas as well, a handful to Olion's hundreds.

When the empire that had once included Aliria first colonized the island, they brought their own gods, as well—twelve of them, which was a good and holy number. And as they'd conquered territory, they'd placed a new temple for every twelve miles they took, at least on the western border; by the time they moved east, they had grown less devout.

In the hundreds of years that had passed since the landing of Ibanar and the independence of Aliria, gods had been passed back and forth across borders, spreading and changing. Scholars said that on the holy street of Ibanar alone, there were three temples dedicated to the same goddess, all calling her by a different name, all interpreting her value differently.

Eloise observed the twelve Alirian holy days, one for each god, and otherwise did not think overmuch about religion; most Alirians didn't, being divorced by an ocean and a dead empire from their own gods. But temples were as inevitable a piece of the landscape as rocks or trees. It would never occur to anyone to search a temple, even in war time— they were sacred. But they were also home to the downtrodden; it made sense that they would fill up, in these days, with various kinds of runaways.

There were more temples on the island than on many other, larger continents. More temples than could possibly be maintained by priests, with the island at war and populations diminished by war and plague. A temple was the perfect place to hide a large group of people.

If each temple was hiding a large group of people, or even a small one, even only one or two men or women—how many people on the island had been driven from their homes? How many hundreds, how many thousands of people had this war displaced?

~

Sylvia brought breakfast, what little they had to spare, to the travellers in the courtyard. It was a very small breakfast—the food in this temple may need to last its occupants through the winter, depending on what happened from here.

There was dust on the horizon; the army would soon be passing.

The travellers had come from the southeast; they were moving northwest. She wondered, as she offered them stale bread, what on earth could compel them to make such a journey. Sylvia herself would move in the same direction, but she had her own motivations, which few enough on this island shared. Moving northwest would take them only deeper into Aliria, into the populated areas, the dangerous areas. Or it would take them clear across Aliria, to the ocean at the other side of the island, but why would anyone choose to move in that direction? If you were sailing off of the island, the southwestern coast of Ibanar was the place to sail from. It was the safest place to reach, and the safest place to leave, and it was nearest to the safest place to land.

The woman was noble. An Alirian noble.

She probably wanted to go home.

Sylvia didn't know how she had come to be so far away from home, in the first place, but she could understand the need to return, even if it was dangerous and foolish.

These people didn't even know the temples were a refuge. They would not make it to the Alirian capital. They would die first. Sylvia didn't care, when most of the soldiers and deserters she encountered died. But these men weren't soldiers, though they seemed able to fight, and the noblewoman—the nobles may have caused this war, but it wasn't this woman's fault. Sylvia had been planning to move northwest already. She might as well keep these people alive, on the way.

She warned the men to stay in the courtyard, though the woman could come inside. She had to keep as much space as possible between them and her women. She did not like causing the women so much fear, in this space that should have been safe when nothing else was. But she did not like leaving people to die when she could help it, either.

All of these women had been through horrible things. But life went on. And they could hardly keep living it if they could not handle the sight of a man with a sword. Many men carried swords, even outside of war time.

She would leave the women here, and they would learn over the next few months, she hoped, to better protect and care for themselves and each other. They may yet continue on this year, but this temple was Sylvia's last stop. Another guide would pick them up from here, whether it was a few days from now or several months. She'd gone all the way to the ports, more than once, when needed, but they had more Ibanari guides now than they had then, and she was more useful farther north, where she knew the terrain best. With the landscape changed by the fire, she didn't know how best to carry out the next leg of the journey south.

They would be stronger, braver, by the time they reached the port. And this one frightening day was one of the easiest things they would endure. The road south had been perilous even before the fire. Sylvia checked on them once more, reminding them that the children must be kept quiet, before she went to the part of the temple where she could best watch the progress of the army.

This was the worst part. When hundreds of men became one, many-headed monster, which she knew she could not fight. Armies seldom took notice of temples, and when they did they usually respected their sanctity. She had her tricks, for when they did not—her Voice of the Goddess, which she had learned in Ibanar, was sacrilege, but it was effective, too, and the gods had not yet seen fit to punish her for it. She had learned the ingredients for a few sacred incenses, at various still-occupied temples across the island, and carried them always with her. Made strong enough, the incense would convince most men that the god or goddess was at that moment in the temple, conferring with a beloved priest or priestess.

The most valuable tool of all, though, was the crossbow. There was one in most temples, distributed by the network Sylvia was part of. They were simple weapons, stolen or bought cheaply, and easy enough to operate. What made them precious was the arrows. Hundreds had been produced by a group of temples in Olion, made to match exactly the arrows of the great god of the sun, which he had thrown down against any blasphemers in the days of old. One of them, aimed at a soldier venturing too close to the temple, would turn the whole army away. No one wished to be struck down by the sun himself, for vandalizing a temple that likely held nothing of real value.

Sylvia kept her crossbow always at the ready, when soldiers passed, and had the supplies for her incense laid out, so she needed only strike her flint if they seemed too interested.

She heard footsteps, which meant that someone had kindly, deliberately made their footsteps heard, for the floors in this temple were designed to soak up and suppress sounds, to preserve an air of holiness. She turned, and saw it was the noblewoman.

"Your men," Sylvia began.

"They're hardly mine."

Sylvia shrugged. "I do not mind your company, but the attic is far from the courtyard, and I would rather you supervised them, if I cannot. The women here have been badly hurt."

"Jo—they would never hurt anyone. Not—not like this. Defenseless women in a temple."

"And why should the defenseless women in the temple believe this?"

She sighed. "You're right. I'm sorry. If I could bring them up here, we could help you keep watch, and you needn't worry about what they may do out of your sight."

Sylvia looked out the window again, at what was still mostly just a great cloud of dust. "Very well. We have things to speak of, and I suppose now is as good a time as any."

~

Joel followed Eloise into the attic of the temple, and the other men followed him. He had not realized that temples had attics, and would never have guessed that a temple attic would have windows angled to give one a perfect view—and a perfect shot—at any intruders, while remaining invisible from the outside.

It made sense, he supposed. The empire had built the temples as they had conquered the territory, which meant they had likely doubled, sometimes, as military outposts. The first structures built in a new land would need to be defensible, dedicated to the gods or not.

"We have some time before the army is near enough to be a true worry," the woman who guarded the temple said. "And we have much to discuss, in this time."

"Have we?" Joel asked.

"You travel toward the Alirian capital," she said.

"And what would make you think that?"

She looked at him briefly, then turned her attention to Eloise. It was, Joel admitted reluctantly to himself, annoying. He had long since shaken off his princess' shadow, and he did not like living under it here, at the whim of some random woman who had decided, for some unknown reason, that Eloise was the one in charge.

Or perhaps it was just that strange men were unnerving, and it was easier to address herself to another woman.

"I think that because you are an Alirian noblewoman," Sylvia said.

Or perhaps that was the reason she thought Eloise was in charge. Joel didn't answer, and neither did the others—what, exactly, did one say to that very accurate accusation?

(They'd gotten so far without being recognized. And now—she was just some random woman. Maybe they hadn't been good at keeping secrets. Maybe they'd just gotten lucky.)

"Don't treat me as if I'm an idiot. You are quite obviously an Alirian noblewoman. It makes no difference to me, except that I doubt your ability to reach the capital safely."

"We've done well enough so far," Eloise said, sounding quite obviously offended, because Eloise could not when her life depended on it resist picking a fight.

(He was a little embarrassed he found that trait so charming.)

"If you hadn't stopped here—if I hadn't let you stay here—you'd have walked right into the army. There's nothing for leagues but temples, and twelve miles is a good distance, when it's the distance you have to run before a soldier spots you. I'm not trying to insult your—

your skill at hiding. I don't much like seeing people dead. And as I'm moving in the same direction you are, I thought I could see to it you didn't die."

"You would escort us to the palace?" Eloise asked.

"Not the palace. I won't go to the palace. But to the city, certainly."

"Very well," Eloise said, without bothering to consult the rest of them.

Joel glanced at Fuller, who shrugged—he saw no problem, then, with the suggestion. Alem only disagreed with Joel when he felt he was being profoundly idiotic, and Fuller was far quicker to call Joel out on idiocy, so if Fuller thought it a reasonable plan, Alem should be amenable as well. Chris was always amenable.

"When do we leave?" Joel asked.

"When the army is past."

~

Armies moved slowly. They waited in the temple for two days. Eloise tried to make friends with the other women, the ones who hid in the oracles' quarters, but they were not friendly.

Eloise had brought strange, armed men into what was supposed to be their safe space. They were suffering from some unknown trauma, which she supposed had, at the very least, involved the deaths of their husbands, as there were several children, and no adult men. The forest around them had burned. An army marched past. They had few enough reasons to be friendly.

Sylvia guarded the hidden attic window with a single-minded determination, refusing to let any of them take a watch until she could no longer manage without sleep, at which point she handed over her post with great reluctance, and for only a few short hours.

"What would you do if we weren't here?" Eloise asked as she studied the incense mixtures, and Joel behind her fiddled with the crossbow.

"I would have one of the refugees take the post, and wake me immediately if anything odd happened. I hate to do it. And this batch is…especially useless. It isn't their faults. But it isn't often that all of the children are so young, and all of the women so meek, and not a man in the group. They're only like this because their husbands—it was an ugly situation. The men died badly, and their wives will pick up and keep going, because there's nothing else to do. But they're not ready yet. The tragedy was very fresh when I picked them up."

"Joel is good with a crossbow." At least, he claimed to be. Eloise had never seen him fire one, but had no particular reason to doubt the claim. "Rest a little."

"The crossbow is only a last resort. We have only so many arrows."

"Yes. You said. It will be fine; they've been passing for hours now with hardly a glance at the temple."

She managed, finally, to shoo Sylvia off to a priest's old quarters, where she would hopefully get at least some sleep.

"All right?" she asked Joel. They'd hardly spoken since arriving. Which was probably for the best, but it felt odd. Wrong.

"Fine. These arrows sure are something. Right out of the stories."

"Where are the others?" Sylvia had become more willing to let them out of sight, as she'd grown more tired.

"Oh, around."

"Not near the women?"

He frowned at her. "Do you think we pester traumatized refugees for fun? Chris is catching up on sleep in the courtyard. Alem is looking through the supplies they keep stored here—and not to steal them, don't even st—"

"I wasn't going to."

"Of course you weren't," he said, painfully unconvinced. "He's checking the status of their medical supplies, seeing if he can help with anything. Fuller's—I'm not entirely sure what Fuller's doing. He might be sleeping. He might be playing with his map. But he's doing it in the courtyard. He wanted to stay up here, with us, but that girl's so jumpy, and it's gotten worse, the longer she's gone without sleep. We didn't think she could handle two strange men hovering about much longer, and I'm the leader, so I got to stay."

"Jumpy?" Eloise asked.

"Not compared to the others, maybe. But she's been anxious since we came through the door. You must have noticed she only speaks to you—I don't think it's just because she thinks you're the one in charge."

"I like her."

"I like her too—that's why I don't want to send her into a panic by surrounding her with strange men."

Eloise sighed. "How is it, out the window?"

He turned to look, briefly. "The same as it has been, for hours. I don't think we'll have any trouble. And with an army this large passing us now, it's unlikely we'll come in contact with another on the way home."

"They're far south, for Olion."

"I've seen battles with Olion farther south than this. Everyone's crawling all over the island. Borders mean nothing."

"I'm so sick of war."

"You're sick of it? It's hardly touched you, El."

"It's ripped my family and my kingdom apart. It's razed the forest and killed men beyond counting and broken my fiancé's heart."

Joel's expression soured. "I can't believe you're marrying him."

"What, because you're back? Jeremy will give me back all the respectability you cost me."

"That I cost you. Seriously, Eloise? You're going to—"

"All right, the respectability that my own outrageous behavior while young and enamored with you cost me. Better?"

"Yes."

"I've no—" She stopped. She shouldn't—shouldn't say anything that could sound as if she was encouraging him. But—they had so little time. A few weeks, perhaps, and their lives would go on, in separate directions. She would likely never see him again. He had always been someone she could speak honestly with—one of the few such people in her life—and she did not want to give that up a moment sooner than she needed to.

"I've no particular desire to marry Jeremy—to marry anyone. I was quite content to be a spinster. But I need to be married, Joel. You must see that—it isn't safe, to be royal and female and unmarried, in war time."

"I understand the risk in general. I understand that a conqueror can solidify his claim on the throne by forcing a marriage to his enemy's daughter. But in your case—who are you expecting you'll be forced to marry? No one has any heirs."

This was true; Aliria was the only country on the island whose future was secure. Or had been, before the war. Eloise's parents had been lucky—she was the fifth of seven heirs.

Olion had, at the start of the war, had three princes and a princess. Then a terrible sickness had been brought over from Kire by a merchant ship. The king had closed his borders to protect the rest of the island, the war, for a time, set aside. His three sons and his son-in-law had all died, leaving him a widowed daughter and two daughters-in-law, all of them with no children. The king was the only child of an only child, and women weren't allowed to inherit, or hadn't been a hundred years ago, the last time the issue had been raised.

(It had seemed, for a while, that Olion and Aliria, at least, would make peace. But in the midst of treaty discussions, Olion had suddenly attacked again. Likely, she knew now, due to the influence of traitors in the Alirian court.)

Ibanar hadn't had a proper heir in years. Their king was on his third wife. The first had died in childbirth over twenty ago, and the baby with her. He had been married to the second for most of the time since, with no children to show for it. She had often ridden into battle at his side, and was said to be a competent warrior. She had died of infection from a wound about a year and a half before Eloise was kidnapped. Though everyone said he loved her dearly, the king was quick to replace her—one last chance at a child. His new queen was younger than Eloise, and had yet to fall pregnant. Even if she did, the king would die of old age, if nothing else, years before the heir was ready to take the throne, and there was already infighting among the potential regents. The king's only sibling was a sister nearly thirty years his junior, and her oldest child, the current placeholder heir, was not yet ten.

"Father is afraid the king of Ibanar will throw over his third wife—the marriage could be easily annulled. And the king of Olion is widowed. He's old, but not too old to bear a child, with a wife young enough to be his daughter. If Olion dies before the war ends, a distant cousin inherits, and he's unmarried still. We don't know what he would do about the war, if he took power. If Ibanar dies, the war likely ends unless his sister persists on her son's behalf; she may, and if she does Maria would likely be married to the young king, in a few years—but that wouldn't be so bad. Not ideal. But they're both young, and it wouldn't be—wouldn't be any less voluntary, really, than a standard arranged marriage."

Joel turned to check the army again; they must have been doing nothing interesting, as he felt no need to comment on their progress. "Your life is quite convoluted, isn't it?"

"I suppose it is."

It hadn't been, when she was young. When she was with him.

She missed those days. More than she wanted to.

~

When the army was safely small in the distance, Sylvia gave her refugees their instructions for their wait, and left, only a few days earlier than she had originally planned, with the five travellers in tow.

She had her duties, on the way to Aliria, stops they would have to make with her. There were the still-priested temples where she would collect supplies, and the abandoned temples where she would drop them for refugees waiting out the winter. She had no orphans now, thank all the gods, to find homes for—that was the worst of tasks, and worse still in winter. Once she had travelled alone through three months of winter and early spring, carrying a child not yet a year old, just her and the baby, until she could deposit him at a temple. Five able-bodied adults would be easy enough to manage; they could even help her carry supplies.

The noblewoman told her they had last passed through Aliria several months ago, but not a full year. They had gone, then, more along the eastern edge. Before the forest had burned.

She tried to think how the landscape had changed, what she needed to warn them of. She had come through from that direction not long ago, and it should be familiar enough to her, but it was difficult to remember what was new, what would take them by surprise.

There was a fort of Ibanari soldiers stationed between here and the capital, guarding the sliver of land they'd taken going up the coast. That would be the most dangerous place to pass, but it would be hard to avoid; there had been a battle along the edge of the forest not many miles east of there, and there could still be soldiers stationed in the area. She was not sure the battle had even ended. They would have to brave the narrow space between those two dangers.

She would speak with Harra, in three days, if she was still where Sylvia had left her. She would speak with George not long after that. They would both have fresher information than her. The priestess of the third god still kept her temple running well; it was one of the great temples, in the one large city they would reach before the capital, not one of the little ones that had been abandoned. The priestess would give Sylvia the best information on the last leg of their journey, collected carefully from any travellers passing through. She would give her supplies, as well, to serve their pockets of refugees between the cities.

Sylvia would see the three little girls she'd left there last year as initiates after their parents had died. She would take more supplies north than she usually could; the devotees of the third god were generous, and she was often offered more gifts than she could carry. These four men would be a great help.

The woman, too, she decided, after they had walked a few hours. She was sturdy enough, for a woman in her position. She would have to be, to have gone this far from home. Of course, many noblewomen were strong enough, but usually they were the ones who had become soldiers. This woman, Sylvia thought, was not a soldier. She held her sword with ease, but she had not the scars, nor the calluses, nor the sense to tie her hair up securely or cut it off.

Sylvia studied the group's dynamics, and did not speak much to them, for the first few days. The first day travelling with a new group was the most important; it was when she learned who they were, and how they were together, and what troubles she may have to sort out through the journey.

They were all five comfortable enough together. There was no particular reverence for the noblewoman, just general politeness. The man with the map, she thought, would rather not be travelling with her, but he was not rude or disrespectful. The boy was friendly with everyone, and Sylvia thought it would not be long before his friendliness was inflicted on her. The oldest man—the foreigner—was quiet, but seemed on good terms with the others.

It was the last man and the noblewoman that were the problem.

The first few hours were fine. It was clear the other three men deferred to him, and not to the woman. It was also clear he was besotted—he was constantly staring at her, in that longing, hurting way people had when love was unrequited, or when they thought it was. The woman seemed determined to ignore him, though she snuck frequent glances whenever he was distracted. They had seemed friendly enough, before, and she was unsure what had caused the new tension between them.

An argument broke out at midday. Sylvia wasn't sure what had caused it, but it was between those two, and the other three shushed them with a swiftness and an exasperation that told her this was a common occurrence.

By the third morning, she had grown used to their pattern—they would avoid each other, and then they would become friendly, and then they would have a dramatic fight that Sylvia did not have the patience to deal with.

"You are like children. If you cannot get along and stay quiet, you cannot play together. You, Senam, you walk with Fuller. Elisabeth, you walk with me."

This arrangement had the added benefit of putting the other woman between herself and the men, who all seemed safe enough, true, but old habits died hard.

"He does bring out the worst in me," Elisabeth said. "I'm sorry."

Sylvia shrugged. "It's because you love each other. It takes people that way, sometimes. You'll settle, with time."

"We don't love each other."

"No?"

"No. It wouldn't matter if we did."

"You're noble," Sylvia remembered. "I suppose you're promised to someone?"

"I am."

"Well, then. It's best you're not in love."

"For the best, yes. Are we nearly to your friend's temple?"

"Nearly. The fire just missed this spot—she's tucked into that copse of trees you see ahead."

Chapter 13

Sylvia was a wonderful addition to their group. It was so much easier, with another woman there, with another person who was not Joel's person there, to avoid being drawn into his orbit. They had a few encounters, still, but Eloise tried to ignore him, and succeeded better than she usually did.

They had spent one night in a temple that was genuinely abandoned, and the next in one that housed a small family—husband, wife, and two boys, perhaps twelve and fourteen. The boys had been fascinated with their swords, and with Joel's and Sylvia's scars. Sylvia was obviously uncomfortable with this, and Joel and Chris had distracted the boys with stories while Sylvia and Fuller talked with their parents, leaving Eloise to help Alem with his checking of the medical supplies. It had been the only time since leaving that first temple that Eloise had not had Sylvia by her side, and it had been fine, since it was Alem. But she very much enjoyed the buffer that Sylvia provided.

She had not spoken with Joel since the morning, a state of affairs she would be content to maintain indefinitely.

This continued until they reach their destination for the night, a temple where they were greeted at the door by a woman perhaps ten years Eloise's senior, with hair the soft orange of a sunset.

"Sylvia!" she said. "I was wondering when you'd be back through. Didn't expect you to have anyone with you."

"We were headed in the same direction, so I'm seeing them home." Sylvia stepped forward to hug the other woman, who Eloise supposed must be Harra. "Any changes?"

"The baby didn't make it, so we're down to eight."

"I'm sorry."

Harra smiled—a tight, insincere thing. "We knew she was too ill. But I daren't push the others any farther yet, not with the death so fresh."

"Contagious?" Sylvia asked.

"No, we're all healthy now. You and your friends can stay safely."

Sylvia introduced them all to the woman—who was, indeed, Harra, and they went inside, where Harra told a small group of people that they would be having guests for the night, but didn't bother with names. She pulled Sylvia into a private area of the temple, leaving the rest of them to their own devices.

The people in the temple all looked sickly and sad. Alem immediately began speaking quietly with the adults, and Chris sat on the floor to talk to the children.

They were so kind. She was still angry with Joel, but she was so glad they were getting pardoned.

Fuller retreated into a corner to study his map, again, leaving Eloise and Joel alone.

"You're angry with me," Joel observed.

"I can scarcely remember the last time I wasn't. Many, many years ago, I suppose."

"I am trying to get you home. I'm trying to fix things."

"I know."

"Will it ever be enough?"

"Enough for you to get your pardon? Yes. Enough for me to love you? No."

"What about enough for you to forgive me, Eloise?"

She brushed past him to sit on the ground between Chris and the two very small girls he was entertaining with some wild story.

She was only sometimes angry with him. She was often angry with herself, for not being angry enough. She couldn't forgive him. Forgiving him would mean letting him back in, would mean putting herself back in the same position she'd fought so hard to get out of. She could not let herself become attached. She had to go home and resume being the princess she spent so many years proving she could be.

These last few months had been fun. It should not have been fun, being kidnapped, or travelling with the man who betrayed her. The journey was nearly over, and she could not afford to keep being the kind of person who had fun this way. She had to leave Joel behind. She had to. She was going to hand this whole mess off to her father, and then she was going to marry Jeremy, move to his estate as soon as it was rebuilt, and spend the rest of her life pretending these last several months—and, if possible, the first several months she spent with Joel as a child—had never happened.

She supported every ridiculous claim Chris made about their journey here, to the deep skepticism of the little girls. Joel watched for a moment before joining Fuller in the corner.

"Did you really see dragons?" the older girl asked.

"Three of them."

"Don't lie to the children, Chris," Eloise said. "It was four. Have you told them about the pirates yet?"

~

"All the way to the capital?" Harra asked.

Sylvia nodded.

"You hate Aliria."

"I hate the Alirian army, and the Alirian government. I don't hate Alirians."

"That woman is clearly—"

"A member of the Alirian governing family, yes. I very much doubt she's ever had anything to do with the directing of their armies."

"The first frost is not so far off, Syl. I don't like the idea of you stuck wintering in the capital."

"I won't. I'll drop them off and continue north. I can be well into Olion before it's too cold to travel, and I'll winter at one of the temples. I can be back down with another group as soon as the cold breaks."

"You think you can get that far? Without a horse?"

"Maybe I can get a horse."

"Oh, and you've learned to ride one, these last few weeks, have you?"

"If there's not time to reach a secure spot in Olion, I'll backtrack a bit, and winter at the temple of the third god. What about you?"

"I haven't decided. Normally I'd take them at least a little farther south. But with the terrain so changed, and with the illness..."

"They might be best left here for the winter," Sylvia agreed. "But will you stay with them?"

Sylvia herself couldn't bear to stay with her refugee groups, crammed into one small space, for all the months of winter. She left them at one of the designated points, and came back for them later, her or another like her. She seldom saw a group all the way from the top of Olion to the bottom of Ibanar, where the port was. She had been all over the island, in her time, but usually they moved the refugees in stages, each guide sticking to their own territory.

"I will," Harra said. "It's too late to collect another group, and I worry, with the illness. It's passed, but they're still weak. Especially the little ones."

She nodded. She especially couldn't bear to stay with a group in this case. She hated it when they died. Especially when the children died. She always distanced herself as soon as possible, when a refugee died on her watch. But Harra was stronger, in some ways, than her. Sylvia could beat a man to death with a club or a quarterstaff—and had—but Harra could much better carry his victims through tragedy, once Sylvia had done the killing.

"It's mealtime," Harra says. "Help me get them fed, and then we'll talk more. Compare maps. I had a deserter pass through two days ago—that's probably fresher data than you have."

"Good. I've a cartographer with me, of all things. He'll want every possible detail."

~

They left Harra, and reached Sylvia's friend George not long after.

"He deserted the Olin army six years ago," she said as they approached the temple where she'd seen him last. "I don't usually tell my refugees that. Deserters have such a bad reputation—well, I've come across more than enough who deserved it. But war is an ugly thing, and you can hardly blame men for wanting no part in it. It's all about how desperate it makes them, after, how far they're willing to go to get what they need, and then how far they'll go to get what they want, once they learn how easy it can be to cross the line. I run deserters and refugees both off the island. And deserters are a lot easier to work with—better at helping themselves. Better at helping the refugees, too. But half my refugees are so frightened by the stories they've heard—or by the ones they've met, sometimes—that we have to separate them into different groups."

Eloise had never met any deserters, only heard stories—many stories—about how horrible and dangerous they were. But then, you would want the people who stopped fighting your war to sound bad to the ones still in it, wouldn't you?

They were perhaps a hundred yards from the temple when a tall, pale man came rushing out to meet them.

"Sylvia! Thank all the gods you're here."

"What's happened?"

"Small family, travelling on their own—parents and an infant. Someone from the garrison shot at them—as far as I can tell they thought the father was me. They made it here, and I did my best, but the wound was infected—the mother passed this morning. The baby's still nursing."

Sylvia swore violently.

"Is there anyone—"

She shook her head. "I've come from the first temple. Haven't seen a single nursing mother along the way."

"Damn it. I'll have to get them back past the garrison. And they're watching now."

They gathered in what was likely once a priest's bedchamber to discuss the logistics. The baby and his father would join their group, as they were already planning to pass the garrison. But getting any of them past it remained a challenge, especially if the last people to try were shot. Eloise half listened to the other, more experienced travellers; she had nothing of value to contribute. She could hear the thin cry of a small baby—a baby who would die if they couldn't get him to the nearest town and to a wetnurse.

"We could start a fire," Joel said, and Eloise checked back into the conversation.

"Are you mad?" she asked.

"It needn't be another forest fire. We could set the garrison on fire."

"And kill all those men?"

"Better them than us and an innocent baby whose mother they've already murdered."

"It could spread."

"No fires," Joel conceded, though he didn't look pleased about it.

"Does the garrison have horses?" Alem asked.

"It does," George said.

"We'll need to steal one. The faster the child can reach the town, the more likely he is to survive."

"It's an Ibanari outpost," Joel said slowly.

"Yes," Sylvia agreed.

"You and George are both Olin. We're in Aliria, and all the refugee groups are coming from the north. I suppose that makes me the only person here who can pass for Ibanari."

"Maybe Alem," Fuller added.

"So," Joel said. "We break in, cause a disturbance, steal a horse. Are you quite sure I can't start a fire?"

"Why do you want so desperately to start one?" Eloise asked.

"It's a very good distraction."

"If you were actually in the garrison," George said, "I suppose we could be sure it would stay controlled."

"Isn't it all dangerous enough," Eloise asked, "without adding a fire to the mix?"

"Cheer up, El. Perhaps I'll be captured and killed, and you can finally be rid of me."

His tone was light and joking, and it cut her like a knife. She stood and left the room. She was useless for the planning, anyway.

~

Joel watched Eloise leave, recognizing the improved posture, the careful gait, that meant she was upset and trying to hide it. (A new tell, for the new Eloise—at sixteen she seldom bothered trying to hide her feelings, and when she did, she wasn't any good at it.)

He didn't have time to worry about upsetting someone who claimed to care about him not at all. Each minute they wasted brought the baby closer to death.

"I can do it," he said. "I happen to be an experienced horse thief."

"They're all trained soldiers," George said. "There's over a hundred of them."

"I can do it," he said again. "Just give me a minute to think." He went over the information he knew. Over a hundred men in the garrison. They generally kept watch along the walls, not coming down into the forest without reason. There were at least a few horses, but they seldom came outside the walls. The soldiers knew there were people holed up in the temple, but wouldn't come after them as long as they stayed there; they wouldn't risk offending the gods. The garrison faced the coastline, with its back to the edge of the forest. There were miles of coast and open land north of it, open land they would have to cross. Most of it was walled in, but not all of it. The gaps in the wall would be guarded, but not all of them well.

George helped Fuller to sketch out a map of the garrison and surrounding area. George produced two Ibanari soldiers' uniform, and failed to produce any explanation for it. Sylvia produced a small, wide horn meant to amplify the voice; when Chris asked what it was for, she told him, "Heresy." Joel prepared, despite what he'd told Eloise, to set a few fires.

It wasn't complicated, really. Joel would wait by the small opening where the wall had been built around a stream that ran through the garrison. Sylvia would scream a scream that echoed for miles. Joel would have a small window, when everyone was distracted by the scream, to slip inside and blend in. Once inside, he would need to unlatch the back gate, open all the stalls in the stable, and create sufficient distraction to get the horses through the back gate.

Unless he could take all the horses, he would probably have to kill the unneeded ones; it would be far too easy for the soldiers to catch them with horses still at their disposal.

Joel was quite experienced with blending in. He had, after all, spent the better part of a decade travelling through multiple countries that he had been banished from.

"I don't like this plan," Eloise had said when he explained it.

"I don't take orders from you," he'd reminded her, and gone to change into his Ibanari uniform.

He waited now, for Sylvia's scream. It was even louder than he'd expected, and he gritted his teeth, since he hadn't a hand free to plug his ears, grabbed at the gap in the wall, and pulled himself through. As George had said, this was a poorly attended area. One man on guard, looking in vain for the source of the scream, and no one else in sight. Joel yanked him to the ground, knocked him out with the hilt of his own sword, and shoved him through the opening he'd just climbed through. After a moment of consideration, he reached back to snag the man's hat, which was in better condition than his own.

Joel was an expert at appearing to know exactly what he was doing and where he was going, and therefore fading into the background. It was a skill that had served him well through a childhood of petty crimes to support his family, and through an adulthood of much larger crime. (There was no blending in, at the palace. He was too obviously other, his skin too dark, his accent too strong, even before there was Eloise, calling attention to him everywhere she went.)

He moved with purpose in the direction of the back gate. Sylvia's screams continued to echo around them, impossible to triangulate, distracting everyone and making conversation all but impossible. She was a very good screamer, which surprised him somehow. He unlatched the gate, quick and casual; anyone watching would think that he was only looking out, trying as so many others were to find the source of the scream.

He began searching for the stables, careful not to look as if he was searching. A group of men were mobilizing to search for the source of the scream. A few whispered, as he walked past, that perhaps that woman they'd shot at a few days ago had died, and it was her ghost that screamed. Others worried that either they or someone else in the forest had angered the gods, that it was one of the goddesses who screamed now.

(They would never find Sylvia by following her screams. The horn was meant to be used by priestesses when they were speaking on behalf of their goddess, and was designed so their voices would seem to come from everywhere and nowhere.)

(Sylvia had made a point of clarifying that she wasn't actually committing any kind of sacrilege; it was the Voice of the Goddess that was sacred, and not the device by which it was amplified.)

There was only one man in the stable, this late at night. He was easy enough to handle. Joel opened all the stalls quickly, and then started his first fire.

The horses were already spooked by the screams, and they fled the stable as soon as they recognized the fire. Joel followed. Alem should, by now, have entered the garrison by the same path he'd taken; a second column of smoke confirmed it. It was after they had, between the two of them, set five small fires that Chris and Fuller would open the unlocked gate, and load Eloise, Sylvia, and their newest travelling companion onto the fleeing horses.

Sylvia had stopped screaming. Hopefully that meant she was now occupied with trying to ride a horse. The fire at the stable was by now quite large, and served as a new distraction. A few men tried to wrangle the horses, and Joel dealt with them as they came. The chaos was sufficient that he didn't feel the need to kill any horses.

He and Alem reached the back gate at nearly the same time. Fuller and Chris were both on horses, and each holding the bridle for another. The rest of their party was out of sight, hopefully well on their way.

They rode through the night. Hopefully the fires and the loss of the horses would keep the garrison occupied for at least that long. Their priority would be putting out the fires, of course. There was little danger of a second forest fire developing; the garrison was mostly stone, and could hopefully contain the flames.

The horses weren't saddled—there hadn't been time—and it was Sylvia's first time on a horse. He could only hope she was managing.

~

It was a long, hard ride, Eloise struggling to manage an unsaddled horse much larger than she was accustomed to, Sylvia in front of her clinging tightly to its neck. Joel called them to a stop perhaps a mile from the town they'd ridden toward, not long after dawn.

"We'll abandon the horses here. No need to bring trouble with us where we're going. How's the baby?"

"Holding on," the father said. Eloise hadn't caught his name, and it was far too late to ask now.

Eloise dismounted, followed by Sylvia, with assistance from Alem. Joel and Chris shooed the horses away—the ones they'd ridden and the ones who'd followed their friends.

They left Sylvia to manage the refugees, that being what she did, and the rest of them walked a few feet ahead. They should probably be moving more quickly, for the baby, but none of them had the energy.

"Did you have fun?" Joel asked her.

"Was I supposed to?"

"You being who you are, I was rather expecting it."

"I think you got the fun part. I was mostly worrying about the baby. I'm still worrying about the baby. But it was a good ride. Beautiful horse."

"I am sorry you had to manage Sylvia for it. I thought she'd be most comfortable with you."

"It was fine. But I expect to sleep before we go much farther."

"Once we find the wetnurse. And I suspect Sylvia will handle that herself."

They'd drifted slowly closer together as they spoke, the rest of the world vanishing as it did too often when she spoke to Joel. She leaned closer still. She was tired—it had been a very long ride—and he had grown to just the right height to rest her head on his shoulder. He wrapped an arm around her waist.

"Almost done, Ellie."

"I was so afraid when you went in," she admitted. "Just you and Alem, with all those soldiers. And Alem wasn't even there the whole time."

"I've taken bigger risks."

"Don't tell me that."

"Sorry."

She and Joel had always fit together so nicely. It was terrifyingly easy to forget, now, that they were no longer—that they could never be—he was still so very Joel. Older, more confident, more hurt, but still the boy she'd loved so much.

They reached town not long after, and Sylvia launched immediately into a flurry of activity. She pulled father and child with her as she spoke to various people, gesturing wildly, all traces of Olion suddenly absent from her accent. Eloise watched, still leaning closer to Joel than she ought to be.

It was the first time she'd been properly in Aliria for months. Being on Alirian soil was not at all the same as being surrounded by other Alirians.

Of course, that increased the odds of her being recognized as Alirian nobility. But it didn't matter so much now, did it? She supposed this Alirian village could sell her out to the Ibanari fort, but surely they wouldn't. If she could trust outlaws, she should be able to trust her own people.

She wasn't sure she did.

She twisted the seal ring on her finger slowly—the seal that had started the war.

"All right, El?" Joel checked.

"All right," she said, and straightened, and took one careful step away. "We should find a place to sleep."

"Sylvia seems to have things well in hand; I suspect she'll manage lodging as well."

Within an hour, the baby was nursing, and the rest of them were at an inn, Sylvia and Eloise in one room, the men in another.

"I'm never stayed in an inn before," Sylvia told her. "Usually we sleep in abandoned buildings, or find someone who'll let us use their barn or shed."

"Things will be easier, now that we're in Aliria."

"Perhaps," Sylvia said.

~

The fort they'd broken into was the farthest north Ibanar had come on the western side of the island, and there were no rumors of Olion in this area. This last stretch of the journey, from the fort to the palace, should be the safest they had. Alirian soldiers were no better than any others, but as long as Eloise had her seal ring, they would be protected.

Still, it would be best to avoid soldiers altogether. Which meant that, for the first time since they'd taken Eloise, staying in towns was safer than camping out in the woods.

Eloise had softened toward him, since they left the last temple. Maybe because he was in danger, maybe because he helped rescue a baby. He doubted it would last too long, but he was doing his best to behave, and not bring it to an end any earlier than necessary.

The terrain here, since they'd swung east again, away from the coastline, was a mix of farmland and small towns. But it was about as safe as they could expect to be. They slept mostly in small inns, leaving the continued run of temples to the refugees who needed them more, and they made it to the next city without difficulty.

Joel hadn't been in any city but Kahir, for one short day, since the weeks he spent sneaking around the Alirian capital, spreading the rumors he knew would draw Eloise out.

He hadn't spoken to her, hadn't even spoken to anyone who knew her, in nine years. But he knew Eloise. When she was upset, she acted out, and she sought space. The best way to do both of those things was leaving the grounds. And when she left the grounds, she always left them in the same direction. He'd just had to hope that he was still enough to upset her.

Things hadn't gone according to plan. Eloise had done exactly what he'd expected of her, but he'd botched things, badly. Had disregarded all his own careful strategizing at nearly every turn. From the moment he'd decided to join the kidnapping party, just as Eloise and Tulip crested the hill, tying on the mask that was supposed to be only a precaution seconds before riding out to meet her.

He'd ruined all his plans. It shouldn't have surprised him; good sense never held up to Eloise.

His last venture into a big city, though, had been a success. He hadn't ruined things until later. It had been a rare city success for him—it tended to be in large cities that things fell apart. He avoided them whenever he could. And this city—this city would be an excellent spot for Eloise to leave him. Surely it was large enough that there would be some Alirian military presence, some political official who would recognize her or her ring. Someone into whose care a princess could place herself, someone who could be better trusted than a band of outlaws to see her home.

He could slip that seal ring right off her finger without her even noticing. He could take her proof of identity, and force her to stay with him.

He could. But he wouldn't. He just had to hope Eloise would stay with him, that the information he'd held for the better part of a decade would see him safely pardoned, if nothing else.

Chapter 14

The temple of the third god was magnificent. It was not the first temple to this god that they had stopped at since they began their journey together, but it was the first of his temples to be still occupied by his acolytes, which made it much more impressive than the others, spread through Aliria.

This temple had designated guest rooms. Sylvia had visited enough temples by this point in her life to recognize this as a highly unusual feature. She left the temple servants to see to her companions, and went to find her flock of little initiates, deposited here at previous visits. She had stolen a handful of candies from a stall they'd passed in the city—anyone well off enough to be selling something as frivolous as candies, at this stage of the war, could afford to spare a few for some orphaned children. The little girls would be excited by them, she knew. They suffered no shortage of food, here at the temple—the third god looked after his own—but it was all staples, no desserts.

Sylvia had not had a dessert in years. She did not steal candies for herself.

~

"This is ridiculous," Joel said. "Obscene."

He was clean and angry. Eloise was clean and happy, or had been, before Joel burst uninvited into her room. Surely he could not be so

149

oblivious to propriety that he thought her bedroom, in a temple, was at all an appropriate place to be.

"Your presence here in my room? I quite agree."

"Oh, come off it, El. Maybe this seems normal to you, coming from the palace, but this is—it's nearly as big as a palace, isn't it? Three countries starving, and the temple has guest rooms."

"Sylvia says this temple contributes more supplies to the relief effort than any other six combined."

"And it's no financial hardship for them, clearly."

"Their clothes are worn."

"And their walls are trimmed in gold."

"What a shame, then, that you kidnapped a princess instead of a priestess."

"I just think it's a waste, all of this here for a god who doesn't use it, while half the island is starving."

"Then complain to Sylvia, or better yet to a priest, and leave me out of it. You should not be in this room."

"This room should not exist."

"Be grateful that it does," Sylvia said, appearing in the open door, forcing Joel deeper into the room. "This room has housed dozens of refugees. All of them have. If you wish to insult the third god and the keepers of his temple, while in said temple, you should at least do it behind closed doors."

"Joel was just leaving," Eloise said. "He can complain behind some other door."

He skirted past Sylvia into the hall. She came more fully into the room, pulling the door closed behind her. She had not yet bathed.

"I was angry too," she admitted, "the first time I came here. Sometimes I still am. But they house and clothe and feed dozens of refugees who have made their homes here, as well as sending supplies for hundreds of others. They grow or make nearly everything they have. All of the extravagances that remain are consecrated to the third god, and to sell them would be sacrilege. I have committed a lot of sacrilege, since the war, and you've committed some of it with me, stepping into all sorts of sacred places. But I suppose that is not something we can ask of priests and priestesses."

"I suppose not," Eloise agreed, and wondered how angry Joel would be when he saw the palace again. They did not have sacrilege as an excuse. True, many crown jewels had been sold, and many fine sets of clothing worn bare. Their food was not as fine as it had been, and paper was saved exclusively for important letters and accounts. But they did not go hungry, their jewelry boxes were not all empty, and their windows were paned with glass.

She wasn't sure how much room Joel had to judge, given the amount he'd demanded in ransom. Surely he hadn't intended to give all that money to the poor.

"Aren't you going to have a bath?" she asked Sylvia.

"Yes. I had some old friends to visit, first. And I wanted to see that you were settled in well."

"Quite well. Will we be here long?"

"We'll leave tomorrow, unless the priestess knows some reason we should not. Someone will fetch you for dinner; I may not see you there. We eat in shifts here, as the only room large enough to hold everyone is consecrated."

~

There was a statue in the hall—not even a statue of the god, just some woman—wearing real gold jewelry. Joel hadn't struggled so hard with the temptation to steal since he was fourteen, in Eloise's bedroom for the first time, faced with her open jewelry box.

The jewelry was almost certainly consecrated. Joel had spent too much of his life too poor to be stopped by piety. But he was on a mission now, which would be thoroughly derailed if he were caught robbing a temple. He was about to get a royal pardon; theft, especially heretical theft, would be a bad move at this stage.

He left the statue, retreating to the room he was sharing with Fuller for their time here. Fuller wasn't there. He'd heard rumors of a small library, and gone to investigate.

It wasn't as if other temples didn't have small libraries, or excessive amounts of gold. But even the Holy Street Temples in Ibanar weren't like this. He'd never seen a temple like this.

To be fair, the Holy Street temples didn't need to house all of their acolytes, because Holy Street had a dormitory building where most of them slept.

He could admit to himself, if not to Eloise, that temples always unsettled him. He had taken refuge in a few, throughout his time as an outlaw, and had met some very kind priests and priestesses. And he had no issue with the abandoned temples they'd been sleeping in. But the fully functional temples, packed with worshippers and workers and priests and oracles—

His father—his birth father, his uncle—had wanted his mother to leave him at a temple as a foundling. She had refused, and so he had convinced his brother to marry her, and spent the next several years resenting her and Joel, especially after his brother had died, and he had been forced to resume some measure of responsibility. "I should have taken you from her and dropped you on Holy Street" was something his uncle had said to him often.

~

Sylvia prepared to leave the temple sooner than she otherwise would have, uncomfortable with how all the men looked at all the gold.

She'd brought plenty of desperate, impoverished people here before. But she was starting to genuinely worry that one of them might steal something, holy or not, and she did not have the energy to deal with the fallout. She left Elisabeth with strict instructions to watch her men, and went to see what the priestess would send off with her.

"I have no supplies for you," the priestess said.

Sylvia stared at her, baffled. The priestess of the third god always had supplies. She always had an excess of supplies, more than Sylvia could possibly take.

"You will not need them. Your journey is nearly at an end."

"My journey ends when the war does." She did not think the war was so near its end.

"Your journey ends where your companions' does."

"I'm dropping them off at the edge of the capital, and then I'm off again. I don't have time to linger. I am needed, still. And so are your supplies."

"You must see your companions safely to the palace. And then you must stay. I have foreseen it."

"I am not bound by the commands of your god."

The priestess sighed. "It is not a command, Sylvia. It is a kindness. If you go to the palace, there will be something there for you. I do not know what, but it is something you want, something you need. You have worked tirelessly for years to protect the victims of this war. You have asked nothing for yourself. My god promises you a gift, if you go to the palace to collect it. That is all. If you do not want what you find there, you may continue with your work. You may come back here, and I will give you all the supplies you can carry, and a direction where your help is most needed."

"And you will not give me the supplies until I have left with my companions, and returned myself?"

"I will not. My god has forbidden it."

"I will go, then. And I will consider stopping at the palace."

~

Sylvia seemed not quite herself when they left the temple, without the large amount of supplies she'd told them to expect.

"Are you all right?" Eloise asked her.

"Fine. Did you keep an eye on them?"

"I did. Will you tell me exactly what I was supposed to be watching them for?" She'd wanted the men supervised that first night, with the frightened women and children, but Eloise wasn't sure what her concern had been in the temple.

Sylvia glanced back at the four of them, following a few steps behind. "I was afraid they would steal from the temple."

"Well, they are bandits."

She stopped walking suddenly. "Bandits?" she repeated loudly.

"El!" Joel snapped from behind them.

She turned to face him. "Well, maybe if you wanted it to be a secret, you shouldn't have gotten sticky fingers in a temple."

"I didn't take anything." He took a step forward, and Alem grabbed his shoulder, then stepped forward himself.

"Sylvia," he said. "It is true that we are criminals. But Elisabeth is not, and our only goal is to see her safely home."

"I will see you safely to the palace," Sylvia said.

"I thought you wanted—"

"The priestess of the third god has advised me to see you all the way there."

"Well," Eloise said. "We will be glad to have your company for a little while longer. Shall we continue?"

~

It was not too far a journey, from the city that held the temple to the city that held the palace. Eloise tried to keep pace with Sylvia, to put distance between Joel and herself. It was almost over. Soon she would never see him again. It was best to—to stop—to not let herself—

It was almost over.

Oh, she wouldn't be rid of him immediately. He would need to talk with her father, with her brothers, with various members of the military and the nobility. He would be in the palace for weeks. But she needn't see him, once she'd delivered him and her promise to her father's feet.

She wondered what Joel's uncle would have to say about his reappearance. Nothing pleasant, she was sure. Hopefully he was on the front. Family or not, she was certain Joel wouldn't want to see him.

Family. Oh, no. Joel's family.

"Joel," she said, dropping back to walk beside him. "I don't know if—if anyone's told you. Your—your mother, your sister."

"Dead," he said.

"Yes. I didn't—I kept track of them, after, for you. There was an illness, in your village, maybe five years ago? I only heard of it after, there was nothing—nothing I could do."

"I know, Ellie. It's not your fault, who dies at the opposite end of the country."

"How—how did you know?"

"I was able to visit them, once. I tried again, and the survivors told me what had happened."

"I'm so sorry, Joel."

He nodded. "You—you kept track of them for me."

"I wanted to be sure they would face no consequences for what you'd—I knew how much they meant to you."

"Thank you."

"Of course." She went to rejoin Sylvia ahead. Perhaps she could just avoid ever speaking to Joel again. That conversation—it hadn't been pleasant, exactly. But it would be, she thought, a good place to leave things. She would like to end on good terms with him, despite everything.

~

Eloise was avoiding him. Her ability to do so while travelling in his company, on foot, in such a small group, was frankly impressive.

They'd been walking the same way most of the time since Sylvia had joined them, the women a few paces ahead of the men. Joel didn't like it, not only because it put distance between him and Eloise, but because he should be in the front, as the first line of defense.

Sylvia, he reminded himself, knew what she was doing. She'd made this trip far more times than he had—made it voluntarily and deliberately, while Joel had spent most of the last few years trying to stay on the outskirts of the conflict.

He knew things would be different once they reached the palace. This was his last chance to really reach Eloise, and she wouldn't speak to him, wouldn't even walk beside him. She'd hardly speak to any of them, and Fuller and Alem could take that in stride, but Chris was young, and he'd thought they were friends; his feelings were hurt by the distance.

And why should Eloise care at all about the feelings of her kidnappers?

He'd made such a horrible mess of everything, and he was out of time to fix it.

(It had been kind of her—unexpectedly kind—to think of his mother and his sister, to check on them.)

(He missed them so much.)

(He had been there again, at the end of things, for what he thought would be just another visit. He didn't tell Eloise that. He didn't tell her that he'd held his sister's burning body, his mother's cooling corpse. That he'd paid for two cremations with stolen money, then left and never returned.)

~

"Eloise," Joel said, as they approached the capital. She hung back, let Sylvia and the others go ahead. They stood there for a moment, staring at each other.

"I love you," he said. It was the first time in years he'd actually said the words, though he'd expressed the sentiment effectively without them.

The others were well ahead, and sky was clear and bright above them, and he was looking at her in that same anxious, reverent way he had as a boy.

She stared at him for a long moment, at the beautiful, familiar face marred by scarring and a broken nose and years of a life lived without her, at the glossy dark waves of hair she'd loved to run her fingers through, at the expression she'd never failed to kiss away.

It would be so easy to do it again. It would feel so right.

Doing what she wanted had never brought her anything but trouble, in the long run.

"Joel," she said.

"Eloise," he answered, half a sigh, understanding her as he had always understood her, and he turned and walked ahead. She hung back, and looked at him only to be sure he was not looking at her. She blinked away a few sudden tears, but she didn't cry, not really.

Their time was over. It had passed. She could not have him back, not really. He was not the boy she had loved, and anyway it had been foolish to let herself love that boy in the first place.

Chapter 15

It had been so long since Eloise had really, properly seen her city. She used to sneak out often enough, with Joel or Ben or a few of her cousins. But with a war on, with her reputation in tatters—Ben and her cousins hadn't been foolish enough to humor her anymore. She'd seen the city for festivals and parades, ever fewer and farther between as the war progressed. She'd seen and been seen in the city as a princess, only ever a princess, and never again just a person.

She had missed it. She had missed it so much.

Everything had changed, when she'd lost Joel. She'd hardly thought, in the midst of all of it, about this loss, the loss of streets she could roam freely, shops she could frequent and casual friends she could make.

There was a new wariness that hung over the city, and Sylvia and the men rushed her along.

She would come back, she promised herself. When it was over. She would come back, would visit the shops and stalls and taverns she'd once loved. She would not let her city be just another thing she'd lost with her first love.

They were approaching the palace from the back. She took the lead, trusting Joel to take the rear, and keep all the others between them.

This was the same door she'd used to leave, on Tulip, fool that she had been all those months ago. It had not been guarded, then. It was

157

now. Three men stepped forward as they approached the gate. Eloise slipped off her seal ring and held it out.

"Princess?" asked one of the men.

Hardly a man. He was so young—they all were. Anyone old enough to be better-trained would be in battle somewhere.

"I would like to see my father. This young woman is my guest."

"And—and the men, ma'am?" He glanced nervously between Eloise and Joel; she wondered if he recognized Joel. His face had been famous once, but he hadn't been here in years, and the soldier was very young.

"Take their weapons," she said.

"Eloise—"

"Take them," she repeated.

"Eloise, you promised—"

"And I'll keep my promise. I'll see you pardoned, but you're not pardoned yet, and I will not escort armed enemies of the state into my father's throne room. Take the weapons."

"Shall we chain them?" one of the other guards offered.

"That shouldn't be necessary," she said. "They'll follow me in. Where will I find my father?"

"In the council chamber, Your Highness."

She began walking there, confident that Joel would hurry after her as soon as he was disarmed, and the others would follow him.

Surely someone had been sent to tell the king of her arrival, but Eloise must have beaten him there, for everyone seemed quite surprised when she threw open the doors.

For a moment everything was perfect, her father and her brother Julian standing to greet her, Jeremy turning away from his conversation as he heard the commotion.

Then Sylvia rushed past Eloise and the others, pulling something out from her braid as she did. She had stabbed Jeremy twice before it registered that what she was holding was a knife, that she was—

Joel took in the scene more quickly than anyone else, running to pull Sylvia away before the rest of them had fully processed the attack. There were soldiers in the room ready to defend the king and the prince with their lives, but no one had been ready for the assault on a fairly minor baron, remarkable only for a wedding that hadn't yet happened.

The room erupted into chaos. Joel wrestled the knife away from Sylvia, who went weak-kneed and weepy as abruptly as she'd gone murderous. Eloise brushed past them to crouch on the ground beside Jeremy. She was not the first to arrive at his side; one of her father's ministers was putting pressure on the worse wound, and Eloise managed the second, staunching the blood flow with the worn red velvet of Jeremy's loose-fitting coat.

He was nearly unconscious by the time she reached his side, fully so by the time she was pressing velvet into his wound. She and the minister were both shoved aside shortly after by a pair of doctor's assistants, who lifted Jeremy onto a stretcher and whisked him away.

Eloise stood slowly, taking stock of the rest of the room. She, Joel, and Sylvia were blood-soaked. Sylvia had crumpled on the floor, and an angry-looking soldier was pulling her back to her feet. Julian had a sword on Joel. Chris, Alem, and Fuller all still stood in the open doorway, largely unnoticed in the chaos. The king ignored them all to embrace Eloise, and she hugged him back, forgetting all about Jeremy's blood, which was now staining her father's limited supply of fine clothing.

"Eloise," Joel said after a moment. "A little help here?"

She pulled reluctantly away from her father.

"He's fine, Julian."

"He's exiled. On pain of death."

"He just saved my fiancé. And I promised him a pardon."

"Eloise, I know you have a soft spot for—"

"He brought me back. I promised him a pardon if he would bring me back and give us information on the conspiracy." She loved Julian, and she had missed him. But he would never stop treating her like a child.

"Eloise, that was over nine years ago. How much of it will still be relevant?"

"Plenty," Joel said, "and I'd suggest you lock down the palace before any of the conspirators take advantage of Sylvia's little episode to escape. I know you're all excited to have your princess back, but has anyone else noticed there are three less men in this room than when we came in? Not, of course, counting your injured baron."

The chaos resumed, the remaining occupants of the room taking note of the missing, orders being barked, Julian removing his sword from Joel's neck to address more pressing issues. Eloise watched; there was nothing more she could do at this moment.

Suddenly she was knocked nearly over; she looked down to find her youngest sister wrapped tight around her. "Hello, Maria."

"They said you were back—Mother's just behind me. Oh, Eloise, you're covered in blood. What's happened?"

"It's not mine; it's Jeremy's. He's been taken to the infirmary—I need—I should check on him."

"Wait for Mother, at least. She's been so worried."

The queen arrived moments later, and Eloise explained again about the blood.

"We'll go down to the infirmary together," the queen said, "and see what's—my goodness, is that Joel?"

Eloise sighed. "Yes. It's Joel."

"Did he stab Jeremy?"

"No! He pulled off the girl who did—probably saved Jeremy's life."

"Well, what on earth was he doing here in the first place? Have you been with him? All this time you've been missing?"

"Not on purpose!"

Before she could go in search of Jeremy, her father handed over the proceedings to Julian, crossing the room to join his wife and daughters.

"We looked everywhere for you. Ben came back from the frontlines, and he and Jeremy coordinated searches. Olion and Ibanar both denied having you, and if it was the rebels they'd have tried to negotiate by now. We thought—we were afraid you were dead."

"You didn't get a ransom note?"

"There was nothing," her mother said.

"Joel," she called across the room, interrupting what was doubtless an important conversation.

"Yes?"

"They never received any ransom demand." As they were in polite company, the "you idiot" was left implied.

"I wrote the note. Fuller delivered it. Didn't you?"

The whole room turned to Fuller, who had, along with Chris and Alem, been ignored until now. "I delivered it."

"I suppose that's what happens," Joel said, "when you have a palace full of traitors. Who knows which of them got the note and decided not to pass it along?"

"Ransom note," Julian said. "So he kidnapped you." He was looking murderous again. Though he'd also sounded a bit relieved. As if maybe he hadn't been certain, before, that Eloise hadn't disappeared with him willingly.

"Yes, and then he un-kidnapped me, and I promised him a pardon. Do you have all the names you need?"

"He has all the names I have," Joel said.

"Then can we wrap this up? I have a grievously injured fiancé to find, and I've been wearing the same clothes for days."

"Yes," said the king. "Anyone who was not part of this original meeting, before the princess returned, may leave."

Chris all but bolted from the room, the rest of Joel's men following more sedately. Eloise left with her mother and sister, trying to provide all the reassurances they needed as quickly as possible. Normally she would be delighted to take her time with the reunion. But Jeremy was more important.

~

"Joel," the king said as he followed the others out. "A word?"

He waved Alem, still in the doorway, ahead—he and the others would wait for him in the hallway. "Of course, Your Majesty."

Nine years ago, asked for an audience with the king, Joel would have dropped unhesitatingly into Eloise's chair. It wasn't about being cocky—everyone knew that was where he belonged. It was where the king had told him to sit, at his first audience. He was tempted to sit there today, but that was about being cocky. His place had changed, and if he was going to last here he had to stop being an outlaw, and become a good little soldier boy again. He stood stiffly.

Joel had had to stand before the king without Eloise at his side a few times, in the past. He had not enjoyed it then, and the king had, at the time, been making a special effort to be kind to the rather anxious boy his daughter was infatuated with. He would be making no such efforts today.

"A full pardon," the king said when the door had closed behind the youngest princess.

"Four pardons. It's only me and Chris who actually committed our crimes here, but since the others have now participated in kidnapping your daughter, you can pardon them for that, at least."

"Four." He raised his eyebrows. "Interesting. Last I heard, you wanted money. Was there not, allegedly, a ransom note?"

"The men who kidnapped your daughter wanted money. I want a pardon."

"It was not you, then, who took her?"

"Oh, it was. I led the band, and I carried out every step of the kidnapping process personally. But the money was for the rest of them. For appearances. My personal plan is more complex."

He risked a glance around the room. Julian was fuming. The others, mostly important older men he'd only encountered when dragged through court by Eloise or when on trial, were harder to read.

"And your plan includes a list of names to end this war."

"It does."

"Would you care to explain to me exactly why this plan couldn't have been carried out a decade ago? Perhaps at your trial?"

He hesitated, but decided to go with the honest response. Seething resentment would have to come out, one way or another. Might as well deal with the whole thing now. "No one asked me for any names then."

"Excuse me?"

"You were too squeamish to handle me yourself. Sir. So you sent the head of the conspiracy to do it. I don't remember there being any actual interrogation. Mostly I remember a lot of torture. And you should know, as long as we're on the topic, that I'm not nearly stupid enough to keep documents containing proof of my treason just lying about. They were probably real documents—I never saw them. But very strategically placed to incriminate only me. I suppose he planted them himself. I suppose he wanted to discredit me before I had the chance to tell you everything. I suppose he knew how many of us joined as some meaningless game when we were children and new recruits. I suppose he knew that I was in love with your daughter, and completely uninterested in deposing her family."

"You had a chance to speak at your trial." He looked guilty.

Well, he ought to.

"I was tortured for weeks. I hardly remember the trial. Until the end. I remember Her Highness' vote. But it was largely a blur."

The king nodded. "Four pardons. You may leave—we'll work out the details later."

Joel left quickly, without looking around the room again. Julian hadn't liked him even when he was a boy, and he didn't care to see his reaction.

He caught up to Eloise in the hallway, just finishing a conversation with her mother. "El!"

"What?"

The queen nodded stiffly at Joel and strode away; he waited to speak again until she had turned a corner.

"I—Sylvia. I'm sorry. I knew she had a knife in her braid. I didn't— I didn't think she was going to do anything with it. I just thought—I saw how skittish she was, with the guards, and I thought just having it would make her feel safer."

"It's fine," she said, voice flat and emotionless. "It's not your fault."

"El—"

"It's over. You brought me home, you shared your information, and my father will pardon you. I'm not angry about Sylvia. I just don't see any further reason for you and I to have anything to do with each other."

"Eloise—"

"Excuse me. I need to find out if my fiancé is dead or alive."

She left him there. Joel stood in the hallway for a moment, unsure what to do next.

"She'll come around," Chris offered, and he turned to see his men gathered a few feet away. "I think her family upset her."

Joel sighed.

"Well," Fuller said, "we're in the palace, princess and all. Have you worked out the next step in your plan yet?"

"Not yet."

"I don't suppose it could involve leaving?"

"I'll need to speak more with the king, go over details, provide evidence, all that. But you can go as soon as your pardon's signed."

"And leave you unattended? Who knows what trouble you'd find."

"We'll all stay," Alem said. "The man with the gold chain told me the steward would find us rooms—Joel, do you know where to find the steward? I forgot to ask."

"I know where we could find him ten years ago—let's go see how much this place has changed. And quickly, before anyone else recognizes me and reacts like the prince." He frowned, thoughtful. "Maybe I should have made the king sign a pardon before I left his sight."

"I thought you were friends with the prince."

"I was friends with the youngest prince—Eloise's twin. Though I'm sure he hates me now, too."

"To the steward, then. We'd best find him before trouble finds us."

~

Eloise was told when she reached the infirmary that Jeremy had not yet woken up, but should make a full recovery. One of the wounds had been quite deep, but neither had hit anything important.

"I want to be notified as soon as he's awake," Eloise told the doctor, and then made her way down to the dungeons, where Sylvia would have been put.

She hated the dungeons. They reminded her, always, of Joel—a silly thing to be bothered by, considering her current circumstances, but now that they had each held up their part of the bargain there was, as she'd told him, no reason to—

But thoughts of Joel were hardly the only problem with the dungeons. Dungeons were, by definition, deeply unpleasant places.

They were seeing more business today than usual, as Joel's intel spread throughout the palace, and men were arrested, and others came down to see whether the rumors could possibly be true. The unknown girl who had attacked a mere baron for reasons unknown had fallen by the wayside, and Eloise found her in a holding cell, where she had likely been forgotten entirely.

"Sylvia," she said.

She was huddled in the corner farthest from the door, and didn't react at all to her name.

"Sylvia," Eloise repeated. "I need you to tell me what happened." She was afraid she knew the answer already. She wasn't sure whether or not to hope she was wrong.

Sylvia continued to ignore her. Eloise might have more luck if she could actually touch her, if she could grab her and shake her and force her to pay attention. But the guards were all too busy to find her the keys, or supervise any grabbing and shaking. She would come back later.

She had not yet changed clothes, and the blood was drying, tacky and disgusting. She would go to her room and change, perhaps even have a bath. And then she would find her family again and explain everything. She had not even seen most of them yet, but of course her other brothers were off at war, and Erika may be as well. Annabelle—she had missed Annabelle's wedding. Annabelle didn't live here anymore.

~

Joel and his men were directed to a suite described by the steward as small and shabby.

"Better than the barracks, where you belong, if you belong anywhere. But there's no telling what a mess you'll make down there—liable to get yourself killed before the king is done with you. The soldiers are the ones actually fighting this war, the ones who've lost friends to your betrayal. I'm sure I'd want to kill you, if I were that kind of man."

Joel was quite relieved to be rid of the steward.

The suite may have seemed small and shabby to princes or dukes or visiting dignitaries. Joel could tell it was less impressive than Eloise's rooms, as he remembered them.

"It's the fanciest place I've ever seen," Chris said. "Well. After that hall we walked through. And the temple."

There were several rooms, with enough space for each of them to have their own down-stuffed mattress.

"Still want to leave?" Joel asked Fuller.

"Maybe we can stay a while," he conceded. "But I don't think a nice soft bed is going to make up for how much these people hate us."

"They hate me—keep your distance and you'll be fine."

"They'll hate us all plenty when news of the kidnapping spreads."

"If it spreads—I think several important members of court being arrested for treason will rather overshadow it."

"You're impossible. This won't overshadow it for her."

"She'll come around," Joel said. "She will."

~

Eloise had her bath, and her reunion with her lady's maids, who were also her cousins. She picked one of her less worn-out velvet dresses, as the palace was rather cool, and fended off questions about Joel as well as she could.

"There's nothing to say about it. About him. He'll be gone as soon as my father's through with him and the pardon signed. I'm betrothed to the baron, and I need to go check on him."

Jeremy was awake this time, sitting up in bed, looking pale and ill.

"Eloise," he said.

She sat on the edge of the bed, taking his hands in hers. "It was her, wasn't it?"

He nodded. "I don't—I don't understand. She was dead. The whole village was razed. And she—why would she—"

"I don't know. No one's had a chance to interrogate her properly. I tried to talk with her, but she—she's gone all odd since attacking you."

"Where is she?"

"In the dungeon."

He sat up straighter, pulling his hands away. "In the—Eloise, you have to get her out of there!"

"She attempted to kill you in front of over a dozen witnesses. I didn't put her down there, and no one is going to free her just because I ask it."

"She can't—she can't stay down there."

"I'll see what I can do. Just let me handle it, all right? She really went at you—you shouldn't be out of bed."

He nodded reluctantly. "You—she came here with you."

"She did."

"But you didn't know?"

"I had no idea until she'd stabbed you; I wasn't certain until this conversation."

"Didn't you recognize the name?"

"Of course I did. She shares it with my grandmother, two of my cousins, the dressmaker's apprentice, my sister's maid, and the mayor's wife. It's a very common name—I didn't hear it and think immediately that she must be a dead girl I'd never met."

"Of course."

"I'm sorry," she said. "It's been a stressful day."

"It's fine."

"I'll see what I can do about the dungeon."

He nodded. "Thank you. Eloise…" He trailed off.

"You'd like to cancel our engagement?"

"Obviously she's upset with me—"

"Obviously."

"But I have to believe she'll come around."

"I know."

He leaned forward. "I only—it was only a few seconds before I…lost track of things, but that first man that came in behind you, was that—"

"Joel? Yes. He kidnapped me, he had a change of heart, and he agreed to finally share what he knew about the conspiracy in exchange for a pardon. Several arrests were made after the doctor took you. I'm hoping he'll be gone again soon."

"Then breaking our engagement now…"

"Same scandal again. It's fine. I handled it when I was a child, and I'll handle it now. They'll assume I've called things off to be with him, but I won't be with him, he'll leave, and it will all die down again." She added, anticipating his next question, "Please don't ask if I'm still in love with him. I swear Julian thought at first I'd just up and run away with him."

"You know how Julian worries about you."

"I know." She shook her head. "That's all done with. I did what I had to in order to get home—don't worry, nothing awful. But I'm done. I'll tell my father about the engagement, then see what I can do for Sylvia. Get some rest."

~

"You want me to release a woman who launched an unprovoked attack on a member of my court."

"No, he wants you to release her. I think he's in a lot of pain right now—physical and emotional—and it will greatly improve his peace of mind if you lock her in an unused room upstairs, instead of down in the dungeon."

The king sighed. "Arrange it however you see fit, as long as she stays locked up. You can come with me to the dungeons now—I have a lot of work to do. It seems your brother and I will have to oversee all proceedings personally."

She followed him down the hall. "I didn't have a chance to ask—I was so worried about Jeremy. How are the others?"

"Good. Annabelle had her wedding—we would have waited for you, if it weren't for the war."

"I know."

"She'll come home to see you as soon as she gets word. Ben just rejoined the army again a few weeks ago; he'll come home for you, too."

"He shouldn't. You need him there. Especially if he's already been back in the meantime, looking for me."

"I'll encourage him to stay; he may not listen to me. Theo and Erika are with the army, as well, Theo at the southern border and Erika at the northern with Ben. The children are still here at the palace. With everything that's happened today, I may send them home with Annabelle when she arrives."

The children were Erika's, four year old twins. No, five now. Erika and her husband, a prince from Geth, had been in and out of battle for most of their lives, and they were usually here, with trusted nursemaids.

"I'll make sure to visit them before bedtime," Eloise said. She was very fond of her niece and nephew. They kept the palace from feeling so empty, with so many of the princes and princesses gone.

Eloise had not been allowed to ride to war—she had not enough combat training, and they could spare no one to train her more thoroughly when they were already at war. Julian was home to help their father with the work of ruling. Theo was the heir, and perhaps should not be risked in battle, but Julian had the better head for diplomacy, and was more useful here than he would be there; Theo had taken his place in battle, and Julian was mostly at the palace with his little sisters.

Annabelle had married for the same reason Eloise had intended to marry, though she was only seventeen. Even if Eloise had married when she was meant to, she would have stayed here with Julian and Maria; Jeremy's estate had been destroyed in battle, and they could not spare the manpower for repairs. He had been living in the palace since, which suited everyone well, as his help in strategy meetings had been invaluable.

The king went to join Julian in his interrogations, and Eloise went back, with two guards, to Sylvia's cell. She had not yet told her father about the engagement, though he may have guessed when she'd told him who Sylvia was. It would keep for a few days, until he was less stressed.

"Sylvia," Eloise said. As before, the girl didn't move. The door was unlocked, and Eloise approached. After a moment of hesitation, she knelt, with regret for the fate of her skirts, on the dirty floor.

"Sylvia," she said again, and Sylvia flinched away from her.

"Jeremy will be fine. He's not even angry with you, the lovesick fool—he's demanding you be moved to a better cell."

She lifted her head slowly; her expression was unreadable, but tear tracks stained her face.

"So move yourself," Eloise suggested, "or these men will do it for you."

Sylvia scrambled frantically to her feet.

"All right. Just walk with me, and they'll follow us, and we won't have any trouble. I know they checked you for any more weapons, and if you try to run, or attack me, you'll have a knife in you before you can blink. But that won't be a problem, because you won't run or attack. Right?"

"Right," she echoed hoarsely, and the four of them proceeded up several flights of stairs.

Eloise had chosen a smallish room in a mostly unused hallway on the same level as her own chambers. It was high enough up, and the window small enough, that escaping through it wasn't an option, and it was largely empty, with nothing that could be fashioned into any sort of weapon. She had often hidden here in the aftermath of Joel's betrayal, when she was the only thing anyone in the palace would talk about, and she needed, for a while, to be completely alone.

"The door will be locked," she told Sylvia. "Food will be brought to you, and fresh clothing." She considered the blood still staining her chest, some of it even in her hair. "Some soap and water, too."

Sylvia didn't react. She stood in the center of the room, unmoving, until Eloise turned to leave.

"He—he's alive?"

She turned back. "He is. He'll be by to talk to you when the infirmary lets him go—a few days, at least."

Sylvia nodded. Eloise left, locking the door carefully behind her.

"I'll keep the keys," she said, and neither guard argued with her. She would give the spare to whoever would be in charge of bringing her food.

Eloise retreated to the comfort of her own rooms. This day had been as exhausting as the last few weeks combined, and it was not yet dinnertime.

Jeremy. Poor Jeremy. Things may have gotten…difficult, with Joel, but at least they had never actually attempted to murder each other.

She wondered, for a moment, where Joel had gone, and pushed the thought determinedly from her mind. She would not think of Joel. She had been largely—well, moderately—successful at not thinking of Joel for some time now, until the kidnapping, and she would be returning to her pre-kidnapping state as soon as possible. He would be gone soon, and she would never have to think of him again.

~

Joel left his men in the comfort of their rooms to attend his next audience with the king. Julian and whoever else he still trusted would be there, as well. Joel was grateful that he would, at least, be spared a reunion with his uncle. Generals were out on the battlefield, not at home with the king—the one good thing to come out of this war, as far as Joel was concerned.

The other members of the meeting sat; Joel stood, as he had not been offered a chair. He understood how tenuous his position here was, and tried to focus on what he was saying, instead of on their faces. He had hated their scrutiny as a child, dragged past them by Eloise, and he hated it now.

There was not much, really, to tell them. He had already offered his list of names, which was the primary thing he knew. Young people had gathered to vent about the difficulties of dealing with the aristocracy. Occasionally there had been older, more important people about, not encouraging them so much as riling them up. Joel didn't know what their master plan had been, or how much of it they may have accomplished since he'd seen them last. He didn't even know what the papers found in his own room had said. He had learned more from being tortured than he had from actually being a part of the conspiracy.

"He tortured me for fun, I think. Or maybe because he'd had hopes, when I met Eloise, and he was mad I didn't come through."

Most of Joel's venting had been about Eloise—they had been the only people he could safely talk to about the danger, the terror, of having a princess focused fully on him, determined to drag him into her circle whether anyone else—including himself—wanted him there or not. The conspirators had likely thought, for a time, that his eventual betrayal of the princess was inevitable. But he had loved her. He had just been frustrated and afraid, as well.

"He told me there would be a great war. He said Aliria wouldn't survive. He didn't say why."

The king dismissed him not long after, and Joel hurried away. He needed—he needed to think.

He had not given them all of the names. He had been thinking about it all through the journey, and all last night, and he had still not decided what to do. He'd named all the big, important people he'd ever recognized at a gathering. He'd named a few who Eloise had told him had become more influential since his exile. But the others—they were people like him, young and overwhelmed and not fully understanding what was happening around them. People who had done nothing wrong beyond complaining to the wrong person. He didn't want anyone largely innocent to suffer like he had. But he didn't know what had happened in the last several years, how many of them were still as innocent as they had been then, and how many had gotten more deeply involved.

The time he had spent in prison—

He knew, because rumors had flown through the palace, that yesterday Eloise had twice gone down to the dungeons to speak with the girl who'd stabbed her betrothed, and the second time she had escorted her back upstairs.

Eloise had never visited Joel in the dungeons.

He would wait, for now, to share his other names. There would be interrogation—likely torture—for the ones he'd named already. Let the other names come out of that. He'd kept his promise to Eloise, or near enough, and he needn't personally condemn anyone else to that place.

~

Sylvia sat on a mattress, bare, but softer than anything she'd touched in her life. She gathered, though no one had said so directly, that she had been denied further bedding because sheets could theoretically be fashioned into a noose.

She wasn't a suicide risk. She happened to be very good at surviving, and she had no intention of stopping now.

Though, granted, this was a setback.

She had not realized Elisabeth—Eloise—was a princess. She had not realized that she was engaged to Jeremy, or that Jeremy would be in the palace at all. And then he had turned, and smiled, and she'd—

She had not learned until after her arrest that the princess was engaged to Jeremy, that his smile had doubtless been meant for her.

This information made her feel both better and worse. He hadn't any right to look at Sylvia like that, after—after everything, but it hurt that he might look at someone else the same way.

She had been allowed, shortly after the princess left, to bathe, under the watchful eyes of three disapproving maids. She had been left with someone's discarded shirt and breeches, which mostly fit.

She had been brought food three times, by various guards, or soldiers, or jailors—some sort of uniformed men, at least. The sun was now setting for the second time since she'd come to this room. It had been over a day. She had gotten no further news of Jeremy. No one since the princess had said anything to her outside of business, and what the princess had said had made no sense.

She had stabbed him. Why should he care what kind of cell she was in? Why should he plan to come see her when the wounds she'd inflicted had healed?

He had burned her village, killed her family, and nearly her as well. Why should she care that he would recover from the stabbing? Why should she care that he was engaged to the princess? Why should she care whether he cared for her?

She had been in the cellar when it happened; her mother, brother, and sister had been upstairs, in the shop. Her father had already been gone, then, to fight in the war.

It had been the dampness of the cellar that had protected her as the others burned. She had clawed her way out coughing and half on fire to find scorched bodies all around. Her mother and sister were gone by then, but her brother—she had heard him scream, watched as he was engulfed in flames. She had run, she had run from him as he died, and everywhere she turned it was the same, the whole village gone or going, no one to help her put out the flames. And marching away, those men in their familiar uniforms, under their familiar flag.

She had run in the opposite direction, trying to put out the flames on her dress without pausing for more fire to catch her. The farmland had all been burned as well, and she hadn't dared to go toward the forest, where fire would catch so easily, burn so quickly. She had thrown herself into the little pond at the far end of the village, where she had passed out, or fallen asleep, or possibly died, and woken up again a different creature entirely, like the phoenix.

It was Jeremy who had told her the story of the phoenix—they did not have such birds in Aliria or Olion, or even, she suspected, in Ibanar.

She had wanted him dead, when she saw him yesterday. She had wanted him dead, intermittently, for years.

She didn't know what she wanted. She didn't understand. She had never understood.

She had loved him. She had thought he loved her too. Even if he had not, she had not thought he would ever—would ever—

She didn't understand. She still didn't understand.

~

Eloise wrote letters to Ben, to Erika, to Theo. To Annabelle, though a messenger had already been sent to her estate, and she would likely be on her way to the palace before the letter left it. She checked on Jeremy, she played with her niece and nephew, she told Maria somewhat edited stories of her kidnapping and journey back home. She let her parents and Julian fuss, when they were not busy with more important work. She assured everyone who asked that there would never again be anything between her and Joel.

She saw him in hallways occasionally, and when she did, she turned and fled. In a very stately, dignified manner. He had not yet come to her chambers demanding to speak with her, but she was afraid it was not far off.

He'd sent Chris to speak to her in the hall.

"Why are you mad at him?" Chris had asked.

She wasn't. Not really. She was just…tired. She'd spent so long distancing herself from Joel. She didn't want to be that girl again.

"I'm not going to talk to you about this."

"Well, you won't talk to him."

She'd spotted a cousin in the hall and taken the opportunity to escape from Chris, before she had to say something unkind to shake him.

They would leave soon. Surely they would leave soon—Joel must have told her father everything he knew by now.

~

When Jeremy was scheduled to be released from the infirmary in the morning, Eloise was forced, at last, to break the news to her family. She started with her mother, hoping she would be more reasonable about it than Julian and her father.

"Jeremy and I aren't getting married."

The queen frowned. "Darling, Joel is no longer—"

"This isn't about Joel. I have no intention of resuming my childhood romance with a brigand and a traitor. The girl Jeremy loves is back from the dead."

"The girl who stabbed him?"

"You're my mother, not his. It's his mistake to make."

"I very much doubt a woman who would stab him is interested in picking up where they left off."

Eloise shrugged. "He wants to try. I want him to be happy."

"Eloise…"

"It's not as if we're in love. I just—you thought immediately of Joel. Everyone will. The entire court, the entire kingdom. I am so sick of Joel. I am so sick of being defined by him. I was a child."

"You loved him very much."

"I did."

"You've never moved on. Even with Jeremy."

"I loved him. I could have loved him forever. But the Joel that exists now—he's not that boy. I can't—I just want to be free of him."

"I'll speak with your father about the engagement. But Eloise— perhaps we don't make it public knowledge. Let the girl know. But Jeremy—I doubt this fancy of his will go anywhere. If it doesn't, you can still marry him. And if he succeeds, and we have to announce the break, at least it will be far enough from Joel's return that people won't jump immediately to that conclusion."

"All right. Thank you, Mother."

~

As soon as he escaped the infirmary, Jeremy took the keys from Eloise and went to Sylvia's room.

~

Her days had fallen into a certain monotony, and she had lost count of their passage. There was nothing to do but think, and that, she did not wish to.

She was woken in what she thought was no longer the morning by a knock at the door—not the sharp double knock that was always followed by the door swinging open, for a guard to leave food and water and take the chamber pot, but a tentative single knock.

"Sylvia?"

Jeremy. She didn't—she couldn't. She couldn't.

"Sylvia, may I come in?"

She didn't answer.

"It's Jeremy," he added, as if she might not have recognized the voice.

There was a long moment of mutual silence, and then a second voice—Elisabeth. Eloise. The princess. "We're coming in. If you're indecent, you have about ten seconds to rectify that."

She was not indecent, and was not entirely sure she would care, if she was. She had felt—so strange, since seeing him again. She thought she had, if not recovered from what had happened, at least moved past it. Now every dragging moment felt like the hours she had spent lying in that pond, waiting to die.

The door opened. Two sets of footsteps came through, and it closed again. She didn't look up.

"Sylvia," Jeremy said softly, sadly. She squeezed her eyes shut.

"We're fine," he said—he must have been speaking to the princess.

"I'll leave you alone as soon as one or the other of you demonstrates some basic sign of sanity."

"Eloise."

"Would you rather have me, or a guard?"

"Fine."

Footsteps—heavier ones, his—came again, approaching her where she lay on the bed. She stiffened despite herself, and he paused.

"Sylvia."

"Sylvia," the princess echoed, and somehow her voice was more bearable.

"I don't want to see him," she said, addressing herself to the princess. She did not sit up or open her eyes.

This was met with a whispered conversation she did not bother to follow.

At last, Jeremy said, voice achingly gentle, "I'll be back in a bit, Syl."

Two sets of footsteps. Door opened, door closed, lock turned. Jeremy's voice, louder again, on the other side. "Fireplace unlit, and there's not a damn blanket in there. At least get her some warmer clothes. And food—she looks half starved."

"I'll handle it," the princess said. "Go lie down. You're still injured."

She squeezed her eyes closed tighter, a vain attempt to hold in the tears.

She didn't understand.

~

He stood in the hallway, waiting for Eloise to finish with Sylvia. Sylvia. She didn't want him there, of course.

It was the first good look he'd got at her since she—since she— there hadn't been time to take it all in, with the stabbing. She'd been burned, badly. He knew exactly when and how that had happened, of course. He wondered if it still hurt. She was both thinner and more muscular than she'd been, and perhaps just a bit taller. She was otherwise the same, externally.

She wouldn't look at him.

Of course she wouldn't look at him. She hated him. She'd tried to kill him.

He would have deserved it, if she succeeded. He should have had much better control over his own men, on his own land.

He could punish himself later. There were practicalities to address, first.

~

"Where has she been?" Jeremy asked, as he followed her on her search for safe bedding, ignoring her attempts to send him to bed. "What has she been through?"

"I don't know. We only travelled together for a few weeks. We talked about—about her work, mostly. Protecting refugees. She didn't talk about her personal life; I don't think she has one. She certainly didn't tell me any details of her past."

"Will you ask her? Please? Will you be there for her until—until she's ready for me to be?"

"You want me to befriend the girl who stabbed you." She had already considered her a friend. Until this. But she had long known she was not a good judge of character. It was not entirely surprising to find her affections, once more, misplaced.

"I want you to befriend the girl I love. It will give you something to do, to distract you from Joel."

"All right. But if she stabs me, I'm done."

Chapter 16

There was a knock on the door, and it swung open slowly. Sylvia was sitting, now, in the center of the bare mattress. She watched as the princess entered, alone this time, and weighed down by an armload of linens, with a large dark fur dragging behind her. She got the fur through the door with some difficulty, and pulled it closed again.

It was foolish, Sylvia thought, for someone as important as a princess to be alone with her. She had carried a sword, when they were travelling, so she must have some combat training, at least. But she was unarmed now, and Sylvia had proven herself dangerous. She was quite capable of killing without a weapon—she'd done it before. And she didn't have to kill the princess, only get past her, to the door.

She didn't move.

The princess approached, dumping her armload of clothing on the bed beside her. The fur, she left on ground.

"Undergarments. Two dresses. One pair of breeches. Two shirts. Stockings. And the bearskin for warmth at night."

Sylvia didn't answer. The princess, sighing, dropped down on the bed beside her. "Jeremy's broken our engagement," she said.

"I'm sorry," Sylvia said, when a long enough pause had passed that it was clear some sort of answer was required.

The princess waved this away. "I don't mind about the marriage. Only the timing was inconvenient. But we needn't announce it until he's sorted things out with you."

"Until he—I'm not going back. He killed my family. He killed my whole village."

The princess leaned closer, looking very earnest. "His men did. He had the whole squad executed. He's mourned you for years."

"I'm not going back," Sylvia repeated. It didn't—it mattered, of course. But she had only the princess' word for it, and even if—even if it was true—it had still happened. Everything had still happened. She couldn't be—be his, anymore. She didn't know how.

"All right," the princess said. She stood. "Your dinner will be here soon; Jeremy's asked for you to be getting more, but I don't know what the point is, when I'm told you barely touch what you're given. Still, what Jeremy wants, Jeremy gets, at least while he's freshly stabbed. I'm sure he'll be by to see you again, soon."

She left. Sylvia spent a moment studying the fine linen, the embroidered details, of the dress on top of the pile. She was fairly certain she'd been given the princess' own clothing, or at least some other noblewoman's. She shoved it all to the side, and dragged the fur up onto the bed—she had been cold.

~

Sylvia had risen, at last, from her pool, unsure how much time had passed. Smoke lingered, but the heat was gone. She had felt the pain of her burns, but in the same way she had felt everything since she ran, far-off and strange. Her leg was—not quite right; she wasn't sure if it was burned or if she'd twisted something. She didn't much care. She had walked slowly back toward the village, feet bare, skirts and hair dripping, the cloudiness of her mind cushioning the agony that came with each step.

Everything was ash. She went to what she thought was her home, though with every landmark burned to the ground, it was hard to be certain where she was. There were a few charred corpses, none of them recognizable. She walked from one end of the village to the other, ash sticking to her wet feet, and stood at what had been the last house, staring across the field at Jeremy's estate.

She had lived here all her life. She would have recognized the uniforms of his soldiers even if she'd never met him. The fact that she had added a much deeper, more personal element to the feelings she would not fully feel for days to come; she had watched her brother burn, and her mind had balked, refusing to properly process any further trauma yet.

She had thought, in some distant way, as she lay in the pool, that she would go to Jeremy. But of course she could not go to Jeremy; that was foolish. Jeremy had slaughtered her family, as surely as if he had lit the first match himself.

She could go up into Olion, or she could go down into Aliria. It hardly mattered; her family would be dead, and Jeremy would have killed them, in any direction she chose. Olion was an enemy, but it was Alirians who had burned her village.

The nearest place she could walk to was Jeremy's estate, and the second nearest was in Olion, which settled it. Crossing the village had been difficult enough; she would never make it to the nearest Alirian town.

She had turned her back for the last time on Jeremy's estate, and had begun the long journey north. She had not made it terribly far before she collapsed, but far enough not to be found by Jeremy, when he returned from a meeting at an outpost the next morning.

~

Joel walked into the room; Chris glanced up at him.

"He's bleeding," he announced.

"Alem," Fuller called without looking up, "he's bleeding!"

Joel collapsed into a chair as Alem came from the other end of the suite, the supplies for treating the wound already collected.

"Who was it this time?" Fuller asked.

"Does it matter?" It had been a man he shared a barrack with, when they were boys.

"You don't have to put yourself through this. Make him sign the pardon, and we can leave."

"The pardon's worthless, signed or not—they all know about it, and it doesn't stop them hating me."

"It's only worthless here, where people know your face. Even out in the city—in the capital—no one would take any notice of you."

"You could defend yourself," Alem suggested, as he took Joel's chin in his hand to study the injury more closely.

"And give them a reason to rescind the pardon? Aggression against the king's men, or something—Julian's itching to be rid of me. And it's nothing, leave off—I'm not letting you put any more stitches in me."

"Stop getting injured, and I'll stop treating your injuries."

"He'd be rid of you if we left," Chris pointed out.

"Not you, too." He stood, pushing past Alem to go to the window. "You're all free to go wherever you like. I'm not leaving this palace without her."

"Joel," Fuller said. "You tried. You failed. She's never taking you back."

"Then I'm never leaving the palace."

"You're being ridiculous."

"Just because you don't like her—"

"If it was up to her you would have hung—you told us so yourself."

"And that was ten years ago. Get over it. I have, and I'm the one it happened to."

"All right," Alem said. "Fuller, you know how he is. Don't go picking a fight with him when he's already been beaten once today."

Fuller flung himself back into his chair, scowling.

"You all agreed to this," Joel said.

"We agreed to your original plan," Alem corrected him. "The one you abandoned immediately?"

"Go, then. I keep saying you don't have to stay. Go wherever you like, just stop trying to take me with you."

"We're just worried," Chris said quietly.

"I'm fine. Everything is fine."

"Last time you were this fine we kidnapped a damn princess," Fuller muttered.

"None of us are leaving you now," Alem said. "But if you won't leave the palace, will you at least stop wandering through it all day? No one notices the rest of us—we can get you food, and news, and you'll not be getting in fights every few days."

"Fine," Joel said.

"She'll come around," Chris said softly, a few minutes later. Joel was nearly certain he didn't believe it.

The palace was full of enemies. It always had been, really. Full of strangers, and then overnight, full of people who despised him. But they had despised him, then, because he was not good enough for Eloise. That she loved him anyway meant they could do nothing worse to him than glare and whisper. Now the reasons for their hatred had amplified, and he hadn't her love to protect him.

He missed her so much. He missed—not just her. The life he'd had here, once. It had been stressful, at times terrifying. But he had had casual friends among the other trainee soldiers, bunkmates, boys who sometimes teased him about the princess, but mostly treated him the way they treated each other. Mason, who had patiently taught him all the names of the royal family, when he learned Joel was from deep in the south and couldn't name even the heir. Remus, who'd been a picky eater, and dumped whatever he didn't like onto Joel's plate. Zachary and Eva and Ward, who'd listened to him vent about everything in the meetings none of them had quite understood were intended to destroy the kingdom. Ben, who'd tempered Eloise.

The moment he'd met the royal family at large had been the most terrifying of his life—then, when his life was so much simpler. He hadn't expected it, hadn't bothered to worry where Eloise was dragging him now until she'd dragged him into a room full of kings and queens and princes and princesses. Eloise hadn't understood why he was afraid, or even noticed that he was, too excited to show off her latest bad decision to the family. It had been Ben, who he'd met—in the much safer environment of the royal gardens—two weeks earlier, who had shot him the look that had promised everything would be all right, who had taken over the introductions from Eloise and introduced Joel as his friend as well, though they were practically strangers. It had been him who talked Eloise out of her absolutely insane plan in that tavern in the city, when Joel had been too afraid to contradict her—a pattern that would repeat several times over the next year or so.

Ben had liked him, and Maria, but Maria had been practically a baby then, and if she had any memories of him now she hadn't shown it. The rest of the royal family had never, he thought, been particularly taken with him. At least they weren't throwing punches, though the threat of execution or re-banishment still loomed, if he stepped too far out of line. And Julian would enjoy a chance to punch him, he thought.

It had been bearable, then, all the quiet dislike.

But now Eloise wouldn't even glance in his direction, and all his friends had vanished, what few former pleasant acquaintances remained turned against him. And he wished for Ben to come and talk sense into Eloise, as he always did, except he was afraid that Ben would decide Eloise was being perfectly reasonable, this time, after all.

It couldn't end like this, after everything. It couldn't.

~

The king and the prince supervised interrogations. Messages were sent, inquiries made. Slowly, the plots of the conspiracy were pieced together, the mystery of war unravelled.

Chapter 17

Joel stepped carefully out of the suite. So he had told them he would stay inside. So he had lied. Had they really expected anything else?

It was late; he was unlikely to encounter anyone looking to pick a fight. He walked the halls he had walked every night, since coming back.

He didn't reach his destination, tonight. Instead, he took a wrong turn in the dark, distracted by the throbbing pain in his cheek, and encountered a man sitting on the cold stone floor, back against a door.

He spoke, against his better judgement. "Wife kick you out?"

The man looked up, squinting in the low light of the hall. "Something like that. Joel, isn't it?"

He shrugged. It was a rhetorical question, he was sure. He didn't recognize the man, but then he didn't recognize most of the people who seemed to know him. That predated his treason. Everyone had known him, because he had belonged to Eloise. He hadn't bothered to learn the names of dozens of courtiers who obviously thought him beneath them.

"I had been hoping to meet you. She used to talk so much about you. She tried not to, but, well."

"You're her fiancé." Jeremy. He had forgotten his title, and didn't want the conversation to go ugly because he was too familiar.

"I was."

"She broke the engagement?"

185

"I did." Hope had, briefly, soared; it came crashing down. Jeremy gestured toward his door. "She didn't tell you?"

"She hasn't spoken to me since we left the audience chamber the day we got back."

He nodded. "The young lady who stabbed me. We were…involved, before her supposed death. She's not pleased with me, at the moment, but—if we could just talk."

"Eloise won't talk to me either."

"So you walk past her door when you can't sleep at night?"

"And you sit in front of hers."

Jeremy nodded. "Sometimes—sometimes she screams. I don't go in; I don't know if I feature in her nightmares, if seeing me would make it worse. But I can pound on the door, to wake her from them."

Joel wondered—not for the first time—if Eloise had nightmares about him. He went back to his own rooms without passing her door.

~

He had inherited the barony at twenty two. His father's health had begun to fail when he was only fifteen, and gradually, his responsibilities had fallen by the wayside. He could not keep up anymore with his position, but he was a hard man, a proud man, and would not admit it. The rest of the barony had been left to fend for itself while he ruled the estate with an iron fist. He would not give Jeremy the training he needed, too stubborn to admit that he needed help, or even that he would someday die and should have a competent replacement.

Jeremy's mother and older brother had both died by the time he was twelve; his father had adored Felix, and hated that in his absence all he had would go to Jeremy instead.

Jeremy had been relieved when his father died. It meant that he could properly take in hand all the neglected far reaches of their land, meant that he could live his own life, make his own choices, not only for himself but for the thousands of people he was responsible for.

It had been a rough start. Sylvia hadn't wanted to marry him, and that—well, she would be ready, with time. But it was the war that made him rush her, and the war that caused all of his problems. The soldiers, having spent the entire war so far under the nonexistent rule of his father, were used to doing what they pleased. He found that often what they pleased was not in the best interests of the barony or the kingdom, though they disagreed with his assessment. The various men his father had left to oversee various parts of the barony had turned out, more often than not, to be corrupt, and in the chaos of war had gotten away with actions so outrageous even his bedridden, half-mad father would have noticed in peacetime.

No one wanted to listen to him, and he had no experience leading. He found himself struggling to negotiate where he should have been able to demand, and have his demands met instantly. He had only a title and some noble blood; the men he should have commanded had all the age and experience and allies to push him back again and again.

He had found that the biggest mess was in a farming area a few days south of the estate, where his father's man was charging all the farmers twice what he should have, and pocketing the difference. That had been bad enough, but then he had heard word the man had beaten a farmer who couldn't pay to death.

He had ridden there, where the man and all his friends and lackeys had denied the death, and denied the taxes, and accused another man of stealing the money, the whole time just barely refraining from openly laughing at him. His soldiers didn't care for him, his overseers didn't care for him, he commanded no respect and had no idea how to earn it—his father had left him unprepared in so many ways for this.

He'd returned home, having accomplished nothing, infuriated with the overseer and himself. He'd been looking forward, at least, to seeing Sylvia; he hadn't meant to spend so long away from her—nearly three weeks—especially after a fight, but he had been so overwhelmed by all the messes his father had left him. He would apologize, and he would explain, and she would understand. He would assure her they needn't marry until she was ready; he was only worried, with the war looming so near.

Her village was nothing but ash. He'd leapt off his horse, left behind the rest of his party to run through it, searching for her, though he knew already it was useless. No one in this place could have survived. He'd come to his senses after a few minutes, returned to his horse and returned to the estate, where he found his own men in the mess hall, bragging about it.

They'd claimed that with the shifting borders caused by the war—a mess he was still struggling to understand, bereft of the training his father had owed him—the village was technically now in Olion. They'd claimed, additionally, that with Olion moving now in this direction, it was best to eliminate any place where they could potentially gather any resources—any place, at least, that they could not defend. The estate was defensible, but the village was not. They had not, from what he could tell as he questioned them, spared a thought for the occupants of the village, Olin or Alirian.

It turned out that a blinding rage, an inhuman fury, was what it took to earn the respect of his father's men. He'd ordered all three dozen men executed. Within a half hour it was done, and none of the men he commanded had ever questioned him again. He remembered that day—the time from his boots touching the ash until he undressed for bed that night, finding blood drops dried into his jacket—as if it had happened to someone else, as if he had been possessed. He was not sure whether he regretted it or not. He had never ordered an execution since, and he hated the moments when his temper rose and he could see that his men feared him. But when he lay down each night he saw Sylvia inside his eyelids, and she chased the guilt away.

(A week later he had returned to the farmlands in question, where the overseer had confessed the truth and pled for mercy. He had gone to prison, and his stolen money was redistributed amongst the farmers. The family of the one who'd been beaten and killed, he'd given a larger sum, and lifelong rights to the small plot of land where they were tenants. In the years since, he had made that farmer's oldest son his new overseer for the region.)

Chapter 18

Joel moved across the grounds quietly, trailing Eloise. She was in the gardens, dead and dying for the season, coated in a light layer of frost, with some cousins and her younger sisters—Annabelle and her husband had arrived at the palace recently.

He was not sure what he was doing here, besides breaking, yet again, his promise to stay in their suite when he could. He half thought, still—if he just had a moment to speak with her. He had been trying since they arrived at the palace, and if they could just speak, if she could just listen—it would be easier to catch her in the gardens than in the winding halls of the palace. The girls would likely disperse, eventually, and even if they didn't—he knew a significant percentage of the palace had disapproved of him from the first. But the girls of an age with Eloise, and younger, had been quite invested in the success of their relationship. It would be easier for her to be herself, to let her guard down, with them than with her parents, or her brother, or any random courtiers.

The Eloise of his memories was pink and gold, giggly and loud. The Eloise of his present reality was cold and quiet and shimmering silver, uncomfortably similar to the Eloise of his nightmares. She had, upon entering the palace, transformed into a completely different woman from the one he had travelled with.

He missed the Eloise of their journey even more than he missed the giggly pink one in his dreams.

If he could just speak with her, with that version of her, away from the trappings of the court—

But he only half thought that would work. The other half of him had followed her all morning in some sort of goodbye tour, and it was that half, now, that was winning out.

Whatever version he'd unearthed for a few beautiful weeks of travel, this was the Eloise that existed here, and he didn't—fit. There wasn't a place for him here.

He had just turned to go when the messenger approached the group—clearly a soldier, in a dirty uniform, message bag swinging as he ran toward the princesses and duchesses and ladies assembled. Joel took no real notice of this until Eloise reacted to the message—a sound that was nearly a wail.

He rushed back, pushing past the other women to reach her. He caught her shoulders, and she turned to face him, eyes caught on something invisible beyond him. She'd brought her fists to her mouth, bitten down in a failed attempt to hold in her scream.

"Ellie. Ellie, what's wrong?"

She all but collapsed in his arms, and he caught her, looking over her shoulder at the messenger.

"What did you say to her?" he demanded, before he recognized her, a soldier, but not a man—Eloise's elder sister, Erika, with her curls cropped short, tear tracks leaving two clean stripes on an otherwise filthy face.

He was too upset to care how he'd spoken to a princess—he'd never seen Eloise like this. He'd never seen her anywhere near like this.

"Ben is dead," Erika said.

Oh, Ellie. Ellie. He looked at the others, picking out the two younger princesses in the crowd. Annabelle, white faced and silent, and Maria, crying quietly.

"Take care of the others," he told Erika, not caring that he had no right to command a princess.

Eloise was shaking in his arms; he could feel her tears soaking into his shoulder. He herded her away from the others quickly, weaving through the garden paths as she'd taught him, until they reached a private place, where once they'd had much happier times.

"Let's sit down," he suggested, and she sunk to the half-frozen ground, skirts billowing out around her. She hadn't spoken. She had let him lead her all the way here, compliant like no version of Eloise had ever been.

"I'm sorry, Eloise," he said, crouching down beside her. "I'm so sorry."

Twins, four years younger than Julian and Erika, eight years older than Annabelle, Ben and Eloise had been much closer to each other than to anyone else, at least when Joel was there. Joel had spent nearly as much time with the two of them together as with Eloise alone. He had considered Ben a friend, had been deeply grateful for the calming influence he had on his more impetuous sister. He had hoped, when he decided to bring Eloise home, that he would have a chance to repair his relationship with Ben, as well.

The aching, disbelieving grief he felt for a childhood friend was a pebble to El's avalanche. He didn't know how to help her.

"Should I fetch your mother?" he offered. No, that was foolish. Her son had died; she would be in no shape herself to comfort Eloise. Who, outside her family, did this closed-off new princess truly trust with her feelings? "Jeremy?"

Eloise shook her head. "Just you," she said, voice hoarse. "Just stay."

"Of course, El."

For a long time, he held her as she cried. No one disturbed them; the whole palace would be in disarray. They hadn't lost a prince or a princess since the stillborn child between Eloise and Annabelle, over twenty years ago.

"I'm so sorry, El," he said again, not knowing what else to say. "So sorry."

A cool wind had risen up, and her curls, half fallen out from their pinnings, blew themselves into tangles and knots. Her skirt rose in the breeze, and he tucked it beneath her legs to preserve her modesty, as she had not the presence of mind to do it herself. Her dress was dove grey with a deep blue brocade, and he memorized the pattern with his fingers as he held her.

She ran out of tears, out of the energy to sob, and still he held her as she shook. At last, she pulled herself away a little.

"Eloise," he said, and she shook her head.

"I don't—I can't."

He didn't know what she couldn't, wouldn't do—he would ask nothing of her at a moment like this. They sat in silence for a long while. It had been midday when the news was broken. They had some time yet before dark, when they would need to make their way out of the gardens, for they were not lit at night, unless there was to be a party.

"Do you remember," she said softly, a long time later, "when the three of us snuck out into the city, all wearing your clothing, and went to that tavern?"

"I remember."

"Do you remember the day we went into the woods and we built a little raft, which sank as soon as we were in the pond with it?"

"I remember."

"Do you remember when Ben taught you to ride on his horse?"

"I remember, El."

She made a sound that was half a laugh, half a sob, and he leaned closer.

"You were a terrible rider, in the beginning."

"You were a terrible teacher," he countered. "I did fine, once Ben took over."

She nodded, made the same awful sound again.

"Eloise…"

She leaned forward and kissed him.

For one eternal moment the world was perfect, the last ten years fallen away. Joel pulled back slowly, reluctantly, to look at her.

Her face was red, her nose just barely running, and her tangled hair clung to her tear-damp cheeks. She had never looked less beautiful. He had never loved her more.

He stood slowly, and held out a hand to her.

"The sun will set soon. We should get you back to your rooms."

"Joel."

"Come on. Don't let's do anything you'll regret in the morning."

She took his hand, and followed him slowly through the gardens and through the palace. They met Julian not far inside; he had likely been coming to search for them.

Joel handed her off to her brother, squeezing her hand once before he let go.

~

"She kissed me," he reported when he returned to his room. The others looked up.

"Really?" Fuller asked.

"She was thinking of her brother."

"Gross," Chris said.

"You're gross," Joel retorted. "She was—looking for a distraction, or something. You heard?"

"We heard," Alem said. "He was the one who was your friend, wasn't he?"

Joel nodded.

"I'm sorry."

He shrugged. "I need to stay, at least—at least for a little while. In case she needs anything."

~

Sylvia sat up and turned to face the door when the knock came. It was the soft knock that meant the princess, not the aggressive one that meant a palace guard.

The princess had made a habit of coming by every day or two; she wasn't quite sure why. They sat in silence together more often than they spoke—the only thing they had in common was Jeremy, and Sylvia didn't want to speak of him. (They'd had plenty to speak about, before reaching the palace. Somehow that time seemed so far away, the casual camaraderie they'd had so unreachable.) It had been three days now since the princess had come, and Sylvia had wondered if she would come again; perhaps she had realized how pointless the whole thing was. But Sylvia enjoyed the company.

The door swung open.

"Oh," she said. It was not the princess. It was Jeremy.

"Um. I'm sorry; I should have said it was me before coming in. I just—I just wanted to make sure you were all right."

"I thought that's what the princess was for." Jeremy had been sending her, hadn't he?

He frowned. "The princess is…indisposed."

"What's happened?"

"Her brother was killed in battle."

193

Sylvia didn't answer—she didn't know what to say. The princess wasn't here to say anything to; it was not Jeremy's brother who had died.

Death was awful, and common, though perhaps less so for princesses. One kept on going; one could do nothing else.

"She—she told you—I mean, you know I didn't—"

"She said your men burned the village without your knowledge," she said. She didn't want to talk about this at all, but she would rather just get it over with than listen to him fumble his way through it.

(It was unlike Jeremy to fumble. But then she hadn't seen him in years. And this was an exceedingly difficult topic, she supposed; she'd overridden all future awkwardness, herself, by opening the subject with a knife to the chest.)

He nodded. He took a step forward, and she leaned back automatically. He stepped back again, glancing around the room; there was nothing to sit on but the bed, where she was perched. After a moment he sat on the floor just in front of her.

"I just—how could you think I would do that?"

She considered, briefly, the possibility of lying back, closing her eyes, and just pretending he wasn't here. But she would have to speak to him eventually, if only to be rid of him in the long term.

"I didn't, at first. I couldn't—couldn't understand it. I thought maybe you had known the attack was coming, and that was why you had pushed me to marry you and come to the estate, but that wasn't— wasn't like you. I—nothing made sense. But when I had been out in the world a while—war turns men into monsters, and so does power. And you got one in the midst of the other, so why should you be any different from anyone else?"

"Sylvia…"

She shook her head. She didn't—she couldn't. Everything was so difficult. Everything had been so hard for so long, and she was so tired.

A silence fell; she hoped that he would leave.

"Where have you been?" he asked instead. "What have you been doing?"

"I went north first. I had my first experience in midwifery with an Olin girl who'd been raped by an Alirian soldier. A few months later I had my first experience in killing with an Olin soldier who tried to do the same to me. Since then I've been up and down and across the island more times than I can count. Taking unwanted babies to temples. Taking refugees and deserters south—turns out I'm good at getting around. You know Kire's been supporting Ibanar since Olion cut ties after they spread the plague there?"

Jeremy nodded.

"Kire had it much worse than Olion—their population was nearly halved, and they haven't enough people to tend all the land. If refugees can get to the right port in Ibanar, they can sail to Kire to start new lives practically for free."

"So you've been helping people, while I've been waging war."

"I've been surviving. The best way to do that is by staying busy."

He changed the subject abruptly. "I've been trying to get you released. The king has been preoccupied with all the secrets of the conspiracy Eloise brought back, and now of course he's in mourning, but as soon as it's appropriate to approach him about such things, I'll make sure he lets you go—after all, I'm the only person you've hurt, and I don't mind."

She cast uselessly for a way to separate herself from him gently, and settled at last on, "When I go I'll go north again; I was on my way back in that direction when I met the princess."

"Won't you—won't you stay? I've mourned you so long."

"You've mourned a dead girl, Jeremy. She's gone, and there's no place for us in each other's lives. I am glad I didn't kill you. But I can't—can't go back. It's too late for that."

He stood slowly, very slowly, like an old, old man. "I'll check on you again, at least until the princess is well enough to come back. I—I'm glad I didn't kill you, too."

~

The court resumed its normal activities gradually. The loss of a son was devastating, but of course he was only a third son, only a fourth child, not fundamental to the ruling of the kingdom, and there was still a war on. His birth order had nothing to do with how much he was loved, how much he would be missed by those who had loved him. But the kingdom would go on running, with or without him, and someone had to run it.

Theo was still at the front line—the only member of the royal family still in battle, and too important in his role there to come home for a funeral. Enemy soldiers, after all, would not care for mourning periods. Men died in battle every day, and the fighting went on.

Julian returned first to his normal life, and then Erika, both of them wanting to spare their parents as much stress as possible for as long as possible. The king and queen had, soon enough, to set their sorrow aside as well. Annabelle did not live here, and Maria was still a child, and so they could take their time in mourning.

Eloise's life had been thrown into disarray by her kidnapping and by her missed and never rescheduled wedding; she no longer had any assigned duties in the court, and no one would think to assign her any now. So she languished alone in her room, turning away her siblings and her cousins, unready to return to a world in which her brother did not exist.

This war had dragged on for ten long years, and she had seen its consequences. In battle reports, yes, but more in less impersonal things. Fewer faces in the hallways, thinner faces in the streets. Fabrics less fine, foods less rich, tradesmen less friendly. She had wept for cousins killed in battle, and she had wept for friends, and she had wept for strangers. But Ben, her brother, the boy she had shared her whole life with, from their shared nursery to their tearful goodbye when he'd returned again to the field, a month before she'd been kidnapped.

She didn't understand, how he could be just—gone, how the world could continue on without him. She had known men died in war, known men who had died in war, but somehow it had never occurred to her that it might be Ben. She had thought, perhaps, that they would share a grave as they had shared a womb, or at least that they would share nurses in their dotage as they had in their infancy. Now long years of life without him stretched out before her, and she—it made no sense, the idea that her life could continue without him.

~

There was a knock on the door; Joel and Alem exchanged puzzled glances. Since they had arrived, there had not once been a knock on the door. The four of them who lived in these rooms came and went without concern for such formalities, and no one else was ever here. No one would ever visit Joel, who was still known more as a traitor than as the man who had ultimately returned with vital information, and the other three were unknown in the palace. If they had been making friends, they had not bothered to tell Joel of it, and also had had the good sense not to invite them back up to the suite.

He went cautiously to the door and opened it slowly; standing outside was Jeremy, whose title Joel still had not bothered to learn.

"Hello," Joel said, wondering briefly if the unknown title required a bow, before deciding that as a recently-pardoned outlaw he could be excused for neither knowing nor caring about such formalities.

"May I come in?"

"Oh. Um, all right."

Joel stepped out of the doorway, casting another baffled look back at Alem, who shrugged. Jeremy came in, pulling the door closed behind him.

"Eloise is having a hard time. Julian asked me to try talking to her, but that…didn't really help. She wouldn't open the door, wouldn't even answer me. I thought perhaps you could give it a try? I know you comforted her when the news first broke."

"Of course. Where is she?"

"In her rooms—she's turned out all of her maids and ladies, and she isn't letting anyone in. Servants set food and water outside the door, and sometimes she takes it. But surely as a leader of bandits you must have some experience picking locks?"

Joel, already with a hand on the doorknob to go, paused. "You want me to force my way into her private rooms, where she's in mourning and utterly alone?"

"I know you've been alone in her rooms before. Likely the whole kingdom knows."

"When I was wanted."

"She needs someone. Whether she wants to let someone in or not."

He didn't want to go. It wasn't that he didn't want to be with her, to support her. But he had dreaded being dragged into her rooms when they were young, knowing how deeply inappropriate it was, and how much more severe his consequences for any alleged defiling would be than hers for being defiled. He had just been pardoned, and wasn't keen to relive that stressful experience with an older, less friendly Eloise who had already once kissed him in the midst of her grief.

He still went, leaving Jeremy behind to introduce himself to Alem.

~

There was a knock on the door, which Eloise ignored, as she had ignored many other such knocks over the last few days. A few minutes had passed when she heard a slow creak, and then footsteps.

Well. It was inevitable that someone would come in uninvited eventually. She had been hiding for several days.

She had not expected it to be Joel, though in hindsight perhaps she ought to have.

"I thought my brother would send someone," she said.

"He did," Joel answered, and Eloise mustered the energy to look skeptical. "Well. Julian sent Jeremy. Jeremy sent me, and now I'm here, more or less thanks to your brother."

"And why should you care if I wish to do my mourning in private?"

He sat uninvited at the foot of her bed. "Because I love you?"

"Still?"

"Always, Eloise." He leaned forward to kiss her, very gently, on the cheek. "I know how hard everything becomes, when you are this sad, when you have lost this much. But your family is mourning too, and they are having a hard enough time without adding worry for you to their sadness for Ben. Jeremy says you haven't been eating much—I took some soup from a maid on my way up. Eat a little, and let me call someone to help you bathe, and then I promise we'll leave you to your own mourning for another few hours."

"Soon," she said. "I'll call for the bath soon. Just—sit with me a while?"

"If you eat your soup," he said.

She suspected he would stay whether or not she ate the soup, but she did not call his bluff, and accepted the bowl when he brought it from the next room. She ate, and he set the bowl aside, and still he sat beside her; she leaned slowly into his side.

"I don't want him to be gone," she said quietly, knowing it was childish.

"Me neither," Joel said. "I had wanted—wanted to see him again. Wanted to apologize, or try to."

"He would have forgiven you. Not—not for hurting me, perhaps, but for the conspiracy. I wrote him a letter when we got back. I hadn't—hadn't received his response yet, but Erika brought it back with her—she slid it under my door, or someone did."

"What did he say?"

"Nothing particularly important. He was glad I was home safe, hoped he would be able to come back again soon and see me. He was worried about the information you'd brought back, but trusted Father and Julian to handle it. He—he was the only one who didn't seem to think I would immediately fall back in your arms, or at least the only one who made any attempt to hide the thought from me."

Joel neglected to point out that she was, at that very moment, in his arms, and she was grateful for this. She was not ready to think about how she felt for Joel, or why his comfort was more comforting than anyone else's. She knew only that happy times with Joel had been happy times with Ben, as well, times when she and Ben both were young and unburdened with the trials of war.

They sat in silence, again, for a long while, and at last Joel said, "Bath time, I think. You'll feel better clean."

"You'll come back, after?"

"It's late—I'll come back in the morning."

"All right," she agreed, and pulled herself reluctantly away from him.

"Seal ring?"

She stared for a moment in confusion.

"To summon maids for the bath. You know no one will listen to me all on my own."

She slipped it off her finger and handed it to him; he kissed her on the cheek again, and then walked away.

She looked down at her ringless finger, and thought of how she hadn't hesitated, even after everything, to give Joel her seal. And then she thought, as she always did now, of Ben.

"You don't have to do this, El," he had said, after the arrest, before the trial, when he found her in the office spare she'd commandeered, surrounded by stacks of paper.

"I do. I know—I know the experts are doing it too, doing it better. But I have to see for myself. I have to be sure."

"And are you?"

She had looked down at the page in front of her, a receipt for an order of cannons from the continent, authorized apparently by her. Only one person outside her family had ever had access to her seal. She'd opened her mouth, but couldn't force the words out. She nodded, instead.

"I'm sorry," he'd said.

Eloise had looked back up at him. "I—I really loved him."

"I know."

"I trusted him."

"Me too. He was my friend."

"He was a good friend," Eloise said, half a question.

"It did seem that way."

Neither of them had spoken for a long moment. Eloise flipped through a few more documents, though there was no point; they all showed the same thing, and that thing was treason.

"Uncle Will is going to check some things at the Ibanari border," Ben said. "I'm going with him. You should come too."

"What use would I be?"

"It doesn't matter. We'll make something up for you. Just—you don't have to be here for the trial, El. I can't face being here for the trial, and I didn't care for him half as much as you did."

"I have to stay. I have to—at least—at least see him, one last time. See his face when we—hear what he has to say for himself. I can't—I can't just leave it like this. I can't bear to."

"We'll be leaving the day after tomorrow, if you change your mind."

She wouldn't change her mind. She had to see this through.

Someone knocked briskly before entering, and started to draw a bath. Eloise let the memory go, for now—it would come back to her, she knew, when she slept.

She missed him so much.

~

A knock on the door, and Jeremy's voice, asking, "May I come in?"

She didn't answer, hoping that he would take it for a no. A minute or two passed, and he knocked again. "Sylvia?"

She ignored his second attempt as well.

"All right," he said at last. "I'll check on you again tomorrow."

She listened to his footsteps fading away. She didn't need to be checked on. She was having a remarkably pleasant time for someone who had been quite justly imprisoned. She didn't need the princess' company, though admittedly she enjoyed it, and she certainly didn't need Jeremy's.

Every word he spoke, every glimpse she caught of his face, was a fresh wound. All of her young dreams had been pinned on him, and everything had unwound so miserably, and she couldn't—couldn't even think of him, without that old familiar feeling of rage and betrayal and desperate longing, the confusing jumble of contradictory feelings that had followed her from the moment she first smelled smoke. She didn't—he wanted her, still. Or thought he did. But she was terribly afraid he was mistaken.

~

Eloise woke to find Joel sitting in the corner of her bedchamber. She was wearing her nightclothes still, and brought up the covers automatically to conceal herself.

"I can go," he said lightly. "Just—I said I'd be back in the morning."

"You can stay. In the next room? Until I can dress myself."

"Should I call someone to help?"

"No, I'll wear something simple." If he wasn't here, she wouldn't bother dressing at all.

He slipped out of the room, and she dragged herself out of bed. Ben had been dead for—she didn't know how long. She didn't know how much time had passed between the incident and Erika's return to the palace; she didn't know how much time had passed between Erika telling her and now. She had been with her family only briefly since it had happened, after Joel handed her off to Julian. She had gone to bed shortly after, and hadn't left her rooms since.

She knew—she knew life would have to go on, like it or not. Joel's presence made that seem both easier and harder. When he was beside her, it was easier to pretend that nothing bad had happened. They were fifteen, and they were in love, and there had never been a war; Ben was not with them only because he was in his own rooms, or out riding, or at lessons.

But it wasn't real. She knew it wasn't real. Joel allowed her to push the tragedy farther away, but it would come home eventually, and

likely hurt all the more for the brief reprieve. And in the meantime—
Joel wasn't the boy she'd loved when she was fifteen, sixteen years old.
It wouldn't do any good to keep him close, to let him think he could
stay close when this was over.

She realized, with a sudden wave of embarrassment, that she had
kissed him.

She had to be rid of him. Before she made a larger mistake.

She had to keep him near, to chase away the agony of Ben's death.

One more day. She would allow herself one more day to wallow
and hide, one more day to cling to Joel, and then she would try—she
would try to go on living.

"I'm dressed," she called, stepping out of the bedchamber. Joel
smiled at her, a small, tenuous thing. One more day. Nothing like—like
the kiss. Just one more day to huddle beneath blankets and cry, one
more day to be held by someone who claimed to love her, who held all
her childhood in his hands.

"I won't need you tomorrow," she told him quietly, hours later.

"I won't come, then," he said, just as quietly. "But Eloise...don't—
don't run from me? Don't hide from me? The rumors will go on now,
no matter what you do, so can't we just...be friends? We were friends
for a while, weren't we? When we were travelling?"

"We can try," she allowed. It was a bad idea, maybe. Probably. But
the world had gone so dark, these last few weeks. Couldn't she just have
this one easy thing? Just for a little while. He couldn't mean to stay here
forever. Just for now. Just until he left again.

~

It took time for the body to travel back to the palace—far longer
than it had taken Erika, as a single rider, to bring the news. She had left
her husband to handle the proceedings; he'd had the body taken care
of, nearer the battle site, to prevent decay, and then brought it back up
with a proper procession of whoever could be spared from the
battlefield. Eloise emerged from her chambers in time for the body's
arrival, in time for the funeral, and then turned to her family for
comfort rather than retreating again.

Chapter 19

"I'm sorry about your brother," Sylvia said.

Eloise glanced over at her, and didn't answer. There wasn't much to say. She changed the subject, instead. "Jeremy said you'd go north when you're released? To help with refugees?"

"Most likely. Though I'll have to winter in a temple, if it isn't very soon."

"My father said the war will end soon. Perhaps there will be no more refugees."

"It takes time for these things to settle. They won't be any less homeless just because their homes were destroyed in the last few days of war."

"What happens when there are no more refugees to help? What will you do then?"

She shrugged. "Keep wandering, I suppose. I haven't a home anymore, either."

"Jeremy loves you."

"He thinks he does."

"Well. Even if you don't want…to be with him again. He would be happy to set you up with a house somewhere. An allowance, a job, even—even a dowry. Whatever you wanted. He'll give you anything you want." He'd told her so, stumbling over the idea of a dowry, last night, the first time she'd spent a moment mostly alone with him since—since Ben.

"I don't want anything from him."

"I'll tell him so. But I don't think he'll give up so easily."

Sylvia frowned. "All I want is to never have to think of him again."

Eloise studied her for a long moment, considering. She thought of how Sylvia had been in the immediate aftermath of her attack on Jeremy, how she'd collapsed and closed off, and remained that way for days after, until Jeremy had come to see her himself, until she had heard his voice, though she'd refused to look at him.

"Do you?" she asked. "Really."

Sylvia didn't answer.

~

Jeremy came to her that night, though she had seen the princess already. She had hoped—foolishly, perhaps—that the return of the princess would mean the absence of Jeremy.

"I don't—I'm not asking anything of you. I just want—to help, however I can. To do what I can to make things right."

The princess had already told Sylvia as much—presumably she had passed Sylvia's answer along. She sighed. "You're asking me to trust you, but that's not a luxury I can afford anymore. I've seen so much trust betrayed, the last few years."

"But it was a mistake, Syl. A misunderstanding. You know I wouldn't—"

"But I lived for four years with the knowledge that you had. That the knowledge was a lie doesn't take away all the pain I've already felt over it."

~

He had come to her in the evening, after several long days apart. She had known, of course, what had kept him. Everyone had known.

He came to her, and caught her hands in his, and told her, "I'm the baron."

"I am sorry," she had said, for it meant his father was dead, and she could imagine nothing worse than learning her own father, off at war now, had died.

"He's been sick forever," Jeremy said, dismissive. He never spoke to her of his parents. "But Sylvia. This means you can move to the estate. We can be married."

She'd taken a step back, drawing their hands apart. "When?"

"Whenever we like, now—he'd never have allowed it. Tomorrow, if you like. Tonight."

"Jeremy!" She'd laughed at him, a little. It was absurd. They'd never spoken of marriage before. She'd—she'd hoped, perhaps. Her mother had warned her noblemen only wanted one thing, and she hadn't—hadn't quite believed it, not of Jeremy, but then she hadn't given him that one thing yet, either. Marriage was—people like him didn't marry people like her. It had been a distant dream, and now he was offering it tonight? "We can't—can't just be married, just like that. What of my family?"

"They can come too! We've plenty of room; I'm my father's only child."

"My mother disapproves of you. And they've work to do. We've work to do—they can hardly spare me, with Father gone."

"Syl, I'm a baron. None of you need ever work again."

"And who will do our work instead? What will become of the rest of the village, without us here, doing our share?"

His exuberance, finally, was fading. "I thought you would want this."

"I—I do. But not—tonight. Not tomorrow. When my mother likes you better. When an apprentice is trained, or at least started."

He frowned. "There isn't time for all that."

"And why is there such a rush, when this is the first you've ever mentioned it?"

"This is the soonest it was an option, the soonest it could be done without my father interfering. I didn't think it needed mentioning, I thought—thought you knew."

"But why the hurry? Why must it be the soonest possible?"

He caught her hands again, this time looking much more serious. "Sylvia, our barony lies on the very northern edge of Aliria, and this is the northernmost village. We stand a stone's throw from Olion—you go there on your market days. All of the fighting has been farther west, so far, but the armies of Olion will continue moving east as well as south. We could have battles here at any time—I've hardly begun learning how best to organize the soldiers Father's left me charge over—and the estate is the safest place to be."

"So you'll let the rest of my village fall to enemy soldiers, while I lie safe in your bed."

"Sylvia, I can't fit an entire village in the estate. I'd move the entire barony in if I could, to please you, but there's only so much space. Of course I'll do whatever I can to keep all of my people safe. But it is so wrong that I would want you the safest of all?"

"I can't. Not yet."

"When?" he asked, releasing her hands reluctantly when she tugged gently in his grasp.

She didn't—she hadn't been prepared. She hadn't thought, hadn't really thought, that they would ever be able to—she was only just eighteen, and with Father gone, her mother needed her at home. "A year?" she suggested.

"A year," he repeated.

"Jeremy…"

"I've work to do. A barony to run. I'll see when I can get away from it next." He turned to go.

"Jeremy," she said again.

He paused, turned back briefly. "I love you, Syl."

"I love you too," she'd said, and he left.

The next time she'd seen him she'd stabbed him.

~

Eloise had kept her promise not to again banish Joel entirely from her life. She had run into him in hallways and been pleasant. But she had been busy, he supposed, with the funeral. She was still mourning, wouldn't want to deal with the stress of whatever friendship looked like between them, when she had so much else to think about. It would take time. He wouldn't push her, not now. Not until she was feeling better.

He tried to spend more time out and about, to catch those brief conversations with her where he could, though the others still all but begged him to stay safely in their room.

He caught Jeremy, though, before he caught Eloise. He'd been loitering in a hallway near her chambers, hoping she would pass by and they could talk for a few minutes. He often saw Jeremy when he loitered here, which he was mostly sure was because Sylvia's room—

her very nice prison cell—was also nearby. It wasn't—Eloise had told him they weren't like that.

He knew Jeremy often lingered outside Sylvia's door, not entering, not speaking to her. Just…being there. He would nod at Joel, usually, as he walked past afterward, off to do whatever it was people like him did with their time. Advising the king, or managing estates, or planning battles—something like that.

He could tell that Jeremy had actually interacted with Sylvia today because he looked exactly as profoundly miserable as Joel often felt after interactions with Eloise.

Astonishingly, Jeremy perked up when he saw him. "Joel! Can we talk?"

There was no reason to refuse, except that he was still waiting to catch a few minutes with Eloise, which wasn't something he cared to admit. He followed Jeremy into another empty room—some sort of office or meeting place, by the looks of it. Jeremy stood in front of him there, for long moment, awkward, unsure.

Finally, he said, "You still love her. Don't you?"

"Does it matter?"

"I—of course it does. I love Sylvia so much it hurts, and she says she hates me, but every time she looks at me she looks like her heart is breaking."

Ah. So he'd sought out Joel as someone likely to be sympathetic to his romantic woes.

"I still love her," he admitted.

Jeremy nodded. "She used to talk about you. Constantly. She tried not to. Tried to hate you. But everywhere I went with her, something would remind her of you."

"Funny thing to talk to your new fiancé about."

"We were friends. Before everything else, and after. I hadn't been at the palace, when she was with you, and I was too caught up in my own grief to care about years-past scandals, and I was…safe, I suppose. To confide in. I know she made a point of never mentioning you to her siblings. Ben mentioned to me once that it worried him."

"Were you—close? With Ben?"

He shook his head. "I only met him a few times. He's been at the front, most of the time I've been here."

"You've never been on the battlefield?" Joel was fairly certain, from things Eloise had mentioned, that he hadn't been, though he couldn't imagine why. Everyone who could fight did, or had, at some point in the last several years.

"I'm not qualified to be anything but an untrained foot soldier, and too important, apparently, for that to be acceptable. My father didn't want me to be his heir. He made a point of denying me access to every sort of training I should have had. I can barely hold a sword correctly. But as it happens, I'm a good enough strategist to be useful to the king here, trained or not. But we're here to talk about Eloise, not me."

"What more is there to say? She thought of me often, when we were apart?"

"She hadn't got over you. I just thought you ought to know."

"Hadn't got over me. But that was months ago. Before our reunion. Before any rosy young memories were replaced with modern reality. I don't suppose there's been any more fond reminiscing since we've come back?"

Jeremy's grimace was all the answer he really needed.

"There hasn't been," Joel concluded.

"I haven't really given her the chance. I've made it all about Sylvia—all about me, really—since you got back. I think she's glad, though—I think she doesn't want to have to think about you, to talk about you."

"Which makes me feel so much better."

"I mean—I think she's avoiding thinking about it at all, because she doesn't want to admit that there's still something there."

Joel shrugged, not entirely sure he wanted whatever hope Jeremy was trying to offer him. It wasn't—it was probably just him projecting, what he wanted with Sylvia. He had pulled Joel into this room all just to work out his own feelings about Sylvia, not really because he knew or cared about Joel's relationships. Why would he? They weren't friends. This was their third proper conversation. Joel still didn't even know his damn title, which was going to be a problem if he persisted in being friendly, whatever his reasons—eventually Joel would have to address him by name, or speak to someone else about him, and it would come out that he couldn't even address him properly.

"Let's not pretend you're here to help me repair my relationship with Eloise. You want to talk about Sylvia."

"Can't we do both?" Jeremy suggested.

"Can't you just ask what you want to ask about Sylvia?"

He sighed. A moment passed before he spoke again. "What was she—what was she like? When you were with her?"

"I'm sure you've gotten it all from Eloise."

"I've gotten her perspective. Maybe yours is different. Eloise is…more sheltered than either of you. I am, too. Maybe you saw something in her that we've missed."

He took a moment to think about it. "Eloise didn't see…how guarded she was, or how frightened of the soldiers. I knew she still had a knife after the guards took our weapons. And I knew she was afraid of the guards—I knew something must have happened to make her afraid of them, the idea of them if not those specific men—so I thought it was best to let her keep the secret knife." He paused. "I am sorry for how that turned out, by the way."

Jeremy shrugged, as if being nearly gutted by his long-dead lover was a matter of no consequence. "Did she—say anything? About anything she'd been doing, anything she'd been through?"

"She said she'd just come down from the direction we were headed, with a group of refugees, and she knew the safest path to take back toward the capital, to avoid any of the smaller fights that had been breaking out around it. We knew it was going to be tricky, and we didn't quite trust her, but we needed her—we didn't want to scare her off by interrogating her."

"She mentioned taking unwanted babies to temples. She didn't say…"

He trailed off, and Joel studied him for a long moment before answering, deciding as he did to just leave off the unknown title. "If any of them were hers? Jeremy, if you want to know whether she's been having babies—wanted or not—you'd better ask her yourself. I don't have anything else to tell you about her."

He nodded. "Thank you," he said, and Joel left.

~

He tried, again, to talk to her. It seemed he was always trying, and always failing.

"When you told me you killed a man who tried to rape you," he started, and wasn't sure how to finish.

"I ran from the first man who tried. I killed the second. I'm still…pure, if that's what you're asking. Not—not that it's any of your business, now."

"I'm not—trying to pry. I just—want to understand exactly how you've been hurt, so I can figure out how to—how to make it better."

She shrugged. "I'm still a virgin. I'm also a murderer. Several times over, in fact." There was a certain defiance in her voice as she said it, as if she expected it to chase him away.

"I'm fairly certain I've caused more death than you have. If that helps anything."

"Oh? And how is that?"

"The soldiers who razed your village? I had them executed, Syl. Every single one. Beheaded."

There was a long pause before she answered. "And are you proud? Did you avenge my death? Did you honor my memory?"

"What do you want me to say?"

"I'm glad they're dead. I'm not glad you killed them. Not you. It should have been me. Do you know what I would give, Jeremy, to feel three dozen necks—those three dozen—snap beneath an axe?"

"I was half mad with grief. I would not do it again. I thought you would be upset."

"Oh, I'm upset."

"Not for the right reasons."

"Go away, then. We have nothing more to say to each other."

He stood to leave, and got halfway to the door before he turned back, unwilling to leave things like this. "No, Sylvia. No. there's more to say. They weren't following my orders. I executed them for you, for my anger, but I executed them because they were traitors, too."

She smiled at him, false, vicious, and half-feral. "Tell me how it feels to be betrayed, Jeremy. Gods know I haven't a clue."

"I didn't send those men."

"Four years ago that might have mattered."

"Why doesn't it matter now? What happened in those four years?"

"I grew up. My charming prince didn't come, so I saved myself."

"I'm sorry I didn't come for you."

"It doesn't matter. It's too late."

"I'm sorry," he said again, and finally left.

~

He spoke with Eloise, and collected stories of a few more violent incidents Sylvia had shared with her, and was more shaken than he could ever admit to either of them.

It was Sylvia. Sweet Syl, who had taken in and bottle fed countless kittens when their mothers' owners would have drowned them. Sylvia, who would pick up and carefully reroute the flies and beetles that others would crush. Who caught spiders and released them outside, who stepped carefully around anthills and found injured wild animals to nurse back to health. Who patched up all the village boys when they got into fights, and scolded them gently, told them fists and kicks would never solve a problem words couldn't. Sylvia, his Sylvia, a remorseless killer.

(And had he not killed, as well? Ordered killing, which felt less personal, less urgent, and therefore somehow crueller? Had he not taken a vicious satisfaction in it at the time? Had he not, for a moment, been every inch the man his father was sure he would never be, and had he not, in that moment, enjoyed it?)

(Sylvia was right; war created monsters. But if they were both monsters, could not they be monstrous together?)

Chapter 20

Olion was willing to make peace. Olion had been willing to make peace years ago, after their plague, until the flames of war were fanned again by lies from conspirators inside the Alirian palace, inside the Alirian government.

Olion was willing to make peace. Olion, whose soldiers had killed Eloise's brother. Eloise no longer wanted peace with Olion, but she knew that the war could not be allowed to drag on, that they must take any chance they could get to stop it. She also knew that she had absolutely no say in the matter.

The plans had been made, no doubt with the help of ministers and barons and dozens of people who knew all the details before the three younger princesses, at least, were informed.

It was at a rare family-only breakfast that Julian and the king explained what would happen next, Eloise only half listening as she entertained her little niece, cutting her food and trying to keep the mess of the meal out of her hair, tight black coils that would bounce back in front of her mouth no matter how many times Eloise pushed them out of the way.

"—and I will marry the Princess Emilienne, and move to Olion," Julian said.

Eloise dropped her niece's fork, which hit the stone floor of the dining room with a great deal of noise. The whole royal family turned to look at her. (Not the whole family. It would never be the whole family again. The family save Ben, gone forever, and Theo, gone for now, still leading their forces at the Ibanari border.)

"You're marrying the princess of Olion."

"I am."

"They killed Ben!"

"Eloise," her father said slowly, heavily. "Men die in war every day. It wasn't a targeted attack against him. It wasn't personal."

Eloise looked around the room, and saw that she would find no support.

"Fine," she said. "Peace, fine. We must have peace. But that's—that doesn't mean you must marry her."

"This is how things are done," Julian said. "The decision has been made."

"Ben—"

"Ben is gone," Erika said, very gently, as if Eloise were a child, or a spooked animal. "The rest of us must keep this kingdom afloat, however we can."

"You don't care. You don't care that he's gone, that they killed him."

"Eloise," her mother said.

"None of you care about Ben. None of you ever cared. You only ever noticed him because he was standing next to me, and you only noticed me because I was doing everything I could think of to get your attention—throwing myself at soldiers and getting caught in closets and making a spectacle of myself in the city. None of you saw either of us as anything but a problem to solve, and even that, I had to work hard to earn."

"That's not true," said the king.

"Isn't it? Do you even know what day our birthday is?"

She needed—she needed—she couldn't be here. She needed—

"Ellie?" her niece asked, worried, in her small, sweet voice. She couldn't manage the full name yet. The only other person who ever called her—

Joel. She needed Joel.

She fled the dining room, going to his suite, the location of which she had pretended to herself, for weeks now, not to know. She pounded on the door, which was opened slowly by Fuller.

"I need Joel. Is he here?"

"I'm here," Joel said, appearing beside Fuller. "What's wrong?"

"I just—I just need you. Walk with me? In the gardens?"

"Of course," he said.

It was all right. As long has she had Joel it was all right. He would understand, if she explained to him about Ben, about Olion. He had known Ben, had seen him as he was, too serious and too afraid of disappointing a world that scarcely noticed him, but so kind, so patient, so happy. Joel had known Ben when he was happy, when they were all happy.

They walked through the dead, frozen gardens for some time, Eloise uncaring, for once, what people might see them, what rumors might be spread. Joel was right, anyway, when he'd said it didn't matter anymore. He had taken her away for comfort when her brother died, had all but carried her home after, had been the only person admitted to her rooms in the days after. Nothing would stop the rumors now.

It was nice, in a way. Not to worry, as she had not worried at sixteen, what the rest of the court thought of her. They would think it no matter what she did—why not let herself be happy?

She looked over at Joel; he smiled at her. Impulsively, she took his hand. His smile widened, and then he ducked his head, looking suddenly shy, as he had been the first time she ever grabbed his hand, over a decade ago now.

It was not long before Julian found them, whatever else he'd planned to talk to her about forgotten when he saw their joined hands.

"Are you really carrying on with him again? At a time like this?"

"And what if I am? You're marrying the enemy; why shouldn't I?"

Joel had loosened his grip on her; she turned to him and nodded, giving him permission to flee and leave them to it. He disappeared quickly.

"This isn't about me," Julian said.

"How can it possibly be about anything else? You're going to be the king of Olion."

"I'm going to be the prince of Olion. Emilienne will be queen, and I will be her primary advisor, as I would have been for Theo if I'd remained at home."

"You think I care about the particulars?" she asked.

"This guarantees a lifetime of peace. Theo and I would never go to war with each other."

"You won't go to war with Theo, but you'll marry into the family that killed Ben."

"You're being deliberately obtuse about this."

"I lost my brother."

"We all did, Eloise."

"Not like me. Not—do you know Theo can't tell me and Annabelle apart? I'm eight years older than her! He doesn't care about anyone but you and Erika. When Ben and I were children, Father only cared about the three of you who were old enough to learn about politics, and Mother only cared about the little girls, and we were alone. We were always alone. The only way I could get attention from either of them was to do something worth scolding me for in person. No one cared about us. No one but each other."

"Eloise, you know I care about you."

"You care about me now, but you only started paying attention to me to keep me in line, to take the burden off Mother and Father. And you still spend half your time disappointed in me for something, no matter how hard I try, how good I am."

"If this is still about—you can't just go breaking engagements and not expect anyone to be disappointed in you."

"I didn't break anything! Jeremy broke it, because he's in love with someone else, and I was only ever the consolation prize, and I knew that all along, I knew we weren't—I didn't love him either, but that doesn't mean it didn't hurt to lose him, and all the life we'd planned to have together, and you never even considered that it might have been anything other than me ruining everything as usual, never mind that I haven't ruined a damn thing since I was sixteen years old."

"Eloise…"

"Jeremy only ever talks to me to worry about Sylvia, and I'm sure once he's married and moved back home he'll never think of me again. There have been two people in my life that have ever really loved me, and one of them is dead. So why shouldn't I have Joel? Why shouldn't I take what he offers me, when no one else gives a damn what becomes of me as long as I don't make a scene about it?"

She stopped, out of words if not out of anger, and Julian took a cautious step toward her. "This isn't about Olion."

"It's about Olion. It's about everything. You care more than the others, at least, and now you're leaving me too. To be with them, of all the ways you could go."

"They all love you, Eloise. We all care. So much. When you disappeared—"

"Don't tell me how you cared when I disappeared, not when you all but accused me of running away with Joel."

"Eloise," he tried, again.

"I don't—I can't do this. We're making a scene. We're in the public gardens—half the court is watching us. And I know you care more what they think than you'll ever care about me."

She made her way back into the palace, absolutely radiating rage and hurt. There was no sign of Joel, but that was fine; she'd told him to leave. Julian hated him, and he needn't be caught in the middle of their fight, any more than he already was. She considered, briefly, retreating to her own room, hiding out until this new scandal she'd caused—and she had thought she was done putting herself at the center of all the drama—had passed. But she didn't want to be alone. Or alone with her ladies, which was often essentially the same thing.

She wanted to be with Joel.

He opened the door himself this time, looking strange and closed off. "You're back."

"I'm sorry," she said. "About Julian."

He stayed standing in the open doorway, neither leaving nor letting her in. "What, did he run out of steam? Do we need to go another round to get him going again?"

"What?"

"Am I even a person to you?" he asked. She saw Chris, in the room behind him, scrambling to get away before he found himself witness to an ugly fight.

"Joel—"

"All you ever do is use me. To upset your family. To distract you from losing Ben. And now—here's a shock—to upset your family again! Has it ever, once, in your charmed life, occurred to you that I perhaps have feelings of my own? I didn't say anything about the kiss, because

I knew how much you were hurting in that moment. But gods all damn it, Eloise. I love you, and I can't go through this thing where you pretend to love me back just to make your brother mad. You know him executing me for soiling you is still on the table? Did you ever know that was on the table at all? Did it occur to you, at fifteen, at sixteen, that if your father had ever truly tired of your antics, you'd have been locked in your room or something, while I'd have gone to the gallows?"

"That was ten years ago. I'm a grown woman—it's no one's business but my own who soils me."

"Really? Well, do please inform the Alirian law books, because I'm quite certain they haven't gotten the memo."

She shook her head. "I'm not using you to make Julian mad."

"Oh? So what are you using me for this time? I'm dying to know."

"Would you just stop—stop being like this? You say you love me, but all you ever do is complain about all the ways I've wronged you since I was fifteen years old. It's not as if you haven't made mistakes too; you—"

"Kidnapped you? Believe me, I wish I hadn't."

It felt, absurdly, like an insult. "Joel—"

"Look, this is all very simple. Do you love me?"

"I—I don't know."

"Then go figure it out." He slammed the door in her face.

She stood there in the hallway for a long time before retreating back to her own room, where she cast out all of her ladies and sat alone in her window seat, looking out the window at the forest that Joel had dragged her through.

She had never, since the moment he was banished, allowed herself to really consider whether she still loved him. She had needed to not care, so she had pretended—and half convinced herself—that she didn't. Everything had been thrown into disarray when she knew she was with him again, and she hadn't wanted to—hadn't been ready to—deal with it, so she had done her best not to think of it at all.

She—she had loved, when they were children, in the desperate, foolish, all-consuming way that children loved. She hadn't felt anything like that since, and had been grateful for it.

She had been—attracted to him, before she knew who he was. She hadn't wanted to admit it, even to herself. But she had been.

And often, after that, all she'd really felt for him was anger, or an exhausted sort of resignation.

But he was still—still Joel. His smiles were the same, and the feeling of his hands on her waist, and the ease with which they handled each other, even after years apart.

He was just also a killer and a traitor and a bandit, and she—she had been determined for so many years not to let her childhood romance define her. Was there anything more defining than winding back up in the same romance a decade later, not because you'd fallen back in love, or never fallen out of it, but because it was comfortable and familiar?

How, exactly, was she supposed to tell the difference?

Joel claimed to love her, claimed to have never stopped. But how could that be true, when the years had shaped her into a different person, one he'd never met? How could he kidnap a twenty five year old woman, confident he loved her because he had when she was sixteen?

If she let herself be with Joel, really be with him, would she ever know if they truly loved each other, or if they were just playing house with dust and shadows?

She wasn't ready to fit back into her sixteen year old self, wasn't confident that was something the new, grown Joel would find he really wanted, once he had it with promises of forever.

How could one tell the difference between loving again and loving a memory?

~

Joel turned to face the empty room behind him. It had not been empty, when he opened the door; since this was the only outside door in the suite, he was confident no one had gone far.

"Well," he said. "I think I'm ready to go now."

"You're not," Fuller said, reentering the room, the others behind him.

"Have you not been trying for weeks to get away from here? Have you not stopped only at dragging me out by force?"

"You're upset. But you're upset because you care. I would love to be gone, but if you leave now you'll regret it."

"She didn't say she didn't love you," Alem offered.

"She didn't say she did," Joel countered.

"Isn't 'I don't know' better than 'no'?"

"We've been together again for months. How can she possibly not know by now?"

"Well," said Alem, older and wiser and ever the voice of reason, "you gave her news of a longstanding and deep-seated conspiracy on the heels of your identity reveal. Then her betrothed was stabbed by his dead lover. Then her brother died. It's possible she's had other things on her mind."

Joel sighed.

He had never stopped loving Eloise, though there had been long painful years when he wished he had. Their reunion had required some adjustments, for the growing they'd both done. But there had never been a moment he hadn't loved her, and known he did. Moments when he resented loving her, moments when he hated her, too, but never moments he didn't love her. He didn't understand how, after all the time they'd been reunited, she could have any doubt about her feelings. But she'd had many problems to juggle, and he had known, today, that she was upset, which meant it was likely not the ideal time to press for a confession of love.

But she only ever came to him when she was upset. She never came to him because she wanted him, as a person, only because she wanted comfort or distraction.

He wouldn't leave now. Not today. But he was beginning to think he'd had the right of it, when he turned to go before the news of Ben came.

~

Eloise sat in her bedroom, watching the sun move through the sky, as her thoughts moved from Joel to the disaster the day had opened with.

She hadn't been fair to her family. She knew that, as her anger died down. Everything she'd said was true, but it wasn't the sum total of their relationships. It was a years-old pain she'd never shared with anyone but Ben.

The truth was that Erika had fought side by side with Ben for years now, had likely known him better, in the end, than Eloise had. And if Theo could not tell all his sisters apart it was only because he'd spent so much time on the battlefields for so many years that he'd hardly seen them. The four of them did all look very alike, or had, at least, before Erika cut all her hair off. They did not look so very different from their cousins, either.

She knew her family loved her. She did. But it had always been so hard, with them.

Mother had said, "Your feelings are too big for a princess." Ben had said, "Your feet are made of ants." Julian had said, "I half think you were swapped with some kind of fairy at birth." The priestess of the god of health and balance had said, when her parents consulted her, "She swings up and down too much, and she's too busy doing and feeling to ever be. She needs to sit with herself and her gods in solitude, perhaps for twelve days, to restore the balance of her mind."

Joel, meanwhile, had said things like, "You're amazing, El," and "You could come to Ibanar with me," and "We can travel together, only I need to learn to swim better first if you want to sail," and "How do they all hold so still all the time?" and "Well, of course you were bored, that sounds awful," and "Who says you have to be a princess forever, anyway? There's enough of them to take on all the boring things without you."

He'd accused her, while they travelled, of choosing him because he was so obviously an outsider. It was partially true.

He had looked...lost. She had felt lost. Ben had taken to their newest lessons in a way she hadn't, had starting seeking out their older siblings more, had started to cut her out, though she was sure he didn't mean to.

She wasn't good at the lessons she took with her brother, and wasn't good at the lessons she took without him, either. Politics and deportment, geometry and embroidery, all of it was pointless and boring and difficult, all of it required sitting stiller than her body wanted to sit. She was sick of being a disappointment. She was sick of feeling left behind, of being surpassed, especially by Ben, who she thought ought always to be right at her side.

When she told her mother she needed to move, her mother offered dance lessons. She'd taken the dance lessons. She'd hated every moment of them, finding dancing far more rigid and structured than she'd expected. She'd asked for sword lessons, which her mother had warned her were also rigid and structured. She'd wanted them anyway, and her mother had said she would make arrangements once Eloise had mastered the ceremonies for the next four holy days.

Well, Eloise was never going to master those ceremonies, but she didn't actually need her mother, did she? She could make her own arrangements. She'd meant to find and enlist a more experienced soldier for her training, but then she'd seen Joel. She had looked at him, so unlike the others, and always a step behind, and she'd thought—she'd thought maybe she would fit with him, the way she didn't with her siblings. Thought maybe he would understand her.

And yes, she'd flaunted their relationship wherever she went.

Joel had always thought that Eloise never cared what anyone thought. But she had, before him. And she had again, after him. It was only in that brief, beautiful time with Joel at her side that no one else's opinions had mattered. Joel had just...liked her. Exactly as she was. Sometimes he'd found her overwhelming, or her ideas alarming, but he'd never been frustrated and baffled when she struggled with her lessons, never been fed up with her inability to hold still, never been impatient or annoyed when she failed to be exactly what a princess was supposed to be. She'd been enough for Joel, and it had been intoxicating.

She'd flaunted their relationship because she'd been so delighted to have something so wonderful, because she wanted everyone to know that she didn't have to be what they wanted to be so, incredibly happy. She'd wanted them to know that Joel was the most important person in the world, and that he didn't care that she wasn't as smart or graceful or patient as her siblings or her cousins. (And, yes, she'd wanted her parents to notice her.) Everything had been so perfect. Their relationship had even drawn Ben close to her again, if only to keep them out of trouble.

And then Joel had betrayed her. And, well, of all the princes and princesses and dukes and duchesses in the palace, Eloise was by far the easiest to betray. The wild, reckless, impatient princess. No one would ever actually call her the stupid princess, but she was sure they all thought it. And none of the beautiful things she'd had were real.

And then he'd come back, and told her that he had loved her, but it wouldn't matter if he hadn't. Which was—it was better, of course, than if he'd never loved her at all. But—but—had he found her annoying, and been too polite or afraid to say so? How much of the acceptance and understanding she remembered had been just a boy in over his head, trying to stay out of trouble?

After Joel, she'd learned to be what everyone but him had always wanted her to be. She'd had to. Had to put as much distance as possible between herself and the girl she'd been, the boy she'd loved. It had been a hard and miserable time. She'd never reached the levels of success her siblings had achieved so easily. But she'd learned that taking notes had soothed the need for motion, and given her the information to review again and again until it made sense to her. She'd handled her special skill of always saying exactly the wrong thing by never saying anything in public unless she'd planned it in advance and checked it with at least one other person. She'd pricked and pricked and pricked her fingers until she could embroider half as well as her cousins. She'd memorized all the tedious dance steps, and all the ceremonies for all the holy days. Julian and Ben had taken turns tutoring and drilling her on all the arithmetic, and for politics—well, she'd mastered the art of saying things that sounded impressive, and meant nothing at all.

Ten years later, all the lessons were done, and she had only to exist every day in court, and it was still so hard. But she'd succeeded. She couldn't throw it all away to make the same mistake she had as a stupid child.

She had loved him so much. He had given her the freedom to actually enjoy her life, just by existing, just by looking at her.

But it was over. It had to be.

Chapter 21

Eloise apologized to her family. She did not apologize to Joel; she didn't know how, or whether it would only make everything worse. She no longer saw him lingering in the hall. She no longer saw him at all. She was fairly confident he was still in the palace, if only because no one had told her different. She tried not to think of it.

Soldiers were coming back from Olion, some to go home, some to be redirected to Ibanari battlefields. (Olion would not be sending any of their soldiers to join Aliria in the war against Ibanar; that had been one of the terms of their treaty. Olion and Ibanar would handle their own issues with each other.)

Erika and her husband went to join Theo at the Ibanari frontlines.

Julian went to Olion, taking Annabelle and her husband as representatives from the Alirian royal family for his wedding. Eloise could not be trusted with such a task. She was not sure she would have been even before her outburst. Before her kidnapping, perhaps. But reappearing with Joel at her side, regardless of the reasons, had shaken what little faith anyone had in her.

"You can come visit," Julian promised, "once things have settled. Perhaps I'll find you a husband in the court at Olion. I think it would be best for you to be away from here."

"Perhaps," she agreed.

He frowned at her. "Eloise…"

225

"Good luck," she said. "I'll write you." She hugged him quickly, and melted into the crowd gathered for his departure.

Losing Julian would be nothing like losing Ben, and not only because of the way she was losing him. But it still hurt. Julian had cared for her the way no one else had, the way her parents and Theo had no time for, the way Ben and Joel had been too young for. He'd protected and prepared her, when things fell apart, and she could not have survived without him.

He had been the one to come for her, after Joel's trial. She had barely held herself together long enough to reach her own chambers, and Julian had found her not long after.

"You're crying," he'd said. "Good."

"What?"

"That little display you put on in the courtroom—I understand the urge. But it was a stupid thing to do. You brought him into our home, and he was a traitor and a spy, probably for Ibanar. Things were already tense—things have been tense for longer than we've been alive. We'll probably be at war within the year."

"War?"

"War. And if you didn't even love him, then what was the point? So keep crying. Go cry out there where they can all see you."

She had gone. And she had hated Julian a little, for a long time. But she'd grown up, and she'd understood. He had been protecting her. It had been cruel, but it had been necessary, and he had been the only one in her family willing to do it, to hurt her so she could be safe.

The entire court had been quickly convinced that she had been only putting on a show in the courtroom, that she had in fact loved Joel deeply. She had been young, and she had been foolish. She had been seduced by a spy, and her kingdom had paid the price.

It had been humiliating at the time. But she'd realized eventually that the pitying distain she'd gotten was the best thing left for her. Better that she loved him, better that he seduced and betrayed her, than that she had carelessly shared state secrets with a meaningless fling.

Better that she had thrown herself so shamelessly at him, and in front of all the court, if she had really loved him, too.

Pretending she hadn't had been the best defense mechanism she could think of at the time. But it had been a very poor one, and she owed what little remained of her reputation to Julian's calculated cruelty.

Fourteen, she remembered, now. Joel had been fourteen. Barely older than her littlest sister. And they thought he'd been fifteen, true, but another year scarcely mattered. They had both been so young. How had they ever attributed such malice, such calculation, to a child? How had her father not—how had he not—

They had tortured a child. They had taken him, injured and feverish, to the border—to the wrong border—and left him alone in the woods.

The most surprising thing about this whole situation, really, was that he had wanted to return to Aliria. To—to her.

To kill them all in their beds, perhaps, and it may be that some of them deserved it.

But no, that wasn't Joel. She still didn't understand why he'd kidnapped her in the first place, but he hadn't—he'd never hurt her. And he'd had more than enough opportunities.

He'd been banished from Ibanar, too. There was nothing for him in Olion, or across the sea. And his mother and sister were dead. He wanted, she suspected, to go home. And the Alirian palace was the closest thing he had.

She had meant to stop thinking of him. She had. Joel was gone as surely as Ben, as surely as Julian. They'd left a boy in the woods to die. The man he'd become was so changed she'd not known his face. If he still loved her, that was only—only another part of trying to come home, and she wasn't the girl he'd fallen in love with, any more than he was the boy that she had.

It was over. It had to be over. Perhaps Sylvia would provide a distraction.

~

The princess had been coming by more frequently. This meant that Jeremy came less frequently, so was, overall, a positive. The princess came, and sat casually on Sylvia's bed, and talked at length about her siblings and about Joel.

(They had introduced themselves to Sylvia as Elisabeth and Senam, but Sylvia had known Senam's true name was Joel by her second day in their company, though she hadn't realized the political significance of the name until more recently.)

"Jeremy says hello," the princess said as she walked into the room, this time.

"Princess—"

"Call me Eloise," she said. "We were friends, weren't we? Before all this?"

Sylvia didn't answer. They had been friendly, she supposed, but they had been travelling companions. There were few people Sylvia trusted enough to call friend. Even George, who she had known and worked with for years, she remained wary of. Her friends—there was Harra, who had driven an Ibanari soldier's own sword through his back while he held Sylvia pinned to the ground. Essad, who had taught her, on the holy street of Ibanar, a half dozen heresies she'd used to save a hundred lives. (Essad who was a eunuch, and sworn to four kinds of abstinence, as were all devotees of the god who wept for what would not be, and was the only man she could truly trust.) The priestess of the third god, who she trusted less since she'd sent her to the palace.

"Eloise," Sylvia said, anyway, and the princess smiled, then frowned.

"He's coming to see you tomorrow. I couldn't change his mind; I'm sorry."

"It's all right." She suspected Eloise could prevent it if she truly wanted to—was she not princess? Could she not command a mere baron to stay away? But Sylvia hardly wanted to encourage overreach of political power, especially as she was technically, she supposed, a political prisoner.

~

Chris found Eloise in the gardens, where she should not have been. Everything was quite frozen and dead.

(She hoped Julian's party had reached Olion safely. It was late in the winter to travel, especially north.)

She'd not seen Chris in weeks. She'd not seen Joel or any of his men. Though the men she'd seen seldom even before her fight with Joel, and looking at Chris, she felt guilty for it, and angry with herself for feeling guilty. They'd kidnapped her, and she'd gotten them pardoned. She certainly didn't owe them anything more.

"Joel's talking about leaving," he said.

"What? To go where?"

"I don't know. But he met with the king this morning, and finally got us all the written copies of our pardons, signed and sealed and all. I thought—I know you're fighting. I wasn't sure he would say goodbye. I think you'll both regret it, if he doesn't."

She didn't go up to his room immediately. She couldn't—they hadn't even spoken in weeks. What would she—

She made it all the way back to her own rooms, changed out of her too-cold boots and into warmer slippers. Sat on her window seat, and stayed there for perhaps fifteen seconds. And then her control broke, and she was off down the hall, to knock on Joel's door.

"Are you leaving?" she asked when he opened it, visibly surprised to see her.

"I didn't have any particular plans to."

"You collected your pardons this morning?"

"For Alem. So he can officially apprentice with the court physician. He's down there now. The barracks are filling up with wounded soldiers, and they need all the help they can get."

"Good. Don't—don't leave without telling me. Please."

"Why? What is there here for me, Eloise? A court full of people who still hate me? A career in diplomacy or war-making? Two things I despise?"

"You could stay for—" She stopped, unsure how to finish the thought.

"For you? I'll stay if you ask me to stay. But you won't. Will you?"

"I can't."

"I know." He sighed. "I won't leave without telling you. I promise."

"Good," she said again, and stood there, awkward, for a moment, before turning and walking away. She didn't know what else to say to him, or how to say it. But he wasn't leaving; she had time to figure it out.

~

"Sneak," Joel said, fondly, later. "You knew why I got the pardons this morning."

Chris shrugged. "Now you know she doesn't want you gone."

"True. But I still don't know what she does want."

"No one knows what she wants," Fuller said. "Herself included."

~

Jeremy stood in front of her; she sat cross-legged on the bed, trying to look polite but distant. She wasn't sure whether she was succeeding.

"I'm sorry to—I know you don't want to see me. But I didn't want you getting secondhand information."

"About what?"

"The troops recalled from Olion have mostly made it home by now, and we're getting better information about them than was available while there were battles going on."

"All right."

"Your father is alive, Sylvia. He's being housed at a garrison with other soldiers whose homes are gone, until we can rebuild."

She hadn't thought of her father in years; she hadn't let herself. It would only have hurt.

"You can have part of your family back, at least. I can send someone to bring him here for you."

"No," she said.

Jeremy frowned. "No?"

"He's already mourned me. And the girl he mourned is as good as dead. Don't—don't make him—don't make me—"

"He loves you, Sylvia. He won't care how you've changed, as long as you're alive." He came closer as he spoke, too close, an arm's length between them, but still too close.

"How could you possibly—"

"Because I don't care, and surely he must love you at least as much as I do."

"Jeremy—"

"I love you," he said, soft and gentle and earnest, and it felt like a slap. He couldn't love her, because he couldn't know her, because she hardly knew herself. All she'd done since the fire was run.

"You're not in love with me. You're in love with the shadow I cast. You're so busy looking over my shoulder for it, you've hardly noticed me."

"I love your shadow, Syl. But you won't let me love the rest of you. You won't let me know you."

230

"You're not trying to know me—you're trying to find something in me that doesn't exist. I died, or near enough. The girl you want is gone."

"I want any version of you I can get."

She shook her head, and Jeremy took one slow step back.

"Don't tell him," she said.

"I won't. Not until you're ready."

She would never be ready. She'd done so many things, had so many things done to her. If she'd been declared neither a heretic nor an outlaw, it was only because no one knew she lived, to assign the charges to her. (And now, because Jeremy and the princess were both too foolish and too kind to want her punished.)

And she had run, while her brother burned.

There was only running. Running the island top to bottom, side to side, back and forth and again and again, never pausing, never looking back. Praying that the war would end, and all the death and pain with it. Praying that the war would never end, or that she'd die in it, so she needn't ever stop and take stock of herself, and learn who she was standing still.

She had been trapped in this room now for months, and still hadn't worked it out, and didn't have even the comfort of a finished war to force her into this introspection.

They should have killed her pulling her off Jeremy's body; surely that was the thing to do when someone attacked a baron.

She didn't want to die. She was just so tired. More tired now than she had ever been, running up and down the island. There was nothing to fill her days, no distraction to keep her sane. She'd never had nightmares like this while she travelled, not even right after—right after—

Well, she'd been through lots of nasty things. Attacked by more men than she'd bothered to count—men who wanted her dead, men who wanted her supplies, men who just wanted her. Held small children as they died, helped terrified, injured women through childbirths they both knew they wouldn't survive, helped others through childbirths then bundled and buried the dead babes before they had to look at them. Killed men with her quarterstaff, with knives, with a golden arrow once, with a stolen sword twice, with a rock she'd picked up off the ground, and slammed into his head three times, until he finally stopped moving, finally stopped reaching for her. She'd suffocated a sleeping woman, once—the infection had spread up from a wound in her leg, and it should have been amputated, but none of them had a blade that could do the job, and even if they had, she might well have died from the amputation instead of the infection. They had been days from anyone who could have helped, and she'd begged Sylvia that morning, "Please, please, it'll only get worse. We all know I won't make it. And I'm risking everyone, slowing us down. I can't—I can't. When I fall asleep. I don't want to wake again. Please don't make me wake again."

Sylvia had killed so many, and buried so many more, and she had watched her brother burn. And she had never had nightmares like this until she'd come to the palace. Until she'd tried to kill Jeremy.

Except of him. For years, all her nightmares had been of him, and even now, even now, those dreams were the worst.

~

Joel encountered Jeremy that night, as he often did at night. They both came here, while the rest of the palace slept, to be near the women they loved.

The women who didn't love them back.

It made them…not friends, exactly, but something like it.

Joel sunk to the floor beside Jeremy, both of them with their backs to Sylvia's door. Jeremy liked to be there, in case she had nightmares— she usually did. Joel didn't have a good reason for wanting to be there, down the hall from Eloise; he couldn't see her, or hear her, or bang on the door to wake her from dreams.

"Eloise spoke to me today," he reported quietly.

"Sylvia, too. It didn't go well."

Joel wasn't sure he would say his conversation went well, either. It could certainly have gone worse. Still, he didn't want to talk about it. Not to Jeremy. "What happened?"

"I told her I'd tracked down her father. Alive. She told me not to tell him about her. She told me the girl we both loved is as good as dead." He sighed. "I don't know how to help her."

"Stop trying," said a voice from behind the door, and they both jolted, startled. "Go to bed."

"Sorry, Syl," Jeremy said quietly, and nodded once at Joel before standing and slipping away.

Joel wondered if she often heard them, if she knew Jeremy spent so much of each night guarding her door. Likely not; they seldom spoke to each other on their vigils. If she had noticed only one set of footsteps walking away, she didn't mention it to him now.

He'd hardly thought of Sylvia since getting here. She had been helpful, and pleasant enough company, but Joel couldn't afford to get attached to people, with the life he lived.

But it wasn't fair. Why should she be locked up for a crime her victim didn't mind? And why should she be forced to see him, to hear him, to think of him, when he was, after all, responsible for the men who destroyed her village, and her family, and her life?

Jeremy didn't know how to help her. But Joel did.

Chapter 22

It was a maid who found Sylvia missing, when she went to bring her breakfast, accompanied as always by a palace guard. Eloise wasn't sure of the exact chain of command for reporting missing a prisoner not held in the prison, but at some point someone had the good sense to ignore it, and send a young woman to report it to her.

"I'll handle it," Eloise told her. "Please don't tell the dungeon master. Or the king."

She checked the room herself—unlocked from the outside, and all keys were accounted for. Missing only Sylvia and one set of clothing— before collecting Jeremy.

"How could she have gotten out?" he asked, staring forlornly around the empty room.

With help, Eloise thought, and didn't say, because it was the only option, but it didn't make sense—who would help her?

"If she'd asked, I would have snuck her out myself," Jeremy said.

"You didn't offer."

"I didn't—I didn't want her to go. But if she'd asked…"

"She didn't pack anything," Eloise said, and went to collect Joel.

Chris stood in the door, blocking her path, looking decidedly shifty. "Joel's—not available right now. He's—he's—"

"Sleeping?" Eloise asked. "Out for a walk? In a meeting? Halfway to the border?"

"Um…"

"We haven't seen him," Fuller said, from deeper in the room. "Don't know where he is. Wouldn't tell you if we did."

"Fine."

Eloise returned to Sylvia's room, Jeremy trailing behind her.

"You think he took her?" he ask.

She nodded. "They'll be back."

"How do you know? How can you?"

"Joel made me a promise. And Sylvia has nowhere else to go."

~

Sylvia followed Joel through the palace silently, noting the twists and turns he took, the abandoned corridors he used to keep them out of sight, the room he ducked into briefly, emerging with two fur lined cloaks.

She followed him out a small side door, down an abandoned path, and into the forest that began behind the palace.

"What are we doing?" she asked, when he finally stopped, leaning casually against a large tree. The sun was rising, by then, not far enough past the horizon to be seen through the trees, but the color of it was bleeding into the small amount of visible sky.

It has been foolish to follow him, she knew. Especially without a single word exchanged until they had reached, apparently, their destination. But she had been exhausted and overwhelmed, and furious that even behind a locked door, she could not truly have privacy. How many times, she wondered, had she slept through Jeremy sitting at her door? How many times had he spoken of her as if she was not right there? When Joel had opened the door, scarcely a quarter hour after she'd sent Jeremy away, her emotion had overwhelmed good sense.

She and Joel weren't friends. They were hardly acquaintances. And she knew better than to trust anyone. She was damn lucky he hadn't murdered her, or worse.

Joel shrugged. "Now you enjoy the fresh air and freedom."

The fresh air wasn't pleasant, exactly; it was winter still, and bitterly cold, and though he'd given her a cloak, the shoes she'd been wearing when they left—not her own boots, but a pair of soft slippers that had come with her other borrowed clothing—weren't meant for tramping around the woods in any season, but especially this one. She was, at least, wearing a pair of heavy wool trousers.

This couldn't last. Surely Joel, who was in love with the princess, and promised a pardon for kidnapping her, wouldn't free a state prisoner trusted primarily to the care of that princess, and risk his relationship and pardon both.

Even if he did intend to truly let her go, it wouldn't work. Her badly burnt face was distinctive, and she could only get enough supplies to survive by going into the capital, and it was too cold to travel far.

She would enjoy the freedom, then, if not the fresh air, for however long it lasted. She found a fallen log a few feet away, and sat on it, lifting her cold feet off the ground.

"This was a stupid thing to do," she said, and it wasn't until she spoke to him that Joel followed her.

"I am a master of doing stupid things. And it's all worked out so far, more or less."

She studied him for a moment. She hadn't seen him since the day they reached the palace; only Jeremy and the princess had ever visited her.

"You're the one who pulled me off of Jeremy."

"I am."

"Thank you. I—I am glad he isn't dead."

"He loves you."

Oh, no. This morning of freedom was not going to be wasted on a pitch for Jeremy. Why should Joel even care, except that he wanted the same thing from a different woman? "And you love the princess," she said, "and all three of you are fools."

"I know," he said, but she was too angry, suddenly, to leave it at that.

"You're exactly like him," she said. "You think you can just reclaim your own past, and the rest of the world will follow. It doesn't work that way. It's over."

"And what about Eloise?" he asked. "What makes her a fool?"

He had gone stiff, clearly angry too, and it was foolish to pick a fight with a man stronger than her, when they were completely alone, and she hadn't her knife, or quarterstaff, or even good boots, but it was a day for foolishness, and she had been subjected for weeks to the princess' conflicted feelings.

"Princess can talk all she likes about how things have changed, and the past is in the past, but she still thinks she can control you, she still can't see how your hands are drenched in blood, and some of it is your own, and on dark, angry days you have wished that more of it was hers, and you are a new creature entirely."

His anger had faded, slowly, over the course of her speech. "You're projecting."

"Am I wrong?"

"No. You're not wrong."

"About her, or about you?"

"I don't see how it's any of your damn business."

"You butt into my nonexistent love life, and I'll butt into yours."

"Fair," he said. He took a step closer to her, and she failed to suppress a flinch. He stepped back again, holding out his hands. "I was just going to sit down."

She nodded, and shifted so she was on the tail end of the fallen tree, and he could sit on it too, with several feet still between them. They sat in silence for several minutes, as the sky continued to lighten. Soon, someone would come with breakfast, and her absence would be noticed.

"You're not like Jeremy," she said. "Not really. You've changed, more than she has—you must have. If you're really stupid enough to love her still, then you'd better let go of the past and make her love you now."

"It's not so stupid."

"It is. You're fools, the whole lot of you."

"And you don't care about Jeremy at all?"

"I'm smart enough to see I shouldn't. To see it could only end badly."

"It might be worth it."

"I am sick of being told how much pain is worth it. It's never worth it."

She was suddenly exhausted. She laid on her back on the log—it had been a large tree, once—and pulled the cloak tight around her. It wasn't a well-balanced position, and it put Joel out of her sightline, but if he was going to hurt her today, he likely would have done it already. She would be safe enough as long as she didn't provoke him.

Time passed slowly. Neither of them spoke. She was hungry, but she had been used to being hungry for long years before arriving at the palace, and learning prisoners were better fed than the average subject.

She had certainly been missed by now. If she had intended to truly escape, she should have gone into the city and begged or stolen supplies immediately, before her absence was discovered, before soldiers were sent to search for her, before the public could be warned of a woman with a half burned face. It was too late, now.

~

Jeremy paced the length of Sylvia's room—of Sylvia's cell. Eloise sat on Sylvia's bed and watched him. The two of them shouldn't be in a bedroom alone, publicly still engaged or not, but that was hardly her most pressing concern today.

There was no talk of reporting the escape, of sending anyone to look for her. Eloise had thought, briefly, of going looking herself. Joel wouldn't have gone far, not without his men, and not with the shoes Sylvia must be wearing. Eloise could think of a half dozen nearby places he might be, all places they had gone to together as children. But she'd been kidnapped, the last time she'd ventured off palace grounds. And there was no point—she understood why Sylvia was being held, but she didn't like it, and knew Jeremy didn't either. If she could get away, they would let her.

"Will the staff keep quiet?" Jeremy asked.

"It depends. I don't know who all knows, and finding out would only draw more attention."

He nodded. "I have a meeting. I should go—keep my usual routine. You'll—you'll tell me, if anything…"

"I'll tell you. I haven't any responsibilities today. I'll keep an eye on things."

"Thank you, Eloise."

~

"What did you think, the first time you met her?"

Joel turned to Sylvia, startled. She hadn't spoken in nearly an hour. And she could only mean Eloise. "I thought she would destroy me," he said.

"Well. That's…dramatic."

"I was fourteen."

She sat up, and met his eyes. "I was sixteen. When Jeremy."

He nodded. "I was fourteen, a foreign child, not there on my own merits or even my own family's money, and she was the princess—not just one of them, but the princess, the one they all talked about, and she loved me. I never belonged there, but less, then, when it started—I lost my Ibanari accent mimicking her. It could never end in anything but heartbreak."

"You still have the accent."

"Well, there's no need to hide it now, is there? No one cares where outlaws come from."

"I suppose not."

He returned to the topic of Eloise. "She was... inescapable. Magnetic. Away from her, you could see how absurd it all was, but you were still drawn to her. She was the eye of the storm, and we all got swept along. She's not like that anymore."

"You've fallen out of love with her?"

"No, she's different. Less alive. I think I killed her."

"Jeremy killed me."

"But you nearly killed him, too."

"And Eloise killed that young, innocent, frightened version of you—when she voted to have you hanged—yes, she told me that, I'm amazing by all the things she tells me—and we are all of us dead now, so what does any of it matter?"

There was a long silence. Finally, Joel said, "I'll have to take you back, you know. If I want to keep my pardon."

"If I cared I'd have run by now. There's nowhere else to go."

"I wouldn't chase you, if you did. Another stupid thing to do, but I—I'd rather be stupid than cruel, I think."

"It's cold," she said. "Let's go back to the palace."

"If that's what you want."

"It's what's best. But—thank you. For this."

They didn't speak on the journey back, as they hadn't on the journey out. She walked behind him, her feet crunching on the frosted ground, so he knew that she was following. He was only a little surprised that she hadn't tried to really escape. The last time he'd seen her—when he'd gotten her off of Jeremy, and all the fight had gone out of her—he had thought that she looked...finished. Like the fight wouldn't be coming back, at least not any time soon.

It was easy enough to sneak back onto the grounds, back into the palace. He'd gotten in so many fights in the beginning because he didn't want to hide—some strange sense of pride he couldn't justify. But he was quite good at hiding in the palace. He'd learned so many tricks and secret routes, from Eloise and from the other unwitting young members of the conspiracy. They attracted no attention until he picked the lock of Sylvia's room, opening the door to reveal Eloise and Jeremy both inside.

Jeremy stepped forward, then quickly back again. "Are you all right?" he asked, clearly addressing Sylvia.

She nodded.

"Good. I'll leave you, then."

He did. Eloise, too, turned first to Sylvia. "I don't think anyone noticed. Not anyone important, at least. I'll have someone bring you some food."

She nodded again, then shrugged off her cloak and handed it to Joel. "Thank you," she said again.

He didn't get a chance to answer; Eloise grabbed his arm and dragged him out of the room and halfway down the hall into the next empty room, not even bothering to lock Sylvia's door behind her.

"What were you thinking?"

"I was thinking that I understood. She was suffocating in here. Eloise, when a woman is half mad with pain and grief, you can't lock her up in a cramped little room for months and expect improvements."

"Take that up with my father—Jeremy would have had her out on the second day, and I have no say in any of this. You realize you just helped a state prisoner to escape? That's illegal, Joel. Did your full pardon cover future crimes? If we didn't still need you we'd lock you up again, too. And we won't always need you. Be careful."

"She's a war hero—a better one than any of the soldiers coming home. She deserves better than this. And a few hours of freedom was all I could give her."

"I know. But if you get caught, I don't know if I can save you."

"I didn't mean to worry you."

"I was more worried about her than you. Where did you get those cloaks?"

"Stole them."

"I gathered that much. Who from?"

"Does it matter? I'm going to return them."

"Good. Do that. I have to make sure everyone knows Sylvia is back, before anyone else finds out she was gone."

It was the first time she'd touched him in weeks.

~

Eloise saw her father for breakfast the next morning. He made no mention of any escaped prisoners. She remained on guard through the rest of the week, but it seemed they'd gotten away with it. There was a war on; everyone had bigger things to worry about than Sylvia.

Chapter 23

The knock on the door sounded like Jeremy. She hadn't seen him in many days, since her temporary escape, and had only heard of him once in that time. The princess had said, "Jeremy wants you to know that he would help you escape, if you asked." Sylvia hadn't answered, and the subject hadn't come up again.

"Sylvia?" he said. "May I come in?"

"If you must."

He did. He was dressed more finely than she was used to, little bits of gold trim on his boots and jacket, and detailed embroidery, gold-threaded and beaded, on his cuffs. (Jeremy had never really dressed as befitted his station, before, but then she'd only seen him when he came to visit her in the village. She'd been surprised by how plainly everyone dressed at the palace—mostly Jeremy and Eloise, but the people she'd seen on her way in that first day, too. Fine clothing, but rather worn. Very little jewelry. Embroidery positioned so that it was likely covering damaged areas.)

"It's a holy day," he said, and presented her with a small, round cake. She counted back the cycles of the moon, marked through her window, and knew what flavor the cake would be, and why he had come to her today, and not on the other holy days that had passed since her arrival.

"The festival of new beginnings," she said, and accepted her cake.

"Repairs on my manor are starting soon," he said, "and I could supervise them, if I liked."

She took a bite of her cake, and waited for him to reach his point.

"I want to make things up to you, Sylvia. It occurs to me that perhaps the best way I could do that is by leaving you alone."

An unexpected wave of panic nearly overwhelmed her, and she dropped her cake.

She was a fool, too. As bad as all the rest of them.

"No," she said, and they stared at each other for a long, silent moment.

"I—I could get you a new cake?"

"Please."

He turned and left; Sylvia crouched on the ground to pick up her cake. They were dry, sweet, crumbly cakes, for this goddess, and a particular favorite of hers, but they made a terrible mess, especially when dropped. She focused on cleaning it, and not—and not—

The idea of Jeremy leaving, of him leaving her here, going home without her—

She picked up the cake, and ate it one small crumb at a time, and didn't let herself think of Jeremy.

It took him about a half hour to return. It felt too long, but he would have to make his way to wherever the cake had come from, and back, and likely stop and talk to many people along the way—he was dressed for a party.

He'd left his party for her, to offer to leave her, to really leave her alone as she had wanted all along, but now—

And what did it matter where he was, and where she was, if she was a prisoner? How could she ever—how could they—

She wasn't supposed to be thinking of him. She ate another crumb, and waited.

He came back with two cakes. She was still sitting on the floor, the remaining crumbs collected in her skirt, and he sat facing her. He handed her one cake, and kept the other for himself, and they ate in silence. She studied his freshly shined boots with their golden trim—hastily applied, she could see this close, and likely not pure gold. (She had seen a lot of gold, in the temples she'd visited.) She studied her own skirt, soft wool woven in three shades of green, with simple blue embroidery along the cuffs and hem, old and worn and still finer than anything she'd ever owned. She studied her hands, cleaner than they'd been in probably all her life, with nothing in this room to dirty them.

She didn't—she didn't know what to do. What she could do, what could possibly come next.

"Do you want me to stay at the palace?" Jeremy asked her.

She didn't look up at him. "Yes. Please."

"Do you want me to visit you, sometimes?"

"Yes."

"Would—would you look at me, please?"

She looked up slowly, and he smiled, just for a moment, before making the face he always made for serious conversations.

"This won't—this won't be forever, you know. The king will release you, and then—and then—whatever you want. Whatever you want, I'll make it happen."

"Don't promise me things."

"I'll try, then. All right?"

"All right."

He stood slowly. "I'll give you some space. But...new beginnings, yes?"

"New beginnings," she agreed.

He smiled again. "Thank you, Syl.”

~

It was one of Eloise's favorite holy days. They varied—some somber affairs, some festivals, some private, some public. This was a festival day, a day to dress in their finest things and eat their favorite foods and celebrate with all their friends.

This was the first festival since they'd ended the war with Olion, and the biggest celebration they'd allowed themselves in the palace for years.

Jeremy had taken cake and disappeared, twice, probably trying for a new beginning with Sylvia. Eloise considered speaking to Joel— they'd spoken briefly after he brought Sylvia back, and when he'd promised not to leave without telling her, but otherwise not since their fight, and she still—she still didn't know what kind of beginning she wanted.

She danced with Jeremy, when he was there, and with her father, and her littlest sister, and several returned soldiers. She ate too many cakes, and thought several times that she saw Joel at the edge of her vision, but could never find him when she turned.

Chapter 24

"Princess," Sylvia said quietly, when they had been sitting in silence together for a quarter hour, two days after the festival of new beginnings.

"Yes?"

"Would Aliria hurt a baby to end a war?"

"No," she said immediately, and then considered. She thought of Erika, who had never wanted anything but to be a mother, and who was a stranger to her children. Of Annabelle, who had always wanted to marry for love, who should have been able to as a sixth child, and hadn't. Of her father, who had started this war wanting only to end it, but had reasoned, eventually, that if everyone else was trying to expand their borders, Aliria might as well do the same. Of Joel, who hadn't wanted to be a soldier because he hadn't wanted to hurt anyone, and who had now killed over twenty men. "I wouldn't," she said, suddenly unsure she could speak for anyone else.

Sylvia nodded slowly. "What do you know of the new queen of Ibanar?"

Eloise frowned, puzzled by the sudden change of subject. "Young— very young, for her king. She was a foundling, wasn't she? Raised in a temple not far from the palace."

"I've been to that temple several times. I bring them foundlings and refugees and supplicants. They give me supplies for my next journey, next group of refugees. I've never spoken with the queen, but I saw her many times, when she was just a girl who lived in the temple. I know her on sight."

"All right," Eloise said, still unsure where this was going.

247

"The last time I took a group of refugees to the port, I saw her. Boarding a ship to Kire with the refugees. There were several people clearly with her, all dressed like refugees as well, but you could see they weren't. Too clean. Too confident, too comfortable. And she was heavily pregnant."

"He sent his wife and heir to Kire?"

"I think so." She frowned. "It makes sense. If I had children, I wouldn't want them on this island, in this war. I don't want it for the children I've seen, helped, but they haven't any parents, or at least any who want them, and you can't board a baby onto a ship alone, so on to the temples they go."

Eloise stood. "I need—I need to think about this. To talk to someone about it."

"Princess?"

"Yes?"

"I am a good killer, despite evidence to the contrary with Jeremy. If that baby dies, you'll die next."

~

An hour later, Eloise found herself back in Sylvia's room, Joel and Jeremy with her. They were the two people whose judgement she trusted most—foolish, perhaps, but true nonetheless. And this was Sylvia's information, and Sylvia's war, in a much more personal way than it was any of theirs.

Sylvia told the story again, and the four of them sat there for a few minutes, thinking.

"If we kidnapped the queen and her child in Kire," Joel said, "we could hold them ransom for an end to the war."

It was exactly what Eloise had feared when she was kidnapped. Except that she was one adult child of a king who had many children, and many of them older than her. This was the king of Ibanar's only child—an infant he'd waited thirty years for, and had not even met— and his wife, as well.

To have your baby kidnapped by the enemy, after you'd sent him hundreds of miles away to protect him, sacrificed all those first moments you'd waited decades to see—it wouldn't matter who technically won the war after that, who wrote the history books, what those books said. Eloise would always know Aliria was the villain in this fight.

"We can't hurt them," Sylvia said. "I won't let anyone hurt them."

Jeremy didn't say anything. Eloise couldn't tell what he thought.

"It needn't be Aliria that kidnaps them," Joel said.

"What are you thinking?" Jeremy asked.

"It's better you don't know details." He turned to her. "Do you trust me, Eloise?"

"Yes," she said. Probably she shouldn't. But she did.

"Then let me do this. Let me end the war."

"The baby—" Sylvia started.

"I won't hurt the baby. I won't hurt the queen. I won't disgrace Aliria. Eloise."

"Yes," she said. "Yes. Do it."

"All we know is that she got on a ship for Kire," Jeremy said. "She could be anywhere. Even if she's still in the port city, that's thousands of people."

"I can do it. I can find her."

"Are you sure?" Eloise asked.

"I'm sure." He stood. "I'm not doing it for Aliria; I don't care about Aliria. I'm not even doing it for you, Eloise. I just want this all to be over."

"I understand."

"Good. Then I need you to utilize your best and most hated skill."

"And which one would that be?"

"Make a scene. In about an hour. Something that'll hold everyone's attention, so no one notices me leaving. I can get around quietly, usually, but I don't want to take any chances. We don't want anyone making connections, later."

"Even if no one notices you leaving," Jeremy said, "won't they notice you're gone?"

"No, I don't think they will. If anyone seems suspicious, Eloise can go to my room and yell a little."

She nodded slowly.

"Don't tell your family. It'll complicate things. I—Ellie?"

"Joel?"

"I—I just—" He bent down and kissed her, not on the lips but on the cheek, and then he turned and walked away.

It felt like a goodbye. It was a goodbye—he would be gone for months, if he was going to Kire. But it felt, somehow, more permanent than that.

"Is he leaving right now?" Jeremy asked. "For Kire?"

"I'm sure he'll talk to his men and gather his things, first."

"And we're trusting him to singlehandedly—"

"I am," Eloise said. "You're free to do as you please."

"Eloise, don't—I just meant that this is a lot, and very sudden. Surely a little more planning—"

"You don't want to know," Sylvia said. "He didn't become a bandit king by accident. The child and the queen will be safe; that's all you need to know."

Jeremy turned to her. "What kind of scene will you make?" he asked.

Eloise took a breath, and then another. Ben was dead, and Julian married. Erika and Theo were on the battlefield still. The least she could do for the war effort was to sacrifice what little may remain of her reputation.

"Well. I think it's time to announce our broken engagement."

~

"I'm leaving," Joel said, and Chris, Fuller, and Alem all tuned to stare at him.

"What, now?"

"Without us?"

"For how long?"

"Yes, yes, and likely several months."

"Joel, what's going on?"

"It's just a little project for Eloise."

"A little project doesn't take several months."

"All right, so it's a big project." He found the bag he was looking for, and began stuffing supplies into it. "If anyone asks after me, I'm sulking in the day and skulking in the night, as I have been since the last fight with Eloise. Stay here, live your lives, but wait to hear from me. No one should know I'm gone. Eloise and Jeremy are covering for me—help them if they ask it."

Eloise and Jeremy spent their allotted hour planning the scene they would make, with occasional input from Sylvia.

(She'd grown much more comfortable with Jeremy, in the short time since the three of them were last in a room together. Eloise was glad.)

"I'm the one who broke the engagement," Jeremy said. "I should be the one to take the blame."

"You have a reputation to preserve; I don't. And if we tell them you broke it, they'll want to know why, and attention from a bored, gossip-hungry court is the last thing Sylvia needs when the two of you are barely starting your new beginning."

"I am still here," Sylvia pointed out. "In fact, you're sitting on my bed."

"Well, then. Do you want the whole court discussing Jeremy's idiotic infatuation with the woman who tried to kill him? Do you want to deal with the petitions to free you for the sake of your romance, and the opposing petitions to return you to the dungeons where you belong, once people take an interest in what we've done with you?"

"Not particularly."

Eloise turned back to Jeremy, triumphant. "See? It's for the best. And it won't surprise anyone. There are still whispers about my display with Joel, and my fight with Julian after, and that was ages ago."

"What are you going to say? You can't say you're leaving me for him; it'll be suspicious, no one seeing you together for months after an announcement like that."

They argued for a while longer—for as long as they could afford to argue—before setting out for a suitably public location.

~

He made his way out of the palace unnoticed, everyone's attention thoroughly occupied, everyone heading the opposite direction from him, whispers spreading quickly—the princess and the baron were having a fight right outside the throne room.

It would be easier if he had a horse, but stealing one was too risky at this stage. So was buying one, for that matter. He had adequate, if not significant, funds; did it really count as stealing if it was all going to be used in service of Aliria?

His best bet was to head for the harbor, get work on a ship off the island, and make his way to Kire from wherever it docked. He should have enough sailing experience to get the job. True, he'd never sailed outside the Basin, but surely it couldn't be too different.

~

"We can't," Jeremy said. "It wouldn't be right."

"Why not? It was never a love match—what does it matter?"

"It matters because you're still in love with him!"

"I'm not," Eloise said, and she felt dozens of eyes on her, and if she was near tears it was only, she told herself, because she was an excellent actress. "I'm not."

"If you marry me," Jeremy said, "you'll regret it. You'll resent me."

She shook her head.

"He loves you. He told me so."

He—she knew Joel loved her, but when on earth had he talked to Jeremy about it?

Her father chose that moment to emerge from the throne room behind them. "What is going on out here?"

"Nothing, Father. Only me, embarrassing myself for your court's amusement, as usual."

"Eloise," her father said.

"Eloise," Jeremy said.

She turned back to him, gathering as much calm as she could. "We won't be married, then. Do please let Joel know, since you're apparently close enough to discuss me, that I don't want to see either of you any time soon."

She wasn't sure that making a scene had been completely necessary. But—Jeremy had gone along with it. He wouldn't have, if he hadn't thought it would help. And this was bigger than breaking a friend out for a morning. This was the end of the war, and making sure Aliria wasn't implicated in whatever plan Joel had.

They couldn't take chances—about a dozen people had been aware of Sylvia's absence before word reached Eloise. She didn't think any of them had made the connection to Joel. But Eloise wasn't the only one in the palace who would have; just the only one who knew Sylvia was gone. And she'd heard a nobleman complain at dinner one night about the time his cloak and his wife's had gone missing for a few hours, then reappeared, just where he'd left them. And there had been whispers, brought to her by cousins because everyone else knew better than to gossip about that kind of thing in her hearing, that Joel had been seen in the hallway with an unknown woman. No one knew enough about Sylvia to accuse Joel of releasing her, but they had seen him that day. So he was right. No one could know he was gone, for this.

Chapter 25

He found a merchant caravan that evening, and bought passage to the harbor, where he quickly found work on a foreign merchant ship sailing out. He gave them the same false name he'd given Eloise; it would let the others learn what happened, if something went wrong, or if his plan changed.

~

She waited four days, during which time she did not speak to Jeremy and did not speak of Joel. Then she knocked on his door, and said to Fuller, who answered, "I need to speak with Joel."

Fuller let her in. He seemed to be the only one there, which she didn't like, but as long as everyone outside thought Joel was there too, it would be fine.

"Did he tell you what he was doing?" she asked.

"Project for you. No details."

"Good." Fuller scowled, and she added, "I don't have details, either."

He nodded. "We're having his meals brought up as usual. Wasteful, perhaps, but it maintains the illusion, and Chris will usually eat the extra."

"I'll need your help pulling this off. Yours, especially—you're the closest in build to him."

"What exactly are you thinking?"

"I'll tell you later. Someone will be coming down the hall soon—I need them to hear me yelling at Joel."

255

She'd timed this visit carefully. They stood there in silence for a moment, until Eloise heard the expected footsteps. She didn't think she needed to make too big a show of things.

"I can't believe you," she said, loudly enough to be heard through the door. "Every time I think that you—that maybe we could—I should have known better."

She opened the door, met the eyes of her father's cousin who was blatantly eavesdropping, and slammed it shut again.

"Not a word," she said to Fuller, still loud enough to be overheard.

A few minutes later she opened the door again, and slunk down the hall. It had gone very well—she had known there would be people passing through, on the way to the duchess' room to work together on their tapestry as they always did on this day of the week, but hadn't realized that particular cousin would be one of them. She was a dreadful gossip.

Making up with Jeremy was a more—though not completely—private affair. She caught him coming out of a meeting, and they went together to the garden; it was still quite cold, and not many people would be there.

"I am sorry," Jeremy said, and didn't elaborate on what, since they still might be heard.

"It worked. I just wasn't expecting..."

"I know. Let's not do that again, please. I don't like making scenes."

She nodded. "Have you spoken to Sylvia? I have, but I didn't want to ask about you; she's sensitive about it."

"Just briefly, to let her know things went as expected. I don't want to—to pressure her."

"You should go see her. It's been a week."

"Tomorrow," he said. "I have another meeting in a quarter hour."

~

Sailing across the ocean was, as it turned out, more difficult than sailing across the Basin. He was a worker, not a passenger, and there wasn't time to be seasick. He worked through the nausea.

~

The next time Jeremy came to see her, he said, "I've met with the men who'll be supervising construction on the estate. I'll meet with them once more before they go to the site, and I wanted your opinion first."

Sylvia sat up straighter, wary. What should her opinion matter? This was a new beginning, and the beginning was certainly too soon for her to be involved in the construction of his home. "Why?"

"I don't need a home as large as my father's. It would be wasteful, especially with the state of things, with the war."

She nodded.

"Do you remember when I told you I'd move your whole village onto the estate, if I could?"

"I remember."

"I want to take advantage of the new construction, to—to help. The people you haven't gotten to Kire yet, the people who need somewhere safe to stay. So. Is it better to rebuild the estate just as large, so people can be there, and protected by the walls? Or is it better to build a smaller estate, and put the rest of the new construction outside the walls?"

"Inside the walls would likely be safer, but it wouldn't feel safer. Most people won't feel comfortable so close to a baron. Especially if they're not Alirian, and if you're taking in refugees from that area, several will probably be from Olion."

"Then we'll rebuild smaller, and focus more funds on the village. Thank you, Sylvia." He smiled at her, then turned back to the door.

"You're leaving?"

"I don't want to—to make you feel—"

"Stay, please? Just sit with me a bit?"

"All right."

He joined her on the floor, back against the bed, and they sat there, not touching but close enough they could, for a long time. They didn't talk. Sylvia thought, for the first time, about the bed behind them, about the closed door, about the utter lack of supervision. These weren't the kind of things one worried about, living the life she had been. But it mattered, now. If anyone other than Jeremy, Joel, and the princess—anyone who cared—knew—well, she wouldn't have to marry Jeremy, but it would be difficult for either of them to marry anyone else.

Jeremy didn't want to marry anyone else. He hadn't mentioned it in a while, but she knew—she knew he still wanted to marry her.

She wasn't sure what she wanted, but if she was ever going to marry anyone, it could only be him.

Jeremy was safe. She could sit beside him, close enough to touch, alone behind a closed door, and she wasn't afraid.

She hadn't been very afraid, with Joel, but it was still—

She had nearly killed Jeremy, and she was essentially his prisoner, and she still felt safer by his side than she had any place since her home burned down.

But what future could there be, when the girl he'd loved had burned with that home, and left behind something so different?

As long as they didn't talk, as long as they just sat here, she could pretend.

~

Eloise made a point of getting caught near Joel's room once every few days. Occasionally she went in, and passed some time making quiet conversation with anyone there, or alternately shouted her half of an imagined argument, while one of the men handled Joel's part quietly enough that no eavesdroppers would realize the voice was wrong.

She spent less time with Sylvia and Jeremy both as they spent more with each other. Her niece, nephew, and youngest sister occupied some of her time; she tried to avoid her parents. She was keeping a monumental secret from them, and knew that they already didn't trust her as much as her siblings.

The weather was warming, and she missed Tulip so much—she might have been angrier at Joel for Tulip than for all the rest of it, by then.

She couldn't expect him back any time soon. She knew that; he was planning to go all the way to Kire and back. But still, every time she went to his room, she hoped. The palace felt different, without Joel in it.

~

They quickly developed a new routine, in which Jeremy came at least three times a week to Sylvia's room, and then sat silently beside her until other commitments forced him away.

He wasn't quite sure what to make of it. But he was happy with any time Sylvia wanted to spend with him.

"Show me your scars, Jeremy."

He'd been sitting there for over an hour now. It was the first time she had spoken in that time, and he didn't understand at first.

"Show me your scars," she said again. "From where I stabbed you."

"Oh." He lifted his shirt to reveal two gashes, still ugly and red, and she reached over slowly, her fingers dancing over the marks. It was the closest she'd come to touching him since the stabbing.

"Do they hurt still?"

"Not so much now."

"I'm glad."

Chapter 26

It was a festival day. The whole court would be out in the gardens until late in the evening, specifically in the garden that Eloise's bedroom window looked out on. It was the perfect time to enact the next step in her plan to keep everyone thoroughly convinced that Joel was still in the palace.

Fuller was…not enthusiastic.

"It's for the whole kingdom," Chris said.

"What do I care about Aliria? What do you care about Aliria?"

"It's for the whole island," Alem said.

Thus convinced, Fuller submitted reluctantly to the careful rearranging of his hair into Joel's usual style. Satisfied that he could carry out the next steps, and meet her as arranged, Eloise went down to the gardens.

There was no rush; their plan was dependent on darkness, and it was still early in the day.

She had an old dress of Erika's to wear, more suitable for the occasion than any of her own, and sisters to entertain. Annabelle was home for the festival, freshly back from Olion, and she and Maria would want to spend the day with their only other sibling still at home.

It had been years since they had the time and energy to celebrate this holy day as it was meant to be celebrated, the entire palace gathered in the gardens unless they'd elected to go into the city instead, to spend the day with friends and family who didn't work within the walls. The music was loud, and the food amazing, and everyone in too good a mood to be unpleasant. People who usually found Eloise painfully undignified, despite years of her best efforts, only smiled indulgently as she tore past the neglected topiaries, chasing her nephew. People Eloise hadn't seen smile in years were laughing.

Seven or eight kitchen maids were huddled around a fountain, tasting the food they usually only carried to others. Everyone had stripes of glittery blue powder on their faces, carefully rationed out so the dukes and the stableboys could be equally decorated.

The one year Joel had been here for this festival, everyone had known by the way the powder streaked, and by the stains on their fingers, that they had been kissing behind the roses, but no one had bothered to reprimand them; it was too happy an occasion.

For several years now, the powder had been distributed amongst the family, staff left to supply their own, and everyone on the grounds had received one pastry—they chose whether sweet or savory—and Eloise had joined her parents and whichever siblings were available to watch the moon rise and the sacred stars fall from the sky.

Tonight, the whole palace would watch the stars together, and then dance until they could dance no more.

It would be a shame to ruin it. But no one had seen Joel in weeks, and the scandal she was about to create would certainly prevent anyone from noticing that he was gone.

"No Joel tonight?" Jeremy asked, as he came by with a basket—he must have been gathering food for Sylvia. Only prisoners were excluded from the celebration.

"No Joel," Eloise confirmed. She glanced around the garden—Jeremy had waited to start their scripted conversation until Eloise was conveniently surrounded by horrible gossips.

"Someday you'll make it a week without fighting."

She sighed. "No more fighting. I'm just…finished."

"If you say so," Jeremy said, and continued on his way.

Eloise checked the position of the sun—a few more hours. That would leave Jeremy plenty of time with Sylvia before returning to the garden so he could report later on the success of their plan. And it would leave her plenty of time to dance with her sisters and her sister's children.

~

Sylvia sat on the floor below her window, listening to the faint music from outside. She couldn't see the proceedings from the window, which was a shame; she was rather curious about how noblemen and women would celebrate this particular festival. She couldn't imagine people in ermine cloaks and golden shoes doing the folk dances her village had.

(It was, in Sylvia's opinion, far too warm now for ermine cloaks, but she had seen a man wearing one through the window yesterday. Though it had admittedly been a little raggedy, as were most of the clothes she saw here. The war was hard even on the rich, it appeared, if perhaps not hard enough.)

Whatever the dances might look like, the music was familiar. Sylvia hadn't properly celebrated any of the twelve holy days, or the occasional Olin religious festivals of her childhood, in years. On the rare occasions when she had been at the right part of the island on the right date, there had been battles to hide from, or wounds to treat, or dead to mourn.

Jeremy came, eventually, with a basket of food from the festival, and a small pot of blue powder which he applied for her. They sat on the floor together to eat, the music still playing outside, her skin tingling where she knew the path of his fingers was marked in blue. It had been two months since the day of new beginnings, and they'd spent plenty of time together since, though little of it talking.

"By the next holy day, I'll have you out of here," he said.

"How?"

"Eloise and I have both tried, but the king—there have just been too many things going on. You're not a threat, obviously. I just have to—it'll be easier, now that there's peace with Olion, now that all the confusion of Joel's conspiracy has resolved. I'll make him understand. I'll convince him to release you."

"And then what?"

"Whatever you want. If you—if you want to disappear again, I'll help you get the supplies you need, and then I won't look for you, I won't..." He trailed off.

"I don't think I want to disappear."

"What do you want?" he asked, and she tried and failed to remember the last time she'd been asked that question.

"Sylvia?"

"I'm thinking."

"All right," he said, and handed her another pastry. She ate it slowly while she searched for words.

"I don't know how to make you understand—I hardly understand it myself. But it isn't that I hate you, or am angry with you, or even that I don't love you—it is only that I feel so dead, sometimes, and I don't— all of the world, Jeremy, all of it is ash, but you are something I am still afraid to lose."

"You won't. I'll be here, as close as you want me."

"I would give you everything I have left, if it could make me believe now that you would stay, and that I would feel for you the way I can remember feeling—if I could feel anything the way I remember feeling it—but I've been so numb, and so frightened, for so long now, and I can't believe in anything yet."

"You don't have to. Tell me what you want, Sylvia. Anything. Solitude, romance—if you want the security of my name with no obligations, I'll marry you tomorrow and never ask you for anything."

"I think—I hope that I will be able to want more than that."

"I'll be patient. I'm good at that."

"I remember." She shifted her body slowly to lean into his side, and he put his arm around her.

She wasn't sure that he would stay, or that he would be happy if he did. He hardly knew her, and she'd hardly given him the chance to change that—she was so afraid of chasing him away, and so afraid that he would regret it later if she didn't. She wasn't sure that he would stay. But he was here tonight.

~

Fuller had made his way into her rooms by the time Eloise returned, taking advantage of the empty hallways. They didn't speak as she set about lighting every candle she could find. Soon, soon, everyone would look up at the moon. And on the way there, they would see her window, huge and brightly lit.

There was about a half hour between the rise of the moon and the fall of the stars, and it was the falling stars that were holy. She would still watch them, though she may not make it downstairs in time to watch them with her family.

It would be strange, to watch them alone. Fuller wouldn't stay—he didn't like her, didn't want to get caught here, and didn't worship the same gods. She wouldn't want him to stay, anyway.

"Is it time?" he asked.

She checked the window, careful not to step fully in front of it. The moon was rising, slowly.

It was time.

She stepped in front of the window, knowing everyone below could see her silhouette, knowing anyone who didn't already know this was her room would learn very soon. And then she reached out, grabbed Fuller's hand, and pulled him into view.

It was awkward. He wasn't Joel; he wasn't even Jeremy. Even Chris and Alem would have been easier. And his own discomfort with the situation didn't help.

She pulled him closer and closer, until they would be one shape in the light of the window. She didn't actually kiss him, because she had some self-respect still, but she brought their faces close enough together that no one on the ground would see the difference.

What did people do? She thought it would come at least somewhat naturally, if she—if Fuller was—but they were performing for an audience, and they hadn't, perhaps, blocked out the scene as thoroughly as they should have.

She'd have lost Fuller if she'd insisted on a full rehearsal. She barely got him here as it was.

Clothing had to come off; fortunately he was wearing plenty of it. She put enough distance between them that any watchers would be able to clearly see how she reached out and slid his vest off.

"Turn me around," she told him as she did, "and undo my laces."

He did, maneuvering her away from the window as he did, and removing his hands immediately after.

"Do you think that's enough?" she asked. He'd had that affair with that duchess; he would know more than her about what it looked like.

"Almost," he said. "Joel was the shy one? When you were children?"

"Yes."

He knocked over a candle, then bent to pick it up, straightening to find himself looking straight out the window, then ducking immediately out of view.

"Start dousing candles; he's just realized we're visible."

"I'll get them. You get back to your room before anyone else shows up." She didn't think anyone would abandon the festival at this sacred moment to protect her virtue, but they couldn't risk it. Fuller being seen in her bedchamber would be catastrophic.

Fuller left; she would thank him properly later. For now, she had falling stars to witness, and a festival to watch from afar. Rejoining it now would spoil it for everyone else.

But perhaps she didn't have to be alone. If someone did come searching, and found her rooms empty, they would assume she and Joel had found another room to hide in.

Jeremy was still in Sylvia's room, which hadn't been the plan—he was supposed to be witnessing from the ground. But she couldn't blame him for it, not when his clothing was smeared in blue from the woman he loved falling asleep on his shoulder.

She had woken when Eloise came in, and the three of them gathered at the window together. The view wasn't the best, but they could still see the stars fall, and when it was over, Sylvia turned to her and said, "You have to show me how the nobles dance."

She did, and Sylvia shared her dances in return, and the three of them fell asleep, hours later, on the floor of Sylvia's room.

Chapter 27

When the ship made port, he bought a horse and a map—with money stolen from various members of the Alirian court—and made his way to Kire as quickly as possible. It was harder than travelling on the island. Few of the people he met spoke his language, at least until he was well into Kire, which had taken so many refugees. With the terrain and customs unfamiliar, he didn't dare to spend nights sleeping wherever he found himself when it was too dark or he was too tired to continue. Time and money were wasted in far too many inns. But he had not landed too far away, and the lack of battles and soldiers to avoid made travel more straightforward.

He had to hope the queen was still in the port city Sylvia said she would have landed in.

It took three days of searching the city to find what he was looking for, a stained glass charm hanging in a window, the symbol of devotion to the Alirian eighth god. He watched the house for another day, to be sure, before breaking into the queen's small room while she was otherwise occupied.

He sat quietly in the dark and waited. The queen entered, at last, alone, and began lighting sconces with the candle in her hand. She didn't notice the intruder. He waited just a bit longer, until she'd set down the candle; he didn't want her to drop it, and start a fire.

"Your Majesty," he said, as soon as her hands were free.

She jumped, and turned in place slowly, fear melting into pleasure as she saw his face.

"Joel!"

She flung herself at him, and he stepped forward to catch her.

Chapter 28

"Hello, Lissie." She pulled back, a little, and Joel held her at arms' length to study her. "Been busy since I left, haven't you? You've grown up."

"I didn't think I'd ever see you again! I left the marker every night, like I promised, but there was no way to get word to you when we left the country."

"I'll always find you, Lissie. Now. I want to meet my—is it a niece, or a nephew?"

"A nephew. Wait here; I'll get him from the nurse."

~

He'd missed his mother's death. He had come home wealthier than he'd ever imagined, and all too aware he could never share it properly with his family, not without drawing too much attention. He shouldn't even be visiting, really.

His mother had died less than a day before he arrived, of the same fever that was doing its best to kill his sister. He'd looked at his bag of ill-gotten goods, and he'd looked at her ashen face, and he'd made a choice. He'd given his mother's neighbor the money to pay for two cremations, because he could afford it, and it would be more convenient, if anyone from his growing list of enemies came looking, for Lissie to be assumed dead. The neighbor would know the truth, of course—she must not have told.

He'd bought a horse and taken Lissie deeper into Ibanar, to the next big city, and paid for treatment. And when she recovered, he'd taken her to the capital and dropped her off at one of the best temples for foundlings and widows.

The only other option had been to take her with him. And he couldn't make his baby sister live like an outlaw.

He had purchased a stained glass window hanging of a colorful, iridescent bird while passing illegally through Aliria, months ago, intending it as a gift for her. It was a religious token, for worshippers of the eighth god, the god of light, sun, and color, though he'd just thought it was pretty.

"Tell them you come from the north. Tell them you swore to your Alirian mother before she died that you would hang the glass at whatever window you slept near, so that the sun god could always find you. Give them your Ibanari name, and tell them you have no surviving family. I'll visit when I can, and use the bird to find your room."

He'd managed to visit her about once a year, until he recognized her name in the king's engagement announcement. But he had no chance of infiltrating the palace, and then he'd heard the rumors she'd been sent away, but no one could tell him where.

It had taken everything in him not to race for the nearest port the moment Sylvia brought it up.

~

"Now what?" Lissie asked, hours later, the sun creeping over the horizon, the baby sleeping soundly in her lap.

"Now I kidnap you."

"And then what?"

"It depends. I told Eloise that I would find you and end the war. But—do you want to go back to your husband?"

"It's not so bad. He's kind to me. And he never touches me unless we're trying to make a baby." She frowned, her nose crinkling up in that way he'd missed so much. "He'll want another one, once we get home. I guess it's risky, having only one heir."

"You don't have to go back to him."

"I do. I will. That and missing you are the only problems. There will be less pressure, now that he has an heir. Especially if the war ends soon. And maybe you can—maybe—"

"We'll be able to see each other. I'll make sure of it. No matter what, we'll see each other. But you don't have to go back."

"You made a promise to your princess."

"My princess hates me. And I promised to protect you before I knew she existed. If you don't want to go back to the king, you won't."

"I want to go back. He—he didn't force me, Joel. He chose me because the gods said I could bear him children, but he gave me room to refuse. The priestesses would never have allowed one of us to be taken by force. I know that you don't like him, I know he banished you, but he's kind to me."

"I'm glad," Joel said.

She nodded. "We made a deal. I'll bear him two children, perhaps three, if anything goes wrong or one of them seems sickly. I don't like making babies, but he only ever touches me for that, not—not for his own pleasure, and he never will again once we have enough heirs. In exchange, I'm safe and protected and want for nothing. Aside from war issues, I mean. He even said I'm welcome to take lovers my own age, once we have the heirs, and he'll raise any children as his own, as long as they're younger and won't inherit the crown. I don't want to take any lovers, but he—he doesn't want to keep me locked away, you see? He wants me to have my freedom."

"And you want your freedom to be at his side."

"I—I do, yes."

"Does he care for you?"

"Yes. I think he does."

"If you were taken, but he still had his heir. Would he search for you?"

"Yes," she said again. "Definitely."

"Travelling with a baby is hard. Can you be away from him for a few months?"

She frowned. "You'll end the war? I'll be reunited with him in a safe Ibanar, and you'll be able to visit me?"

"That's the plan."

"Would it be dangerous for him to come along?"

"Yes. Children his age have done it, but it would be much safer for him here. Your staff would be able to take him directly home. There would be guards to accompany him. You and I will be taking a much longer, harder route. We'll have to evade Alirian and Ibanari soldiers. We may encounter any number of outlaws and bandits, many of whom have reason to dislike me. We might not have consistent access to good food. If you need him to come we'll make it work, but it will be safer and easier without him."

"You promise you'll bring me back to him?"

"I promise."

"All right," she said. "All right. To end the war. His wet nurse is from Olion, and she's already agreed to come back to the island with us when the time comes. She'll care for him while I'm gone. Just give me tonight with him, please? We can leave tomorrow."

"Tomorrow," he agreed.

"What time?"

"I'll surprise you. Remember, it has to look like I'm taking you against your will."

"I know. I wish—he'll be so worried."

Joel frowned. "You understand you can't ever tell your husband the truth."

"I do."

"I mean it, Lissie. Never. I could hang. We could both hang."

"I understand. I'm not a child anymore, Joel. I made oaths to my kingdom along with oaths to my husband, and the kingdom comes first. If this is how we end the war, now, without further bloodshed, I can keep a secret. It's not as if I'm new at this. I've kept yours, haven't I?"

Chapter 29

In Julian's absence, the task of lecturing Eloise fell to her mother.

She had woken still and sore on Sylvia's floor, in time to intercept the maid and the guard bringing her breakfast. Sylvia and Jeremy were still asleep, twined together, more comfortable with each other than they could be awake, and she didn't want to disturb them. She left the breakfast and crept back to her own room, and her waiting attendants had the sense not to ask where she'd spent the night. It was about an hour before she was summoned to her mother's study.

"Do you know what happened last night?" the queen asked her.

"I have some idea, yes."

"You're not a child anymore. I understand that you have never valued your reputation as you should, I understand that your engagement was broken, I understand that I cannot control what you do behind closed doors. But to allow your indiscretions to be viewed by the entire palace—"

"I didn't mean to be seen."

Her mother sighed. "Dare I ask how far things went?"

"Not as far as I would have liked," Eloise lied, and watched her mother close her eyes and take two deep breaths, a sure sign that she was struggling to control her emotions.

"Well. Thank all the gods for that. Will you marry him?"

"I doubt it."

"You realize how unlikely you are to marry anyone else."

"I realize."

She sighed. "Eloise, what am I going to do with you?"

"I'm sorry, Mother."

"I need to think. Get out of my sight. Stay out of everyone's sight, if you can manage it. I would tell you to relay that order to Joel, but no one has seen much of him lately."

"Too many soldiers coming through. He got sick of being punched."

"So one of you has some sense. Such a shame it isn't you."

"Yes, Mother."

"Go on, now. I'll call for you when I've decided what to do with you."

~

Jeremy woke in the morning, and realized three things.

Sylvia was sleeping in his arms, he had missed at least one meeting, and he didn't care about meetings at all.

He knew Eloise had been there when they fell asleep; he hoped she hadn't left too long ago. He didn't know how the Sylvia of today felt about the matter, but before, she would have been mortified to know she'd spent a night alone with a man who wasn't her husband.

A meal had been brought, likely gone cold now—he really hoped Eloise hadn't left long ago, hoped that she had been there to prevent the maid and the guard seeing them.

He was tempted to go out and find a new, warm breakfast for them both, but he didn't want Sylvia to wake up alone. He would stay here, holding her as long as he was allowed to.

He had to get her out of here. She'd been confined to the same small room for months now; he didn't know how she hadn't yet gone mad. She had nothing to do but sit and pace and think. It was, he supposed, not as difficult as being in a prison cell, which would have a similar lack of space and entertainment, while being far less comfortable. But "not as bad as a prison cell" was not nearly good enough. He had to get her out. He had to convince the king. But his relationship with the king had deteriorated since the very public dissolution of his engagement, and the king was busier than ever, having had to take back all the responsibilities previously handled by Julian. He needed to arrange an official audience to make an official request, but the king was booked out for weeks.

It wasn't long before Sylvia woke, turning to face him, but not pulling away.

"Oh," she said. "We fell asleep on the floor?"

"We did."

"And the princess?"

"Gone when I woke; I'm not sure when she left."

Sylvia nodded. "Your whole face is blue."

"Yours, too. I suppose we should wash."

"Later," she said. "Unless you have to go?"

"I don't have anywhere more important to be."

"Good. I want—I want to be with you."

~

Joel spent the hours before the kidnapping purchasing two tickets to sail back to Ibanar, leaving that day. He could work for his own passage, but he wouldn't ask Lissie to. The money for the tickets was stolen from her or her companions; he was sure she wouldn't mind.

They would land at the same port she'd sailed out of, the same port most refugees sailed out of. From there they would go up the coast, into Aliria, nearly into Olion, and then travel east. It would be easier to cross the island, west to east, while they were still in Ibanar; they looked Ibanari, and travelling with an also-Ibanari woman would make him look less suspicious than travelling alone, or with others clearly from other parts of the island. Lissie had not been queen long enough to be recognized by most. But he needed to stop by the Alirian capital, so they would have to put off the journey east for later.

Perhaps it would have been easier to go back the same way he'd come, but he was more comfortable travelling on his own island, and this way they would be out at sea before anyone could mobilize to track her down.

The kidnapping was easy enough. He'd considered putting on a bigger show, but that would likely require him to hurt someone, and these were all people his sister knew and cared for.

He came back when she was in a room alone with the baby. She kissed his little forehead goodbye. Joel dropped his ransom note in the cradle. Then she screamed, to draw attention, and they quickly knocked some furniture about, to make it look like a struggle, before leaving through the window.

An hour later they were at sea. Ships left for the island only once every three or four days; it would be enough of a head start, he hoped, even if her people figured out immediately what direction they were taking.

He thought they would. He hadn't signed the note, but he'd used his own language, a language unique to the island, and he'd requested a ransom in Ibanari currency.

Of course, they may assume it was another refugee, here in the city. But he would send another note directly to the king once they landed, which should clear things up.

"You're sure this'll work?" Lissie asked him.

"No," he admitted. "But I'm hoping."

~

Eloise returned to her mother the next day, and received a list of new responsibilities and expectations.

"If you don't intend to marry Joel," her mother said, "if you plan to stay here in the palace, unwed, you must have a role."

"Surely you don't want me to marry Joel."

"I didn't. But after your display the other night…"

"I'm sorry, Mother."

She sighed. "I wish Julian were here. Or Ben. They always knew what to do with you."

They had; her parents never did.

She was a woman grown; it shouldn't matter that her parents didn't understand her.

"Give me the list," she said. "It may take me a while—you know I'm a slow learner."

Chapter 30

Jeremy had gone. Not forever, not even for long. But Sylvia hated the knowledge that he wasn't in the building.

He would be away for a week. He had gone to oversee the start of construction on his estate; he would be there for two days only, the rest of the week taken up in travelling back and forth.

Things were improving, between them, and she was afraid the time apart would compromise that. She was finally learning how to talk to him again, finally finding the courage to really confide in him. She had told him last night, "This war has hurt me in ways I didn't know I could be hurt, and I'm not your Sylvia anymore. I don't know who I am."

He had said, "You're Sylvia. Any Sylvia that ever exists is my Sylvia, as long as she wants to be."

But then he'd gone away.

The princess has been in her room most of the morning. She had been quiet and listless since the night of the festival. Sylvia knew what her plan had been, to make a show of Joel being absolutely here still, and could imagine it had been poorly received, though of course Eloise wasn't talking to her about it.

She visited a little less often now, probably so that Jeremy could visit more often. But Sylvia was feeling increasingly trapped and miserable in her room, and would happily take more visits from both of them.

277

"I should go," the princess said, after most of a morning sitting mostly in silence. "I've a meeting with a housekeeper."

"A housekeeper?"

"I'm learning about the management of an estate. I have meetings with everyone."

"You haven't learned about estate management before now?" She thought of Jeremy, of the way his father had refused to teach him what he needed to, had made it so difficult for him to seek the knowledge elsewhere. She thought of Jeremy's father's resentment of him, and how Eloise spoke so seldom of her large family, and usually to report one of them was angry with her.

"It's not—like that," Eloise said. "Like Jeremy."

Of course, she'd been engaged to him too. And she knew Sylvia well enough by now to follow the pattern of her thoughts.

"I'm a poor student; I always have been. My training in many areas was cut short because I wasn't yet where I ought to be when war broke out, and then all my instructors had more pressing tasks than my continued education. And these are new lessons; I oughtn't to have been managing any estates. It's busywork, something for my mother to do with me now that I'll not likely marry, and foist my inadequacies on some other family."

"So, a bit like Jeremy," Sylvia suggested quietly.

"They love me. They just don't know what to make of me."

She left not long after.

~

The meeting with the housekeeper went well enough. Eloise wandered listlessly about, when it was finished.

The halls were so empty. Ben gone, Julian gone, Joel gone. So many soldiers headed back for the battlefield, including her remaining older siblings.

At least there was Jeremy. Only because his home was destroyed and his beloved imprisoned, so she felt guilty for being glad he was there. But it was something.

She let herself into Sylvia's room often, and saw Jeremy as much as she could; now that they were no longer engaged, and that the pressures of war had lessened enough for people to think of gossip again, it wasn't appropriate for them to be too good of friends.

Neither she nor Theo had married, and they hadn't any prospects. Theo would marry eventually; he had to. He was the heir. But it could be years yet, until they were not just stable again but prosperous, until they had something to offer a princess from another land.

Eloise was fairly certain she would never marry—how could she marry anyone but Joel? How could she marry Joel, after everything? She could have married Jeremy. She could have been happy with Jeremy. But she couldn't imagine reaching that level of comfort and familiarity again, starting over with someone new. She'd had one doomed romance and one close friendship; she could hardly ask the gods for more.

Theo would not marry soon. Eloise would not marry at all. Her responsibilities had been few, and her political value was little. She was being trained now to fill her mother's role, to be the lady of the house until Theo married a queen to replace her.

Her parents weren't elderly; Theo would likely still marry before they passed. And the palace was full of people better qualified than her to manage a household the size of a village, aunts and cousins and such. She knew this new role was more to keep her occupied than to fill any real need.

It had been a hard—she didn't know how long it'd been hard for, now. Certainly more than a year. The last round of rumors about Joel, the kidnapping, realizing who Joel was, the journey across the island and back, the discovery of Sylvia, Jeremy's injuries, the breaking of her engagement, Ben's death, Julian's departure, Joel's departure. She appreciated her mother's attempt to distract her, even if it was also a punishment. But she had no interest in managing an estate, and no real skill for it, either.

When she was quite young, she had thought that she and Joel would live a life of endless adventure, coming and going between her family's properties as they pleased, and otherwise travelling throughout the island, and perhaps beyond. When she was engaged to Jeremy, she knew that she would be the lady of his estate, someday, but first there would be the war, and then the rebuilding—it had all felt impossibly far away, and in the meantime she was an unattached princess, untrained in combat, far from inheriting the throne, free to live the life she had always lived.

She hated the palace, without Joel in it. She tried to decide whether she had hated it all these years, and not let herself notice; she thought it was likely.

She didn't need to be in love with Joel to know she'd been trying desperately not to be herself since the moment he'd been charged.

What if he didn't come back?

He would; he had to. He'd left his friends behind. He'd made her a promise. He'd gone through all the trouble of worming his way back into her life. Surely he would be back. He hadn't even been gone long, not considering all he had to do.

She should go to his room again, perhaps stage another fight.

No, she hadn't the energy for a fight, pretend or not. It would be a friendly visit. With any luck, she'd find the room empty, and she could just sit there, in Joel's space, alone.

Alem was seldom in the room anymore, except to sleep, busy helping the doctors and training with them. Fuller had begun to talk to some people about shifting borders, and she suspected he would be asked along as one of the cartographers on a survey soon. Chris had made friends with several young soldiers; they had rotated out, sending those who'd been working as palace guards down to Ibanar, assigning some of the soldiers back from Olion to take their place, and the new guards happened to include several young men about Chris' age.

This had been her home all her life, and even pardoned criminals found a place in it more easily than her.

~

His trip home was brief, and he would have felt guiltier were it not for Sylvia, waiting for him. He had visited various parts of his barony over the last few years, attending to whatever business couldn't be addressed by messenger, but he hadn't set foot on the grounds of his estate since it had burned.

He had been away at the time of the attack, addressing a dispute between tenants several miles south. Having failed to find anyone of political significance to take hostage—not that Jeremy had much political significance, then—the attackers had looted, and burned, and left.

Jeremy's father had, fortunately, been a paranoid man, and much of the wealth tied to the estate had not been actually onsite. Jeremy had lost little beyond the building. There had been some question of whether Aliria would retain the northernmost portion of his barony, where the estate had been, or whether it would go to Olion in the new treaty. But Olion had ceded this territory in favor of others that had been more in contention throughout the war. With the surrounding village burned to ash, and the whole area abandoned, there was little of value for a treaty.

Years after the fire, it was still abandoned, and it hurt to see. All the surviving residents of the estate had been relocated to the best of his abilities. He himself had been relocated to the palace, at the king's invitation. The only survivors of the village were Sylvia and five men who'd been away, fighting in the war; two of those men had since died. Jeremy would, of course, offer whatever he could to the remaining three, once he got around the difficulty of one being the father Sylvia didn't want to see.

He hoped that construction would go quickly, and that the area would soon be occupied again. But for now there was nothing but ash and ruin for miles, and he and all the builders were sleeping in tents.

He'd asked them to prioritize smaller outbuildings that could be constructed quickly over the actual manor house, so that they could sleep in them while they continued to work.

Two days, to approve the finalized plans on site, to supervise the groundbreaking, and he was headed back to the palace. Back to Sylvia.

He had tried and failed to arrange a private audience with the king. He could raise the matter when he wasn't alone with the king, of course, but he didn't want to draw anyone else's attention to Sylvia, who'd been largely forgotten by the court in all the political chaos that followed his stabbing.

He would submit another request. Or he would ask Eloise to raise the matter, and request an audience for him. But her father was still quite angry about the incident on festival day; she wasn't likely to get far with him for at least another week or two.

Soon. Soon he would have her released. And he thought that perhaps, when he had—things had been going very well between them, of late.

Chapter 31

The days dragged on. Eloise tried to calculate how long it would take to go to Kire and back, but it depended heavily on the weather, and besides, she didn't know whether he was going straight there and back—she suspected not. Surely his plan was more complex than that—simply bringing the queen here would not solve the issue of ending the war without making Aliria forever the villain.

She visited Joel's room. She made a point of creeping about late at night. She hadn't been really convinced that no one would notice Joel's absence; she had thought that eventually she would need to make an excuse for his departure, perhaps a worse fight than they'd ever had. But his meals were delivered, and her visits made, and if anyone was suspicious, they hid it not only from her, but from Jeremy as well.

Perhaps they had never really seen Joel as anything but an extension of her.

Her new list of responsibilities was possibly more boring than doing nothing at all. She planned to skip her next scheduled meeting in favor of a visit to Joel's room. It was exactly what everyone expected of her, after all.

~

"I'm meeting with the king tomorrow," Jeremy told her. "Finally."
"And you think he'll release me?" Sylvia asked.
"He will. He has to. You're not a danger to anyone."

283

"I've dreamed for years of killing you."

"Sylvi—"

"They were nightmares."

"Well, I suppose I'm glad of that."

"And then I—I didn't even plan it, you know. I had no idea you would even be here. I just—you shouldn't want me. You shouldn't trust me."

"You didn't mean it."

"I did. When I did it, I did."

"But you regretted it?"

"Of course."

"Then what does it matter?

She sighed. "You're never going to leave me alone, are you?"

"You think I—if you want me to go, Syl, I'll go. Just tell me. I won't—I don't want you hurt anymore, but especially not by me."

"No. I won't—I want you to hurt me forever, Jeremy."

He leaned away. "Was that supposed to be romantic? Because it's quite troubling, actually."

"I mean, things aren't going to get better. Not the way you want them to. I'm not going to be who I was, or who you want me to be, or— I know you only want me to be all right. I know that. But I'm not going to be. I'm so—angry, and afraid, and I don't know how to—how to— and I'm asking you to stay with me anyway."

"Always."

"And I'm asking you not to expect anything easy."

"I don't."

"And I'm asking you to kiss me now."

He did.

~

"Jeremy," the king said, which was a relief—he hadn't spoken directly to the king since the official, public dissolution of the engagement, and he hadn't been certain he would still be addressed so informally.

He bowed. The king may be as informal as he liked; Jeremy could not.

"I would like your permission to marry."

"Someone other than my daughter, you mean?"

"Yes, Your Majesty."

"You hardly need my permission; all arrangements between the princess and yourself have been called off."

"I know. But you see, my betrothed is currently a prisoner of state."

He frowned. "A prisoner of...oh, you mean that woman who stabbed you?"

"Yes. I have filed multiple petitions for release, and I believe Eloise has filed at least one, as well."

"You know we haven't had time to review things like that."

"I know, sir. I was hoping, now that things are settled with Olion, that perhaps you might have a chance to consider."

"I'll take a look at it."

"She's been instrumental in helping refugees displaced by the war, all across the island. I understand she has a number of connections in all three countries who are unhappy with the effects of the war on the average person. I think a pardon, if publicized properly, could help to ease certain tensions. I've put together a new request form with the most updated information."

He handed a sheath of papers to the king, who flipped through them briefly. "I'll take a look," he said again. Jeremy thanked him, and bowed, and left.

~

"How long does a look take?" Sylvia asked.

Eloise shrugged. She had appeared that morning, determined to discuss wedding plans, despite the fact that Sylvia was still a prisoner of state, and therefore not guaranteed a wedding.

"I'll try to hurry him along," she offered.

"Is he still angry with you?"

"I don't think so. But honestly I've been avoiding him. I'll see what I can do. I should have pressed harder earlier—much earlier, really. I'm sorry. I was caught up in my own drama."

"And your drama has since relocated to Kire?"

"Exactly."

"Will you—when he comes back." She stopped, not sure how to phrase the question. She didn't want to upset her.

Eloise looked away. "No. That time has passed."

"What do you have left to lose?"

She glanced at her briefly, then away again. "You wouldn't understand."

"I might. If anyone would."

She shifted to face Sylvia properly. "There's—too much has changed. It might—for a while—but it wouldn't last. I would have to lose him again, and then keep standing right at his side for the next forty years, with all the good things about us gone. I would—I can't trust him. How could I trust him?"

"You trust him with the queen and her baby. You trust him with the war."

"I trust him with my life. But not with my happiness."

"I think—I think he's a good man."

"I do, too."

"Well. Do you love him?"

"I don't know. He kept asking me, and I don't know. I don't feel the way I did when I was fifteen. But I hate that he's not here with me. But I can't—it wouldn't be fair to him, you see? Because he loves me. And I'm…not sure."

"I know I love Jeremy," Sylvia told her. "But I'm still afraid. Of all the other same things."

"And how do you know?"

"It hurts when he's gone."

~

They had made port safely, and he'd been able to buy two horses. Not good horses; those were all involved in the war effort. And it had taken an absurd amount of stolen money. But they would speed up the journey significantly.

He'd ventured into the capital, leaving Lissie behind with his sword and the horses at an abandoned farmstead a few miles out. He delivered the ransom note not to the palace but to the temple where Lissie had lived. It was stamped with her seal, the seal of the queen, and the priestesses would make sure the king was informed. There was too much chance involved in getting a note directly to the king.

He lingered in a side street and watched until an urgent message was sent to the palace, then went to collect Lissie and begin the journey north.

~

She didn't know how she felt. She kept trying to put it into words—for Sylvia, for Jeremy, for herself. Especially for herself. But none of it quite made sense, quite fit together, when she said it out loud.

She'd spoken to Jeremy and to Sylvia about it once each, in the aftermath of their engagement, which had forced her to think about it again. And then she'd realized that it was selfish to be talking to them, of all people, about it. That it would remind them both of Sylvia's fears and complicated feelings, and they hardly needed that, now.

They were the only friends she had. And soon they would be gone.

Soon, she hoped, Joel would be back. But what then?

She had spent the better part of a decade putting Joel and everything he represented behind her. And it had been so much hard work. To throw it all away now—

But she had already thrown it away. She had thrown it away when she unbuttoned Fuller's vest in her brightly-lit bedchamber, and she didn't even have Joel to show for it.

He had kidnapped her.

Even if he hadn't meant to be a traitor—and she believed that he hadn't, that he'd just been a boy, swept up in something he didn't understand—he had still kidnapped her.

He was dangerous. He hadn't been dangerous to her, not really, but he—

It was a terrible idea. And she was late to meet Sylvia. With Jeremy back at the manor build for a few days, it was her job to deliver the good news.

~

Sylvia looked at the paper Eloise had given her. It said a lot of things, in tiny, spiky writing she could hardly make out. But what mattered was the verdict, and the king's signature, in large letters at the bottom of the page.

Pardoned.

"He didn't sign it until just after Jeremy left—not on purpose, he doesn't keep track of barons' schedules. But I didn't want you to wait. Jeremy will find out when he gets back."

"Now what?"

"Well, it's conditional."

She sat up straighter, dropping the paper as if it had burned her. She should have read the spiky little letters.

"It's nothing bad," Eloise assured her. "Jeremy told him you have lots of connections with groups helping refugees. And the general public has been…less and less impressed with the king as the war has dragged on. He tried to stop it, you know. He tried so many times to make peace, but people we trusted kept stirring things back up, until Joel came and revealed the conspiracy."

"Eloise," Sylvia said.

"Sorry. That doesn't matter now. My father would like you to reach out to your contacts, and let them know that new homes are being built for refugees of any nationality, with the backing of the crown."

"Jeremy's homes?"

"Yes. He doesn't know yet that my father is providing what money he can to expand the project—but there's a great deal of empty land in that region now, and frankly we need the good publicity involved in sharing it. Jeremy was already going to build as much as he could afford to, so he won't mind."

"So all I have to do is tell everyone how wonderful your father is, and I'm free."

"You don't have to tell them he's wonderful. You just have to tell them that if they don't want to leave the island, they can go there instead, and be provided for. And perhaps that you'll be the local baroness, and can therefore vouch for the whole thing."

Sylvia frowned. "Baroness. I hadn't really thought about that, yet."

"But you'll do it? You'll accept the pardon?"

"I'll do it. I needn't go the whole route—I can stop in key places, like the temple of the third god, and leave messages. It will probably be my last chance to see any of the others."

"Good. You needn't go immediately; it's conditional on you agreeing to do it, but there's not a deadline. Would you like to move to a proper suite?"

"Could I—could I just stay here? With the door unlocked?"

"If you like."

"I'm…comfortable here. And so much else is changing."

"You can stay here. But not all the time. You are officially free, and I am officially getting you some fresh air. To the gardens, I think. Oh, won't it be fun, when Jeremy gets back, to meet him at the gate? It'll be a lovely surprise."

Chapter 32

"I just don't understand why she wants to stay in her prison cell," Jeremy said.

"She said it was comfortable. Familiar. You're overthinking this."

He changed the subject to his other, more pressing concern. "Your father shouldn't have asked that of her. Hasn't she been through enough?"

"She has," Eloise said. "But I think it will be good for her. To wrap things up. And to still be helping."

"It could take months."

"Are you afraid she won't come back?"

"No. At least not on purpose. But it's still dangerous out there."

"She can take care of herself."

"I still worry."

"Have you talked much about the wedding?"

He nodded. "After she comes back. Though we haven't decided when she's leaving. I asked to go with her, and she said no. I asked her to take someone else with her—Joel or one of his men, maybe, since she knows them, and I know she'll never feel comfortable around an Alirian soldier. But she said she has friends along the way, and anyone else would slow her down."

"Well, we certainly don't want her slowed down. Go to the kitchens before you meet her—I have someone making up a basket for you. You're having a picnic."

"You know, I might have had plans."

"Did you?"

"No."

"Then enjoy your picnic. I have to help my mother review a budget."

~

Sylvia laid in the grass; it was prickly, and she could feel it through the layers of linen she wore.

It was so good to be outside.

She had brought Jeremy to the place where Joel had brought her. They had wanted to be out of sight, which generally meant off the palace grounds, and this was the only place she knew the way to.

When she'd mentioned leaving the grounds, Eloise had said, "Don't get kidnapped." But she had filched a long, serrated knife from the kitchens, for protection, and neither she nor Jeremy were important enough to warrant a kidnapping.

Jeremy was sitting on the same log she'd sat on with Joel, inspecting the contents of the picnic basket. She was ignoring him, for now; she'd had Jeremy for weeks, and the grass beneath her and trees and sky above for only a few minutes.

"We should talk about your father," he said.

She sat up and turned to face him. "Must we?"

"All of the surviving soldiers are coming home. We can hardly turn him away from the haven we're building, especially without giving him a reason."

"I'm not ready."

"But you will be?"

"I don't know."

"Sylvia…"

"I don't want to talk about it."

"How is reuniting with him any different from reuniting with me?"

"I said I don't want to talk about it."

"We can't put it off forever."

"He's my father. He loved me. He mourned me. He remembers me as someone worth loving and mourning. I ran while my brother burned. I've killed. I've committed heresy against every pantheon on the island. And I'm marrying the man whose soldiers murdered my family. I don't want to see him."

Jeremy slid off the log, onto the ground, close enough to touch. "You couldn't have saved him. You could only have saved yourself. Running was the right thing to do. You've killed in war, to defend yourself and others, just as your father has for the Alirian army. You've committed heresy in defense of the defenseless, with aid from priests and priestesses, and no god has struck you down."

"And you? And your soldiers?"

"He would be justified in killing me, just as you would have been. But I think that if you blamed me you would not have agreed to marry me. Do you think he won't understand, if you speak to him, if you explain?"

"I'm not ready."

"All right. Just, think about it?"

She nodded. He leaned forward, and held her face, and kissed her. "Picnic, then."

Chapter 33

Joel left his sister in the city, and returned to the palace. He made no particular effort to hide his presence; if all had gone according to plan, no one would think he had ever left. Besides, it was the middle of the night.

He went first to Eloise's room, and left a note on top of her jewelry box, saying, "Send a trusted squad to the barony at the twelfth hour on the eighth day of the eighth god.

- Senam"

She would have to come up with her own reason to send them, but he'd picked a location he hoped would be easy for her. He could have woken her, and told her in person, but if he saw her now, it would be so hard to leave her again. He didn't even allow himself to check on her, asleep as she was.

He went next to the room he'd shared with his men. They slept less soundly than a princess, and he found himself pinned to a wall before being recognized.

"Joel?" Alem asked, releasing him slowly.

"You're back," Fuller said.

"Just for a bit. Chris, I need you with me. We'll be back in a week or two."

"And us?" Fuller asked.

"Keep up the charade. Trust the princess. Chris?"

"One minute—let me pack."

295

They met Lissie an hour later.

"Chris, this my sister, the queen of Ibanar."

"The what?"

"We'll talk later; I want us far from here by nightfall." He had the newest map he was able to find, and if they moved steadily they should arrive in three days. They could spend the nights in temples, as he and Lissie had been since they crossed into Aliria, at least when they were empty or when other residents were comfortable with them.

"Your sister is the queen of Ibanar."

He hadn't even said hello to Lissie, which would be horribly rude even if she wasn't technically a queen. Joel sighed. He had chosen Chris because he thought someone younger would be less intimidating, more comfortable for Lissie. But the others would have had better manners.

Maybe. One never knew with Fuller.

"Yes, and I will explain. But we need to leave now."

~

Eloise read the note once, twice. Definitely Joel's handwriting.

He had snuck into her bedchamber in the middle of the night. And he hadn't even woken her to say hello.

She went to find Jeremy, the only baron of Joel's acquaintance. It would be easy enough to arrange another trip out. Finding a way to include herself on the trip might be more difficult, but she didn't intend to miss whatever happened next.

~

"Did you lie?" Chris asked. He and Joel were sitting outside the temple; it was at the time Joel had agreed to take over the watch, but Chris hadn't gone in to sleep yet.

It was such a relief to have a third person. He didn't like having Lissie on watch; he could hardly protect her while he was sleeping and she was awake. But he had to sleep sometime.

"About what?"

"When were you going to tell us your sister was the queen of Ibanar?"

"I wasn't."

"I thought you trusted us."

"I did. With everything else. But no one in the whole world knew about Lissie. Do you know how many enemies I have? How many people hate me?"

"Did you lie to us?"

"About what?" Joel asked again; Chris had never answered the first time.

"The princess. Did you just want to use her to get to your sister? So you could be a prince, and meet the queen?"

"No. I never lied about Eloise. I did hope that if our plan—any of our plans—worked, it would be easier for me to get to my sister. But everything with Eloise was primarily about Eloise."

"Good." He stood up. "I'm going to bed."

~

"You understand the plan?" Joel asked, as he prepared to leave.

"I understand," Chris said.

"The timing is essential. If this doesn't go right—"

"I understand," Chris said again.

He nodded, and turned to his sister. "Lissie? You're all right with this?"

"You trust the king of Aliria? After everything?"

"I trust him to try to do what he thinks is right. And I trust him to understand the opportunity I'm dropping in his lap. And if all else fails, I trust Eloise to shame him into making the right choice."

"Then I'm all right. We'll see you in a few days."

~

"I really don't see why you need to be involved in all this," the queen said, when Eloise announced her intention to ride out to Jeremy's estate.

"Jeremy is bringing along his betrothed, and it wouldn't be appropriate for her to be the only woman there. She needs a chaperone."

"And that chaperone needs to be you?"

"Yes. I'm the only woman here that Sylvia knows. It would be unkind to make her travel surrounded by strangers."

"Very well, then. You'll take an attendant, of course."

"That really isn't necessary. It's a short trip, and Sylvia and I have both managed to attend to ourselves in worse conditions."

"You'll take an attendant," the queen repeated, "for my peace of mind if nothing else."

What she meant, of course, was that Eloise could not be trusted as a chaperone. It hardly mattered; Joel wanted witnesses, if she was understanding the request for a squad correctly, and an attendant would be one more.

~

Joel made the trip back to the palace much more quickly, without the burden of travelling companions, one his baby sister, and with the route now familiar.

It was daylight, and he couldn't count on any drama inside to distract from his movements, so he went down into the city first, getting properly cleaned up, then using the last of his stolen money to purchase a necklace, for camouflage.

He walked up to the front gate, where one guard attempted to turn him away, before a second recognized him as the princess' traitor.

"Is that what they're calling me now? I'll have to tell Eloise."

The guards exchanged glances, deciding, apparently, to ignore both his improper use of the princess' given name and the threat to tell on them.

"We didn't see you leave," the first one said.

"I didn't use this gate. Can I get in, please? I need to give this to the princess before dinner." He held up the box, labelled with the jeweler's name, and the guards exchanged another glance.

"If you plan to bribe her every time you fight, you're going to be destitute within a week," the second guard said, and stepped by to let him through.

So he and Eloise were fighting. That was good to know.

The second guard seemed familiar, and spoke to him familiarly, too, after the initial name-calling. Someone he'd shared barracks with, perhaps?

Someone who still considered him a traitor, so it was irrelevant; he wouldn't be renewing any friendships there.

He went directly to Eloise's chambers, where his knock was answered by a woman he vaguely recognized as one of her cousins, who was probably, given her presence, also one of her ladies.

That was good; he'd always been surprisingly popular with the cousins, even after everything.

She stared at him for a long moment—his face, then the box in his hands, then his face again.

"What did you do?" she demanded.

He ignored this. "Is the princess here?"

She turned away and walked deeper into the chambers. He stood in the doorway, noting what little he could make out of the conversation she had with Eloise and whoever else might be there.

"Came to your room—he hasn't been here since—and he brought you a gift!"

A total of three probably-cousins exited the room shortly after, the last pulling the door closed behind her, leaving him alone with Eloise.

She was clearly in the process of dressing for dinner, in her stocking feet, with her hair half done, and only one earring in. She smiled when she saw him, and he was—he was—

"I heard there was a gift?"

He offered her the box. "I needed a reason to be coming in from the city."

She opened it slowly, staring down for a long moment at the necklace inside.

It was nothing special, really. He hadn't had much money left. A thin, simple bronze chain, with a rose quartz pendant.

"Put it on for me?" she asked.

He did. She stepped away quickly when it was done, and turned around to face him again. "You were here. You were in my room. You didn't even speak to me."

"There wasn't time."

She let it go easily enough; she must not have been truly angry. "Now what?"

"Now a squad rides out to Jeremy's estate, the day after tomorrow."

"And when they get there?"

"We'll see."

"Joel."

"Are you going to be there?"

"Of course. We all are. Jeremy and Sylvia and I."

"Then it's better if you're surprised. I'll let you finish getting dressed—don't forget your left earring."

The cousins were all huddled just outside the door, not that it would have done any good. He had gone far enough from the outside door, and spoken quietly. Eloise would have to make up a conversation, when they asked.

He wondered what they were supposed to be fighting about. He should have asked before he left.

Chapter 34

Jeremy rode out to his estate in the company of his betrothed, his former betrothed, Joel, and a small squad. The squad was ostensibly for the protection of the three women—there was an attendant, as well. That Sylvia and Eloise could both protect themselves, and that Sylvia had a deep distrust for soldiers, besides, were minor details that everyone was politely ignoring. They needed a squad at his estate. Since he'd ridden out to the estate without a squad multiple times, the addition of young women to the travelling party was the best explanation for the presence of one.

He hadn't spoken properly to Joel since his return, which had only been a day and a half ago. He had spoken to Eloise yesterday, but she hadn't told him what, exactly, the plan was, and he suspected it was because she still didn't actually know. He hadn't the faintest idea who the soldiers were meant to fight, or why. But he trusted Eloise, and Eloise trusted Joel.

He didn't distrust Joel, himself. He just wished he knew what, exactly, required him to bring his traumatized fiancée back to the site of great tragedy while surrounded by men who resembled its perpetrators.

They spent three nights on the road, which went well enough, except that the presence of a dozen soldiers and one lady's maid prevented the rest of them from speaking freely.

301

He had not planned to bring Sylvia back here until construction was complete. But now, on the final morning of their journey, he was wondering why he had considered bringing her back at all. Surely he could build his new estate somewhere else, anywhere else. It wasn't a particularly large barony, but there must be another bit of land, somewhere, suitable for a small manor. Why had he thought to bring her back here?

Sylvia, having extremely limited experience on horseback, had been lent an elderly pony, and she had, after the first few hours, taken well enough to it. She was still and tense again now, clutching the pommel tightly, face white. He was fairly confident it was the location, not the pony.

They were several miles out from the village, just approaching the crumbling remains of the old mill; it had been built generations ago by a particularly antisocial miller, well away from anything else, and had not been in use in Jeremy's lifetime, or perhaps his father's, the newer millers preferring to be rather more in the thick of things. It wasn't burnt down, only dilapidated.

He glanced at the rest of their party; Joel was watching the passage of the sun—they were rapidly approaching the twelfth hour, and he had slowed things down this morning, undoubtedly on purpose. Jeremy had intended, based on his interpretation of the note, for them to be at the build site by this time. Eloise was watching Joel. The ladies' maid was flirting with a soldier. All of the other soldiers appeared, understandably, bored. Their presence was hardly needed.

"Help!" a woman shouted, just as the sun reached its peak. "Somebody help, please!"

The three soldiers in front peeled off from the group, moving toward the old mill.

"No!" Sylvia snapped, and they paused, turning back to look uncertainly between Jeremy and Eloise. Likely they weren't sure who was actually in charge; Eloise outranked him, but they were on his land.

"The last thing a woman in distress wants is soldiers," Sylvia said.

"Hello?" the woman called. "Is anyone there? Please, help me."

"It could be a trap," one of them suggested.

"For who?" she demanded, apparently forgetting the princess in their midst. She slid off her pony and pulled out the staff she'd insisted on bringing. "Stay here. If I'm not back in a quarter hour, two of you may come after me."

"Sir?" someone asked him, as Sylvia strode quickly toward the mill.

"As she says," Jeremy said. He wasn't too worried; he was fairly confident that the shouting woman was the queen of Ibanar.

~

Sylvia entered the mill cautiously, though given the timing, it wasn't likely dangerous. There was a young woman on the floor, hands and feet tied. A good chunk of the back wall of the mill was missing, but she was tucked into the corner, her face in shadow.

"Are you alone?" she asked, and the woman nodded. Sylvia set her staff aside and crouched to begin undoing the knots. This close, she could make out her face, and confirm her identity. "Queen Lissan."

"Yes," she said.

Joel hadn't just left her here. There was no source of water within her reach; she would have died of dehydration in this time. And her skin wasn't raw beneath the ropes as it would have been after several days.

"Do you know where you are?" Sylvia asked.

"Somewhere on the island."

"You're in Aliria. You'll be safe now. We'll get you home."

She led the queen out of the mill, watching how she scanned the crowd on horseback.

"She was alone," Sylvia reported. "All tied up."

"Lissie?" Joel asked, as they came closer to the others. "Lissie, is that you?"

He slipped off his horse much more gracefully than Sylvia had, and approached; he took only a few steps before the queen ran forward and threw herself into his arms. This, Sylvia admitted to herself, was an unexpected turn of events. Did every woman Joel kidnapped fall for him? What a peculiar talent that was.

"You weren't in the palace," Joel said. "I couldn't find you. What are you doing in Aliria?"

"They—I was in Kire. They took me from Kire, and they brought me here, and it's been—they went this morning to get supplies, and I heard the horses, so I shouted—what are you doing in Aliria?"

"Joel?" Eloise called from her horse. "Do you have introductions to make?"

He let go of the queen, and turned to face the others. "Right, yes. This is my sister, the queen of Ibanar."

~

She was going to strangle Joel, she really was, just as soon as there were no witnesses.

His sister. His sister, the queen of Ibanar. His sister who was supposed to be dead.

She collected herself as best she could. "It's a pleasure to meet you, Your Majesty. You said you were taken from Kire? Kidnapped?"

"Yes."

"All right." She turned to address the leader of the squad. "I want half of you to search the area for any suspicious figures." She hoped that Joel didn't have any friends lingering about; it would look terribly strange if they didn't try to locate the queen's kidnappers. "Two should escort the baron to his destination and back. The rest will accompany us home. Sylvia, would you like to continue on with Jeremy, or come back with us?"

Sylvia glanced at Jeremy, then at the queen. "I'll come back."

The squad separated as directed, and Sylvia and Jeremy said their goodbyes. Eloise debated how to manage an additional person with no additional horses. If the queen was Joel's sister, they could share a horse. But she was still a queen, so that was hardly proper. Eloise and Sylvia had shared a horse before; they could do it again, and give the queen the pony.

They rode back south until nightfall, and made camp. Sometime in the night, the half squad joined them, having failed to locate any potential kidnappers. Eloise sent one of them ahead to inform the king she would be bringing back a guest.

There was no opportunity for private conversation. She couldn't strangle Joel; she couldn't even question him. She made an effort to be much more proper and dignified than usual, since she was in the presence of a queen, and tried not to be too irritated as Joel and the queen acted as if they hadn't seen each other in years.

304

She was fairly certain it had only been about a week. But the charade was necessary for their audience. She would drag all the details out of Joel later.

They followed all the correct procedures, when they reached the palace, for visiting royalty, with a high-ranking minister escorting the queen immediately to the throne room, to be greeted by the king and queen. Joel, Eloise, and Sylvia followed.

Her parents acted as if Queen Lissan was a normal, expected visitor, ignoring for now both the kidnapping and the war. Her identity was verified by seal ring, as well as Joel and Sylvia's accounts—though admittedly neither of them were necessarily reliable sources of information in the eyes of the crown.

After an appropriate amount of pleasantries had been exchanged, the queen was escorted upstairs by the same minister; a suite had been prepared for her, and a bath drawn. Joel and Sylvia both followed; Sylvia, Eloise thought, was still concerned about the queen's safety in enemy territory.

The pleasant but distant masks her parents had been wearing vanished as soon as Eloise was alone with them.

"The queen of Ibanar?" her father asked.

"Eloise, darling," her mother said, "why do these things always happen to you?"

"It's hardly my fault someone kidnapped a queen," Eloise lied. "And it's the best possible thing that could have happened to us—surely Ibanar will be willing to make peace, when they learn we've rescued their queen."

For a long moment, Eloise stared steadily at her parents, and they stared back at her. Would someone suggest the less friendly and possibly more effective option of holding her hostage and demanding an end to the war?

"It could have been me," she said.

The king sighed. "We'll start drafting a letter to her husband immediately; it will have to be worded carefully to avoid any... misunderstandings. Queen Lissan is of course welcome to join us tonight for dinner, though we would understand if she needs more time to collect herself after her ordeal. She should write to her husband as well. A variety of clothing options have already been made available, but your messenger was not able to provide adequate information for sizing. Eloise, you may handle the queen's wardrobe yourself, or delegate as you see fit. I am putting you in charge of determining and meeting her needs for the duration of her stay. We will have a meeting with the council regarding this matter tomorrow morning."

"Thank you, Father."

"Eloise," her mother said, as she turned to leave.

"Yes?"

"Did you know that she was Joel's sister?"

"No. I had no idea."

~

Joel sprawled across Lissie's enormous bed, watching as she explored her suite. He had been expelled from the room, briefly, while she bathed, and had used that time to confirm Chris had made it back safely, but had returned as soon as he was able.

He was fairly certain that Eloise was angry with him, and he didn't think she would let herself in to the queen's room to yell at him, no matter who she was related to.

"Do you think I should go to dinner?" Lissie asked him.

He considered for a moment. "Not yet. You should have been in horrible distress for months now. You need time."

She nodded, turning away from the wardrobe. "Are you avoiding your princess?"

"I told her you were dead."

"Surely she can't be angrier about that than she was about the conspiracy and the kidnapping."

"One never knows, with Eloise."

"Go find her. Let me rest."

"I'd rather not leave until we get confirmation they'll see you safely home."

"And what difference will it make, having you here, if they do decide to hold me hostage? Go find her."

There was a knock on the door before he could answer. Lissie went to answer it; Joel rolled over and propped himself up on his elbows for a better view.

"Princess," Lissie said. "Please come in."

Eloise entered the room, barely glancing over at Joel. Like Lissie, she had bathed and changed; he was still wearing his dirty travel clothes.

"I'm sorry to bother you when you're just settling in, but I wanted to let you know that the king is working to arrange your safe return to your husband as soon as possible. We'll have ink and paper delivered shortly so that you can write him. I see we've found something that fits you not too badly, but with your permission I'll send in a seamstress to take your measurements, so we can have a few more dresses altered to your size."

"Of course," Lissie said.

They were both talking like the royalty they technically were, and Joel didn't like it. The words themselves were no different from what they might normally say; it was something in their voices, in their postures. Eloise usually only felt like a princess when she hated him. He hadn't seen her do it until the day she voted for his death.

This wasn't about him, though. It was about politics and diplomacy and both of them doing their jobs.

He got off the bed, and made his way toward the door. Eloise, without looking away from Lissie, reached out and grabbed him by the wrist.

"My rooms," she said, and then released him and went back to talking about—something. He'd stopped listening. Dinner parties, perhaps?

No one answered when he knocked at her door, so she must have cleared everyone out in preparation. He let himself in. He could have ignored her instructions, and put off their confrontation for a few hours at least, but they would have to talk eventually.

It had been torture, riding beside her for three days and having to act like—like—none of the squad would actually have been surprised by their usual interactions, and neither would Lissie. But their presence, and his newly revealed relation to her, did demand a certain degree of decorum.

Eloise couldn't be too angry, if she wanted to meet in her room, and had sent him here to wait unsupervised. He thought about what little information he'd collected from Alem and Fuller, between getting back and leaving again. They had, apparently, convinced everyone that he was still at the palace by convincing everyone that he and Eloise were more...involved than they'd been even as children, though not consistently on such good terms. It hardly mattered, having him alone in her room, when she'd been creeping about the palace at all hours of the night, apparently returning from meetings with him, and spending sometimes hours at a time in his rooms, and apparently undressing him in front of the entire palace.

All of this time she was willing to spend with him, but not when he was actually there.

It wasn't about him. It was about the war. He knew that. He knew it. But he wished—

He chose a chair in her sitting room, and waited. It didn't take long.

"Your sister?" she asked as she walked in.

He nodded.

She sat down across from him. "Your dead sister."

"I lied."

"You often do."

"I hadn't seen her since four months before the king chose her. And then he sent her away, and no one—no one could tell me where. I've been so afraid, El."

"So you need a pardon from Ibanar, too."

"It would simplify matters, yes."

"Did she want to be the queen of Ibanar? He could be her father. He could very nearly be her grandfather."

"I did ask. I—I want this war over. But not as much as I want my sister safe. I wasn't sure I'd come back, really. If she'd wanted me to, I'd have taken her deeper into the continent, and we'd have disappeared."

"I should be angry," Eloise said. "I thought I could trust you."

"You should be," he echoed. "But you're not?"

"I don't care how valuable Ben was on the frontlines. If I could have kept him safe—or if Julian hadn't wanted to go to Olion—or if Father tried to marry one of my little sisters to an old man they hated—" She stopped.

"Damn Aliria," Joel said quietly, "and damn the war. Some things are more important."

"Yes."

"Which, I suppose, is why it's such a very good thing that neither of us regularly has much of an impact on the government."

"I would," she said, "if they trusted me. I'm essentially the third child now, with Julian in Olion and Ben—well."

"How convenient, then, that they don't trust you."

She didn't answer.

"You don't want to run a government, Eloise."

"And what do I want?"

"Adventure. Freedom. To be who you are without worrying about whose eyes are on you, or what they see."

"And if I can't have that—which I can't—I'd rather at least be useful."

You could have it with me, Joel thought, and didn't say. She knew how he felt. She didn't want to hear it again.

She changed the subject. "We'll get her home as soon as we can. It'll likely be several weeks. We're not holding her hostage—we just have to communicate with Ibanar, so he won't think it's an invasion or a hostage situation when we appear on his land with his wife."

"I understand."

"I assume you'll want to be in the party escorting her home?"

He nodded. "It'll be the best time for it. Hopefully he'll be so happy to have her back, he'll forget he hates me."

"Will you—will you come back, after?"

"I don't know," he said, and waited to see if she would ask him to.

She didn't.

"I need to find dresses to be altered for your sister. I've given too many of mine to Sylvia; I'll have to raid Erika's closet. She's not using her good clothing, anyway."

She stood. Joel took it as the dismissal it was, and left.

He would see Lissie safely back to Ibanar. He would almost certainly be pardoned when they arrived; Lissie would make sure of it. He could stay there. See his sister every day, and his nephew, and whatever nephews or nieces were yet to come. He would look like he belonged, there—he and Lissie had both taken much more after their mother than their fathers. He would not be constantly recognized as Eloise's, anywhere outside of Eloise's home.

It was what he should do, probably. Lissie would be glad of it.

And Eloise—Eloise probably wouldn't care at all.

Chapter 35

I am in the Alirian court. Don't worry; they aren't the ones who kidnapped me. I don't know who the kidnappers were working for, but they brought me back to the island. They went to get supplies one day, and left me tied up in an abandoned village near the Olion-Aliria border; that's where the Alirians found me. I heard more noise outside than just the kidnappers would make, and I shouted and shouted until they heard me. The kidnappers didn't come back; they must have seen the baron's party where they'd left me and gotten scared off. I did give descriptions, but they say the island is full of bandits and deserters and refugees, so they're not hopeful about finding them.

They didn't know about the baby, or they'd have taken him, too. I hope so much that he's safe, that I'll be reunited with him when I'm reunited with you.

And the best news—my brother is here in Aliria. I can't wait for you to meet him!

The Alirians say they'll get me home soon, and without a ransom, and I think I believe them. Do please be nice to the messenger they're sending, and give my love to the baby if he's there.

Yours,
Lissan

Chapter 36

He went to Sylvia as soon as he was back, though it was late in the evening, and she'd probably be preparing for bed. He understood why she hadn't continued to the estate with him, but he had missed her. And he had hated not knowing what was happening, with the queen. It wasn't as if the build actually needed his supervision; he'd only been going to put them in the path of the queen. And then he had missed all the excitement.

Sylvia's insistence on remaining in the same room, and her refusal of any sort of attendant or maid, was actually very convenient. It remained as easy as it had always been to be alone with her, in private.

She told him, when he knocked, to let himself in. She was sitting on the bed in her nightgown, braiding her hair; he sat behind her and took over the task.

"I could have been anyone," he said.

"I know the sound of your knock." She didn't turn around, head held carefully still for him to work.

Her hair was fine and silky, difficult to work with. He hadn't braided it in many years, but his fingers remembered.

It was an old Olin tradition, braiding your lover's hair, a form of intimacy not restricted to married or even betrothed couples. And Jeremy, like Sylvia, had spent much of his childhood in Olion. The estate and the village were firmly in Aliria, but the nearest large city was in Olion, which meant Olin festivals and Olin markets, Olin foods and linens and pottery and woodwork.

"There will be a party travelling to Ibanar with the queen," Sylvia said.

"Yes."

"Who will be going?"

"People the king can both trust and spare, I suppose."

"So, you?"

He paused, having reached the end of the braid. She reached back without turning to hand him a ribbon, which he tied slowly.

"Perhaps."

"I could go, at the same time. We could both have journeys, and come back together when they're finished."

"You think I should ask to be in the party?"

"You'll worry, if you're sitting here waiting for me. Best to keep busy." She turned around, finally, and smiled at him. "I'm sorry I didn't make it all the way to the estate."

"You weren't ready. I wouldn't have asked you to, if it wasn't for the plan."

She nodded, running her fingers absently down the finished braid.

"If you're not—if you don't—you don't have to be ready. It was foolish and selfish of me, asking you to go back there at all. We can live somewhere else. Everything they're building can be for the refugees, and we can go farther south in the barony, or stay here in the capital. Or—anything you want. You don't have to go back there."

She stared down at their folded legs, just meeting at the knees, for a long moment without answering. Finally she looked up again, and said, "No. No, I want to go home, I think. Not yet. But soon. I think, when I've done this task, when I come back and see you again. I think I'll be ready. For you, and for home, and I hope for my father."

"All right. If you're sure."

"I'm not. But I want to be."

~

"You'll be going to Ibanar," Fuller said.

Joel nodded.

"Will you be coming back?"

"I haven't decided." Lissie, unlike Eloise, would actually enjoy having him nearby. But was he really ready to give up?

"Mission's over, then?" Fuller asked.

"Your part of the mission ended a long time ago. If you're asking permission to disband—well, you didn't need to wait on me to sort out my romantic woes, for that."

"We wanted to see you settled," Alem said. "Because you're our friend."

"I'm not going anywhere now," Fuller said. "I'm just not sure I'll be here when you get back. If you get back."

"Did you get officially asked to join the survey team?" Chris asked him. Which was the first Joel had heard of it—he felt so disconnected, now. Fuller had been angry, when he found out about Lissie. It was possible he was still a little angry; it had been a big secret to keep from his closest friends. Alem had been more exasperated than angry. It seemed Alem was always exasperated with him. But his relationships with all of them felt a little different, a little distant, since he'd gotten back. He wasn't sure if it was the long absence or the secret sister that caused it.

"They're putting together the team the day after tomorrow. I'll be at the meeting. And I have more experience—or better experience—than most people here. Mapping the terrain in northeast Olion is a lot more complicated than anything in Aliria."

"I hope you get it," Joel said. "Chris, do you have plans?"

"I'm hoping to get an apprenticeship, in the city. There's a lot of openings from all the men who went off to war. But I haven't settled on anything yet."

"Have Eloise write you a recommendation. She'll do it—she likes you. And an endorsement from a princess is bound to help for any job."

At least he was planning to stay in the capital, where Joel would probably be able to find him if he came back. And Alem was staying here, would reliably be still in the palace, though likely in different rooms. He would work with the court physician at least until he was ready to practice medicine independently, which Joel understood would take years.

It wouldn't be the same, though. Things would never be the same, even if he came back.

The queen of Ibanar was an easy guest to have, despite the odd circumstances. She had turned down offers for any sort of attendant, saying she'd done without assistance longer than she'd done with it, and she'd rather not be surrounded always by strangers. She attended court dinners most nights, which required them, of course, to also invite Joel, but in a rare show of good sense, he'd turned down the invitation.

(Perhaps, Eloise had thought, this journey, this reunion, had been good for him. Their single one-on-one interaction since his return had gone remarkably well.

And then he'd added that he'd always hated going with her to court dinners, and leaned close to quote a line from "Senam and the Mermaid," not fully singing it, but voice lilting up and down a little, almost singing, "For though I love you dear and true, your home I cannot abide."

She had said, "Good," and left quickly.)

It was easy to avoid any discussion of politics; the queen, having been hidden away in Kire for some time, knew little of what was going on locally, and knew better than to raise the subject with Alirians.

She spent the majority of her time with Joel, outside the dinners. Which meant that Eloise seldom saw Joel, which was—a relief, surely. It had to be.

But Eloise had been given the role of looking after their guest, so she did try to arrange things for her to do. She'd invited her to go riding, but the queen had admitted she'd not ridden until her marriage, and then seldom, and though she was not bad at it, she found horses rather frightening. Invitations to various gatherings of young women in the palace had also been turned down, as had the offered tour of the capital. Although that, Eloise could admit, had not been her best idea. She was the queen of a kingdom with which they were at war. Public appearances could be…tricky.

The problem was that Eloise was beginning to worry that the queen disliked her. That Joel had—well, why shouldn't she dislike Eloise, whose disastrous relationship with her brother had very nearly ruined his life?

But she didn't like the idea of Joel's little sister disliking her. It was—it felt too much like Joel disliking her.

She offered, next, a stroll around the gardens at a time when they would be largely unoccupied, and to her surprise, the queen accepted.

"No one else will be here?" the queen checked, when they reached the gardens.

"I thought you might like to be—to have some privacy. I've had this section blocked off." It had occurred to her that everything she'd suggested so far had involved being either in a group or in a crowd or supervised by guards for her own protection (no more solo rides, after Eloise's kidnapping), and that it was likely difficult being a technical enemy, and one who was quite recognizable, at that. There were few enough people in the court with skin as dark as hers, and all the others had been there for years. She couldn't disappear into the background the way another woman with curly blonde hair would.

She smiled at Eloise, then slipped off her shoes and toed them carefully to the edge of the path, her posture sliding into something a little looser, a little more open.

"Good. It is so hard to be always a queen—I was still learning, when he sent me away, and then in Kire I wasn't supposed to be acting like a queen, and it's just—strange. But I don't have to get it right with you, do I? After all, we were almost sisters-in-law."

"You don't have to act like a queen for me," Eloise confirmed.

"Good," she said again.

So. She didn't dislike Eloise. She was just trying to put on the right show.

They walked through the garden for a while. Their countries weren't so far apart that there was significant difference in the flora, but there were a few flowers that flourished in the slightly cooler summers of Aliria, and a few bushes that some ancestor had brought over from the continent, and the queen was interested in those.

Eloise could hardly keep thinking of her as the queen, now.

"Is your true name Elisabeth or Lissan?" she asked.

"My true name is Lissie. Except that Lissie is also a child's name, so I suppose it's Lissan, now. Elisabeth is my Alirian name, and Lissan my Ibanari name, but both parents called me Lissie, always."

"Does Joel have an Ibanari name, too?"

"No. My mother left the naming of him to my father—Joel…told you, didn't he?"

"About your uncle?"

Lissie nodded. "Mother felt letting him choose the name was the least she could do, after he married a stranger and claimed her child. By the time I came, they were—it was a real marriage, by then."

"Have you met your uncle?"

"No. He never visited. He only sent us enough money to feed Joel."

"He is rather awful. I have half a mind to tell my father about it—I wouldn't, without Joel's permission, of course, and anyway not until after the war—we need him, now, he's a good general. But he—he's married to my cousin, you know. Well, my father's cousin. He has been for thirty years, well before Joel was—I can't imagine his wife knows."

Lissie shrugged, and Eloise realized she was rambling. "You have a baby, don't you? Do you miss him?"

"So much," Lissie said.

"Tell me about him?"

She did.

~

They had written the king of Ibanar. They had received a response—he was eager to be reunited with his wife, was grateful that the Alirians had rescued her, and would be willing to discuss the possibility of peace following her safe return. They were asked to head south as soon as possible.

There was then the matter of who, exactly, would be heading south. Jeremy's offer to assist had been accepted, and the supervision of his barony handed off temporarily to an assistant. A few ministers to handle the negotiations. Attendants and assistants. Soldiers to escort them safely to their destination.

"The difficulty," Eloise's father explained at breakfast one morning, speaking primarily to his wife, "is that really we ought to have a representative from our family."

Eloise looked up from the task of convincing her niece to eat a piece of fruit—something Maria was succeeding much better at with her nephew.

"The party could collect Theo or Erika on the way down," the queen said. "They would have to be caught up on everything, and it may take a slight detour to pick them up."

"Or you could send me," Eloise suggested, "since I'm already so near at hand."

The king frowned. "Eloise, I'm not sure—this is very sensitive. We haven't been on truly good terms with Ibanar in generations."

"You wouldn't want me to handle the negotiations. I know that. But you don't need me to make a good treaty; you just need me to represent the royal family. I'll let the experts do their jobs, and I'll sit there quietly, and be a princess who has never personally participated in waging war against them. I know—I know you trust Theo and Erika more than me, but they're soldiers. And Annabelle has a husband and a life, Maria is a child, and Julian is in Olion. I'm your best option for this."

"I'm not a child," protested Maria, who had recently turned fourteen. "Not that I want to go."

"Joel will be there," her mother pointed out.

"I can get along with Joel."

"That's what I'm afraid of."

"I can get along with Joel to an appropriate degree."

"You'll have to," her father warned.

"I will," Eloise said. "I promise."

"Very well, then. You are familiar to the queen, and the fact that you're not currently in battle against Ibanar is certainly an advantage."

Chapter 37

"I need to speak with you," Chris said. "Before you leave."

Eloise had hardly seen Chris in weeks. "All right. I've nowhere to be at the moment."

"In—in our room?" he suggested. "No one else is there now—Joel is with his sister, and the others are working."

She really did need to get out of the habit of being alone in private rooms with men to whom she was not married. But anyone who noticed would certainly assume she was there to see Joel, and they were all certain she was doing that anyway.

When they reached the room, Chris paced a bit, and then stood in front of her fidgeting for a moment, while she sat and waited.

"Joel's never told you why he kidnapped you. Has he?"

"No."

"He's—I think he's embarrassed. But I think you deserve to know. So—I'm telling you. He'll be mad at me, but if you can wait to let him know until you're in Ibanar, he'll be over it by the time he gets back."

"Tell me."

"He wasn't supposed to be there. For the kidnapping. He was supposed to come later, but he decided at the last minute to join us, so he put on the mask. He definitely wasn't supposed to take the mask off. He expected it all to be over then—we all expected you to recognize him. After—after that, we didn't really have a plan anymore."

"And the plan originally?"

"We were going to kidnap you. And then he was going to rescue you. And then you wouldn't hate him anymore. And maybe you would love him again."

Well. She had wanted to know why he'd kidnapped her; it had never made much sense. She closed her eyes and took a breath, her mother's strategy for managing emotions—her own, which involved a great deal of shouting, would be no help in finishing this conversation, in collecting any information Chris had to offer. "And if I did? He would, what, spend the rest of our lives lying to me?"

"Alem and Fuller told him it was a bad idea. And he realized almost right away that he couldn't—that he couldn't actually do that to you. And then he couldn't just take you home, because he still had to tell you about the conspiracy, but you wouldn't believe him if you didn't know who he was. So we were all just stuck, pretending, while he tried to make a new plan."

"And the best thing he could come up with was to take me to that island, and surround me with men who weren't pretending, who were actually dangerous to me?"

"He took you home. It wasn't a very good home, but it was all we had."

None of this was Chris' fault. She wasn't going to lose her temper with Chris. He had gone along with Joel's plan, but Joel was his leader, and she had been a stranger. And he was telling her now.

She stood slowly. "Thank you for telling me."

"Are you—are you angry?"

"Not at you."

"I—this is probably a bad time to ask a favor. But you're about to leave, so."

She sighed. "What do you need?"

"Joel said I should ask you to write me a letter. So it'll be easier to get an apprenticeship."

"I can do that. I'll bring it by later."

She left quickly.

He'd—he'd planned to—but he hadn't. It was fine, because he hadn't.

It was fine.

It was fine.

If he had rescued her—if he had seemed to rescue her—would she have—

She absolutely would have fallen back into his arms.

He hadn't actually done it. So it shouldn't matter.

It didn't matter. It couldn't matter. She was travelling to Ibanar with him. She was representing her kingdom and her family. She couldn't back out now, couldn't prove that her parents were right not to think of her for something so important.

She wouldn't—if she wanted to talk to him, it had to be now. Within the next three days, before they left. Here at home, she could get him alone, could have a proper conversation with him. Once they were travelling, she wouldn't have a chance to speak with him in private. And she certainly couldn't be alone with him in Ibanar. It was now or never.

Never, she decided.

He was likely going to stay in Ibanar. Their recent interactions had been polite. They had not—it was better to let things end. A conversation would turn into a fight that would just—would draw out feelings they didn't have time for, resentment and regret and nostalgia. If she didn't speak with him now, she could more easily maintain the appropriate level of polite distance for their journey.

She wouldn't speak to Joel. She would write a letter, and sign and seal it, and give it to Chris. Then she would go see Sylvia.

Sylvia was planning to leave on the same day as them. Between preparations for the trips and leaving Sylvia and Jeremy to spend what time they could together, Eloise had seen little of her. But Jeremy was in a meeting just now, and Eloise wanted to say goodbye, and wish her luck.

~

"You'll be careful," Jeremy said, half a question, half an order.

"I'll be careful," she said. "I've been doing this for years. I don't even have anyone else to protect, this time. And I have supplies from the crown, and even money for more."

"I know. I still worry."

"You be careful," she told him.

"I have several trained soldiers with me, and orders from both kings for both sides of battles to let us through."

"Be careful," she repeated.

"I will." He bent down to kiss her. After, she leaned against him for a long moment, her forehead on his shoulder, her eyes closed, memorizing the feel of him, their fingers entwined, her body moving with his breath.

She pulled away slowly, reluctantly. "It's faster to travel alone. I'll be back before you, I think. I'll be waiting for you."

"And then we'll be married."

"And then we'll be married," she agreed.

"I love you."

She stood on her toes to kiss him once more, and left.

~

Eloise was avoiding him. It was fine; he had Lissie to worry about. She didn't much care for horses, as he'd learned on their last journey. She was anxious to see her son, and nervous about lying to her husband, and dreading an extended period of time surrounded constantly by near strangers. And since she was his sister, and he was a person of no particular importance, he wasn't really expected to maintain any sort of formality in her presence. He would focus on Lissie, and let Eloise try to be the perfect princess.

The number of people in their party slowed them down, of course. But the fact that they didn't have to struggle to avoid battlefields or enemy soldiers sped them up again—they had letters from both kings indicating that they should be let through. And the soldiers accompanying them reduced the danger from bandits and deserters, and ensured plenty of people to keep watch, so they needn't worry so much about finding the best shelters. And they didn't have to make it all the way down to the capital.

No one had bothered to officially tell him the details of their plan, of course. He'd gotten his information from Jeremy, though he was sure Lissie would have told him if he'd asked.

It had been arranged that they would meet not in the Ibanari capital but at a manor farther north. Ibanar would be happy to host a party of Alirians for the purpose of negotiations, and one squad of soldiers would be permitted to accompany them. Ibanar was grateful for their treatment of the queen, and hoped for a resolution of conflict.

He was sharing a tent with Jeremy, which was fine, and three diplomats, which was...less pleasant. Male assistants and attendants were in another tent. Eloise, Lissie, the one female diplomat in their party, and the one attendant they were sharing had another tent. Whichever soldiers were not currently on duty guarding the rest of them had a fourth tent.

It was fortunate the highest ranking people in their party were Lissie and Eloise, both of whom were on the hardier side for noblewomen, and both of whom were invested in reaching their destination quickly.

Though he still wasn't entirely certain why Eloise was in a hurry; it might be because she was angry with him, and looking forward to leaving him in Ibanar as soon as possible. But he was trying not to assume that he featured as prominently in her thoughts as she did in his; likely it had nothing to do with him.

~

"Are you all right?" Jeremy asked Eloise quietly. They'd been travelling several days, and she had been withdrawn for most of that time, less enthusiastic about leaving the palace, and about being trusted with this task, than he would have expected.

"Fine," she said. "And you?"

"Worried about Sylvia."

It was harder to talk to Eloise than it used to be. When they were engaged, and when they were working together to look after Sylvia, there had been—a certain intimacy, perhaps, to their interactions.

"She can take care of herself."

"I know. It's just—"

"The last time you were apart for any length of time, she was dead."

"Yes. That." He glanced around to be sure no one was paying any particular attention to them. "You and Joel have been remarkably civil lately."

There was an iciness to that civility, at least on Eloise's side, and it worried him.

Joel was his friend, too, though they'd had little enough interaction since he'd returned with a queen.

"Don't defend him," she said.

"I'm not. I don't even know what he did to defend."

"I don't want to talk about it."

"All right. Are you ready to meet the king?"

"I can do it," she said. She seemed to be feeling quite defensive today.

"I know you can. But it's big. A lot of things to get right. We can go through it all a few times, if you like. Practice."

"I'd like that, yes. Please."

~

Sylvia had moved south, first, toward the temple of the third god, stopping at any smaller temples along the way to spread the news. At empty temples she left notes. Not everyone could read, but there was a good chance that at least one person in any group passing through would be able to. She did not think too many were likely to pass through and find the notes; the northern half of the island had been at peace for months now, and no new people should be losing their homes at this stage.

For once, there was no urgency to her travel. She needed only to finish by the time Jeremy did, and his journey would be interrupted by a long period of diplomacy.

She met with the priestess, and admitted that she had been right about going to the palace, and shared her news. She continued south with the overabundance of supplies the temple of the third god always provided. The priestess had let her know the safest routes, as she'd heard them from the last traveller; it had only been a few days, so the information should be accurate.

It was so good to be here again, to be wandering and free and on her feet.

She would be free again, when she and Jeremy were wed. He would let her wander when she needed to, though he would worry. She just needed to hold on until the estate was rebuilt, until they were able to leave the palace and truly live their own lives.

The estate, so near the burnt village. The rebuilt village, which would likely house her father. Her father, who thought she was dead.

Well. She had the rest of this journey to prepare herself.

Chapter 38

They were approaching a battlefield, likely the only battlefield they would approach on this journey. Hostilities had been largely paused, although there were likely soldiers who hadn't received messages to that effect. And there may still be some Olin soldiers, but Eloise had heard Ibanar and Olion were negotiating peace as well.

Eloise checked that her sword was still in its sheath on her saddle, even though she knew it was, and knew she wouldn't need it, and still wasn't certain how to use it while on horseback.

No one was actually fighting, though Eloise thought they were rather annoyed about it. There was a lot of restless pacing in the Alirian camp they reached first. Their party stayed mounted, waiting, while one of the soldiers on guard read the king's note, then went to collect a superior of some sort. The diplomats talked quietly among themselves. Some of their guard struck up conversations with friends stationed there. Several minutes passed.

A general came striding over quickly, the soldier who'd taken the note struggling to keep up with him. Eloise recognized the uniform first, and the man second, as he came closer.

"I hope one of you is finally going to explain why we've been ordered to stand down," he said, addressing himself to the squad leader.

"Read the letter," Eloise suggested. She wouldn't bother with manners or formality; he was married into her family, and besides, she hated him.

"It tells me to let you past," he says. "Doesn't give a single good reason I'm not in battle right now. Surely you haven't taken up with him again?"

It was the closest she thought he would come to acknowledging his son, who was right behind her. She glanced back at Joel; he was expressionless. Unreadable.

"Joel is a part of the diplomatic mission that you are currently holding up by attempting to interrogate us." Her father would not, of course, have mentioned in a letter, which could so easily fall into the wrong hands, that the queen of Ibanar was in their company. Likely, given his military position and his wife, it would be acceptable to share the truth with the general in person. But Eloise didn't trust him, and the others would follow her lead.

"You'll camp here for the night," he said. "Nightfall is approaching; you won't be more than a mile past the Ibanari camp by full dark. I don't trust them."

It was an understandable suggestion, since they were at war still, and Eloise could hardly explain to their whole party that she was refusing because she personally disliked the man, and didn't want him near his son or his niece.

Not that he seemed to recognize his niece; they had never even met.

"Fine," she said.

"And in the morning I'll send two more squads with you through the Ibanari camp."

"No. We've been given permission from Ibanar to travel with one squad. I won't violate the terms of our agreement for the sake of your peace of mind."

He nodded once, then started calling out orders to the nearby soldiers, to tend to their horses and help them set up. Eloise looked back at Joel again; he was leaning over to speak quietly to Lissie. She needed to talk to him, to check on him, but it would be difficult to do without an audience.

~

No one had thought to warn him that his uncle was leading the army they'd have to pass through. Though Eloise, he thought, hadn't known. She'd sounded surprised.

The man wouldn't even make eye contact. He'd hated Joel long before he'd become a traitor, and given him a convenient reason to do so. And now they would be spending the night in his domain.

Joel looked to Lissie. Lissie, who he'd have gladly let starve to death, though she was both his brother's daughter and his son's sister. Lissie, who obviously didn't know who he was. He leaned over, reluctantly, to explain.

An hour later their tents were assembled, and Joel separated from Lissie and Eloise both, as he could hardly intrude on the space of the other two women sharing their tent. He stuck close to Jeremy, the only other man in the group he had any kind of relationship with. Hopefully he wouldn't actually need a buffer against his uncle, but it was better to be prepared.

It was not long after the tents were set up that dinner was prepared for the camp, and they were all invited to join the army.

Even beside Jeremy, even with the knowledge that being quite clearly in the company of a baron would protect him, Joel couldn't—he couldn't—

His uncle was bad enough, but he wasn't the only man here Joel knew.

He retreated to the temporary privacy of the tent.

It wasn't the first time he'd recognized a soldier. There had been several altercations, back at the palace. But the man he'd seen now—they'd been not just training together, not just sharing barracks, but genuinely friends.

Mason. Mason, who had taught him the names of the royal family. Who'd patiently worked him through all the different titles they held, and how to address them in the rare case of a direct interaction. Who had explained the relationships and the history and the tricks to at least appear to recognize dozens of people who expected to be identifiable by everyone they encountered. How the king, his brother, and his cousin had married three sisters from the continent, who all looked alike and all produced children who looked alike, so if you saw a girl or a woman with golden ringlets she was almost certainly a princess or a duchess. How everyone in the king's cabinet wore a special sash. How the lower-ranked nobility wore less elaborate clothing, how barons had an outfit indicating their station, but never wore it, and still expected to be recognized. When to attempt to make it through an interaction with a nobleman, and when to run or hide if you saw one approaching.

Mason had spent hours preparing him to safely navigate the palace, when few others had bothered to help him at all. Joel wasn't going to stick around long enough to have an altercation with him.

The tent flap opened, and Eloise slipped in.

"You shouldn't be here," he said.

"Jeremy is keeping an eye on Lissie, and I have no good reputation left to salvage, at least not in this country. Are you all right?"

She sat down beside him, and held out a bowl, which he took reluctantly; he was far too stressed to be hungry.

"Fine," he lied.

"I'm sorry; I didn't know he'd be here. Or how to refuse spending the night."

"It's fine," he said again.

"He hasn't spoken to you?"

"No. I'm sure he won't."

"We'll leave first thing in the morning."

He nodded. They ate together in silence, then Eloise took his empty bowl and left again. A few minutes later, Jeremy and the other diplomats returned.

~

They left early in the morning, as Eloise had promised. Passage through the Ibanari camp went well; they had a letter from the Ibanari king, as well, sent to them as they made arrangements to get Lissie home, and the Ibanari soldiers escorted them quickly past the camp.

They encountered no more soldiers or battlefields.

Chapter 39

They were met at the gate of the manor by the king, a squad of guards, and a few assorted courtiers. The king of Ibanar was a tall, narrow man, much darker than his wife, with graying hair. He looked very serious, almost severe, until he saw the queen. He stepped away from his guards, and she pushed past Joel to throw herself at him, a surprising move for a woman who had been clear that her relationship with her husband was not a romantic one. (Of course, Eloise loved Jeremy, also without romance. But Jeremy wasn't a man twice her age. Jeremy wasn't the king of Ibanar.)

He caught her, and held her close, and kissed the top of her head. They held a whispered conversation while his guards moved forward to resume their positions around the king.

After a few minutes, Lissie—Queen Lissan—took her husband's hand and pulled him toward their party, leaving his guards behind again.

"This is my brother, Joel," she announced. "He wasn't going to come, because he says he's exiled, but I told him you'd just have to un-exile him, then, unless you wanted me going up to Aliria all the time to visit him."

Eloise watched the king; he looked fond and a little exasperated. She didn't think they would have any trouble here as long as the queen was on their side.

She had spent hours practicing and memorizing all the formalities associated with being introduced as her family's representative in a foreign court. None of these were utilized, swept away by Lissie's enthusiasm. She introduced the king, casually, to Joel, Eloise, Jeremy, and the four diplomats they'd brought along. And then she asked to see her baby, and the king requested that all political matters be postponed until the next day.

"Of course," Eloise said. It would be the first time both parents were with their child at the same time.

~

"I think that went quite well," Joel said, and enjoyed the way Eloise jolted probably a bit more than he should have.

She turned to face him. "I am supposed to be on my best behavior as my father's representative."

"I know."

"So what, exactly, are you doing in my bedroom?"

"It's a very old manor."

"Yes, I know that. It doesn't—"

"Walk me through what you know of regional architecture—you'll get there. You are the one who taught me."

"Most of our surviving architecture is in the style favored by the empire. Even after they left us, we maintained their techniques. More recent builds tend to favor new trends from the continent. But there are still a few remaining estates in the old Olin style, though none within the current Alirian borders." She paused. "It's an old Olin manor house? This far south?"

"Olion did have the run of the island at one time."

"We'll have to request a proper tour."

"If you like." He made himself comfortable in an overstuffed chair near the window. There was no risk of inappropriate behavior being noted unless someone else was also behaving inappropriately. The manor had a guest wing in which all the rooms were linked by a series of hidden hallways, allowing guests to go about their business without their hosts or their hosts' servants prying into anything. Joel had learned this from the man who'd come earlier to invite him to a royal breakfast. Joel, from there, had peeked behind every tapestry in his suite—the walls of which were covered in them—until he'd found the hallway, which he'd been exploring ever since. No one else in this wing likely knew about the passages, and if they did, they would, unlike him, have the good manners not to use them for intruding on the princess' private space.

She sighed. "Joel..."

"I promise there was no one to see me sneaking in. The passages were empty. As long as you don't raise your voice, no one will have any idea I was here. Which means that you and Jeremy and I can have private meetings without those damn diplomats."

"Fine. But keep away from the window."

He slid reluctantly out of the chair, onto the floor. "I know nothing actually happened, and he hated every moment of it, but I am still wildly jealous of Fuller."

Eloise joined him on the floor. "I don't think I've ever been in such disgrace in my life. And I didn't even get to do anything to earn it."

Pressing herself up against a man in her bedroom was inappropriate even when that man wasn't Joel, but he knew what she meant, or hoped he did—that she would have at least enjoyed herself, if he had been the one there with her.

"I missed your lessons," he said, returning more or less to the safer subject of architecture.

"I only passed them because of you."

"What?"

"I was always so bad at my lessons. Focusing was so hard, and the information didn't stick in my head. But you wanted so badly to hear about them, I tried to hold onto everything at least until I could tell it to you, and the telling of it made remembering it easier. Ben used to help me, but the gap between us was growing, then—you brought him back to me, I think—and you just helped so much. Just by wanting to know."

"You made it look easy."

She didn't answer. After a few minutes she said, "I do have an attendant, you know."

"Your poor attendant has been exhausted since we left the capital. Not nearly as sturdy as the one we took to find Lissie. Has she ever travelled at all? I'm sure she's quite soundly asleep now, and anyway she wouldn't just barge into your room."

"No, but she might be suspicious if I made her wait in the hall until you were gone."

"Then it's a good thing she's sleeping," Joel said.

"These buildings fell out of favor because rather than using the passages to allow guests to move freely without speculation, they were being used to spy on the guests."

"No one is spying on us. I've just been through all the hidden passages; I would have seen any spies.

"Tonight no one is spying on us. But they could."

"And surely any Ibanari spies are far more interested in our indiscretions than whatever political discussions they may be having in the next room."

Eloise sighed. "Go back to your own room. We both have appointments in the morning."

~

Joel was scheduled to have breakfast with his sister, nephew, and brother-in-law. He reminded himself, as he dressed in the fine clothing that had been hastily provided in Aliria, in acknowledgement of his relationship to the queen, that this was a good thing. He hadn't seen Lissie since she went to get her baby yesterday, and the fact that he was invited to a family meal was a good indicator that the king was planning to pardon him.

But he hadn't liked the king, at their previous meeting. And he didn't like that the king was married to his baby sister, that he'd had a child with his baby sister.

Although he was, admittedly, looking forward to meeting his nephew again in less fraught circumstances.

Lissie and the king were already there. And the baby, in a high chair with intricate carvings.

"Good morning, Lissie," he said, and then wished he hadn't, because he could hardly say good morning only to her, and had no idea how to address a king who was also his brother-in-law who also probably hated him.

"Tell him," Lissie said, before Joel had a chance to work it out.

The king sighed. "All criminal charges are of course being dropped."

"And?" Lissie asked.

"You are of course welcome at any of our royal holdings at any time, and for any length of time."

"Thank you," Joel said.

Lissie beamed at both of them, then stood to remove the baby from his chair, and deposit him instead in Joel's lap. "Meet your nephew," she said. "Sweetheart, this is your Uncle Joel."

The baby said—something. It sounded as if it meant something, not just baby talk, but Joel had no idea what.

"He keeps saying that," the king reported. "His nurse tells me it's some sort of Kirian greeting, but she didn't know the exact meaning."

"Tarin's terrible with languages," Lissie said. "All those months in Kire, and I don't think she picked up a single word." She turned to Joel. "I have to make fun of her for that, you see, because she's so much better than me at everything else."

"Do you know what it means?" the king asked her.

She nodded. "The literal translation is 'Tell me a story.' It's a Kirian greeting for old friends."

Joel very carefully didn't react. If he was being greeted as an old friend—but the baby was not yet two years old. Surely he couldn't remember their one brief meeting months ago.

He glanced up at the king, who looked fond and amused and not at all suspicious. "Well, then. It seems he's acquired a great many old friends in a very short time. He's been saying that to priests and priestesses, ministers and military officials, chambermaids and chefs and gardeners, every single dog, cat, and horse he's encountered, and on one memorable occasion a wasp, which, alas, was not receptive to his overtures of friendship."

Lissie reclaimed her child. "Oh no," she said to him. "Did you get stung?"

He nodded solemnly.

"Where?"

He pointed to his left hand.

When Lissie had finished fussing over the baby, she turned back to Joel. "I know you'll want to go back to Aliria. But you'll come to the capital for the naming ceremony, won't you?"

"Of course," he said.

Ibanari tradition demanded that the royal heir's name not be written down or shared outside the immediate circle of his caretakers until a religious ceremony had been performed. Typically this was done within a few days of birth. But the ceremony required a number of Ibanari priests, and could not be done in Kire. Which meant that Joel did not yet know his nephew's name, and the king had not known his own son's name until he was brought home from Kire.

It would be interesting; Joel, of course, had never been to such a ceremony. It was only required for the first child of the king, though it was often done for later children, and for the children of other noblemen, and occasionally children of particularly wealthy merchants who were striving to move upward in the world. Certainly it was never done in Joel's hometown, which hadn't even enough local priests to correctly perform the ceremony. He thought it had been done once in the nearest large city, but he had been too young, then, to be interested in such things.

The rest of breakfast went well. They didn't linger; the king had several meetings scheduled for the day. But something had been bothering Joel. It had been bothering him, actually, for several months, but recent events had brought it to the forefront.

"Did you recognize me?" he asked the king. "Yesterday, when we arrived?"

"You were by far the most likely of the group to be Lissan's brother."

"No, I mean, not as Lissie's. From before." Should he be drawing the king's attention to their previous meeting? Probably not. But he needed to know.

"Of course. We'd been assuming you'd be at least willing to betray Aliria, if not enthusiastic. Your reaction was…unexpected. And then there was the ring. You were quite memorable."

$$Chapter\ 40$$

It occurred to Eloise that several days had passed since she'd seen Joel outside of the dinners to which they were both invited. This was odd; she'd expected him to take advantage of the secret passages to pester her frequently. He hadn't even joined the rest of their party on a tour of the historic manor.

"Do you know which room is Joel's?" she asked Jeremy, the next time she caught him without too many people around.

He frowned at her. "He doesn't have one."

"What?"

"He moved out of the guest wing, into the family wing. Days ago, now. I think it was after the first night. He didn't tell you?"

"We haven't spoken."

He frowned harder. "The passages are exclusive to each wing, and we're expected not to wander elsewhere. You'll have to catch him in public."

"I don't need to speak with him," she said. "I was just wondering."

"You're running out of time, Eloise."

"Time for what?"

"Time to keep him."

She didn't answer. She retreated to her own room; she had a break before her next meeting. As she was primarily there for appearances, not handling the actual negotiations, her schedule was more open than anyone else's. Some afternoons she spent with Queen Lissan, and others she spent alone.

She remembered how achingly empty the palace had felt without Joel in it. How achingly empty her life had felt, these last several years, but that wasn't—it wasn't because Joel was gone, surely. It was because he had ever been there at all, because she'd spent those years trying to atone for him.

She'd missed him so much, as soon as she'd stopped trying to hate him.

She didn't go looking for him the next day, or the next. She checked in with the diplomats—their negotiations were progressing well enough, and there was nothing for Eloise to help with, nothing to distract her.

"I think they're a little uneasy that we're now connected by marriage to Olion," Jeremy offered, being the only one willing to actually confide in her. "It puts Ibanar at a disadvantage for any future intra-island conflicts. They do like having you here, though, even if you're not particularly involved in the actual negotiations. They like that you've never personally waged war against them, and they say the queen is more comfortable with you than she is usually with even most members of their royal family."

"They don't care that it was my childhood romance that launched the war in the first place?"

"The war would have started regardless. It may have been somewhat sped along by the need to discredit Joel before he caught on and told you or your father, but the actual plan to destabilize the government and create conflict on the island had nothing to do with you. Have you spoken to Joel?"

"I've been busy."

"With what, exactly?"

"Being friendly to our hosts and collecting data on the progression of negotiations to write back to my parents."

"It could be argued that Joel is now one of our hosts, and you should be friendly to him as well."

"If he's in a different wing, I'll have to speak with him publicly. Joel and I have not, historically, done well publicly."

"I'll handle it," Jeremy said, and left.

~

He slipped past the tapestry into Eloise's room that night—he'd entered the passages through Jeremy's room.

She frowned at him. "That's not one of the outfits you brought along."

"Lissie said I looked too Alirian." There hadn't been time to make new clothing, but she'd had some altered, as they'd done for her in Aliria.

"You are Alirian."

"Am I?"

Eloise didn't answer, not directly. "So you're staying, then."

"Is there any reason I shouldn't?"

She studied him for a long moment. "You're angry."

"I'm not."

"You are. You've been avoiding me, you moved out of our wing, and you're planning to stay in Ibanar."

"I'm not angry. I'm just not asking you for anything I should have known all along you would never give me."

"But you were, before. So what changed?"

"I realized how foolish it was to hope for anything from you, how little I meant to you."

"You don't mean little to me," she said.

"Everyone else recognized me, Eloise! My uncle recognized me. The king of Ibanar recognized me, and we barely met. We walked into your father's throne room, and they all knew exactly who I was. Your father, your brother, random people I'd never even spoken to. But you. You said you loved me. And then you spent every day with me for months before figuring it out."

"I didn't—"

"Did you ever even care?"

"I loved you."

"Then why didn't you know me?"

"Because I didn't want to know you. I spent the better part of a decade doing my best to forget you, and apparently I had some success. And you acted different, when you were Senam."

"Oh, and I was acting so much like my old self in the throne room?"

"It was the way you looked at me."

"What?"

"I asked Julian, before he left. It...bothered me, that I hadn't recognized you, and he had. He said that you still looked at me just the way you always had."

"The way I always had. Like I loved you, and knew it would end in disaster?"

"I suppose so."

"I still do, you know."

"I know." She sat down in the chair by the window, and he perched on the window sill, waiting to see if she would protest.

She didn't.

"I spent years seeing you everywhere I turned, and years trying and failing to pretend I'd never seen you at all. I didn't not recognize you because you didn't matter. I think I didn't recognize you because you mattered too much. Because—because it couldn't be you, because I was sick of seeing you everywhere, because—because why should it really be you this time, when it never had before? By the time you took off the mask, I'd gotten used to the bits of Joel I couldn't help seeing in Senam."

They sat there quietly for a long moment. He didn't know what else to say, didn't know how to—he meant more than a little to her. But that didn't mean—didn't mean anything, really.

"It's late," she said, finally.

"Eloise…"

"Come back tomorrow?"

"All right."

~

"Chris told me about your original plan," Eloise said when Joel slipped into her room the next night.

"Did he."

"He meant it to help you. I'm not—well, I'm past being angry about all that. I do appreciate that you didn't go through with it. I just—was it because you still loved me, or because an Alirian prince had a better chance than an outlaw at reaching the queen of Ibanar?"

"Being a prince of Aliria wouldn't have stopped me being an outlaw in Ibanar. I had hoped that if I got back in your good graces, I would be able to tell everyone what I knew—what I did tell them. And putting that information toward ending the war would have gotten me a little closer to Lissie, but it wasn't about her. I would have made a better plan if she was the main goal. I'm not stupid about Lissie the way I am about you."

"So you admit it was stupid."

"Of course it was stupid. I kidnapped you so that I could rescue you from myself. It's quite possibly the most idiotic thing I've ever done. And you'll recall I did once join a conspiracy against the king."

She smiled despite herself. "I did miss you," she admitted.

He sighed. "What do you want from me, Eloise?"

"I want you to be here."

"As what?"

"I don't know."

"You couldn't figure it out, in all those months I was gone?"

"I just—I don't want a life without you in it."

"Then make me stay. Marry me."

She studied him for a moment, thoughtful. "You're the brother of the queen."

"I suppose I am."

"A political marriage—"

"I don't want a political marriage with you, Eloise."

"But you do want a marriage."

"Eloise..."

"Marry me, Joel."

"Because you love me, or because I'm convenient?"

"You were away for months. I—I didn't like you being gone."

He didn't answer. It wasn't enough. She knew it wasn't enough. She wasn't ready to say she loved him. But she wasn't ready to lose him, either.

"We don't need a political marriage. Aliria and Ibanar are both willing to end the war. You gave that to us. You ended the war, and no one will ever know. We can do without any more marriages. No one is demanding this of me. No one is even asking it. Don't marry me for politics. Marry me because you want to. Because I want you to."

He stared at her for a long moment, and then he sighed. "All right. Let's get married."

It wasn't romantic. But it was Joel, and what she had to give him, and the threat of a life without him.

~

Eloise requested—and was granted—an audience with the king. She brought Jeremy along, because she trusted Jeremy, but didn't mention it to the others. He would support her, and not interfere with her plan.

"With Olion and Aliria now joined by marriage, Ibanar is at a disadvantage. As my father the king's representative in Ibanar, I would like to offer you a marriage treaty of your own."

"And who do you propose we marry for this treaty?" the king asked, though she suspected he already knew; there was one rather obvious option. Even were it not for their history, Ibanar had no other relatives of marriageable age, and Eloise was the highest ranked person in Aliria of compatible age.

"I would offer myself in marriage to your brother-in-law," she said.

"And you are authorized to make this arrangement?"

"I am," she said. It was true. She may well be in trouble for it later, but it was a good political match, and she was acting in her father's stead, which meant that she was technically authorized to do anything that he was.

"Very well. Are your other negotiators aware of this offer?"

"Not yet."

"I will of course need to speak with my brother-in-law before accepting."

"Of course."

"His acceptance is likely. I would advise you to make your colleagues aware so that we can begin discussing the details tomorrow."

~

"That was a foolish thing to do without consulting us," said the head minister.

"Well, it's done. I'll leave you to handle the details."

"Your father—" another began.

"My father trusted me to handle things here, and this is how I've chosen to do it. If he disapproves, I will discuss it with him directly, not

342

with you. Can you deny that a marriage alliance will simplify our treaty?"

"There are rumors that Joel and the king have a bad history. A marriage to him may not be a deterrent to future conflict."

"My understanding is that a marriage would be more for his peace of mind than ours. And the king adores his wife, who adores her brother, which should be deterrent enough. I'm done discussing it. The offer has been made; you're too late to talk me out of it. It will be the primary point of negotiation tomorrow. I'll leave you to discuss your strategy."

~

Neither Joel nor Eloise sat in on the discussions regarding their marriage. The king and queen of Ibanar weren't present, either. It was Jeremy's duty, then, as a friend of both parties, surrounded by others who cared little for either of them, to ensure the best possible outcome. It was arranged that Joel be officially named a lower prince, as he had not yet been titled, and that a certain amount of wealth, though no property, be attached to the title. It was arranged that the wedding would be held in Aliria, after the Ibanari heir's naming ceremony, and that the queen would attend as a representative of Ibanar, accompanied as she felt necessary, but with no stronger military escort than a single squad. It was agreed that the details of the ceremony could be decided by the primary participants. It was agreed that while the war would be officially over the moment the agreed-upon treaty was signed, and hostilities would cease immediately, the new trade agreements would not go into effect until after the wedding.

Jeremy had, he thought, done as well for Joel and Eloise as could be expected, giving them space and time to plan their own wedding, making sure Joel had an official title to protect him, arranging it so that Joel's sister was guaranteed to be present. The long delay was unfortunate but unavoidable.

Joel and Eloise would be given the details officially the next day, separately, by the head negotiator for each country. But Jeremy would tell them now, tonight, so they needn't worry about it; he'd already arranged for Joel to meet him in his rooms, and they could collect Eloise easily enough.

Chapter 41

Sylvia returned to the palace earlier than expected. She had seen both Harra and George. She had helped an injured man reach the nearest village, and helped a woman give birth. She had found several refugees who no longer wanted to continue south with the news she brought, and had helped them back north a way before finding someone to hand them off to.

She presented the seal the king had given her—well, the seal he'd given Eloise, to give to her—at the palace gate, and waited there for nearly an hour as news of her arrival travelled through various parties, and instructions on what to do with her were then passed back along the same route.

Her pardon was official, the condition met. They invited her in. She could return to her old room or be settled in a new suite closer to Jeremy's while she awaited his return.

"May I have the seal back?" she asked.

"What for?" asked the guard who'd taken it.

"I don't want to stay here. But I will return, to meet my betrothed, and I would like to be let in when I do."

This required further consultation, and further waiting, but eventually the seal was returned.

She headed north.

~

"When should we do it?" Joel asked.

"In the spring," Eloise said. She didn't look at him. They were alone, both sitting on her bed; it should have felt much more intimate than it did. "The first day of spring. The holy day."

"In the morning?" he asked.

She remembered telling him, once, that she wanted to be married in the morning, wanted to start her new life and start a new day together. But that had been a long time ago. "At sunset, I think."

"All right."

They were sitting on the same bed. They were engaged. They felt so far apart.

Did he regret it? Would he rather—

She knew he didn't just want to be married, he wanted to be loved. Of course he did; it was what everyone wanted most out of marriage, wasn't it?

She just…couldn't. Not yet.

"I'll stay here with Lissie until the end of winter, then. We'll be back in time for the wedding."

She nodded, then looked up at him; he was looking at her, unreadable—she always used to be able to read him.

"I should go," he said, and stood, and did. It was their last private meeting in Ibanar.

~

As Joel's future wife, and therefore the king's future sister-in-law, Eloise was invited to family meals.

Joel had joined Lissie and the king for one meal daily since their arrival. And he hadn't been so nervous since the first one.

He sat between Lissie and his nephew. Eloise would be across from him, beside the king. He wasn't—

She'd agreed to marry him. She—she wanted to marry him, even if she didn't—didn't—

She said she hadn't recognized him because she was so used to seeing him where he wasn't. He had been, at least, on her mind.

Eloise arrived, curtsied, and greeted Lissie and the king. Then she turned to Joel, frowning. "I don't know how to address you," she admitted.

"Generally you use my name."

"I mean, they said you were a lower prince, now. I don't know how to speak to a lower prince. Are you a highness? A lord? A grace?"

It was an old Ibanari tradition, dating back to their time on the sea, and mostly fallen out of favor now, not shared with the rest of the island.

"I don't know how to speak to a lower prince, either," he said. It had certainly never come up when he was a child; they lived nowhere near the capital, and he had never encountered a prince of any kind.

"We'll have documents with that information prepared for both of you," the king said. "In the meantime, as you are betrothed, and this is a private family meal, I believe Joel will continue to suffice."

Eloise nodded.

"Sit, please," the king said. "Traditionally we would have seafood at the first family gathering after a finalized betrothal. But alas, the estate is landlocked. We have fish from the river, instead."

There was little difference, as far as Joel was concerned, between seafood and river food. Different types of fish, perhaps?

"I'm sure it will be lovely," Eloise said. She sat, and the table was narrow enough that he could have reached his feet out to touch hers; he didn't.

She was going to marry him. She was actually going to marry him.

He wished it felt more like a victory.

"Have you made any plans for the wedding yet?" Lissie asked.

"Just a date and time," Eloise said. "Won't you tell me about yours? I've never been to an Ibanari wedding."

Lissie lit up, and it occurred to Joel, belatedly, that he probably should have asked her more about her wedding, months ago. He remained uncomfortable with the marriage as a whole, though the king has been perfectly kind since he arrived, but a wedding to a king would certainly have been an exciting event that she would have things to say about.

Joel and Eloise didn't speak at all over breakfast, Lissie dominating the conversation with wedding talk. But she looked over and smiled at him, twice, and that was—it was something.

She would leave soon; with the marriage arranged, the treaty was all but finalized. And with the date she'd chosen for the wedding, it would be some time before they were reunited.

He thought of going to her that night. He thought of going to her most nights, especially as she couldn't come to him, didn't even know where to find him, here. But the engagement felt, bizarrely, like losing her. He didn't—he still didn't know where they stood. If possible, he knew even less than he had before. Her refusals and denials had been straightforward. This engagement was less so.

He still didn't know how she felt. So he didn't go to her. And far too soon, she was leaving, without him.

They left early in the morning. There had been a dinner last night, at which Lissie and the king had officially said their farewells. Only Joel and a few members of the Ibanari court were present to see the party off.

He stood off to the side, and let someone whose name he ought to have learned by now say all of the official, appropriate things, and watched Eloise.

She was wearing pale pink, against which her dark leather riding boots stood out oddly, her hair tied back for the coming ride. The pink was an odd choice—it would dirty easily—and he wondered if it was because of him, if she even knew that he loved her in pink, that it reminded him of their early days, when it had been her most worn color by far.

He watched as Eloise said all the official, appropriate things back. He watched as the whole group turned to leave, mounting the waiting horses.

And then Eloise lifted her skirts, ran back, and kissed Joel, quick and barely there. "In the spring," she said, and before he had processed she was on her horse, riding away.

~

Sylvia reached Jeremy's land quickly. She got as far as the mill with no issue—as far as she had gotten before—and froze. Just ahead was everything she'd lost.

None of the people she'd known would be waiting, on the other side of the mill. None of the buildings she'd known. Even the trees she'd known would be gone.

Her whole life had burned here. Why had she thought she could come back?

She sat in the grass behind the mill; there was a large rock there that she could lean on.

She couldn't—she couldn't—Jeremy was building a home for them here. She had to go back.

He wouldn't make her. She knew that. If she told him she couldn't go back, he would find them a new home. He would give up the barony altogether if she asked him.

But this place had been hers. It had been hers long before she even knew Jeremy. This place held her mother's ashes, and her sister's, and her brother's. This place held, maybe, her living, breathing father.

The men who'd burned the village were long dead. She couldn't let them win.

Time had passed. An hour or more. But there was still plenty of daylight left. She could sleep in the mill tonight, but that would leave her with long, boring hours to wait, as her dread continued to build.

She stood, and forced herself forward, one step at a time. She could hear the sounds of construction, and faint but cheerful conversation.

This was her home. Hers. The fire couldn't keep it.

She made her way, slowly, through the last several feet of trees, smaller and more spread out until at last they stopped altogether, and there was nowhere left to hide.

There were several men working on several small buildings; one spotted her, stopped working, and took a moment to confer with two others nearby. One of them—the smallest of the three, which was undoubtedly deliberate—set down his hammer and approached slowly.

"Hello," he said. "Are you here about the refugee encampment?"

"In a way."

He nodded. "We're not done building yet. We can find you a place to stay today, but it may be a bit crowded for a while."

"Oh, no," she said, "that's not—" It occurred to her that, while she had a letter in the king's hand, stamped with his seal, there was absolutely no proof of her relationship to Jeremy. "I may stay for a few days, only. I'm looking for my father; I think he's come here. This used to be our village."

"Well," he said, "I'm just a builder, but if you go about half a mile that way, you'll find the woman handling intake. She can tell you if your father's here."

Sylvia thanked him and went on her way. It wasn't too late; she could still turn and leave. Her father didn't know she was here yet. No one who knew her did. But she was so close. So close.

She went in the direction he'd indicated. There were people everywhere. Small houses and various other buildings at various stages of construction. A large garden. There were stakes laid out to mark something—locations for buildings and for streets, she assumed. A few children were running about, a few people working the garden, a few carrying things back and forth, several working construction. She could see the larger project of the manor ahead; if it was being put in the same place as the old one, it would be a few miles from the edge of the village.

There was a collection of tents about a half mile from where she'd started. A young woman standing just outside one spotted her, turned to call out to someone, "We've got a new one," then waved Sylvia over.

"Hello!" she said. "We'll get you settled right quick—I just need your name, age, and nationality to start."

"I'm not staying. Just looking for my father."

"All right, then, let me fetch Mary. She knows everything."

Sylvia stood waiting for a few minutes, until Mary was located. Mary, it turned out, was familiar to her, a woman she'd encountered several times in her years of running refugees across the island.

"Sylvia, darling. They told me you'd be here eventually. Not staying, though? Or at least not yet? This is your part of the world, isn't it? What's your father's name, dear? Most of the men are either helping with the construction, or working the field out on the eastern edge of town, this time of day."

Sylvia had never actually enjoyed Mary's company, finding her ceaseless cheerfulness and constant chatter rather overwhelming. But she was a good woman who did good work; if she was running things here, they would be well run. She gave her father's name, and was told he was likely working up at the manor. She was also told, because Mary always had more to tell, that most of the village residents so far were doing either construction or farming, but once everyone had a stable home, and the crops were better-established, they would transition over to working in their own trades. She was told that they were monitoring origin points of incoming villagers in case of tension, but everyone had been getting along well so far. She was told that a person or small group of people had been arriving every two to three days for the past month. She was told that they were expecting the population of the village to at least double, if not triple, before they were through.

"I know you said you aren't staying," Mary said, as Sylvia tried, again, to extract herself, "but you will be back, won't you? No one knew when you would arrive, but they did say you'd be helping run the place. And it's a fair bit of work already; I don't know what I'll do when more come, or how to transition from a refugee encampment to a proper village."

This was the first Sylvia was hearing of this, but it made sense—a baroness had to do something, she supposed, and helping manage the surrounding village was a good option.

(But must it be with Mary?)

"I will," she said. "After my marriage. Now I must find my father."

It was over an hour's walk to the manor; her eagerness to escape Mary propelled her most of the way there. She was very close before she remembered again to be anxious about her father.

The manor was coming along nicely. It all was—there was much to build yet in the village, but several finished buildings, as well.

The new manor was much smaller than the old one, less than half the size, but still extravagantly large. Jeremy had explained to her that one of the requirements of a baron's residence was that it must be able to comfortably house the king and any other guests he wished to have present. He was not too worried about the current king or the next straining the bounds of his hospitality, but didn't want to leave a mess for his descendants with a too-small manor. Also, one of Eloise's brothers had married into Olion, and Jeremy's estate would be conveniently placed for the royal family to meet, or to rest for a night while travelling back and worth.

There were many men working busily, none of whom took much notice of her. The workers nearer the edge of the woods likely saw travellers frequently, and were therefore looking out for them.

Most men were up on ladders. She found one nearer the ground, and gave him her father's name; he directed her around to the other side of the building.

After asking directions twice more, she found herself inside the manor—inside her new home—watching from behind the door. The man she thought was her father turned, confirming it, and she stepped forward before she could lose her nerve.

"Father?"

He dropped his hammer. It was a good thing he hadn't been up on a ladder. "Sylvia? Is it—is it really you?"

She nodded, and he stepped forward and wrapped his arms around her, and it took her too long to remember she should hug him back.

"Sylvia, sweetheart. I thought you were dead."

"I—I left them. They were burning, and I ran."

He pulled back, and studied her face for a moment, fingers hovering over her scars, but not touching. "Let's go somewhere more private, yes?"

She nodded again.

They wound up sitting on the ground several feet behind the manor. From there, Sylvia could see a few more tents, and the part of the forest they must have been cutting down for all the building.

"I'm sorry," she said.

"What for?"

"I ran. They burned, and I ran."

"And what was one slip of a girl to do against a raging fire and three dozen soldiers?"

"I could have burned with them," she offered. She'd wished she had, often enough.

"I'm glad you didn't," he said, firmly. "Where have you been?"

"Oh, everywhere. Up and down the island more times than I can count. You've been—you've been back here for some time now?"

"A few months. There were just a few of us at first. Got the crops started, and cleared out the ash so the river could run again. Dug a new well. Tried to start rebuilding. And then the baron's men came, and then the refugees, and things have moved quickly since then. I have a house of my own, finished, larger than most—reparations, the baron called it. But it's full of people every night, until we can get enough built. The baron—you know he's marrying?"

"Me," she said, a little nervous to admit it, after everything. "He's marrying me."

"I'm glad. But you came here alone? On foot?"

"He's in Ibanar now. Politics. I've been travelling. I wanted to—to tie up some loose ends, before the wedding."

"Well, then. Your house will be finished before the week is out."

She looked back over at the manor. They'd made good progress, surely, but she didn't think it was that far along.

"We're prioritizing getting shelter for as many as possible before the first freeze. The baron's house is to be prepared for the winter weather, but we're only fully finishing a space large enough to comfortably hold the two of you, a few servants, and a kitchen. Once that's done—in a few days now—the detail work, the painting, the other rooms, all of that waits until the spring."

"Good. Tell me what else is happening?"

"We've planted the crops with the shortest cycle, and we have people canning and salting as fast as they can in some of the finished buildings. We're trying not to cut down too much of the forest, since we'll get most of our meat this winter by hunting there. But there's livestock coming, at some point. I'll be getting some of that for the reparations, too, likely goats and chickens. We're making use of all the empty space in the manor to build furniture and make bedding. All of us helping with the construction, for the manor or the village, are being paid by the baron. Between that Mary and the foreman, everything is going smoothly, although I think Mary has had about enough—she's waiting on someone else to come take charge."

"That's me, too, apparently." The disadvantage of having one of the most popular names on the island—he'd known she was coming without knowing who she was. "Refugees are my business. Though usually we're travelling, not settling. I've been escorting groups down toward Ibanar, to sail out to Kire from there."

He nodded.

"Will you—will you show me your new house? If you can spare the time from working?"

"I'm sure the baroness can excuse me. And now is a good time—it's not so crowded in the day."

They made their way back to the village slowly. Her father walked with a limp, now, likely a war injury. She didn't ask. She didn't want to think about him, on a battlefield, fighting and killing. She didn't want him to pay more attention to her burns, or ask about the fighting and killing she'd done.

It was a larger house than the one they'd lost, though it would house fewer people. It was built, as most things here were, from a combination of new wood and salvaged stone from the old village. There was a fence in the back, and a little covered area she thought was the beginnings of a stable. Inside there were mostly thin mattresses all over the floor.

It would never be her home.

In front of the fire were several round, flat stones, large, and some chiseling tools. Her mother's name was mostly carved into the first stone.

"We'll make a graveyard," her father said, "or a memorial, at least. It's slow going. But one less stone, now."

"One less," she agreed.

"Is the baron joining you here, or are you meeting him elsewhere?"

"Elsewhere. We'll be back after the wedding. But for now I can stay a few days, perhaps a week."

"You won't want to sleep here. It's all men. But we can find you a spot, for a few days."

The week passed quickly. While her father worked construction, Sylvia met with Mary, and started work of her own. Math, mostly. How many they had, how many they could expect, how many shelters were being built and how quickly, how much food they would need, how much time they could expect until the first hard freeze.

It was a good thing she was there, and leaving again—she could give all the numbers to Jeremy, and they could bring what supplies they needed from the capital when they returned.

A few days passed before her father raised the question of her wedding. He would enjoy attending. But there was no set date for the wedding—there wasn't even a set date for Jeremy's return. It was better her father stayed at home, ready to welcome her back.

She was relieved, and tried not to show it. It was so strange, having a father again, having a family again, and after all they'd been through, they still felt half like strangers. Better to readjust to each other at home than in a palace.

Chapter 42

Jeremy was worried about Eloise. She had been quiet and withdrawn for the whole journey home, and had neatly redirected any conversation he tried to start about it. In private, he could have pinned her down and worked out the problem, and maybe helped her solve it, but there was no privacy on the journey.

By the time they reached the same battlefield they'd passed before, news of the war ending had preceded them. The army was in the process of packing up and heading home, and several more soldiers joined their party. She had taken to avoiding him, and it was easy to do, with so many of them travelling together.

He wanted to really talk to her, when they reached the palace, when they could finally escape the audience. But there was Sylvia, standing just outside the gate, dusty and worn as if she too had just arrived, but smiling brightly when she saw him.

Later, he promised himself. He would talk to Eloise later. He swung off his horse's back, handing the reins to one of the many grooms who'd come out to meet them, and went to Sylvia.

She wrapped her arms around his neck, there in public, and leaned close, and kissed him.

"Missed you," she whispered, when she pulled away.

He took her arm and led her into the courtyard, trusting the grooms to handle his things. "When did you get back?"

"About an hour ago. They said you were expected today, so I just sat down and waited."

"Do you need to talk to the king?"

She shook her head. "All taken care of. Fully pardoned. Now when do we get married?"

~

Eloise hated returning home with neither Joel nor Lissie. She had not made friends with the other women in their party—admittedly, she hadn't tried to—and sharing a tent with them was awkward. She had only Jeremy to talk to during the day, and there was little they could comfortably talk about, surrounded by others. And besides, she suspected him of wanting to talk about Joel.

Her parents already knew what she'd done; messages had been sent ahead. She had no idea whether they would be angry or not. She would find out soon enough; she'd been summoned to meet them immediately upon the return.

"Are you sure this is what you want to do?" the queen asked as soon as Eloise arrived.

"Yes."

She sighed. "Very well, then. Will your primary residence be here, or in Ibanar?"

"We haven't discussed it."

"You'll have to write him to find out. And we'll have to prepare a suite of rooms suitable for a married couple; you'll be here for the days following the wedding at least."

Eloise nodded, and turned to her father, who hadn't spoken yet; was he angry with her?

"I am glad," he said slowly, "that you are finally able to have this."

"Thank you."

"Theo and Erika will be arriving within the week. We will celebrate your engagement and their return together."

"It will be your duty," the queen said, "to inform Julian of your engagement."

And for the first time, Eloise was glad her brother was far away in Olion.

~

There was hardly time to miss Eloise. Granted, he missed her regardless. But there was so much to do.

They returned to the capital. There was a formal introduction, a ceremony signaling the end of the war, and a ceremony solidifying his new title. There was a full wardrobe to be made, and a number of temples to visit, and several lessons on what was expected of a lower prince.

Not much was expected, fortunately. Well. There were many expectations for how he behaved and how he interacted with others, most of which he struggled to meet. A number of events he was expected to attend while he was there, mostly meals and the occasional outing. But there were no associated responsibilities.

He wondered if there would be responsibilities in Aliria. He rather thought not, if only because surely no one in Aliria would trust him with any. That was likely the reason he hadn't any here, either. Perhaps he ought to be offended, but he didn't actually want the kinds of responsibilities that princes were supposed to have.

He received a letter from Eloise, the day before his nephew's naming ceremony. It was short.

"I've arranged a suite for us; it's in a corner, and faces the sunset on one side, and the forest on the other. We never discussed long term living arrangements. Do you intend to stay in Aliria? Or would you rather we return to Ibanar?

Eloise"

He responded by writing out the entire text of "Senam and the Mermaid," and then, realizing this may be unclear, added, "I have a plan. A surprise. You'll like it."

He posted the letter, then went to make a plan.

~

Sylvia had wanted to be married immediately; after all, they had been engaged for months. She had wanted to be married, and move to their mostly-built house, and be with normal people again, be with her father again, live in a village and help people settle and be free to live her own life.

Things were not so simple, when one was marrying a baron. There were arrangements to be made. Traditions to observe. It would take weeks.

"It would normally take months," Eloise informed her. "We've sped things up significantly."

"Months? Why should it take months? You get the approval of your parents and a local priest, you put on your best clothes, and you braid your hair right."

Granted, a few weeks often passed between betrothal and marriage, but she'd seen a couple married the morning after their betrothal, too. And she and Jeremy have already been betrothed for months.

"It's more complicated when you're a baron," Eloise said. "But soon. Definitely soon."

"Before—before, he offered to marry me tomorrow."

"Well, then, it's more complicated when you're a baron living in the king's palace. Perhaps you can cut corners, away up north, but here in the capital it has to be done right." She glanced around Sylvia's room. "Where is he? I hardly ever see you without him anymore."

"Meetings. Something about furnishings for the manor, and something about finances for one of the farms, and something about paperwork."

"My fault, then. All the work that built up when I dragged him to Ibanar. He'll be a while yet?"

"Hours, he said."

"Come with me, then. Off the grounds, where we can relax. We can talk about your wedding dress."

"What is there to talk about?" Sylvia asked as she followed her down the hall.

"Cut, color, material, decoration. Shoes, jewelry, hair."

"Must we? I don't care, as long as it happens soon."

"It is rather important."

"Then I want whichever of all of those things can be prepared the fastest."

Eloise frowned, and didn't speak again until they were in the forest behind the palace, in the same place she'd come to with Joel and with Jeremy. Eloise paused there for a moment, looked around, and shook her head. "Pond, I think," she said, and led her a little further.

At the pond, Eloise sat in the wet grass, pulled up her skirts, pulled off her shoes and stockings, and put her feet into the water. Sylvia sat nearby, feet tucked under her legs—it was a bit too late in the year, she thought, to comfortably play in the water.

"The dress won't slow anything down. So it might as well be exactly as you want it. Didn't you ever think about it, before?"

"I never really expected Jeremy to marry me. And then everything went wrong so soon after he asked. And normal people don't have fancy new dresses for things like that—I suppose I would have just worn my best dress, the same one I wore to festivals and holy days. It was blue, I think."

"Do you want the traditional Olin wedding braid?" Eloise asked.

"Yes. I know that much."

"That's a start. I know you were near the border, and a lot of things you used and did came from Olion. What did your dresses look like? Would you rather have one that looks more Alirian, or more Olin?"

There were very few things less important to Sylvia than the shape of the dress she married in. But this was what one must endure, she supposed, to marry a baron.

(Well, what one must endure to marry a baron with the wedding hosted and witnessed by the king. None of this would have been necessary for Jeremy, at home. At home, she could have worn her own best dress. It had been blue, hadn't it?)

"I still like blue," she offered.

Eloise nodded, and fortunately didn't ask for a specific shade of blue. "Silk? Linen? Wool?"

Sylvia collapsed backwards onto the grass, sighing.

"I'll just pick one, shall I?"

"Please."

~

Eloise read Joel's letter twice, and then carefully folded it and hid it away. The last bit was in his own familiar handwriting, but for "Senam and the Mermaid," he'd mimicked almost perfectly the script of a famous Ibanari historian; she recognized it from a few of his texts in their library. She didn't need her family to find out just how good a forger he was.

Erika and Theo were back, but she'd seen little of them. There were apparently all sorts of details to be seen to at the end of a war, and they'd been locked up with her father in his office for days. Erika and her husband were spending every spare minute with their children, and Theo had, in addition to post-war tasks, all the usual crown prince responsibilities that had been mostly neglected in recent years.

She was still waiting to hear back from Julian, after writing him about her upcoming wedding.

Annabelle was pregnant, and anxious about it, and not travelling. Maybe Eloise would go and visit her for a week or two, after Jeremy and Sylvia's wedding. She could bring Maria along—she would enjoy that.

Fuller was gone. Chris was in the city, working. Alem was still here, but busy. Not that they were exactly her friends, without Joel there.

Eloise's new responsibilities had vanished upon her return, confirming her suspicions that they had all been only busywork, to keep her out of trouble. All she had to do now was plan her wedding. And to avoid thinking about that, she was instead planning Jeremy's.

It would be happening a month from the day they'd returned from Ibanar. Which was in fact incredibly fast, whatever Sylvia thought about it. There was much to be done.

Her own wedding to Jeremy had been planned and scheduled when she was kidnapped, the dress sewn, the details arranged, mostly by her family, as she had not herself been terribly invested. It would be easy enough just to make her wedding to Jeremy into Sylvia's. Sylvia certainly wouldn't mind. She had very little interest in the wedding itself, except as an unfortunate barrier to the marriage she was waiting for.

But Eloise thought that she would mind. She hadn't loved Jeremy. Well, she had. She still did. She hadn't been in love with Jeremy. But she had still planned a future with him, still looked forward to it. A safe, steady future, lost to her, and she hadn't the faintest idea what a life with Joel would really be like. She didn't mind not marrying Jeremy, not really. But somehow it still hurt, just a little.

~

Lissie slipped into his room, late at night. He was a light sleeper, a natural consequence of being an outlaw, and was sitting up, reaching for a knife, before she was close enough to be recognizable in the moonlight from the window. He lifted the covers, and she slipped into bed beside him, as she had when she was a little girl, before their uncle called him to Aliria.

She didn't speak for several minutes. He waited her out, no longer at all tired.

"I'm pregnant," she said, finally. "The doctor confirmed it this morning."

"That's wonderful, Lissie."

She nodded. "I—it is. I'm glad. But I—he missed the birth, last time. It was to keep me safe, but it hurt him, to miss it, to lose so much time. And this second will probably be the last. I don't want him to miss anything."

"The wedding."

"I do want to be there. But I—I know I should be back before I'm due—but I don't—it would be close."

"I understand," he said. She shouldn't be travelling across the island heavily pregnant.

"I'm sorry."

"Don't be. I suppose I'll miss the naming ceremony, this time—I'm sorry for that."

They laid there together in silence for a long time, long enough he thought she had fallen asleep.

"Joel?"

"Yes?"

"Do you think she loves you?"

"I hope so."

"Do you think you'll be happy?"

"I hope so," he said again. She'd kissed him, before she left. That was something, surely.

"I'm sorry," Lissie said quietly. They didn't speak again. When he woke in the morning she was gone, and at breakfast with the king, neither of them mentioned it.

Chapter 43

"You've been avoiding me," Jeremy said when he found her.

"I haven't."

"Eloise. You've been avoiding me since Ibanar. Somehow, despite organizing the majority of my wedding."

"Mine is next."

"I know."

"You'll come for it? Both of you?"

"Of course."

She nodded slowly, and didn't answer.

"Eloise. Do you want to have a wedding?"

"I don't know," she said.

"Do you love him?"

"I can't."

"Do you love him?" he repeated.

"Of course I love him! I love his smile, and the way he ducks his head and shuffles his feet when he's anxious. I love how he calls me Ellie, and I love how he can never decide whether to use his real accent or not, and how it always bleeds through when he's emotional, even when he wants to hide it. I love all the things about him that he shares with the boy he used to be, and that's not—that's not fair to either of us."

"And how much of a role is your fear of renewed gossip playing in your current feelings?"

"I am sick of being the punchline of half the jokes on this island. Is that so bad? To not want to be haunted forever by one childhood mistake?"

"But was it a mistake? You loved him. He loved you. And he never truly conspired against you. Where, in that situation, was your mistake?"

"I made so many mistakes. There were the times I pulled him into my private chambers, the times I kissed him in front of half the court, that time I convinced him to sneak out into the city and—"

"Eloise. None of those mistakes are—none of those have to do with being with Joel, loving Joel. They're all mistakes you could have made with anyone—they're not about him."

"I know," she said. "I know. But I'm afraid."

"You don't think you could be happy with him?" Jeremy asked.

"I think the damage we've done each other is beyond what can be repaired, and we can enjoy each other's company for a while, but a forever together is only going to hurt."

"You were friends, after you loved him. Even if—if you're only in love with the memories. There is nothing wrong with a marriage based on friendship."

"But we were friends before I loved him, too. And then it all fell apart."

"So it's hopeless? Eloise. You realize you're having this conversation with a man who's getting married tomorrow to a woman who has actually attempted to kill him?"

"I can't—you have always been far more forgiving than me. And Sylvia is…Sylvia, and you weren't really the one who hurt her—it all started from a misunderstanding. Joel and I—I don't know how to— how to sort out the distant past, and the recent past, and the present. I don't—I don't know how to talk to him. Not about the things that matter."

"Eloise, you've agreed to marry him. There will have to be conversation."

"I know. I just—we've tried this before, and it hasn't exactly ended well. In fact, it ended in a devastating war. I'm just hoping we can get through this with minimal casualties. Happy family life would be overreaching."

"You aren't the sort of couple to have a happy family life, anyway. We would have had a happy family life. You and Joel will have chaos and tension and joy, and it will all be worth it."

She shook her head. "We're focusing on the wrong wedding here. Tomorrow, Jeremy. How is Sylvia holding up?"

"All right, I think. She won't let me see her just now, but apparently that's a traditional sort of wedding thing? I mean, it's not because she's angry or having doubts."

"I'm sure she's not."

"One more night. We'll be on our way home by tomorrow evening, and it will be all new for both of us. A fresh start."

"I'm glad."

~

It had been their secret, that first betrothal. Not a betrothal at all, she supposed, since it had never been announced or approved by anyone official. Her father had not yet known. But everyone had been waiting for it, expecting it.

They had been hiding in some small corner of the palace when he had asked, shy and unsure of himself the way he still sometimes was in those days, "You'll marry me, won't you, Ellie?"

She had laughed, and kissed him. "Idiot. Of course. You pick the date, I'll pick the time. We can wait to announce it until we have all the details worked out—that way they can't ruin our plans, and they can't slow everything down. You know how adults get about these things."

"And I'll have to get you a ring."

"Mm. You're penniless. We'll improvise. Maybe I can steal some money from Julian for you."

"Julian. He's going to hate this."

"He'll cope. As long as you take good care of me."

Joel had kissed her then. "You know I will."

A week later he was arrested for treason. They had never told anyone—she was only grateful that he hadn't mentioned it at the trial. But then he was probably a bit distracted, with the torture and all. Torture had never been authorized—you couldn't do that to the boy your daughter loved, no matter what he was guilty of.

He had been a boy. He had been just a child, and he had loved her, and he had not deserved to suffer as he did for it.

But it was far too late to solve these problems now.

He never had gotten her a ring.

~

Eloise helped Sylvia prepare for the wedding, as she was the only other woman anywhere in the vicinity that Sylvia knew. She was sitting, tense, hands in her lap, staring into the mirror as Eloise wove flowers into her braided hair.

"It would have been nice to have Joel here," Sylvia said. "Jeremy is—they're friends. Jeremy doesn't make friends easily. Neither of us does." She fingered the fabric of her dress. "I feel like I'm wearing a costume."

"You look wonderful."

"I think I'll spend the rest of my life in costume."

"If you still can't be yourself with Jeremy—"

"It isn't that. It's—I'm sure about Jeremy. It's everything else. Living in the manor. Being a baroness. He could—well, he could have married a princess. And my stupid scars. You would still be yourself with flowers in your hair."

"Everything will be fine. And you look beautiful with flowers in your hair."

"Did I tell you I saw my father?"

"No."

"I told him I'd see him again when we got back. I told him not to come."

"If you want him here, we can postpone. We can get him."

Sylvia started to shake her head, then stopped, mindful of the flowers. "No, ignore me. I'm just nervous."

"If you're not ready to do this, Jeremy will understand, Sylvia. You can still—"

"No. I'm fine. I'm fine. Whatever else happens, I want—I want to marry him."

"All right." Eloise attached the last flower. "Time to go, then."

~

366

She could hardly recall the details of the wedding, later. It all seemed so unimportant. Just something she had to get through, a show to put on, before she could be allowed to have her husband, and her life, and her home.

She remembered the steady presence of Eloise beside her, Jeremy's smiling face, his eyes never leaving hers. She said the words she was supposed to say, and made it somehow through the endless meal that followed the ceremony, and then they were on the road, having both flatly refused to wait until the following morning.

(They'd had a morning wedding, to allow for travel time later, the only detail Sylvia had taken a true interest in.)

She fell asleep in the carriage, her head on Jeremy's shoulder, her hand in his, and didn't wake until they stopped at an inn for the night.

"Not the best place for a wedding night," he said, looking disapprovingly around their room, which seemed to her to be a perfectly nice one.

"It's perfect," she said, and tugged him to the bed.

Chapter 44

"It was a lovely wedding," Erika said, later.

Eloise nodded. They were alone; she'd come to Sylvia's room, knowing it would be empty. She wasn't sure when Erika had joined her, or how she'd known to.

"I'm sorry it wasn't yours."

She shrugged.

"And Joel. I'm sorry about that, too."

"Sorry?" Eloise asked.

"I know it wasn't what you wanted. And I know everyone has immediately forgotten that."

It was possibly the first time since the betrothal that anyone had considered all the time she'd spent getting over him, had considered she might not have wanted this. And she was, embarrassingly, wrong. "I didn't have to," she admitted. "It wasn't essential to the treaty."

"But it helped."

"Yes." Things had all gone very quickly, very smoothly, once the betrothal was made.

"At least you know him," Erika offered. Her first meeting with her husband had been on their wedding day. And Julian had met the princess of Olion before, but he had only met her; they had never done more than exchange pleasantries.

"Sometimes I think it would be easier if I didn't."

She thought of Senam. She could have loved him, if he had existed. Joel, grown up, without all the ugly things between them.

She could have loved Senam. She could have.

But Senam was only Joel.

She stood.

"Eloise?" Erika asked.

"I need to go plan another wedding."

~

It was strange, planning a wedding alone. Somehow, she hadn't expected it to be. When she was sixteen, and planning to marry Joel as soon as possible, she'd had dozens of wedding ideas, and hadn't at any point consulted Joel about his. She found she wanted to, now.

But he wasn't there.

She wrote him again. "A winter wedding seemed gloomy and almost ominous, but spring is so far away. I miss you."

It wasn't enough to say, she knew. Not for Joel, and not for the messenger, who was carrying two lines over so many miles.

She just—there was no guarantee of privacy, with a message. When she next spoke to Joel, she wanted to be speaking to him and only him, face-to-face, not on a slip of paper anyone between here and Ibanar could read.

In the spring. In the spring they would speak.

She added several questions about wedding planning to the bottom of the letter, as much to justify the expense of sending it as to get his opinions.

~

Sylvia had a screaming nightmare the first night they spent in the manor. Jeremy was trying to wake her; the door flew open, a lantern illuminating their bedroom, just as he succeeded.

"Sylvia?" the woman in the door asked. She was the cook, he thought—the light wasn't much, and they'd only met briefly, earlier this afternoon. One of the three staff members living in the manor. "Are you all right? Did he—"

"No," she said, voice hoarse. "No, just a nightmare."

"You're sure?"

"I'm sure. Thank you, Ingrid."

The woman left, pulling the door closed behind her.

"Did she—did she think I was hurting you?" Jeremy asked in the sudden blackness of the room.

"It happens," she said. "Not to us, but they don't know you, yet. They know me; I'm one of them."

It was good, he decided, that people were looking out for Sylvia. Though he hoped Ingrid's opinion of him—and anyone else's—would improve with him.

"Are you all right? You haven't had one like that in a long time. Not—not since we were engaged, at least."

She found his face in the dark, and kissed him. "I love you," she said. "But love's not magic."

"Do your nightmares wear my face?" he asked.

"Sometimes. Do yours wear mine?"

"Sometimes," he admitted.

"Nightmares don't matter. What we have in daylight is real."

~

When Joel got Eloise's letter, he seriously considered going to Aliria immediately.

But there was Lissie. Lissie, who wouldn't be coming to the wedding. Lissie, who he hadn't lived with since he was barely fourteen, and who he would likely never live with again. He didn't particularly care for the Ibanari court, where there were dozens of new rules to memorize, where most people clearly only tolerated him for his sister's sake, where he always felt awkward and wrong and in the way. He wanted badly to be at Eloise's side again. But he couldn't leave Lissie early.

He didn't care about the wedding. It would be whatever it had to be, to make Eloise happy, and to let him be with her without judgement and criticism and gossip, without having to sneak around and hide away. He wrote back with a few Ibanari traditions he knew Ibanar would expect to be observed, and offered opinions on a few things she seemed indecisive about, hoping it would be helpful. There was only one detail of the wedding he really cared about, and he saved that for the end of the letter.

~

She accepted the message absently, thoughts on the suite she was preparing for the wedding night. They wouldn't be there long, as far as she knew, though Joel had given her no details. But it was their wedding suite, and it would be where they stayed any time they were in the palace for the rest of their lives, and it had to be perfect.

It was well over an hour later that she actually bothered to open the message, finding a long letter from Julian, at the very, very end of which he'd written, "Your betrothed sent me a bag of coins and the name of the town in Olion where he sold Tulip; I sent someone to pick her up. She should be waiting for you in the stable."

She left the letter sitting there, and ran down to the stable as quickly as she could.

The loss of one horse, beloved though she was, had been—well, they were at war, and her brother was dead, and another had married and moved far away. Tulip's sale had hardly been the most difficult thing she'd been through lately. But she was—she could have Tulip back. She couldn't have Ben back, she couldn't undo any of the awful things that had happened, but she could have Tulip back.

She had, selfishly, her own private reunion with the horse before fetching Maria, who also adored Tulip, who had learned to hide on her and probably had spent more time with her than Eloise had.

Wherever Eloise went, she likely wouldn't take Tulip along. She would leave her here, for Maria, for Annabelle when next she came to visit. For her nieces and nephews when they learned to ride. But she was here now. Joel had gotten her back. With Julian's help, but that almost made it more impressive; they had never got on, even before the conspiracy, and she couldn't imagine Joel had enjoyed asking him for help.

~

The king had grown on Joel. He had seemed unpleasant, at their first meeting, but then war was stressful for everyone, and Joel had robbed a member of his court.

He was kind to Lissie, and wonderful with their son. He treated Joel like family.

Joel had, consequently, become comfortable enough to argue with him. The matter of the party travelling to Aliria for his wedding had become a point of contention.

"You are going to Aliria as a representative of Ibanar," the king said. "It must be done properly. What will they think of us, if we send you alone? How will we know the wedding happened, if there are no Ibanari witnesses?"

"I realize I'm not particularly trustworthy, but I should think you could at least trust me to marry the woman I've been rather famously in love with for a decade."

"It's not a matter of trust, Joel. It's a matter of protocol."

"It's not a matter of trust for you. It is for me. Most of your people don't like me, don't trust me, and I don't feel safe travelling across the country with them, without Lissie for a buffer."

He frowned. "Tradition indicates we can send along one to three priests, and whatever assistants they deem necessary. Do you find any priests preferable to the court?"

"Yes."

"Take some sort of vow that requires you to stick close to the priests, to room with them over our other representatives, even to avoid speaking directly to anyone else. Pick your favorites, or your favorite temples, at least—individual priests and priestesses may of course have commitments. Will that do?"

"I suppose."

"If we send too small a group, it will be seen as disrespectful. Or too large a group. It's a delicate balance. But I will aim for the smallest acceptable number, and attempt to find people acceptable to you. Surely you don't distrust the entire court?"

"Not the entire court, no. There are a few who don't despise me."

"It's not personal, you know. They were opposed to me marrying outside of nobility. The advantage to choosing a foundling, as far as they were concerned, was that there would at least be no common relatives to manage."

"And then me."

"And then there was you, yes. Speak with Lissan; see if the two of you can come up with a list of tolerable travelling companions. And think about which priests you'd like to invite."

~

It felt like forever before Joel's next letter arrived. Several partially-made plans had been put on hold while she waited, and people were beginning to be annoyed with her.

She made careful notes on his opinions, to be shared with the necessary people for preparations to be made. Then she set about a far more exciting task.

"There's a loose stone below the window in your sitting room. I'm afraid you'll have to try them all; I don't remember which one it was. There should be a wooden box. I put it there the day before I was arrested."

She sat on the floor and began testing each stone beneath the window—it was not a terribly high window, but there were still several options.

Finally, one stone came sliding out.

It was a small box, made of a pale, unfinished wood. She opened it carefully to reveal a silver ring set with a small, irregularly-shaped blue pearl.

Engagement rings were an Alirian tradition shared with neither Olion nor Ibanar. (Jeremy and Sylvia hadn't had rings, which she attributed to their northern upbringing, or perhaps to Sylvia's background; rings could be expensive, and it was possible they were a tradition exclusive to the wealthy.) Pearls for weddings were an Ibanari tradition, from their seafaring roots.

At fifteen, on a trainee soldier's income which mostly went home to his family, Joel had bought her a pearl engagement ring.

(There was a not-small chance he'd stolen the money for it, actually, but Eloise couldn't bring herself to care.)

The shape, size, and color would all have contributed to reducing the value, but it was still a significant expense, and that was just the pearl itself. The ring may not be pure silver—it may not be real silver at all—but she didn't care.

He'd bought her a ring. Ten years ago, he'd bought her a ring, and it had been sitting in her own sitting room, just out of reach, ever since.

Soon. Soon they would be married, and ten years of waiting would be worth it.

Chapter 45

Sylvia and Jeremy arrived three days before the wedding, to find Eloise frantic.

"He's not here."

"Well, where is he?" Sylvia asked.

"I don't know! He was to arrive yesterday at the very latest. We haven't heard anything. What if he's dead?"

"I'm sure he's not dead," Jeremy said.

"Death," Eloise informed him, "is the best case scenario. The alternative is that he changed his mind."

"After a decade? After kidnapping you, crossing the island twice, and going to the continent alone for you?"

"That wasn't all for me."

"He wouldn't have changed his mind," Sylvia said. "Travel is unpredictable. You know that."

Eloise didn't answer.

"Let's go out to the forest," Sylvia suggested. "Jeremy can get our things settled."

Jeremy nodded. Sylvia kissed him, quickly, before herding Eloise out to the same place Eloise had herded her, months ago. They sat there quietly for a long time. Neither dipped their toes in the pond; it was only barely spring, and the water was far too cold.

"I'm sure he'll be here," Sylvia said, because she was; it was inconceivable that Joel, who had clearly been mad about her from the

375

moment Sylvia met them both, would fail to turn up for his own wedding.

Eloise hummed thoughtfully. "Distract me?" she asked.

Sylvia did. She knew Jeremy and Eloise had written, at least a few times, but she was a poor correspondent, and hadn't written anything herself.

"We've just resumed building. We had everyone in houses by the time winter truly started, though some of them were still sharing. And Jeremy paid for most of everyone's food, which I think was harder on him than he'll admit. But now we'll be able to do the work buildings, and the last few houses, and get proper crops in. We've people from most of the trades a village needs, but people like the blacksmith and the miller haven't been able to do their jobs, really, without the proper space and supplies. Soon all of that will be done, and we'll be mostly self-sufficient. We didn't get many new people in through the winter, but I suspect more will show up again now that travelling is easier. But I can find places for them. It's good, having things to do again."

"I'm glad," Eloise said. "And you're happy? You and Jeremy?"

"Yes." It was hard, sometimes. She thought it always would be. Her nightmares had gotten worse, returning home with him beside her. And sometimes old pain or newer guilt overwhelmed logic and even love, and she needed to be away from him. But there was work to do, and her father to visit, and she would always come back, and he would always be there, and it was so much better than any future she could have imagined. "Yes, we're happy."

~

He found her on the balcony of their new suite, her golden hair standing out against her silver-grey dress, silk and satin, staring at the sky.

"Eloise."

She didn't turn around. "You're very late."

"I know."

"When you said 'in time,' I thought you meant at least a few days."

"I'm sorry."

She faced him, finally. She was wearing the rose quartz necklace and the blue pearl ring. "What happened?"

"You're going to laugh at me."

"What happened?"

"We were set upon by bandits."

"Joel. Really? Were they—"

"Bandits of my personal acquaintance? Yes. It was very awkward for all of us."

She didn't laugh at him. But she was smiling, and that, he thought, was worth the bandits.

"The tailors made your suit," she said. "They still had your measurements, from before we left. Unless you've grown. It'll ruin everything if you've grown. Or shrunk."

"I haven't grown or shrunk."

"Good."

She turned away and leaned over the balcony, searching for stars in a still-bright sky.

"Eloise," he said, and she turned to face him again. "I love you. I know you don't, but I—I just—ten years and a thousand horrible things between us, and I'm still in love with you. And I want to marry you, so badly, and I know we have to now for the treaty, if nothing else, but I don't want you to spend a lifetime hating me, or even only tolerating me."

She took a step forward and leaned close, until their foreheads were nearly touching. "I love you, Joel. I do. I loved you when you were a child, and I loved you when you were a stranger, and I love you now. But I don't know how to do this."

"Well. I had an idea that might make it easier."

"Yes?"

He took her hands, and she let him. And she loved him. "Run away with me, Ellie. As soon as the vows are said, the treaty is set, and they don't need us. I have two good horses, and money from the king. We can go to Kire, or Geth, or anywhere in the world. We can be whatever we want to be. We can be free."

"Anywhere in the world?"

"Anywhere. Everywhere. Always, as long as you're with me."

"All right. Let's run away. After the wedding."

She leaned forward again, until their foreheads really were touching, and then she tilted her head and kissed him.

"We should go," she whispered. "I don't want to hear the rumors about why we were late for our own wedding."

"You love starting rumors."

"And we'll start plenty when we run away. You need to get dressed."

He kissed her again, quickly, and nodded. "Anything for you, Ellie."

Acknowledgements

Special thanks to my Patreon supporters, Jeff and Sue Prater, Sharp_Cheddar, Lynn and Lowell Nystrom, DSC, Mushki, Beth and Steve Cragle, Animone, and Margeling. You make writing so much more enjoyable, and I appreciate not only the financial support, but also your engagement and encouragement on my page. Thank you also to Taylor, wherever you are; we don't talk anymore, but this book wouldn't be what it is without all those years spent talking writing with you. Double thanks for Jeff and Sue Prater, who get bonus points for being my parents, and triple thanks for Sue Prater, who copy edited the first twelve chapters.

Jenny Prater is a medical scribe and fairy tale enthusiast. She lives in a cottage in Minnesota with her dog and cat, Wendy Darling and Alfred Lord Tennyson. *When the War Ends* is her third novel, following *Lindworm* and *Shards of Glass*. She is also the author of the short story collection *The Shoemaker Prince*, and several books of poetry. You can find more information at <u>jennyprater.com</u>, or at <u>patreon.com/ konglindorm</u>, where she shares weekly fairy tale blogs, updates, and assorted bonus content.